A
SEARCH
FOR
STARLIGHT

A SEARCH FOR STARLIGHT

THE FIREWALL TRILOGY

JAMES MAXWELL

Text copyright © 2021 by James Maxwell
All rights reserved.

Published by 47North, Seattle

www.apub.com

Amazon, the Amazon logo, and 47North are trademarks of Amazon.com, Inc., or its affiliates.

ISBN-13: 9781542005272
ISBN-10: 1542005272

Cover design by @blacksheep-uk.com

Cover illustration by Larry Rostant

Printed in the United States of America

For my daughter, Evelyn, with all my love

1

When viewed from a great height, the ugly stains on the landscape could have been patches of dark gravel, but whenever she saw them Selena felt ill.

Death had come to the wasteland.

Selena was farcasting. Like her parents before her, she was a mystic. The ability to farcast was something she had been born with, and over time she had developed skill. She was separated from her body as her awareness flew over the wasteland. Under the light of two suns, a rugged landscape of red dirt, boulders, and man-sized cactuses passed below her. Her gaze was on a group of distant black splotches that began to reveal themselves in detail.

Drawing closer, she lost height, and finally hovered to inspect the area. Ash coated the ground. If she had been able to smell, the sour odor of char would have filled her nostrils.

She was looking at what had once been a small settlement: a cluster of three homesteads that now lay in ruins. Everything was burned away, with each house only distinguished by the shape of its cinder pile. Selena was familiar with the races inhabiting the wasteland. From the layout, she knew this had once been home to a group of humans. Their bones would be in there somewhere, but she had already seen enough bones and bodies to last a lifetime.

She wasn't just coming across human settlements, all razed to the ground. Although the wasteland was sparsely populated, Selena could cast far enough to find entire bax villages destroyed in the same manner. She had seen caves set into hillsides where the rock itself was scorched and the bodies of skalen lay sprawled outside the entrances.

After a look of despair at the forlorn piles of ash, Selena climbed the sky once again. As soon as she had gained enough height she stared in all directions. For some time, she had been trying to observe one of these strange attacks firsthand. She wanted to understand what was causing such devastation. Only then would the city of Zorn be able to fight back.

A bright light flashed in the sky.

Her attention snapped into focus. An instant later she saw sunlight sparkle from metal. She sped toward the location, yet the object disappeared back the way it had come, leaving a wispy white trail like a thin cloud. Selena wanted to pursue it, but her lifeline was stretched almost to the limit. Instead she headed for a newly created plume of smoke rising from the ground.

When she arrived, her heart sank.

The bax village lay nestled in a low valley by the edge of a cliff. Just the day before she had seen the hunched creatures who lived there innocently going about their business: tending fires, repairing huts, hunting, and foraging. There was no point in going closer, for what had once been a thriving settlement was now a smoldering ruin.

Selena was both saddened and angry. She was desperate. Some kind of machine in the sky had suddenly appeared and then was gone. She needed to understand what it was.

There was one thing she knew for certain. These attacks were the work of a powerful new enemy—the bonded—and their scouring of the wasteland had already begun.

Four weeks ago, Selena and Taimin, along with their companions, had returned to Zorn. Even more time had passed since they had witnessed the fall of the firewall that had trapped them in the wasteland all their lives. Selena now worked with Elsa, the leader of Zorn, using her abilities to find out what was happening beyond the city. She had learned that entire homesteads and settlements were being systematically destroyed. The pattern of the attacks always came from the same direction—and was drawing nearer and nearer to Zorn.

Selena had been told why. The strange race known as the bonded were engaged in a long, drawn-out war far from this world that Selena called home. Their tall, powerful warriors were aggressive hunters and killers. Long ago, early in the war between worlds, they had taken prisoners from the five civilizations who were their enemies and penned them in a hunting ground.

Everyone trapped within the firewall had been put there as prey, quarry for the bonded to hunt and take trophies from. Zorn and its arena had been built several centuries ago as a place of temporary lodging, and a destination where bonded warriors could watch each other prove themselves in fights.

But then over time, as the firewall started to cause searing storms and the war in space continued, Zorn was abandoned. Most of the bonded lost interest in their hunting ground, aside from the military elite who still followed the old ways.

Among the prisoners inside the firewall, the memory of who they were was lost.

Everything changed when Taimin and Selena encountered Ungar, a bonded warrior. Taimin and Ungar fought and, during the struggle, the machine that powered the firewall was destroyed. Now there was nothing separating the wasteland's inhabitants from the enemy civilization outside.

And this terrible destruction was their reaction.

Selena had been farcasting constantly in the hope of understanding the threat that Zorn was facing. It was all part of Elsa's plan to prepare for an attack. But fatigue was weighing her down. Turning, Selena saw her lifeline, a white cord connecting her to her body, which was far away in Zorn's tall central tower.

Despite the grave situation, she experienced a brief flash of pride. Her lifeline stretched much farther than it ever had before; as a mystic, she had never been stronger. Milton, her father, had helped her to accept her talent, before sacrificing his life trying to help her.

Selena's role was similar to when she had been forced to farcast for the Protector—the tyrannical leader of Zorn before Elsa—only this time it was her choice. Her father was dead, and her mother too, but wherever they were now, she hoped they understood that she no longer worried about who she was.

Selena wanted to continue her search, but her lifeline was faint. She needed to return.

She took hold of the ethereal white line and pulled. Faster than thought, she shot toward the horizon, and then toward a white-walled city with a tall spike in the center. In a heartbeat the tower loomed large and an open-sided chamber at the summit beckoned. Inside was a slender young woman with long coal-black hair. Her odd-colored eyes—one green and the other brown—were open and unfocused.

Selena rejoined her body, seated in a chair in the middle of the tower's observation room, and gasped.

———

Selena and Elsa faced a rectangular table with a large map spread out in front of them. They were in Elsa's workroom, a wide chamber with walls of white stone in one of the tower's lower levels.

Abundant natural light filled the space. The air was dry and cool. Everything about the workroom was functional: the sturdy desk, the long table, and the chairs that had been pushed to the side.

Elsa, the leader of Zorn and architect of the rebellion that removed the Protector, leaned forward and inspected the map. Selena had made it, based on her travels in the wasteland, incorporating the map she had found on the wall at the bottom of the tower. Elsa's brown hair, streaked with gray, fell in front of her piercing green eyes. She wasn't young, perhaps fifty years old, with thin arms and a wiry build.

Elsa drummed her fingers on the table. Her gaze roved from one black mark on the map to the next. "Describe to me again what you saw."

"Something in the sky. It reflected the sunlight, so it might be metallic. It was . . . fast." Selena wished she had been able to see the attack more closely. "I'll keep looking and I'll have something more—"

Elsa raised an eyebrow. "You're feeling guilty?" She shook her head. "Selena, without you we would know next to nothing. I have faith in you, believe me."

Selena tried to disguise the pleasure she felt to know that Elsa placed so much trust in her. She had always wanted a proper home, and a place for herself in the society around her.

Elsa continued to peer at the map. "The attacks are getting closer. But why haven't they gone straight for Zorn?"

"From what I've seen, they're clearing the wasteland in a line that gets closer and closer to us here," Selena said.

"Hmm," Elsa said. "They could be preparing for a ground attack. Or perhaps they're just being thorough, and they think we can't defend ourselves." She scanned the swathe of destruction that was nearing Zorn. "Either way it's happening faster than we had predicted." She met Selena's eyes. "How long, in your view?"

Selena's worried eyes inspected the map. "Not long."

"How long?" Elsa pressed.

"It would be a guess."

"Then guess." When Elsa became irritated, she showed it.

Selena hesitated. "Two weeks."

Elsa let out a breath. "And we still don't even know what we're up against."

"We should evacuate, shouldn't we?" Selena asked.

"No." Elsa shook her head. "I'm not ready to do that. We need to find out what it is that's heading our way." Her voice firmed. "This is no homestead or village built of wood and mud. We have a tall wall. We have strong buildings of stone. We have a population ready and willing to fight. If we flee, we've already lost. We must remain united."

Selena thought again about all the destruction she had seen. "But—"

"Believe me, Selena. I have thought about this long and hard, and continue to do so. There are thousands of people here. It is my job to protect them. First, let us understand the nature of this threat."

Elsa gave the map one last look before leveling her gaze at Selena. The older woman's eyes were intent. "Continue your work. Find out as much as you can. Meanwhile, we can also access our other source of information." Selena's heart sank. She had a feeling that she knew what might be coming next. "Our prisoner," Elsa concluded.

After the fall of the firewall, Selena and Taimin had brought someone with them back to Zorn. Ingren, a bonded female, had been the constant companion of the warrior Ungar, who had sought out Taimin for a battle to the death. But Ingren was nothing like the bondmate she had traveled to the wasteland with. She said that in the pairs that made up bonded society, she had no choice but to follow her bondmate on his quest; her role was merely to advise.

6

Where Ungar had been savage beyond belief, a gleeful taker of the heads of his victims, Ingren's manner was calm—almost serene.

"Our situation is urgent," Elsa said. "There must be more she can tell us."

Selena's anxiety grew. "I'll talk to Taimin."

"Do it right away," Elsa said. Her expression changed as she scowled. "I offered him the command of the city guard, but he refused. I asked him to work at my side, as you are, but he turned me down. He doesn't want to fight. While we prepare, he spends all his time with our prisoner."

"You've said it yourself," Selena said. "We have to learn about our enemy if we want to survive."

"Yet what has he learned? We know that they are strange, these bonded. Taimin tells me their society is divided between those who use their bodies and those who use their minds. He says the majority of their lives are spent in pairs, but the warriors are in charge, while their advisors are subservient. All very interesting, but it doesn't help us fight off an imminent threat." She stared directly into Selena's eyes. "Talk to Taimin. Tell him that unless he produces results I can use, I will get the information I need in my own, unpleasant way. I have to think of the people under my protection. Tell him that I can only give him one more day."

Selena felt that she had to explain Taimin's position. "It's not that he won't fight. He doesn't think we can survive. He thinks it's going to be—"

"I know," Elsa said curtly. "A massacre. He tries to tell me every chance he gets. Maybe it's a good thing that he spends so much time with our prisoner." She again faced the map in front of her. "I don't want his negativity to affect anyone else."

Knowing Elsa's moods, Selena turned to depart.

Elsa spoke over her shoulder. "One day, Selena. Tell Taimin that he has just one day."

2

"Torture her?" Taimin asked incredulously. "No. I won't allow it."

"You don't have a choice," Selena said. "You know what she'll say: if it can save lives . . ." She trailed off, clearly uncomfortable with the idea.

Taimin knew that Selena had found a sense of purpose at Elsa's side and he didn't want to get between them. But he also knew in his heart that the idea of fighting the bonded on even terms was madness. Elsa could force Ingren to talk, and learn about every weapon the bonded possessed, but still the wasteland was doomed. Taimin had seen inside the machine that powered the firewall. The awe he had experienced was still with him. The bonded had an entire world, and an advanced civilization, at their disposal. The wasteland was just a forgotten playground.

Taimin felt isolated, even from Selena. He knew that she just wanted to help, in any way she could, and use her talent where it was needed most. He understood that and respected it. What he wanted was a solution that didn't involve fighting. He didn't want everyone to die.

He had been on his way to talk to Ingren when Selena found him in one of the tower's wide, high-ceilinged corridors. Daylight shone through an oval window nearby. Selena wasn't currently farcasting, so Taimin knew that Rei-kika, a mantorean and Selena's former teacher, had taken her place to allow her to recover.

As Selena looked at him, Taimin was aware that his bristling brown hair was unruly, and he needed to shave the stubble from his cheeks. Unlike many of the soldiers and administrators he often encountered in the tower, he was dressed in the clothing of a waste-lander: trousers, rugged vest, leather boots. But despite his difficulties with Elsa, he was just as desperate as she was to save Zorn, and he had no time to worry about his appearance.

He still couldn't believe what Selena had just told him. "One day?"

Selena was pale as she nodded. "You know what Elsa is like. You won't be able to talk her down."

Taimin shook his head. "I have to go."

"Wait," Selena said, taking his arm and gazing into his eyes. "Whatever happens with Ingren, she might not give you the solution you're looking for. What are you going to do then?"

"I want to help," Taimin said. "I really do." He was desperate for Selena to understand. He would do anything for her. "This isn't a war. It's not like when Blixen wanted to conquer Zorn. No one could guarantee who would win, back then. This is different. This city is going to be turned into dust."

"We need to have faith—"

Taimin knew she would hear the frustration in his voice. "Selena, you were with me. We're the only people to see inside the machine. The power they have . . . Everyone should evacuate—immediately. Elsa's wrong to offer false hope. She needs to start getting people out of the city. Two weeks is no time at all."

Selena let go of Taimin's arm. For a moment she couldn't hide her fear. "It could be less."

The dread that Taimin was already feeling became something more visceral. There were so many lives at stake, not just in Zorn, but throughout the wasteland. Selena's among them.

"Elsa is clever," Selena said. "We'll learn more about what we're up against and we'll find a way to defend ourselves. We have to stand and fight together."

Taimin stared into the distance. "No," he said. "There has to be another way."

⌣

"I'm here to see the prisoner," Taimin said.

He hated using that word. He had been imprisoned in the arena and it went against every fiber of his being to deny someone else their freedom. The inhabitants of the wasteland had been prisoners, confined within the firewall until it fell. They should all know better than this.

He stood at the end of a corridor, outside a huge, securely locked wooden door. As with everything in Zorn, the corridor in the white tower was designed to accommodate the impressive size of those who built it long ago. The guard, a burly man armed with a hardwood sword, narrowed his gaze.

"I want to see her," Taimin repeated.

"Again?" the guard asked flatly.

Taimin met the man's eyes. "Yes, again. She's my prisoner. I'm the one who brought her here." As he fought to keep his tone even, he thought about Elsa's ultimatum: he had one day to get useful information or Ingren was going to be tortured.

The guard tilted his head as he considered. With a sigh, he turned and slid the bolt. He pulled the door open and glanced inside, before stepping back and jerking his chin.

Taimin entered and the door closed behind him. He heard a clunk as the bolt was thrown once more.

Ingren had been given as much comfort as possible. Her room wasn't small; even the bed pallet was massive. Sunlight glowed at the high window, revealing an untouched plate of meat beside a water jug on the table.

"Ingren," Taimin said firmly. "We need to talk"

The bonded female sitting on the bed raised her chin.

Ingren's size was impressive: when she stood, her eight-foot-tall frame towered over anyone next to her. But strangely, she couldn't lift a finger in her own defense. On the journey to Zorn she had never protested; in fact, she had been surprisingly forthcoming as she explained the true nature of the wasteland.

Her skin was tinged red and her short, pointed horns gleamed as gold as the sun Dex. Grooves dominated her crown and her face was triangular, with a sharp chin and a black-lipped mouth. Her eyes were like cold coals.

Taimin wondered what she made of his size—he was tall for a human, but far smaller than her—as well as his brown hair and his much lighter eyes. Did he look as strange to her?

"Ah, it is you, Taimin," she said. Despite the fact that she was seated on a bed, they were almost eye to eye.

"I need you to tell us something, anything that will help us," Taimin said.

Ingren sighed. "We have been over this."

"Selena says something is destroying settlements one by one. Something fast. I need you to tell me what it is."

"What would be the purpose in sharing information you will find difficult to understand? It does not matter what I say. You are all going to die."

Taimin's eyes narrowed. "Why destroy us like this?"

"It is the warriors' way," Ingren said. "The wasteland no longer serves a useful function. And that includes those who live inside it."

"But you said it yourself," Taimin said. He thrust an arm toward the open window. "The real war you are fighting is out there, among the stars. We mean nothing to you. You forgot about us."

"Most of us did," Ingren harrumphed. "Only those like Ungar, aspiring to high office, still favored the quests."

"Why don't they just rebuild the firewall?"

"You saw the machine, Taimin. Rebuilding it would take time and energy. Meanwhile, you are no longer separated from our civilization. You have intelligence. In time, you would organize and threaten our lands. To the warriors back home, you are vermin that must be eradicated."

Taimin began to pace. He glanced at Ingren while he thought about Elsa's ultimatum. He experienced a mixture of emotions.

On one hand, the bonded were at war with the five races of the wasteland. It was a conflict that had raged for centuries in the void between the stars: ship against ship, homeworld against homeworld. The warriors who led the bonded had taken Taimin's ancestors and those of everyone he knew and trapped them within the firewall, purely to satisfy their primal urges to hunt and kill.

At the same time, Ingren was not a bonded warrior. She said she valued knowledge above all else. She even enjoyed it if Taimin corrected the occasional mistake she made when she spoke the common language of the wasteland.

It felt wrong to blame Ingren for the actions of the warriors who were in charge. Elsa was looking for practical information, and with torture she might be able to get it. But what Taimin wanted was something more: a real solution . . . an end to the conflict.

As Taimin walked back and forth, he looked at his right foot, which was now just as strong as his left. The bonded warrior Ungar had instructed Ingren to heal Taimin's crippled foot so they could battle as close to equals as possible. Ingren's device had been lost during the machine's destruction, but what it had done was just another sign of how advanced the bonded were.

"Whatever the case," Taimin said, "Zorn is going to be targeted in two or three weeks. Maybe less. You have to help me. Give me something useful, something that can help us hold off the assault. This is your one chance." He stopped to face her and stared into her black eyes. "Ingren . . . They'll torture you."

Taimin clenched his jaw when Ingren shrugged once more. "If they were going to torture me, they would have already done so," she said. Then a thought sparked in her eyes. "Unless . . . Ah." She leaned back. "You have been protecting me."

"I know you can't defend yourself," Taimin said. "But I can't protect you anymore. Ingren, please. There must be something."

Her next words surprised him. "Very well then, little human."

"You'll help?" Taimin asked. Her sudden change made him suspicious. "Why?"

"Despite my best efforts, you still do not understand." Ingren touched one of the short golden horns that crowned her head. While her bondmate had been alive, they had been pale yellow, rather than the stronger shade they were now. "You have noticed this change," she said. "A bond is only made once. I am no longer Ungar's advisor. My bond is broken, and I am now an elder. My role is similar to what it was before—I seek knowledge and offer advice. However, rather than serve a single warrior, I must now serve a group of the most powerful bonded, which we call the assembly. The change in me that is most relevant to you, Taimin, is that I am free to make my own decisions."

"That doesn't explain why you would help us."

"Let me try again. There is no room for knowledge in the middle of an endless war. The distances in space are vast. The conflict

13

between worlds has endured for centuries. There have been many casualties, and you here in the wasteland will soon join their number. I have no love of death and destruction."

"You want the fighting to be over?" Taimin asked with a frown. "Why don't you do something about it?"

"My society does not function in the same way as yours. We are at war; the warriors are in charge. When they are the principal member of the bond, their needs come first. When we are at peace, then the advisors and elders are dominant. Then, Taimin, we bonded serve knowledge. Our society is completely different."

"Would you like it if the warriors were no longer in charge?"

"It does not matter what I would like. Even if I would prefer us to explore the realms of knowledge, as I said, we are at war."

Taimin thought about everything he had learned from his many talks with Ingren. Much of it was strange, but he understood that the warriors in charge of bonded society were the ones seeking the total annihilation of the wasteland's inhabitants. Whereas Ingren and the elders and advisors like her were completely different. Unlike the warriors, they were incapable of violence.

"What would bring about the change you are talking about?" he asked. He held his breath as he waited for her next words.

"Total victory," she said. She pondered. "Or perhaps total defeat. All I can tell you is that the warriors must give up power willingly."

Taimin's heart sank.

Ingren spoke again. "You must believe me when I say that I have no love for blood and death. I have no personal interest in seeing so many die. The warriors are in charge. It is their way." She paused. "Here is what I can tell you. I was not certain, but the approach the warriors will take is now clear. The destruction you speak of will be caused by strikers—winged machines armed with projectile weapons. This is just the initial stage. The strikers will destroy what they can. Ground forces—most likely devastators—will then scour the wasteland for anything left living."

Taimin focused intently on her. "These strikers. Can you draw one for me?"

Ingren nodded.

"Hold on."

Taimin rapped on the door and spoke urgently with the guard outside. Initially surly, the man's manner changed when Taimin explained that he had detailed information for Elsa and needed paper and charcoal.

"What else?" Taimin asked Ingren.

He listened carefully, asking probing questions, as she described the ground forces that would advance on the wasteland. But rather than excitement at learning something useful, all he felt was dread.

"There must be something else . . ." he muttered. He was pacing again, back and forth, desperate to find a way to avoid conflict altogether. As she watched him, Ingren's eyes were surprisingly sympathetic.

All Taimin had wanted was to get to the paradise on the other side of the firewall. Instead, he had uncovered the truth about the world he lived in. The firewall was gone, exposing everyone in the wasteland to the hostile race outside the former barrier. He had to put right what he had done.

He decided to ask more questions. "Who leads the assembly?"

"The sky marshal. His name is Jakkar."

"A warrior?"

"Yes."

"Where is he?"

"He rules from our capital, Agravida. The city I call home."

"Your assembly is also in Agravida?"

"Yes."

Taimin's brow furrowed. If only he could talk to them. He explored the notion as he paced. Talking had worked with Blixen. Lives had been saved.

He focused on Ingren again. "Isn't it easier to let us live in peace? Surely that makes more sense than to hunt down every human, bax, skalen, mantorean, and trull."

"Peace is not a warrior's way. Surely you learned that from Ungar. Fighting, proving his worth, was all he lived for. To the sky marshal, you are troublesome pests who must be destroyed rather than allowed to roam free."

Taimin looked through the oval window. His eyes were on a clear blue sky, but he was seeing something else altogether. He was thinking of the sunburned plain that surrounded the city, but in his mind the plain became filled with a multitude of grim-faced bonded warriors. He imagined row after row of tall figures marching inexorably toward the city. They were bigger and stronger than any of the races of the wasteland. Their skin was wrinkled and leathery, the same shade as the terrain, with long grooves above fiery eyes. Curling horns crowned their scalps. Mouths displayed rows of sharp teeth. And there weren't just a few of them. Zorn was a populated settlement, but according to Ingren the bonded vastly outnumbered the city's inhabitants.

Desperation made his thoughts whirl. There had to be some way forward.

"What if we came to an agreement?" he asked. "We agree that we will never leave the wasteland. You guard the wasteland's boundary, and if we cross it you have the right to take whatever action you think necessary. Would that work?"

Ingren considered this idea. "As an elder, I can see that it is simpler to guard a border than it is to kill so many. I cannot promise, however, that the sky marshal and the warriors of the assembly, will agree." Her tone became musing. "There is strength to your idea.

16

The warriors live for fighting, but they are reasoning beings. They do listen . . . when it suits them." She paused. "Of course, they would need to hear this proposal from you."

Her last statement was full of meaning.

Taimin's eyes widened. Was this his chance? Could he meet with his enemies and come to some kind of arrangement?

As a plan slowly formed in his mind, he realized what he would have to do in order to speak to the leaders of the bonded personally. He would need Ingren's help, yet she was Elsa's only source of information on the enemy. Elsa would never voluntarily let her go.

He lowered his voice. "If I got you out of here, would you take me to Agravida?"

She spoke seriously. "I would."

Taimin wondered if he could do it. For the first time, his hopes rose. Could he get Ingren out of the tower?

But then he remembered what Selena had told him. There wasn't time. The assault would come in a matter of weeks, while Ingren's city, Agravida, was far from the wasteland.

His despair returned. Ingren had described frightening weapons. Everyone he cared about was going to die.

"It won't work," he said. "I'd never get to Agravida before it's too late. There's no time."

"Actually, Taimin, there is."

Taimin stared at her.

She continued. "It would take some time to reach the edge of the wasteland, that is true. But a few days from the boundary there is a place, something we call a station. We have a machine called a quadrail that travels faster than you can imagine. It is how I and Ungar arrived. Once we reach the station, we could get to Agravida in a single day."

"A day?" Taimin was stunned.

All of a sudden, he knew that this was the opportunity he had been looking for. An alternative to the destruction that was already in progress and would soon reach Zorn.

"We could get there before Zorn comes under attack?" he asked urgently.

"Yes, I believe so."

"But would I get a chance to talk to your assembly?"

"In my world, I must admit, you would be something of a curiosity. I am an elder, and my status is very high. I cannot guarantee it, but I would do my best to help you."

Taimin became suspicious once more. "How do I know I can trust you?"

"I want to go home," Ingren said simply. "As you know, the wasteland is dangerous. I would not survive the journey without you. I also cannot get myself out of this tower, and out of this place you call a city. I need your help."

"But what about once we're in your world, rather than mine?" Taimin persisted. "You could just hand me over."

"That is true. I could. But what choice do you have? I promise you, what is coming is not a battle but a slaughter. There will only be one outcome. I can take you to Agravida. You will have an opportunity to bring about peace."

Taimin's head was spinning. The idea of leaving the world he knew, of traveling to Ingren's home, the city of Agravida, was something he could barely grasp.

"Remember," she said. "We would travel together. You are capable of violence, but I am not. And as I have said many times, I am no lover of bloodshed. I want to help you."

Taimin released a breath he hadn't realized he was holding. He could do this. He was desperate, but also determined. He had a chance to save everyone.

He realized that Ingren was looking at him, waiting for a reply. "I need to think," he said.

"I understand." She slowly spread her arms. "This is all you have known. But there is much, much more beyond the wasteland for you to come to terms with. If you choose to leave, you will be risking your life. Be in no doubt about that."

3

Taimin walked with determined strides. He had no qualms about interrupting the meeting underway in Elsa's workroom. As he approached, through the open doorway ahead he saw Elsa's advisors and administrators seated on chairs around a long wooden table. An intense conversation was underway.

A dozen men and women filled the room and Taimin recognized several faces. Selena sat beside the stick-thin figure of Rei-kika, another mystic and the only mantorean in the room. Rei-kika's beady black eyes were focused on the man speaking and her triangular head was cocked to the side.

Elsa's council also included Jerome, a white-haired man in charge of the infirmary, round-faced Harvin, who oversaw the city's supplies, and a burly man named Grom, who had a background in construction and had been tasked with building shelters.

The first to see Taimin was Ruth. Her eyes widened with surprise—Taimin never attended Elsa's council meetings. After their return from the distant desert, Ruth had volunteered her skills as a healer. She was taller and curvier than Selena, with short, wavy hair the same dark-red shade as the wasteland.

Grom was speaking. He had kind eyes, smile creases, and shaggy brown hair that was always unruly, but like his companions his expression was worried.

"—building as many shelters as we can, working day and night," Grom was saying, his booming voice matching his size. "We're doing our best, but still . . ." He trailed off when he saw Taimin stride in and come to a halt behind Elsa.

Elsa hadn't noticed. "Keep at it," she said. "If you need more workers—" Her head turned. A frown creased her face. "Taimin?"

Elsa was staring directly at him, but it was Selena's attention Taimin was most aware of. Her mismatched eyes, tight with concern, made him think about the perilous journey he was considering making with Ingren, someone he didn't even know if he could trust.

Yet Selena was the very reason he knew he had to do it. Zorn would soon be attacked, just like all of the scorched settlements and homesteads Selena had described. He had to try to reason with this sky marshal in Agravida before the assault on Zorn took place.

Taimin responded to Elsa's impatient stare. "Here," he said. He took the bundle of paper he had under his arm and placed it on the table in front of Zorn's leader. "You'll want to look at these drawings."

As Elsa looked perplexed at the pile in front of her, Taimin drew her attention to the piece of paper on top.

"This is what to look out for. Machines that fly called strikers. They're fast and they launch projectile weapons that explode when they hit the ground. Ingren also made drawings of their other machines." He leaned down and shuffled through the sheaf. "This is called a field laser. It's like a bow and arrow but more accurate and more deadly. Their warriors carry them." He spread the drawings out on the table. "This is a devastator. It's an armored machine on wheels, like a wagon. That there—on the dome on top—is a powerful field laser."

For once, Elsa was stunned. She examined the drawings and then turned to Taimin. "Ingren gave you all this?"

Taimin nodded. "She did."

Elsa spoke to no one in particular. "Whose side is she on?"

With many eyes on him, Taimin described Ingren's role, explaining that she valued knowledge and peace, and personally didn't want to see lives lost if there was another way.

However, he kept to himself the idea of traveling to Agravida. Selena would say that Taimin was taking too big a risk. She would never understand it, but Taimin had to take the only opportunity he had to save her life, along with so many others. He had to try to talk to the enemy, to come to a truce of some kind. He had no other choice.

As Elsa spread the drawings out across the table so that everyone could see them, Taimin turned to leave. "I hope it helps," he said.

He meant every word.

———

The rising sun Dex bathed the white buildings and paved roads in slanted morning light. The city of Zorn shook off the last vestiges of a chill night and woke with vigor. The tall walls glistened, and the soaring tower watched over the purposeful citizens and newcomers as they scurried below.

Selena had to walk swiftly to keep up with Elsa, who had a determined look on her face as they both left the tower and crossed the surrounding plaza. Elsa clutched the drawings that Taimin had given her as if her life depended on never letting them go.

The plaza was busy as people browsed the market. Animal skins hung from racks, tools and weapons lay on tables, and food aromas wafted from a stall where a fat woman stirred a big bowl with a ladle. Children tossed stones and chased them over the paving stones. A pair of bax walked past with sloshing water sacks hoisted on their shoulders. Not long ago Zorn's well had dried up, but with peace holding throughout the wasteland, the city now had a supply of water coming in from outside.

As Selena navigated the plaza, she passed the insect-like figure of a mantorean bargaining with a human vendor selling bows and crossbows. The vendor scowled and shook the bundle of arrows they were arguing over, while the mantorean waved his arms and rasped back at him. Selena scanned more passersby as she walked. Most were human, but she saw a couple of skalen working together to roll a barrel down the street. An old bax dressed in leathers walked alongside a tired-looking wherry with plump sacks piled up on the animal's back. In the distance she even saw a trull, marked out by his solid build, upturned nose, and protruding incisors.

There was a time not long ago when the scene would have been unimaginable. The five races of the wasteland—human, bax, skalen, mantorean, and trull—now had a mutual enemy.

"Why are we going to the barracks?" Selena asked Elsa when they had left the commotion behind.

Elsa walked on, eyes straight ahead. "We need to show these drawings to my son, Dale. I've given him command of the city guard. It's important that you meet him. You're going to tell him when our enemies are coming, and he'll do something about it."

Selena wondered why she hadn't seen the new commander of the city guard at council meetings, but then Elsa answered her unspoken question.

"He's always busy with his new recruits," Elsa said, "so we have to go to him. Until now there wasn't much we could plan by way of strategy." She indicated the sheaf of papers. "This changes everything."

As Selena navigated the bustling city, she wished the temperature would remain just as it was, but soon the red sun would climb and the heat would grow. The breeze felt humid and moist, rather than the dry air that had permeated the wasteland before the firewall fell. She thought about the rain clouds she had seen while farcasting. Even settlers in remote regions would know that something had changed.

Selena saw a lot of worried faces. Like her, everyone was fearful about what the future might bring. The city's numbers had swelled—mainly due to the bax coming and going from the Rift Valley—but many humans had left, deciding to take their chances outside.

She found it strange to think that bonded once walked these same streets. They watched fights in the arena. They watched the plain from the observation room at the top of the tower, where a sighting would create a frenzy of warriors eager to make a kill. They stalked more distant prey, but always kept their presence secret, so that their quarry never learned to organize and take the thrill of the hunt away for good.

Selena and Elsa passed a human family burdened with heavy packs, evidently about to leave the city. Many thought it safer to take their chances in the canyons and caves after learning about their strange new enemy. She watched the father plead with his crying daughter.

"Come on, Bess. I'm your father. We can't stay here!"

Selena felt the tension in the air. Two well-dressed men outside one of the houses drew her attention. She overheard them talking.

"I've lived in Zorn my entire life. Where else is there to go? We built something here—civilization. We can't just leave it all behind."

Selena glanced at Elsa. As always, the older woman's face gave little away, but she must have seen and heard the same things. People trusted Elsa. If she gave the order, they would leave their homes behind.

Elsa believed that Zorn could hold out against their enemy.

Selena prayed that she was right.

Dozens of men and more than a few women stood side by side, arranged in rows as they waited in the burning sun. A few of them cast curious glances in Selena's direction but most maintained their discipline. They were all close to Selena's age, some younger than twenty, others older. All wore blue uniforms over leather armor, blazoned with a white tower. She could pick out the new recruits by the anxious looks on their faces.

Selena had never visited the barracks before. Stone walls enclosed the long, rectangular space where she stood at one side while the lined-up soldiers filled the center. A series of hut-like outer buildings framed the paved floor, with high, narrow entrances and barred gates in front of them. Creatures snorted and stirred behind the gates, and Selena saw a wyvern lift its wedge-shaped head to give her a narrowed stare.

Elsa had asked Selena to wait as she spoke with her son. They would then address the soldiers who would be defending the city. Selena's introduction would come at the end.

Selena spied movement at the largest building, where Elsa had vanished with papers in hand. Elsa emerged from the tall doorway, and a man now walked by her side.

Dale looked a lot like his mother. He had striking red hair, a dusting of freckles, bright blue eyes, and a sharp nose. Clean-shaven and smartly dressed in a brown vest and trousers, he wore an expression that was friendly but determined.

As Dale moved to stand in front of the city guard, he suddenly noticed Selena. His eyes widened with surprise. It was too late for Selena to look away; she had been watching him and felt as if she had been caught.

Meanwhile Elsa left her son and came to stand beside Selena. The focus of attention, Dale waited for a moment, preparing his words.

"Soldiers," he addressed the group in a firm voice, "I have important news. Listen carefully." The uniformed men and women shuffled. "The last time I asked you to gather, I told you about how little time we have before Zorn is targeted by our enemy."

Selena realized he was referring to the assessment that she had made. Her jaw was tight. The faith that Elsa had in her was a heavy burden to bear.

"Now," Dale continued, "we have an idea what we will be facing." The barracks became silent. Not the slightest cough broke the stillness. "And what we have learned fills me not with dread, but with hope. Our enemy will come with strikers—winged machines made of metal. These air machines possess formidable speed and are able to launch explosive projectiles at targets on the ground." His determined gaze swept the ranks of soldiers. "Why does this fill me with hope? It is unlikely that they know we have wyverns, and you, soldiers, are growing more skilled at riding them with every passing day. Our plan is to capture more wyverns from the mountains near the Rift Valley. Our stocks of aurelium-tipped arrows are growing. Undoubtedly, aurelium's destructive power will be effective against these strikers. Together, men and women of the city guard, we will defend Zorn."

Selena was impressed. Already she was seeing Dale's words have an effect on the young soldiers in front of them. His resolute expression was mirrored on their faces.

Someone called out.

"Yes?" Dale looked in an older man's direction. "You have a question?"

"What about ground forces?"

"It is a reasonable question," Dale said with a nod of acknowledgement. "However, the imminent danger comes from these strikers. We will worry about them first. Now," he continued, "I don't need to remind you that people are scared. They will see your uniforms and ask you questions. It is important that we try to keep the city calm. Make sure that everyone knows about the shelters we're digging and where their nearest shelter is. Soldiers, we will meet again to discuss tactics. You will learn about these strikers in detail. I will also be dispatching some of you to capture wyverns." He concluded, "You may now go about your duties. That is all."

The soldiers dispersed, chatting in small groups, and Dale headed toward his mother. His eyes were on Selena as he gave her a warm smile. "You must be Selena," he said. More confident than she had expected, he stared directly into her face. "I heard about your eyes . . . but it's not the same as seeing them."

"Dale . . ." Elsa said in a low growl. "We aren't at one of your taverns. This is business."

Selena kept her face carefully blank. "You gave a good speech," she said.

"You gave me good information," he swiftly returned.

"It didn't come from me." Selena cleared her throat. "I'll do it, though. I'll see one of these strikers for myself."

Dale spoke softly, with complete seriousness. "You can do things that no one else can."

Elsa harrumphed. "Well, now that you've met, just remember that you're both critical to our survival. Work together. Get along. Anything else?"

"I've got something," Selena said. "It's about the observation room."

"Go on," Elsa said.

"The tower is at the heart of the city. If Rei-kika or I are up in that room, and we see something coming, we need a way to warn not just the commander, but everyone. I think we should install a warning bell."

"Good idea," Dale said. "Makes sense."

"I'll ask Grom to see it done," Elsa said with a nod.

"Get him to do it quickly," Dale said. "Then my men can help spread the word. The sound of the bell means everyone should flee to the nearest shelter." He turned to scan the soldiers busying themselves about the barracks. A new recruit sat unsteadily on a wyvern's back while his instructor explained the basics of riding. Half a dozen uniformed men and women practiced their archery on a target. "I'd best get back to work." He nodded at Elsa. "Mother." Selena couldn't help but return the crooked smile he gave her. "Selena."

Selena watched his departing back.

A few moments later, Selena glanced at Elsa. "He looks like he knows what he's doing."

"He does." Elsa's mouth tightened. "And yet I can't help picturing Taimin here too. We need him, Selena. He can help us find the best way to fight these machines in the sky. People will follow where he leads."

Selena decided that the time had come: she had to do something about Taimin's despair. As she watched Dale approach the recruit seated on a wyvern's back, she thought about Taimin, and had another idea.

She spoke to herself, as much as to Elsa. "Maybe Taimin needs to be reminded about what we're fighting for . . ."

4

"Where are we going?" Taimin asked.

"You'll see." Selena glanced at him and her eyes sparkled. "It's a surprise."

Taimin rubbed his temples; it was early as he and Selena walked the city streets. But with a beautiful young woman beside him, a woman he had woken up alongside in the room they shared in the tower, he instead knew he should treasure every waking moment they had together.

Soon he would be gone.

It was a moody morning, with wide bands of red cloud in the sky, layered one on top of the other and streaked with gold and blue. Zorn was quiet and the air was cool. The smell of baking razorgrass bread wafted from the white stone houses. Carts trundled toward the market, laden with water, cactuses, and tubers. A group of field workers chatted as they passed, on the way to the city gates.

Selena led Taimin around a corner and onto another wide avenue. He started when he saw the opposite half of the sky, in the direction of the Rift Valley.

"I've never seen clouds that thick before," Taimin said.

"Nothing to be afraid of," she said quickly.

Taimin watched the darkness shrouding the sky as the thick blanket of gray clouds continued to spread. Since the firewall's disappearance, everything had changed. The sky he was looking at was not the sky he had known his entire life. "I hope you're right," he said under his breath.

After a time Taimin forgot about the evil-looking clouds and as Selena walked on with purpose he instead looked at her. He wanted to talk to her, to explain what he was planning, but at the same time he couldn't.

Selena would try to stop him. She wouldn't want him risking his life. If she chose to, she could thwart his plan—even though he was doing it for her. It was best if she didn't know he was going to do something that Elsa wouldn't like at all.

She turned toward him, and her expression became puzzled. "It's nothing bad, I promise."

Taimin cleared his throat. "I'm just worried . . . Do you really think wyverns can stop them?"

"I'll know better when I see an attack firsthand," Selena said.

Taimin fought his own desire to talk about his plans. "I don't think there's anything more we can learn from Ingren," he said slowly. He watched Selena's expression. "How do you feel about keeping her prisoner?"

"To be honest I'm so busy I haven't had much time to think about her. If I didn't have Rei-kika's help, I wouldn't see you at all."

Taimin kept his face blank. "Maybe we should let Ingren go." He continued to gauge her reaction. "She's already told us about their weapons. She's tried to explain their society."

"You and I both know that Elsa would never release her. Elsa's in charge. We have to trust her. She's doing everything she can."

"But survival requires more than faith."

Selena met his eyes. "We can't just give up. We have to try."

Taimin hesitated. He was coming to the crux of his probing questions. "We're in a losing situation. Shouldn't we try to bring about peace?"

"Peace?" Selena frowned. "You keep telling me that they're led by warriors like the one we fought. He took heads as trophies." She came to a halt and turned to face him. "I know you're scared. We all are." Her tone softened. "But we also have to forget our troubles sometimes. Come on. We're nearly there."

Taimin knew he should be curious about where Selena was taking him, but he couldn't stop thinking about his conversation with Ingren. As he continued to follow Selena, they reached a broad archway that faced onto the avenue, and he started when he recognized the location. He remembered when he was taken captive by the city guard and dragged through the same archway, out of the barracks and onto the streets. Beaten and in a haze of pain, he had been marched all the way to the arena.

Selena saw his face. "What is it?"

"Nothing," he said.

She pursed her lips but focused her attention on the uniformed man who stood waiting for them outside the archway. With his red hair, piercing eyes, and sharp features, Taimin wondered why he looked so familiar, and then realized who it was he resembled.

"He's Dale, Elsa's son," Selena murmured. "The new commander of the city guard."

Taimin rubbed the stubble on his jaw. He had never been able to make his chin so smooth.

"There you are," Dale said warmly as he came forward to greet them. "I was beginning to think you might not be coming. Good to see you again, Selena."

Dale's smile made Taimin frown at Selena. She hadn't mentioned meeting Dale, let alone the fact that he was far from a bad-looking man. But if Selena noticed the way Dale's eyes were on her, she gave nothing away. Instead she hugged Taimin quickly.

"Here he is," she said, a fond expression on her face as she glanced Taimin's way. "Dale, this is Taimin."

Dale held out his hand. Taimin reached out and the two men gripped palms. Dale's handshake was strong. Taimin had to resist putting more pressure into the handshake than was necessary.

"Of course I know who he is," Dale said with an admiring smile. "Now, let's not keep your surprise a secret for too long." He gave a wave of his hand, indicating the archway. "Come inside. Your wyverns are waiting."

Taimin cast Selena a swift look and the sparkle in her eyes returned as she grinned at him.

The barracks were just the way Taimin remembered. Wyverns glared between the bars that kept them penned in their huts. The rectangular floor was paved and swept clean. So early in the day, they had the place to themselves.

Dale approached two wyverns saddled up in the middle of the floor, stirring against the ropes that fastened collars around their necks to hoops nailed into the ground. One was larger than the other, but both had leathery, rust-colored skin, long wings that fluttered, and tapered faces with grooves above their dark eyes. The big one opened its jaws to reveal sharp teeth the size of a man's fingers as it growled at Dale, but Dale was obviously accustomed to his charges and rested a hand on the wyvern's flank to calm the creature before turning to face Taimin and Selena.

Dale raised an inquiring eyebrow at Selena. "You said you've both been on wyverns before?"

"Ah . . ." Selena glanced at Taimin. "Yes."

Taimin and Selena had both flown on Griff's back, but that was a long time ago. Thinking of Griff made Taimin wonder about how his old companion was faring after his transformation from wherry to wyvern. He glanced at the bars keeping the other wyverns penned, and was glad that, wherever Griff was, he was free.

"You'll be fine," Dale said. "They're both well-trained and know their way home. Selena, yours is Flame, this one here. She's the leader." Turning to Taimin, he indicated the smaller of the pair. "Growler here will follow Flame. Ready to go?"

Dale pressed down on Growler's shoulder and the creature obediently dipped to allow Taimin to climb up onto its back. Taimin settled himself onto the saddle and then looked up to see that Selena hadn't waited for Dale and had already climbed on. Her head turned and she grinned again; whatever she had planned, she looked excited and ready to go.

Taimin tried to get comfortable. Something felt different compared with riding Griff. Griff wasn't trained, or caged, or bowed into submission. Griff was his friend. He forced himself to relax in his seat.

"Where are we going?" Taimin asked Selena again.

She gave him a bright smile, along with the same reply. "You'll see." She waited as Dale untethered her wyvern and then she took a deep breath. "Follow me."

Dale came over to untie the rope that held Taimin's mount in place. Selena's wyvern spread her wings, beating them down to propel her lean body into the sky. Taimin barely had a chance to prepare himself as Growler strained, eager to follow suit.

An instant later the pressure of launching into the air pressed him into his seat. He climbed at a steep angle while, up ahead, Selena banked. Taimin gripped hard with his knees and leaned forward to hug the creature underneath him.

His stomach lurched as Selena soared over the city wall and he shot after her like an arrow. He was so high above the rugged plain that boulders looked like tiny pebbles; when he lifted his gaze, he could see all the way to the wrinkles of the Rift Valley. The terrain below him sped past, but looking made him dizzy, so he straightened and focused his attention on the wyvern ahead of him. Wind rushed into his eyes and forced him to blink away tears.

It was still early in the day, but both suns were rising, with the crimson orb of Lux chasing golden Dex. Up ahead, the spread of gray clouds formed an ominous presence on the horizon, past the mountains that bordered the canyon. Taimin was surprised to see that Selena was taking him straight toward the angriest part of the sky.

The Rift Valley came closer and soon Taimin was passing over the multitude of seams in the ground far below. Part of him wanted to scan the landscape but he kept his attention on Selena, who cast him a quick look to check he was behind her. She smiled as she met his eyes, and the sharp peaks of the small mountain range approached with speed. When she cast him another glance over her shoulder, he grimaced. He had a feeling that she was about to do something rash.

Flame tucked in her wings and Selena plummeted toward the gap between two of the peaks. Growler followed without hesitation and Taimin flattened his body against his mount to grip with every muscle he had. He experienced the strange sensation of his stomach moving to the top of his torso. The sheer face of the nearest mountain's summit grew as it approached, jagged and forbidding. Selena took her wyvern far too close to it, banking sharply at the last moment to skirt its edge. There was nothing Taimin could do as his wyvern performed the same maneuver. He gritted his teeth and then the mountains were behind them.

Another plain beckoned. Taimin's anxiety grew when he saw that the black clouds shadowed the region ahead. Foothills passed below them, and Selena lost height as she descended toward the ground. Taimin saw her point at a hump-shaped rock formation. She swooped toward it and the rust-colored plain approached with speed. Taimin braced himself. Selena pulled up hard and Flame's wings slammed down at the ground, raising up clouds of dust before the creature settled on its clawed limbs. Growler came up behind her and Taimin's heart raced as the wyvern pulled up to hover just a few feet above the dirt. Growler's wings fluttered for a moment, then Taimin sensed solid ground beneath them.

He shakily slid off his wyvern's back and saw that Selena had already climbed down. She took Flame's reins in her hands and then glanced back at him to point again toward the rock formation. "We should lead them under that overhang."

"Why?" he called back.

"You'll see."

Growler was willing enough as Taimin led him toward a hollow in the formation's wall, creating a place sheltered from above. Taimin saw Selena tying her reins around a knob of rock and did the same thing. The two wyverns sank down to the ground, weary after the flight.

"Now what?" he asked.

"This way," Selena said with a grin.

She walked away from the rocks and headed back to open ground. Taimin's brow furrowed as he followed her; he couldn't see anything she might be heading toward. As a sudden change took most of the light away from the day, he glanced askance at the sky above. The black clouds were fighting each other, boiling like soup in a pot. There was no blue left anywhere at all; instead he was in shadow, with the suns hidden from view.

Selena came to a halt. She turned and watched him approach and spread her arms, as if finally revealing her secret.

"What is it?" he asked. "Why are we here?"

She lifted her eyes to indicate the gray clouds that clustered overhead. "I farcasted this for you." She took his hand. "Once you made me see the moon in a different way. It's my turn to show you something."

Taimin opened his mouth, but then he shut it abruptly. He was sure that something wet had stung the bare skin of his forearm. He looked at his arm and, sure enough, saw moisture. He turned his hand up and spread his fingers. As he watched, a droplet of water fell from above and splashed onto his open palm. Falling water struck the top of his head.

Then the heavens opened.

He looked in all directions and saw countless clear droplets descend vertically from the sky to strike the ground. In a light trickle, and then a torrent, streams of water fell continuously. Gentle fingers tapped against his crown. Warm liquid trickled down the back of his neck. His face was wet in a heartbeat. He looked at Selena with wide eyes.

"It's rain." She laughed.

Taimin couldn't help but laugh along with her. Selena tilted her head back and opened her mouth. Taimin did the same, astonished as sweet-tasting water slid down the back of his throat. His laughter grew as Selena began to dance, looking up at the heavens and spinning in circles with her arms spread at her sides while her clothing grew wetter and wetter. Her face lit up as she saw him standing still and she came over to take his hands.

They both danced together, and soon they were completely sodden. Taimin had never experienced anything like it. The water felt cleansing; it washed away all his cares. He never wanted the rain to end.

But slowly the rain lessened until it stopped altogether. The clouds shifted overhead and the sky became lighter, with patches of blue visible through the pale gray.

Taimin and Selena stood holding hands and smiling at each other.

Selena came forward, looking up to meet Taimin's gaze. She closed her eyes and her mouth moved toward his. Taimin bent his head and pulled her close, and as they kissed, he loved her for what she had done. He knew it was something he would always remember.

But then guilt started low in his chest and climbed, working its way through his body.

He broke off the kiss and stared into Selena's eyes.

"What?" she asked. "What is it?"

"I want you to know I would do anything for you."

She smiled and brushed her lips against his. "This is what we're fighting for. You and me. We'll find a way to get through this. As long as we stay together. Don't you see? If we lose hope, then we've already lost everything."

Taimin loved Selena. Together they had searched for a city, fought for each other, and seen the world of beauty that lay outside the firewall. Taimin knew he shouldn't feel guilty. Journeying with Ingren to Agravida, and doing everything he could to find a path to peace, was what he had to do.

He couldn't tell her he was going, even though they would no longer be together. Although she might never understand, he had to do everything he could to protect her.

5

Selena stirred in her sleep. Something drifted through to her troubled dreams; she imagined a head bent forward and lips that gently kissed her forehead.

A soft voice spoke. "I love you."

With a smile and a roll of her body, she reached out to pull Taimin closer. Her hand rested on warm bedlinen. A hint of surprise penetrated her slumber, but the moment was fleeting. In seconds her breathing was heavy, in and out, as her body completely relaxed.

———

In the depths of night, Taimin opened the heavy door at the bottom of the tower that was its sole entrance. The door was huge and Taimin's shoulders were tense as he listened for a loud creak, but the hinges were well-oiled and used often. He barely heard the door groan.

He peered out through the narrow crack. The thin guard outside turned and saw him, and then tapped the side of his nose to signal that the way was clear. Like many who had taken up positions under Zorn's new leadership, the guard had been held prisoner with Taimin in the arena.

Taimin opened the door the rest of the way. He then stepped aside as Ingren exited first. Her breathing was louder than a human's and her height meant that even in darkness her silhouette would be remarked on. Taimin followed, wary as he scanned from side to side, but the plaza surrounding the tower was empty.

Now hurrying, he headed over to the wiry guard. As he approached, the man grinned and held up a flask. "I thought if I start drinking now I'll smell just right come morning. Don't worry, I haven't seen a thing."

Taimin gripped the guard's shoulder. "Any sign of Lars?"

"None, I'm afraid."

As he searched up and down the street, Taimin muttered under his breath. He glanced at Ingren, whose expression was apprehensive. Before either of them could think about the long journey they were planning, they had to get safely out of Zorn.

Taimin heard a clatter.

The sound grew louder: a rattle and squeak. Facing the direction it came from, he saw a big man pushing a handcart.

With a bald head and a thick black beard the same color as his hairy arms and legs, Lars was grimacing as he struggled to keep the handcart moving. With two long handles, the cart had a tray deep and wide enough to suit Taimin's purposes, but with every roll of its wheels it made a squeal that set Taimin's teeth on edge. The wood at the sides was splitting in places, bound together with rope. Wherever there was metal, there was rust.

Lars came to a halt. He leaned the pair of long handles on the ground and scowled at Taimin as he panted. "What's that look for?"

The guard sipped from his flask and grinned.

"I asked you for a—" Taimin began.

"You asked me for a cart and you didn't give me any money to pay for it. This is the result." Lars's scowl deepened. "Look, all it has to do is get her out of the city."

"Will it even get us to the gates?" Taimin looked askance at the dilapidated cart. "Haven't you heard the sound it makes? We'll wake half the city."

"You asked me to help. This is what help looks like. In truth, I'd rather get a decent night's sleep for once." Lars nodded in Ingren's direction. "Are we going to do this or not?"

Taimin turned to Ingren, and then back to the cart. "Ingren?" he asked.

She knew the plan. Without another word, she lumbered over to the cart and soon Lars was taking the handles to balance it while she curled herself up on her side; despite the handcart's size, she still had to squeeze herself into it. As she grabbed the blanket in the cart and draped it over herself, Taimin tugged it around her body, creating a misshapen bulk. He decided that the deception was as good as it was going to get.

"Hurry up," Lars grunted. "Are you going to take a handle or not?"

Taimin hefted one handle while Lars took the other. "Ready?" he asked Lars.

"This is a foolish idea."

Taimin ignored him. "Let's go."

———

Taimin looked back at the white city of Zorn, glowing in the light of the crescent moon, and remembered seeing it for the first time. It was isolated on the plain, with tall walls and a soaring tower, strange and otherworldly, not made by human hands.

He kept moving and returned to peering into the night. Wheels ahead of him squeaked, Lars panted, and the handcart threatened to fall apart with every bump and strike against rock. Taimin's arms groaned from pushing his pole. He wondered how Ingren was coping; she hadn't made a sound.

Taimin heard a low whistle. With sighs of relief, he and Lars stopped, setting down their handles.

A moment later Vance stepped out of the darkness. The slender, brown-haired man anxiously scratched at his trimmed beard and moustache.

Taimin had first met Vance in the arena. A weapons trader, Vance had grown up in Zorn, but after traveling the wasteland, he was now as confident outside the city as any of them.

"Part of me was hoping you wouldn't come," Vance said. He glanced at the cart. "So you did it?" He shook his head and gave Taimin a worried look. "Blast it, Taimin, you're taking a risk."

Taimin saw that Vance was carrying two packs, one on each shoulder and both stuffed full. Vance set them down on the ground near the cart.

"Did you have any trouble getting the things we need?" Taimin asked.

"Me?" Vance snorted and turned his attention to the packs. "You've got dried meat, water, blankets—"

Vance broke off and took a step back. Taimin followed Vance's gaze and saw that Ingren had clambered out of the cart. The tall bonded female scanned behind her to take in the distant city before returning her attention to the three humans. Taimin was relieved to see that she looked ready to travel; he wanted to get as far as he could from Zorn by morning. Elsa would be vengeful when she learned that Taimin had left and taken her prisoner with him, and the city guard had wyverns.

Vance tore his eyes off Ingren. "You're sure you want to do this?" he asked Taimin.

"It's no use," Lars said, throwing Vance a look of resignation. "I've already tried."

"I'm sure," Taimin said.

Vance shook his head. "You're brave, I'll give you that." He raised his voice to address Ingren. "You will keep your word?"

"Taimin has nothing to fear from me," Ingren said in her low, gravelly voice, "and I will do what I can to get him to Agravida and give him the opportunity he seeks. However, you are right to tell him that what he does is dangerous."

"This is madness," Lars growled at Taimin. "After everything we've seen, you think these monsters will give you peace, just because you ask for it?"

"And do you think we can beat them in a war?" Taimin replied.

"No," Lars said flatly.

"Then I have to try."

Lars harrumphed. "Well, I suppose this is goodbye." He put out his hand, and Taimin stared into the older man's eyes as he shook Lars's hand firmly.

Vance came forward and opened his arms. He and Taimin embraced. "Be safe, you fool. Farewell."

"Tell Selena . . ." Taimin said to Vance. "Tell her I did this for her." He clapped Vance on the back and then the two men drew apart.

"It won't make any difference," Lars said.

Taimin gazed at the white city on the horizon. "We all know she would never let me go. This was the only way."

Vance turned to look in the same direction as Taimin. "She'll be angry."

Taimin smiled sadly. "I know. But if I'm successful, she'll be alive."

Selena was again at the table in Elsa's workroom. This time, she and Elsa were seated across from two visitors to Zorn: Rathis, a respected clan leader among the skalen, and Pron-mik, a man-torean. Taking advantage of the opportunity, Elsa had asked for their help to elaborate on their map, marking out settlements for Selena to investigate, along with useful information such as popula-tion size. If Zorn could hold out against the enemy, there were great numbers beyond the city—of all races—who could join them as they began to fight back.

"There should be skalen here, here, and here," Rathis said as he pointed out places on the map. "These are the big groups I know about, but you will find smaller clans among the mountains."

Rathis was old, with any feathers on his scalp long gone and his diamond-patterned skin faded enough to blur the segments together. His tilted eyes were wise; like Rei-kika and Blixen, the warden of the Rift Valley, Rathis had played an instrumental part in establishing communication between the different races and ensur-ing that the new peace lasted.

Selena used her charcoal to draw marks on the map to go with the annotations she had already made.

Pron-mik spoke in his clicking voice. "I know of a large skalen clan here as well. Perhaps a hundred individuals. Bax villages here, and here." As his thin finger touched the map in multiple places, Selena was reminded that mantoreans were nomadic.

"Large villages?" Elsa asked.

Pron-mik turned his multi-faceted eyes on Elsa. "A few hun-dred bax in each."

Selena leaned forward to make more marks. Satisfaction welled within her; slowly their knowledge of the wasteland was growing.

All of a sudden Selena's hand stopped moving.

She turned to face the door. A clatter of footsteps grew louder with every passing moment. Her pulse began to race. Someone was running toward Elsa's workroom.

The door burst open.

Dale stood framed in the doorway. He was out of breath and his fiery hair was disheveled. Dread gripped cold fingers around Selena's heart. She wondered if the city was under attack. But when she saw Dale's face, her intuition told her it was something else.

"Our prisoner is gone," Dale panted.

Elsa started. "What?" She frowned. "How? Who was standing guard outside her door?"

"He says Taimin came to relieve him last night. Told him that you gave the order."

"Where is Taimin now?"

"Nowhere to be found."

Selena's heart beat out of time as soon as she heard Taimin's name. Little by little, she realized what had happened. She knew Taimin; as soon as she thought about the misgivings he had voiced, she understood what he had done. He had set Ingren free.

And he hadn't told her he was going to do it.

Elsa cast her a sharp look. "Do you know anything about this?"

"No," Selena said. She couldn't believe it. But what were his intentions? She hadn't seen him in the morning.

Then she remembered: she had heard his voice in the night.

Her stomach churned. The pieces began to fit together. Taimin had brought up the idea of letting Ingren go. Why? He had always persisted with his view that there was no purpose in fighting. What else was there?

Thinking about his probing questions and his talk of peace, Selena knew. Taimin planned to go with Ingren to her home, to the very heart of the enemy's domain. He was heading directly into danger. He would try to talk . . . but the bonded would kill him.

"Do you want me to hunt them down?" Dale asked.

"Yes." Selena lifted her chin to stare at Dale. She had spoken unthinkingly, but she knew what she wanted to happen.

Then Rathis spoke before Elsa could give the order.

"Wait," Rathis said in his reedy voice. Elsa's head swiveled to focus on the old skalen. "He told me of his plan." Selena's mouth dropped open. "I am sorry, Selena. He asked me to say nothing to you." He returned his attention to Elsa. "You must understand. Taimin has made his choice. While we ready ourselves for war, he is trying to find a path to peace. He is taking a great risk. His life is on the line. Should we not let him try?"

Elsa stared down at the map, gnawing at her lip as she pondered.

Selena couldn't hold back her frustration. "Elsa, we have to go after them."

"No, Selena," Elsa said slowly. "I am afraid not. Our skalen friend speaks sense. I could have used Taimin in the fight to save this city, but he has a plan of his own. I don't think he will succeed, but I would be a fool not to let him try."

Without another word, Selena got up and raced from the room.

———

"Selena."

She kept walking, striding furiously, even as a man's voice called after her. "Selena!"

A strong hand grabbed her arm. She turned and saw Dale.

"Where are you going?" he asked as he met her eyes.

They were out on the street, and a few passersby glanced at them curiously, but both Selena and Dale ignored them.

Taimin had left in the night. He knew the wasteland. He would be aware that the city guard on their wyverns might be hunting him. Even with her talent, he would be difficult to locate. If she was going to find him, she had to start right away.

Selena's voice was like steel. "I'm going to get a wyvern and I'm going to go after him. I'll farcast on the way."

"I'm sorry, but I can't let you do it." Dale still held her arm, along with her gaze.

Selena's eyes flashed. "What do you care?"

The corners of his mouth tugged upwards. "Well, for a start, the wyverns belong to the city guard, which means that I have a certain . . . responsibility for them."

"Let me go," she demanded.

"Selena!" he snapped. "What do you think would happen? Do you think he would turn back, just because you went after him? He didn't tell you. I don't know why, but I'm sure he had his reasons."

She tried to make her voice sound calm. "Dale. Please . . . Let me go."

As the moments passed, Dale's lips stayed sealed and all he did was stare into her eyes. The sickening feeling in her stomach grew stronger. She knew that if she yanked her arm out of his grip, Dale would only stop her again.

"Remember what the skalen said." Dale's voice was grim. "Taimin is taking a risk—the greatest risk there is. It may be a foolish idea, but he has courage. You can't take his choice away from him. He doesn't think we can defend ourselves." Dale released her arm. He put his hand on his uniform, near his heart. "I do. What do you believe?"

Selena wouldn't give up so easily. "I'll go with him. He'll need my help."

"And leave this city defenseless? We need you to farcast for us. You know the mantorean can't do it alone. You're the strongest mystic we have."

Selena stared into the distance. Realization struck home. Taimin was heading directly into danger. A human life meant nothing to a bonded warrior. He was never going to return.

It was a long time before she spoke. "He left me," she said softly.

"I know," Dale said. "But remember: he's trying to save you."

6

After one day passed, and then two, Taimin knew that he and Ingren had successfully made their escape, but if anything his sense of urgency grew. He had to travel the wasteland, cross the blackened ground where the firewall once was, and enter Ingren's world. He had to trust that Ingren could get him to the station and onto the quadrail she said would take them swiftly to Agravida.

Taimin spent much of the time thinking about Selena. He knew he had hurt her, but surely she would understand that he had no other choice? He had recklessly tried to find a way through the firewall, and then sought to bring it down altogether, without a thought about who had created it and why. He had to put right what he had done.

Eventually Taimin turned his thoughts from the woman he had left behind. As he set a hard pace, Ingren often cast glances his way, but she left him to his thoughts. Zorn vanished into the distant horizon, and at first there was little conversation, but then the necessities of travel opened a dialogue as they shared food and water and discussed landmarks and bearings. Taimin hunted with his bow while Ingren looked out for dangers. She helped to choose good places to make camp and willingly worked to set up each evening.

Yet still he found himself sometimes looking sidelong at Ingren. Would she honor the bargain they had made? He had got her out of the city. He would keep her safe as she journeyed through the wasteland. But what would happen when they were in her world, rather than his?

Taimin also pondered his destination: Agravida, where the sky marshal ruled the bonded. As he traveled with mountains at his back and a broken landscape of cliffs and gorges in front of him, he realized he would need to learn as much as he could from his companion.

"Your city, Agravida . . . How big is it?" He glanced up at the imposingly tall figure walking beside him.

"Very big." Ingren's face was carved with unfamiliar angles but could still be expressive. She gave him something close to an amused smile. "The place you call Zorn would be swallowed by Agravida many times over."

"Are there no other cities?"

"There are many, but Agravida is the most populous by far."

Taimin was desperate to get to Agravida before Zorn was razed to the ground. "Tell me again how long it will take us to get there."

"Most of the time will be spent getting to the other side of the barrier—" Ingren broke off as she corrected herself. "That is, where the barrier once was. After that we will pass through farmland to reach the quadrail station." She met his eyes as she considered her words. "The quadrail is a series of compartments that travel on four metal rails, hence the name. As I said, if we make it that far, the quadrail will get us to Agravida quickly."

As always, Taimin struggled to understand the things she told him. "So it will take us longer to cross the wasteland than it will to get from the wasteland to Agravida?"

"Yes." A warmth crossed her dark eyes: more amusement at his lack of comprehension.

Taimin found her reaction irritating. "Do my questions make me sound foolish?"

"No, Taimin." The wrinkles in her face creased in what he had learned was a smile. "Not foolish. You seek knowledge. It is to be applauded. You know more about your world. I know more about mine." He cast her a swift look but she appeared to be serious. "I also have sympathy for the position you find yourself in. The humans I am accustomed to, the ones we are at war with, along with the bax, skalen, trulls, and mantoreans . . ." She pointed at the sky. "They understand technology. All of this is new to you."

Taimin scowled. He hated not understanding. Trying to calm his thoughts, he gazed out at the rugged terrain. Still in the foothills, he was high enough to see to the next plain. He remembered long ago, on the same plain, when a firestorm had passed through, and he and Lars had escaped the skalen who had captured them. Ingren said that firestorms were the result of the firewall behaving unpredictably, and were one of the reasons why the bonded had abandoned Zorn, more than four hundred years ago. Taimin supposed that no one would ever have to worry about a firestorm again.

He was lost in thought as he tried to imagine what dangers his journey might bring. Ingren was right. He knew his world, but he had to learn about hers if he wanted to have any chance of success. His survival depended on it.

"You and Ungar spoke a different language . . ." He trailed off as he glanced at Ingren.

"That is correct. Our language is called Ravange."

"Does everyone speak it in Agravida?"

"The language you speak is a common tongue, devised long ago to allow communication between the five allied races, whereas all bonded speak Ravange. Almost no one in Agravida understands the language you speak. I can, due to the study I undertook to support my bondmate's quest."

Taimin looked up at Ingren's face. Despite her fearsome appearance, she was someone who had labored to learn new words and phrases. "You speak it well," he said.

She shrugged. "I learn quickly."

"Ingren . . ." Taimin knew that what he was about to ask of her wasn't part of their bargain. "Will you teach me your language? Will you teach me Ravage?"

"Ravange," she immediately corrected him, and then smiled. However, he continued to wait for her reply, and it was a long time coming. "You want to learn, I can see that."

"Isn't that a good thing?"

"It is. Nothing is more important than knowledge, at least, to one such as myself. I must tell you, though, that you may not be able to learn. It would be difficult to teach you."

Taimin had to do whatever he could to increase his chance of success when he spoke to the assembly and the sky marshal in the strange world he was to visit. "Ingren," he said. "Please. Can't we try?"

Ingren thought for a moment and gazed out at the harsh vista filled with various shades of red, broken up only by boulders, gullies, cliffs, and the occasional gnarled tree or drab green cactus. As she considered Taimin's request, a distant firehound's howl drifted to Taimin's ears, carried on the wind. The sound reminded Taimin that if they were attacked Ingren couldn't defend herself. She needed Taimin's help.

"Very well then," she finally said. "I enjoy a challenge. You have until we get to Agravida to apply yourself."

⌣

Taimin pulled the pricklethorn bush away from the ground, careful to avoid the sharp tendrils that were eager to tear at his skin. He remembered a time when he had thought that the bush was alive, but now it was clearly dead, brown and dry, withered so that it no longer completely obscured the passage in the cliff behind it.

Ingren stepped back as Taimin hoisted the bush and planted it down to the side. Now Taimin stood in front of a crevice, a tunnel in the cliff that burrowed until shadow darkened the interior.

"You knew the bush was hiding something?" Ingren asked, her head tilted to the side.

"I've been here before," Taimin said. "A skalen . . . Syrus. He helped me." He hesitated and then voiced his thoughts. "I thought this might be a place we could replenish our water, but now I'm worried about him."

"Why?"

Taimin stepped inside; the ceiling was low, but he didn't need to duck his head. "He was always firm about keeping this passage well-hidden." He glanced back to see Ingren stoop to squeeze into the tunnel. She pulled the bush back into place without him asking. The thorns she had gripped didn't appear to bother her at all.

Taimin was silent as he led the way. The tunnel wasn't long, and in moments he emerged into a steep-walled ravine. Ingren straightened and looked around her. Tall cliffs bounded the space on both sides. Scrub grass clung tenaciously to the dirt floor.

The sense of emptiness was eerie, and Taimin's hand rested casually on the hilt of the steel sword he wore at his side. Vance had given it to him, and along with the bow on his shoulder; its presence was comforting.

Up ahead, the ravine opened to reveal a basin surrounded by rocky heights that formed a natural protective barrier.

Taimin didn't go any farther.

Once there had been fields that bordered Syrus's homestead. The cactuses and clumps of razorgrass had stood in orderly rows. A timber shack, surrounded by a ditch and a twelve-foot-high fence, had brought back memories of the place where Taimin grew up.

Now everything was black. The rock itself was coated in soot. The fields had been burned to the ground. The homestead was gone, with just a coating of ash in its place.

He didn't walk any closer to the lump that was Syrus's body, but there it was, not far from the ditch.

Taimin released a slow breath as he felt a terrible sadness. Syrus, a skalen raised by humans, had helped Taimin and Lars when they had no one else to turn to. They would have died if the kind old skalen hadn't taken them in. Syrus had enjoyed deep thoughts and deep talks. He didn't have the fear of strangers that many settlers did—after all, Syrus had said, he would meet his end at some point anyway.

Taimin had hoped to ask the old skalen for advice. Syrus had shown Taimin that the different races weren't natural enemies and could live together in peace. What would Syrus have made of the bonded?

As he surveyed the destruction, Taimin was given a stark reminder of the fate that awaited Zorn—and Selena—if he wasn't successful in his quest.

When his sadness shifted to something else, he threw a look of venom in Ingren's direction.

"Before you ask, the answer is yes," Ingren said. "A striker did this. We are systematic beings. Every place that provides a home will be targeted. Like walking through a garden, plucking weeds one by one." As she saw Taimin's expression, she hesitated and then spoke again. "I am sorry," she said. "I can see from your face that you are upset."

"I am."

Ingren nodded at a nearby rock. "We have been traveling hard and we need to rest. Sit. Tell me about Syrus."

Taimin slipped his pack off his shoulder and sank onto the rock. He sighed. "He was old, a survivor. This isn't how he should have died." He forced himself to look again at the skalen's body. "You wouldn't understand."

"We have emotions, just as you do," Ingren said. "Go on. Tell me more. The lives led by others never fail to interest me."

"I think he knew all along," Taimin said. "He spoke about the fact that water once flowed in the wasteland. He said the tales of Earth, a world of rivers and oceans and a single yellow sun, might be memories of a distant past, rather than a place we go to when we die."

"Now there is a name I have not heard in a long time," Ingren said. She met his eyes. "Earth is the world of your origin. It is still the home of humans. We attempted an invasion three hundred years ago. Many died."

Taimin had heard stories of Earth, many times—they were how he knew about rain, rivers, and oceans—but the concept of the afterlife had been confused with the truth. It was strange now, knowing that it was a distant world where the first humans came to be.

He had a sudden thought.

"What is the name of the world we're on now?"

Ingren started. If she were human, she might have put a hand over her mouth. "You do not know. This had not occurred to me. This world, my homeworld, is called Lumea."

"Lumea," Taimin said the name slowly. He wished he could have told Syrus. His thoughts then turned to Earth, and he tried to picture a world with a single golden sun, under attack as bonded fought human. "Why is there a war between the bonded and the five other races?"

"Why does anyone fight? Because we feel threatened."

"But what about people like me? What about us here in the wasteland? We're no threat to you."

"You are. You would not be content to remain within the bounds of where the barrier once was. You are our enemies. Sky Marshal Jakkar could never allow you to roam free."

Taimin clenched his jaw. He stared into Ingren's eyes. "The same two suns watch over us all," he said. It was a phrase she had taught him, and he said it in her language.

Amusement creased her face. "Your accent needs work."

7

Selena always met Dale at night, when Rei-kika took over farcasting. Selena and Dale shared something in common—they were both so busy that it was easy to neglect normal things like feeding themselves. As the days passed, they developed a pattern, and joined each other at The Mason's Lodge to share an evening meal.

In a hurry, Selena passed a pair of bax as she entered the tavern's dining hall. They gave her a cursory glance but when Selena nodded, they grunted an acknowledgement back. Most of the other patrons were humans, but as Selena continued inside she saw a table where a mantorean sat with a pile of dried grubs on a plate in front of him. Swiftly scanning the crowded room, where murmuring men and women sat at round tables made from cactus trunks, she spied Dale seated across from an empty chair.

Desperate to talk to him, she headed straight over.

Dale was still in uniform and his red hair was combed, but his eyes were tired, and there was stubble on his square jaw. He jumped to his feet as Selena approached. "There you are. I was waiting to order." His warm smile disappeared when he saw her face. "What is it?" he asked as he sank back down.

Selena pulled up a seat and leaned forward to stare at Dale intently. "I saw one," she said. "A striker. It was alone, but I saw it destroy an entire bax village."

After a sharp intake of breath, Dale also leaned forward, so that he and Selena were gazing into each other's eyes. "Describe it."

"Ingren's information was accurate. It was a winged machine, the size of a big wyvern. Forty feet from nose to tail. Bright silver."

"How did it move?"

"It didn't look as agile as a wyvern but it was fast. I was watching the village when it came out of nowhere. I saw tubes underneath it and flashes of light. Something detached from the striker's body and shot toward the village. In an instant the whole village was gone." Selena paled. "And all of the bax were dead."

"What happened then? Did you see it leave?"

Selena nodded. "It turned around and went back the way it came. That's why I think it can't turn as quickly as a wyvern." She lifted her hand to demonstrate, following a line and then turning a slow arc until her hand was pointing in the other direction.

"I suppose that's something we won't know until we face them," Dale said in a grim voice. "And we still don't know the answer to the most important question of all: would they use the same weapons to fight an enemy in the sky? Or something else? We might be lucky—perhaps they can only attack targets on the ground."

"I'm sorry," Selena said. "I wish I had answers for you, but I don't."

Dale raised an eyebrow. "You've done more than anyone could have asked," he said. "Can you think of anything else about it that might help us?"

"If I do, I'll let you know."

Dale continued to ponder. "Aurelium damages steel. If we dart around them and make them turn, we could focus our arrows . . ." he mused. With a start, he glanced at Selena. "Sorry. I have some tactics to plan tomorrow."

Selena changed the subject. "How are the new recruits?"

"As well as can be expected," he said. "We don't have long to prepare, but they'll do what they need to when the time comes. It's our lack of wyverns that's the problem. I now have more riders than I have wyverns." He shrugged. "I suppose things could be worse. I'm able to get the best archers from a large pool." After a moment's silence, he glanced at Selena. "I feel alone, truth be told. Even when I'm surrounded by the people I'm supposed to lead. I can't talk to anyone the way I'm talking to you right now. My mother's given me a great responsibility and then, well . . . she's left me to it."

Selena gave a slight smile. "Sounds like Elsa."

"Yes, you know what I'm talking about," Dale said, "and you probably feel even more alone than I do."

"I have my friends," Selena said as she thought about Ruth, Vance, and Lars.

"You don't have to do that, Selena," Dale said. "Don't diminish it. Taimin left you. He did something noble, but it must hurt. How are you managing?" He held her gaze, and then all of a sudden he reached out and placed a hand over hers on the table. After a quick squeeze, he let her hand go. Selena was surprised, and then grateful.

"He did what he thought he had to do," she said.

"Just as we are," Dale said. He didn't speak for a time, waiting to see if she had anything more to say. "Let's move on from serious topics." He considered her for a moment. "You're from the waste-land, aren't you?"

"Elsa told you."

He shook his head.

"Then how do you know?"

"I can tell. You're strong." His blue eyes twinkled. "You speak your mind."

"You're from the wasteland too?" she asked curiously.

"Ha. No." He smiled wryly. "I'm a soft city-dweller."

As Selena examined him, she thought he was tougher than he made out. "What made you join the city guard?" she asked.

"In truth, I always wanted to be a soldier," he said. "I would have joined a long time ago, but my mother hated the Protector and she hated the city guard. So did I." He chuckled. "But I still wanted to be a soldier."

"Is being a soldier what you thought it would be?"

He barked a laugh. "No one could have predicted the situation we find ourselves in."

"We're getting serious again," Selena said.

"We are." He grinned at her. "I'm famished. Let's order some food."

8

"Among bonded, roles are clearly defined," Ingren said. "Advisor, elder, warrior, worker. All bonded are one and not another. Our roles are in our bones and in our blood. Say the four roles to me."

Taimin gathered his thoughts and uttered a series of the guttural syllables that comprised the bonded language.

"Good," she said. "You are improving."

Taimin and Ingren were crossing a broad plain. Taimin set a hard pace, and Ingren's long stride meant she had no difficulty keeping up with him. Boulders and strange rock formations filled his vision. Every footstep took Taimin closer to a hill up ahead, where two massive rocks leaned up against each other. It was mid-morning and the golden sun was alone in the sky, creating wavering shadows in front of the two travelers. In the distance, Taimin saw the first hint of another series of cliffs. He always remained alert for danger.

"We will continue with more names for things," Ingren said. "I will say the word in the common tongue, and then follow with the word in Ravange. You repeat as I go. Understood?"

Taimin nodded when Ingren glanced at him.

"Rock." Pause. A sound like a man being sick. "Tree." Pause. A confusion of grunts. "Sun." A snort. "Star." A chortle.

Taimin spoke the names for roads and the vehicles that traveled them, tall buildings that brushed the clouds, and ships that traveled between worlds. Learning Ingren's language meant learning about her civilization.

As he struggled with the words, he tried to remain calm when Ingren chuckled as he mistakenly uttered obscenities. He pushed on, despite the fact that her constant criticism caused his head to hurt. If he wanted to meet with the assembly and the sky marshal who led the bonded, it could make a key difference if he were able to speak their language.

When they had left the plain to follow the towering cliffs, and Taimin thought about how far they still had to go, his worry resurfaced.

"You said you have weapons that can break mountains," he said. "Why not use them against us?"

"It is true," Ingren said. "We possess weapons that could melt every rock in the wasteland. However the council of elders would speak up, and would never allow such harm to be caused to our world. Hence the use of more conventional weapons."

When Taimin imagined fire raining down on Zorn, his blood ran cold. He and Ingren had been traveling from dawn to dusk, but still he worried about how long it was taking to cross the wasteland.

"Can Zorn hold out against your strikers?" He watched Ingren's face.

"Initially, perhaps. In the long run . . . no. Strikers possess an array of weapons. They are extremely effective."

He continued to look at her, and wondered again if he could trust her. She was his only chance at saving everyone he cared about. At the moment, she needed his help to return to her home. But when they left the wasteland altogether, would she just hand him over to warriors like her dead bondmate Ungar?

He wouldn't know until the time came.

Taimin abruptly halted. His eyes were wide as he stared at the sky up ahead. For a moment he couldn't believe what he had seen, but then it happened again. Light flashed in the clouds and then gave birth to jagged forks, like isolated rays of the golden sun but far, far brighter. The spears of light struck the ground again and again.

He watched apprehensively and wondered if he was looking at some kind of weapon. The wide area of menacing black clouds was above the towering cliffs and escarpment he was heading for.

"It is called lightning in your tongue." Ingren had stopped up ahead and turned when she realized he wasn't with her. "In Ravange, the word is . . ." She made a sound like a repeating grunt, mingled with a hiss. "It is like rain, a natural process. We will soon hear thunder as well."

As soon as she finished speaking, a sound like breaking rocks reverberated over the small plain, as if the sky were splintering into pieces. Taimin's frightened eyes shot to Ingren, but this time she didn't laugh at him.

"Thunder." He said the unfamiliar word below his breath. "Is it dangerous?" he asked. Ingren didn't seem concerned, so he resumed walking, but he kept his anxious gaze fixed firmly on the black strip of sky and the spiky lightning that appeared and disappeared like flickering fire.

"Not especially dangerous," she said, "although I would not hold your sword in the air." Another boom resounded throughout the heavens. She waited for the thunder to finish before nodding in the direction of the escarpment. "Lightning is attracted to metal, particularly if it is held by a human with the name of Taimin."

He knew her well enough to see the twinkle in her dark eyes. "Very amusing," he said drily. "Is it truly attracted to metal?"

"That part is true." She was silent for a time as she squinted at the clouds. "Never fear, little human. I can see that the storm will soon pass. However it will be dark soon." She glanced at him. "Where shall we make camp?"

"There are hundreds of caves at the bottom of the cliffs. I know a good one, with fresh water."

"I remember the caves," she said with a nod. "Do not forget, I came this way with Ungar."

Another flash of lightning made Taimin think again about an imminent attack on Zorn. "We'll rest tonight and climb up the trail tomorrow," he said. "I want to leave the wasteland as soon as possible."

"Good," Ingren replied. "So do I."

———

Taimin woke with a gasp. He wondered what had startled him. He thought he had heard a scuffle, a whisper of something dragged across the dry cavern floor. His head flicked to the side and then his eyes widened. He sat up swiftly.

Ingren was gone.

His gaze immediately shot to the mouth of the cave. The last stars were disappearing from view as the glimmer of early dawn lit up the sky. The golden sun was yet to rise but already the dark blue of night was shifting to a lighter shade. With a silent curse, he leaped to his feet and ignored the sword by his bedside to burst into a run.

He couldn't believe he had been such a fool. He knew it would happen. He had brought Ingren safely across the wasteland. They were close to where the firewall once was. Ingren had left him to continue her journey alone.

He sprinted as he left the cave, but then slowed until he had stopped altogether.

Ingren stood on the expanse of rocky ground that spread out in all directions along the base of the towering cliffs. Her head was tilted back and her eyes were lifted to stare up at the sky above. He wondered if she was looking at the stars, but there were just a handful left to see, and she wasn't looking straight up; her attention was above the escarpment.

"What are you—?"

She held up a hand to cut him off. Taimin fell silent as he joined her. His eyes followed hers. The escarpment was high and it was difficult to see in the low light. Perhaps she had caught sight of some of the wyverns that laid eggs on the ledges. No, she was definitely looking at the sky, not the cliff.

Ingren turned. "Can you hear?"

Taimin frowned. Now that he was listening, he heard a whooshing sound, a guttural gasp of air that grew louder and louder. The sound was similar to the thunder from the previous day, but more constant, with less of the jagged crescendo that gave the impression of rocks breaking in the heavens.

Like Ingren, Taimin craned his neck and watched the cloudless sky. He wasn't sure where the sound was coming from, but it was definitely from somewhere up above. He focused his attention on the top of the cliffs.

His jaw tightened. Normally, at all times of day, he would see wyverns soaring near their nests, but there wasn't a hint of a flying creature, not even a bird. It was as if the noise had forced every living thing to hide, which made him wonder if he should do the same. The powerful roar grew in volume with every beat of his heart as it took on the nature of a screaming whine.

Then he saw them.

He gasped. Three winged machines shot over the top of the cliffs. They streaked through the sky, and in moments they were overhead. The three machines were sleek and angular, shaped like throwing knives, and gave off a metallic, silver sheen in the morning light. They were unbelievably swift. Unlike a bird or a wyvern, their narrow wings appeared to be fixed in place, and didn't move at all. It was unclear how they stayed in the sky.

Taimin's heart thudded in his chest as the three strikers flew overhead. White horizontal trails formed cloud-like plumes in the air, lines that proved how straight their passage was, without turn or deviation.

Taimin had to spin to follow them. He tracked them with his eyes until they were gone. The noise hovered in the air, along with the long lines of pale mist the strikers left behind them.

"Three of them," Ingren said. She gave Taimin a grim look. "Enough for Zorn."

Taimin used the white lines in the sky to guess the strikers' direction of travel. There was no way of knowing for certain, but if the winged machines were heading for Zorn, they were going the right way.

He wanted to run, to race after them, even though he had seen them for only a moment before they were gone from view. Fear sank into his chest.

"Selena," Taimin said out loud.

"Even if she is in danger, there is nothing you can do," Ingren said. She met his eyes and her voice was surprisingly gentle.

Taimin gazed in the direction the strikers had gone. What if he were already too late? What damage could they inflict on the city? His stomach churned. He should never have left.

"Taimin." Ingren said his name, dragging his attention onto her. She nodded at the cliffs. "You can do nothing but keep going, and get to Agravida swiftly. If you are ready, we can commence the climb right now."

Taimin knew she was right. He had to cling to hope. The strikers might not be heading for Zorn. Hope was all he had.

He was surprised when her huge hand with claw-like fingers gripped his upper arm and gave him a squeeze.

"Come," Ingren said. "Lead the way."

9

Selena was in darkness. Her limbs twitched. Her eyelids fluttered. Was she asleep? Weariness tried to drag her down, sucking her into unconsciousness, but something inside her fought it.

All of a sudden the darkness was no longer complete. Three silver triangles, like distant stars, appeared against the black. The shining shapes grew larger and larger. The triangles were sharp, like arrowheads made from steel, honed until they had edges like razors. She rolled fitfully in her sleep. This was different from a nightmare. She reached out to touch the tiny triangles and they stabbed her palm.

As she tried to surface from her deep slumber, her fingers flexed. She groaned. This was a sensation she recognized. Before she learned to control her abilities, dangers out of view would start as feelings of unease. But this was more than unease. She knew that in the real world, she was gasping. Something was coming. Something was coming.

Something was coming!

She lifted her head and sucked in a breath as she opened her eyes. The deep-blue sky glowed outside the oval window of her bedchamber in the tower. A solitary star twinkled. A faint hint of pink and gold tinged the heavens. It was early dawn, barely light enough to be called morning.

The fear stayed with her. Her heart raced, beating with a swift tempo. Was it just a terrible dream? Now that she was awake, she had to know.

She sat up on her bed and rested her hands on her knees.

Her eyes lost focus.

She imagined a radiant orb inside her mind and visualized a pair of hands reach out to grab it. The orb became lighter than a feather; it wanted to float. Casting was familiar to her; she could do it with a moment's thought. She allowed her symbol to pull her awareness free from her physical body.

Immediately she turned her attention upward. Her consciousness climbed through the floor separating her from the observation room, then above the tower itself and the surrounding city. She ascended the sky as fast as she could and the ground fell away until Zorn became smaller and smaller, until finally it was a miniscule disc enclosed by white walls.

With the jagged fear still swamping her thoughts, she spun around and around, searching in all directions.

She stopped turning. Something was moving, to the right of the small range of mountains that bounded the sunburned plain. A pinprick against the dawn sky gave a twinkle as the rays of the golden sun sparkled on its surface. A second speck glimmered also, and then a third. The three specks became silver triangles, moving at speed. The way they grew in size made it clear: they were heading directly toward the city.

Selena knew that there was no time to see them up close. The three triangles were far too fast. They would be at the city in no time at all.

She dived down toward the city and with an abrupt jolt returned to her body. She had fallen asleep fully clothed, and raced from her bedchamber and down the corridor. Reaching the stairway that climbed to the observation room, she threw her body upward, struggling with the steps that weren't designed for a human's stride. At the top step she stumbled and fell face down to land painfully. With a grimace she shot up again and sprinted for the center of the chamber. She lunged for the long rope that hung from the ceramic bell.

The observation room at the top of the tower was open on all sides. Selena turned to watch the sky even as she hauled on the rope. With her naked eye, she now saw the three triangular shapes clearly. A low noise filled the air, a coarse whooshing that reminded her of the sounds given off by the machine buried under the desert. The bell casing jerked back and forth as the bell began to clang. Keeping the rope in her hands, she rushed to the edge of the floor and gazed down at the city as she pulled again and again. Despite the early hour, a few workers and traders moved in the streets below. As soon as the bell began to herald that danger was near, they ran for the shelters. She heard screams.

The bell continued to peal, making a loud, jarring sound. In between the jangles the hiss that reverberated through the sky became a high-pitched, mechanical whine. The triangles had grown in size. Now they had form. The flying machines had narrow, tapered tips, sleek bodies, and sharp, tucked-in wings.

The three strikers flew together, triangles that formed a larger version of the same shape. The first winged machine was still outside the city wall when Selena saw flashes from below each of its wings. Something bright and crimson streaked ahead. The striker was quick, but whatever it had released was swifter by an order of magnitude.

Selena's chest tightened. The two projectiles almost hurt her eyes to look at as they sped through the air and twin bright lines lost height to reach the ground. They struck a pair of neighboring houses, a block inside the wall of white stone.

The two houses exploded simultaneously, instantly obscured by a cloud of flame and dust. The strikers released more projectiles. The thudding boom of each detonation caused the tower to tremble beneath Selena's feet. In moments the silver machines were past the walls and over the city. Together they launched salvos of bright lights at the structures below them. Building after building shattered into pieces.

People were dying. Selena was watching it happen. She rang the bell as if she could somehow save them. But families would hear the bell while still in their beds. Parents would wake with startled glances at each other as their thoughts immediately turned to their children. Then everything would turn red, before it became black forever.

Her eyes followed the three silver machines as they shot past the tower, leaving destruction in their wake. The strikers turned as they reached the far side of the city, preparing to make another pass over the structures below.

Then they slowed. The strikers hovered, as if demonstrating to the inferior creatures below that they owned the sky, and that the settlement that was home to thousands was theirs to destroy at will. Selena hated them with every fiber of her being. They were utterly cold, filled with malice.

A glimmer at the wing of the lead striker heralded another projectile. Watching the streets, Selena saw Grom, the burly, shaggy-haired administrator Elsa had tasked with building shelters. He was waving his arms and bellowing at every person he could find, no doubt telling everyone to get to the nearest shelter. The bright flash streaked down to burst onto the street. The resulting cloud of flame enveloped the section of road. Dozens of people disappeared in flame, Grom among them.

The strikers now moved slowly through the air, taking their time. Clearly they wouldn't leave until the whole city was rubble.

But then Selena felt a kindling of hope.

She let go of the rope connected to the bell and clutched one of the columns at the edge of the floor. She squinted as she saw something lean and lithe with rust-colored skin beat down its wings to climb into the air.

A wyvern was flying out from the barracks. More followed behind it, one after the other, until dozens filled the sky, with their riders demonstrating impressive discipline as they formed up to make a wall of flying creatures.

The city guard had come to Zorn's defense.

As soon as their group was complete, the wyverns sped forward. Selena had never seen them move so fast. They flew at the three strikers from behind. Selena guessed there must be close to fifty wyverns or more.

The strikers ceased firing on the structures below and turned as they became aware of the new threat. The two groups were now close enough to the tower for Selena to see the men in blue uniforms on the wyverns' backs. The soldiers held bows. Even as their mounts closed the distance to the strikers, the riders aimed their arrows.

The first of the strikers completed its turn and released a stream of sparks that enveloped a section of the wyverns. Selena cried out as both the wyverns and their riders were ripped to shreds. But the rest of the city guard kept going, clear in their aim of getting close enough to use their bows. Soon all three strikers had opened fire.

Selena saw a red-haired rider at the center of the line. "Dale," she whispered.

Dale waved an arm and the line broke up as the wyverns performed evasive maneuvers to escape the hail of sparks. Even as they weaved, ducked, and swooped, they never stopped closing the distance to the three machines. Selena watched Dale closely;

he had flattened his body so that he was low on his wyvern's back. He straightened and raised his bow to pull the string to his cheek.

Selena watched breathlessly as a moving green light was the only sign of Dale's arrow. The arrow was fashioned with an explosive aurelium head, designed to detonate on contact, and carved its passage through the sky. It struck one of the strikers and a boom split the air as a burst of flame clouded the machine's silver wing. The other soldiers of the city guard released their own arrows. Another aurelium arrow slammed into the crippled striker and it shifted into a wild spin, descending in circles before it crashed into the street below.

With renewed vigor, the soldiers of the city guard closed in.

———

Lars had seen a lot of death, but nothing like this. As he raced along the street, he skirted a crater filled with charred bodies; it was only luck that the explosion hadn't caught him too. He passed terraced houses on both sides; all he knew was that he wanted to get to the nearby city gates. His instinct to survive was strong, overriding everything else.

His eyes roved wildly, searching for danger. A high-pitched whine came from the sky above him. A moment later he saw the source as a striker fell into a crippled spiral, losing height until it vanished behind a city block to make a boom it made when it hit the ground. He caught a glimpse of the arena down a side alley. Smoke poured from somewhere behind its tall, enclosing walls.

The two remaining strikers streaked overhead, trying to evade the wyverns pursuing them. Lars admired the bravery of the city guard, but he was glad he wasn't up there. Despite the wyverns arrayed against them, the strikers continued to fire at the city below. Tubes under the strikers' wings released projectiles that arced down toward the white-walled houses. As buildings shattered, slivers of stone flew in all directions.

A woman's scream made Lars's head jerk to the side.

"Gretel!" The scream came from the next house in the terrace. Just ahead, Lars saw a two-storied dwelling with an open doorway. A second scream was even louder. "Gretel!"

Moments later, a man bellowed along with her. "Gretel!"

A small girl with a crown of curls exited the house and ran onto the street. Lars didn't know why the girl was trying to run from who he assumed were her parents.

Everything happened fast.

A bright light flashed from high above. The projectile was so swift that if Lars hadn't been looking, he wouldn't have seen its passage.

The house exploded.

Smoke, dust, and debris flew outward in all directions. In an instant there was no house, only flame. Anyone inside was dead in a heartbeat; they wouldn't have even known what had hit them.

Lars stopped so suddenly that he skidded. He wasn't the only one.

The little girl fell onto her hands and knees. Wide-eyed, she turned to face the house she had just come from. She didn't scream, or call for her mother or father. Her expression was stunned.

Lars burst into a run. He reached the girl and wrapped his arms around her in case she tried to run toward the smoking ruin that had once been her home.

"Don't go in there!" he growled, staring into the girl's eyes. He remembered her name. "Gretel, is it? Don't move."

He heard a change in the whining sound that the strikers made. Even as he held the girl, he scanned the sky until he saw the winged machines climb the sky. Seeking to get away from the wyverns, the surviving pair of strikers separated. The high-pitched whine became

72

louder until it overwhelmed any other sound. As the two strikers put on speed, the powerful roar made the heavens rumble. Then they were gone.

The attack was over. The wyverns had beaten back the enemy.

But for Gretel, it was too late.

Lars let out a shaking breath. He brought himself down until he was at eye-level with the young girl. He knew nothing about children; what was she, four years old? Six? All he knew was that he had to find someone to look after her.

"Gretel? Can you hear me? Have you been hurt?"

She stared at him with blank eyes.

"Come on."

He grunted as he picked her up, holding her with one strong arm. Leaving behind the ruins of her home, he headed up to a doorway across the street and knocked at the tall wooden door. When no one came, he pounded harder, but still to no avail. Meanwhile he inspected Gretel's face. She didn't say a word. Nor did she protest at the stranger holding her to his shoulder. He wondered what was going through her mind.

After raising a din and calling out, he decided that the house was vacant. With a sigh, he left the doorstep and headed to the next house in the row.

"Hello!" he bellowed, pounding his fist against the door. Gretel was becoming heavy, so he shifted her weight. "I need help!"

He sighed with relief when the door slowly opened. A middle-aged woman with dark hair cautiously revealed her careworn face. She was almost shaking. No doubt she had been cowering from the attack, terrified of the battle in the sky.

"What is it? Are we safe?" she asked.

"The attack is over," Lars said grimly. "Do you know this girl?"

The woman hesitated and then nodded. "I've seen her face. I think she lives up the street."

Lars glanced again at the smoking ruin of the girl's home. "Not anymore. See for yourself."

The woman peered out from the doorway and gasped when she saw the aftermath of the explosion.

"Does she have any family in the city?" Lars asked.

The woman shook her head. "They only just arrived. Newcomers. They don't know a soul." She paled as she corrected herself. "Didn't know, I mean."

Lars's mouth tightened. He indicated the girl. "I need you to take her."

"Not on your life!" the woman snapped. "I have four children already."

"Then what am I supposed to do with her?" Lars demanded, before the door shut in his face.

With a scowl, Lars set Gretel down and took her hand as he led her back onto the street.

He needed to find someone else to take the girl. He didn't know the first thing about children. He was a free man, had always been a free man, a rover, traveling far and wide, living by his wits. Responsibility was the last thing he should be given.

He inspected Gretel more carefully as she looked up at him. She still hadn't spoken, nor emitted a sound at all. She had plump cheeks, blue eyes, and blonde, curly hair.

All of a sudden, she burst into tears.

Lars didn't have a choice. It might take him some time, but he would find an appropriate home for her. She had lost everything in one swift, deadly moment.

He took her hand again.

"Come with me," he said gruffly.

10

"Mystic . . ." the thin man with his arm in a sling said. "Are there . . ." He hesitated. "Are there any more survivors under there?"

There was no use softening it. "I'm sorry," Selena said. "The woman we're looking for is the only one."

His narrow face was covered in dust. Tears had carved tracks down his cheeks. "My brother," he said. "My uncle." He covered his mouth with his hand.

Selena faced a wide pile of charred stone where an entire terrace of houses had shattered. She watched with mingled hope and fear as a dozen brawny men worked at the rubble to remove one heavy block after another. A crowd looked on from a distance.

She glanced at the sky; it would be dark soon, but she desperately wanted the light to last just a little longer. After visiting all quarters of the city, she had never seen so many bodies. People sought her out and she followed them from one ruined house to the next. Frantic faces watched her as she tried to sense living souls under the rubble, her eyes becoming unfocused. But more often than not she was forced to shake her head. Her talent enabled her to sense the living, but there was nothing she could do to find the dead.

Nonetheless, those who searched for loved ones refused to give up, and she couldn't blame them. The rubble would take a long time to be cleared. More bodies would be unearthed. It didn't matter whether they were children, adults, or the elderly; the attack had been indiscriminate.

Zorn wasn't yet in mourning; that would come. The aftermath of the dawn attack was something that had to be dealt with.

Selena glanced away from the chain of laboring men hauling the stones. Not far from the rubble, she saw Ruth. The healer was crouching next to a boy, who sat with a dazed expression and savage burns on his bare legs. Jerome, Ruth's older colleague from the infirmary, was checking the boy over while Ruth spoke softly to him. The boy's face was shocked. Selena couldn't hear what Ruth was saying, but the boy nodded when she asked him something. A linen sheet lay over a body next to them.

A cry made Selena return her attention to the workers. A burly man with thinning hair waved furiously at his fellows. The human chain broke up as the gang rushed forward. The workers threw rocks the size of their heads as if they weighed nothing at all, then four men labored together to lift away a heavy stone slab. Selena swallowed, hoping that the frightened woman she had sensed under the rubble wasn't seriously injured.

The burly man gave a bellow. He reached down with both arms and spoke to someone, and then a moment later he slowly pulled up an old woman with gray hair like a bird's nest. She was obviously shaken, and covered in white dust, but miraculously she was unharmed. The man who had found her helped her away from the ruins of her home.

As soon as she was clear, the gray-haired woman sat down heavily, but she looked up when she heard a cry: 'Grandma!' Despite his injuries, the boy with the burned legs pulled away from Ruth. He ran toward the old woman and they embraced.

Selena let out a slow breath.

She turned when she heard a voice call her name and saw Elsa approaching. The leader of Zorn was alone, and the dust in her hair made her look even older than she was. Like Selena, Elsa had been rushing from one part of the city to the other.

"Are there any more?" Elsa asked wearily.

Selena shook her head. "She's the last one."

Elsa's weathered face was grim. "Well, at least we survived, for the time being." She glanced at Selena. "How are you holding up?"

"I'm fine," Selena said.

"You're tired, and you feel guilty," Elsa said. "Get used to it." She harrumphed. "It could have been worse," she said. She spoke low enough that she wouldn't be overheard. "Our enemies weren't expecting the wyverns. Next time won't be so easy."

Selena took a last look at the scene. There was nothing more she could do. "I should head back to the tower—"

A round-faced older man called out; he waved his arm as he hurried toward them. "Elsa!"

Elsa turned sharply. "Eh?"

"It's your son. He was injured in the attack."

"What?" Elsa gasped. "I was told he was unharmed."

"I only just found out. He's at the infirmary."

Elsa started to walk. "Selena," she called over her shoulder. "Come with me."

Selena caught a rare glimpse of Elsa's inner workings as the older woman took a deep breath, set her face like stone, and then entered the infirmary.

Selena glanced around. She had been to the infirmary before to visit Ruth, but today, despite being one of the city's largest buildings, it was packed with wounded people. The long room was laid out like a mess hall, but, rather than tables, contained rows of benches and beds. Archways separated one section from another, and the high ceiling helped disperse the murmured conversations and occasional cry of pain. Healers dressed in white smocks moved about. Ruth was going to be busy.

While Elsa led the way, heading farther into the interior, Selena recognized the men, women, and children she had helped to locate after they were buried under the ruins of their homes. She saw the young parents with the little girl, all suffering from burns but well enough to give her a nod of acknowledgement. The old washer-woman she had found early in the day held a baby to her breast, rocking from side to side as she made shushing sounds. The babe's mother was conspicuously absent.

Elsa navigated the infirmary until she passed through one of the archways. Selena followed her toward a man seated on a stool with his back to her. Clad in a blue uniform, he was alone and waited patiently: clearly the healers had other charges with more urgent needs. His fiery red hair marked him out.

As Elsa cleared her throat, Dale turned. If Elsa was relieved, she didn't show it.

He looked haggard. A few smudges covered the dusting of freckles on either side of his angular nose and his blue eyes were reddened. His sighed with resignation when he saw Elsa.

"Mother," Dale said. "I'm barely hurt. I didn't even want them to bring me here." He stood awkwardly, wincing as he put a hand against his side. "It's nothing," he said. "A bruised rib is all." He glanced at Selena. "I hope you had a better reason to come than to see me."

Elsa slowly looked her son up and down. She nodded to herself, and then turned to Selena. "I have a thousand things to do. Stay with him until one of the healers comes. Make sure he's telling the truth."

"But I have to farcast—" Selena said.

Elsa cut the air with her hand. "It's after dark. Another attack won't come today." She returned her attention to Dale. "If you're lying to me, we'll be having words." She stood on her toes to kiss him on the forehead, before rushing away to leave Selena and Dale behind.

"Never work for your mother," Dale said. As he focused his twinkling eyes on Selena, she felt a flutter in her stomach.

"You should sit down," Selena said.

"I—"

"Sit," she said, pushing down on his shoulders as she put some of Elsa's firm tone into her voice.

He gave her a grin and returned to his stool.

"What was it like up there?" she asked seriously. Dale immediately sobered. Selena couldn't imagine how it must have felt to fly a wyvern directly at those sinister machines while they destroyed building after building below. She remembered seeing Dale at the forefront of the line of wyverns, heading directly into the stream of sparks that tore apart his companions.

"Frightening." He let out a breath and looked away from her. "I lost some good men."

"You drove the strikers away. We all owe you our lives."

A cry of pain made them both glance back at the beds and the people groaning as they waited their turn to be attended by the healers. Selena watched for a moment and then returned her attention to Dale.

"Did you hear the bell?" she asked.

"The whole city did."

"Next time I'll do better." She felt a surge of guilt. "I should have seen them sooner."

"You're only human, Selena."

"Do you think they'll come back?"

He sighed. "Of course they will."

Selena spoke firmly. "And you'll see them off again—"

Selena heard a voice call her name and glanced over her shoulder to see Ruth heading her way. Ruth's short, wavy hair was unruly and dust covered her forearms. Grime and blood stained her healer's smock.

"Vance wants you," Ruth said.

"Where is he?"

"Outside."

Selena frowned. "Is it urgent?"

"You know Vance," Ruth said wearily. "With him, everything's urgent."

"Ruth," Selena said quickly, before her friend could leave. "Elsa asked me to find out what's wrong with Dale."

Ruth barely gave him a glance. "Bruised ribs. Low-grade burns. His chest needs binding and he needs rest. You'll have to excuse me," she said.

As Ruth departed, Dale gave Selena another grin. "See? I was telling the truth."

"Do what she says and get some rest," Selena said. "I have to go." She was surprised to hear the regret in her own voice.

"Until we meet again, Selena." He gazed into her eyes. "When you go to sleep tonight, just remember: we can do this. Together we'll save Zorn."

She felt his eyes on her as she walked away.

———

Vance watched from just inside the infirmary's broad entrance. Past the rows of beds he saw Ruth near a bench. There were several healers dispersed through the long hall, but she always seemed to be with the same colleague. He had white hair, but he wasn't an old man. He stood quite close to her. When she unrolled a length of bandage, he cut it. She poured a cup of water from a jug, and he took it from her hands. They brushed against each other. They murmured. He spoke into her ear. She nodded. They walked away together.

"Vance?"

He realized Selena was standing beside him. She looked tired. Her long black hair was lank and there was a tightness around her eyes. Slight and slender, her appearance always made him think she was frail, but he knew that she could keep going when other people would have faltered.

Vance tore his eyes away from Ruth. It took him a moment to remember why he had asked for Selena. "I'm trying to find something that will work against those machines." His determination grew as he met her eyes. "The right weapon could make a difference."

"What can I do?"

"I need aurelium, but it's in short supply. Will you talk to Elsa for me?"

"I'll do what I can. How much do you need?"

"As much as I can get."

Selena looked past Vance to gaze outside the infirmary. "I can't believe it's night." She let out a breath and then nodded. "I'll go and find Elsa now."

She left without another word, and Vance called his thanks to her departing back. He had things to do, but he watched Ruth for a moment more as she bustled around the infirmary. Flickering torches now lit up the interior: aurelium was too valuable as a weapon to use for lighting. The white-haired healer went over to squeeze Ruth's hand and then led her toward the beds. Vance frowned.

"There you are," a rough, gravelly voice called, loud enough to cause some of the healers to glance in Vance's direction.

Vance turned and saw Lars out on the street. The old skinner was unperturbed by the fact that his voice was far too loud for the calm murmurs inside the infirmary.

Shaking his head, Vance left the doorway. The street was dark and quiet, and by some miracle had been spared the destruction visited on so many other quarters in the city.

"I went to your house but you weren't there," Lars said flatly. "I need somewhere to stay. And, before you say anything, an inn is no place for a child."

The big man moved and Vance's mouth dropped open when he saw a little girl with a crown of blonde curls half-hiding behind Lars's thick body. She gripped the skinner's hand tightly and looked at Vance with frightened eyes. He guessed her age at five or six years old.

"This is Gretel," Lars said. He leaned in to speak into Vance's ear so she couldn't hear. "Her parents were killed in the attack. Died right in front of me. They were wastelanders, new to the city. She's got no one else." He stared directly at Vance with his disconcertingly dark eyes. "Well? Can we stay with you?"

After traveling across the wasteland with the skinner, Vance knew that he and Lars rubbed up against each other in all the wrong ways. But he also knew when someone needed his help. He looked down to meet Gretel's eyes and smiled at her. "Hello, Gretel." He hoped he was doing it right; he had almost no experience with children. When she shrank farther behind Lars, he returned his attention to the older man. "Of course. You don't even have to ask."

"Good," Lars grunted. "I'll go there now. You have food, don't you?" He gave a short nod. "Of course you do. I'll see you there."

The big man crouched down and met Gretel's eyes. His expression softened.

"All right, Gretel?" Lars asked. "We're going to go to Vance's house."

Vance was surprised. Even the tone of Lars's voice had completely changed, and was more gentle than he had ever heard it before.

"Vance and Ruth are friends of mine," Lars continued. "You'll like them both."

Vance's heart went out to the girl when her face remained blank and she didn't reply at all, but Lars was unfazed as he led her away.

Vance watched them set off down the street, hand in hand, and then glanced back inside the infirmary. Ruth was once more murmuring, with her head close to the healer with the white hair. Vance knew she wouldn't be home for a long time.

With a sigh, he hurried to catch up with Lars and Gretel.

11

Taimin had once faced the firewall and watched his parents' bodies burn to ash on the ground he was now about to walk upon.

Ingren glanced at him. "This will be a new experience for me too," she said. "The last time I came this way I wore protective clothing. However, I am certain that it is safe."

Taimin still didn't move. "Why is everything so hazy?"

He had grown up not far from the firewall, where the sky had been tinged a menacing shade of pink that deepened to red with every footstep taken closer to the barrier. Within the wall of searing heat, the rust-colored terrain had visibly blackened, like char.

Now everything was different.

Where the firewall had been, a thick gray mist, like steam or smoke, clung to the landscape. It looked viscous, as if entering it would be to walk into something solid. Taimin could only see a short distance before the blackened terrain blurred and vanished.

"The ground has been hot for a long time," Ingren said. "I would surmise that the heat is colliding with the air around it."

For the first time, what Taimin was about to do truly sunk in. He was about to leave the world he knew. He had no idea what he would find on the other side.

Ingren saw his hesitation. "It takes courage, what you are doing," she said. "You are strong, Taimin. And I do not refer to your strength as a warrior."

The air tasted foul on his tongue, like ash combined with stinking mud. "Is it safe to breathe?"

"I hope so."

He cast a swift glance at his taller companion. The familiar look of amusement wrinkled her face.

"We will not be breathing this air for long," she continued. "And what choice do we have? We will be fine, little human."

"How long will it take us to get to the other side?"

Ingren looked over her shoulder. The two suns, one close and golden, the other a smaller crimson circle, had just begun their ascent of the sky. "It will be a long day, but we will get to the other side before nightfall."

"Good," Taimin said.

He took a cautious breath. His senses told him that the air was breathable.

With determination, he took a first step, and then another.

The region of foul, smoky air swallowed him up, while Ingren walked at his side. At first he was treading on the familiar rust-colored ground, but then it became darker, until it was black. The gray haze clouded his vision.

Taimin focused his attention straight ahead as he left the wasteland behind.

———

The two blurred suns climbed the sky, but it was difficult to judge the passage of time. Taimin walked with long strides, but Ingren was frequently ahead of him. Clearly she was reluctant to wait, and wanted to get through the haze as badly as he did.

The ground was black in all directions. Taimin had never walked on a surface like it. The grains beneath his boots crunched like dirt, but nothing grew, and through his soles he could feel warmth seeping up from below. He was hot, and blinked sweat out of his eyes. At first he had tried to take short breaths, wary of the sickening stench that made his stomach churn, but he couldn't fight the urge to get air into his lungs.

He was grateful for the fact that every now and then Ingren checked over her shoulder and stopped to wait. If she had simply plunged into the haze, he never would have found her again. The only landmarks were hulking black boulders and the occasional crack that split the ground wide open. He glanced at a steep gully to his left. He didn't like the idea of falling down and becoming injured.

Slick patches began to dot the landscape. As Taimin wondered what they were, his boot sank into a puddle of hot ooze—a mixture of blackened dirt and water. He grimaced and struggled to free his foot, but at least the sludge wasn't scalding.

Ingren called back to him. "Be careful. It must have rained here recently." She then glanced down at the ground at his feet. "Ah, I see my warning came too late."

With a grunt he yanked his leg free. "Yes," he said drily. "It did."

"Soon the weather will change all this." She waited for him to catch up to her and then waved her arm as she resumed walking. "The ground here will then be much the same as the ground anywhere else. Plants will start to grow. It may be hard to imagine, but it will happen."

Taimin didn't reply. He did his best to keep his mouth shut and his lips firmly sealed. His nostrils flared with every breath, but his tongue needed some time without tasting the air.

Ingren noticed his expression. "I also find this unpleasant. The sooner we are through, the better."

Taimin nodded. Ingren again began to outpace him.

But then he came to a sudden halt. He froze and cocked his head. He thought he had heard something.

He wasn't sure at first, but then a low howling sound, muffled by the thick air, caught at the very edge of his senses. It was gone as soon as he noticed it.

"Ingren," he called. "Wait." She frowned and looked back at him. "Do you hear anything?"

She snorted. "I can hear—"

Taimin shook his head, cutting her off. The howling sound droned through the air again, followed by a distant baying. It was the last thing he had expected to hear in this place.

"Firehounds," Taimin hissed. He kept his voice as soft as possible. "Stay quiet."

He placed his hand on the hilt of his sword and carefully drew the blade from the scabbard. The steel made a slight whisper, but nothing that would give him away. He wondered if the foul air would prevent the firehounds from smelling them. A sonorous howl sounded closer this time. Another came right after it.

He stood with his sword drawn, turning his head to peer in all directions as he struggled to see through the haze. He cast Ingren a swift look. "Do you have a weapon?"

"I cannot defend myself."

He had expected the reply, but it still surprised him. "Not even from an animal?"

"It is unusual for an elder to be so far from the protection of home."

He thought furiously as he took in her commanding height and her huge hands, which looked strong enough to rip a man's arm from his body. "Get behind me and stay there."

Brandishing the steel blade in front of him, he continued to stare into the mist that clung to the terrain and clouded the sky. If he hadn't been forced to protect Ingren, he could have kept turning, but with her behind him he was forced to judge which direction the howling had come from. He blinked; it was impossible to see far. He thought something had moved when the air cleared for a moment, but it could just have been a distant boulder.

Then three lithe shapes lunged out of the haze.

The firehounds were already racing toward them. Leathery skin covered their bodies, the same rusted color as Ingren's. Oversized jaws dominated their wedge-shaped heads. Sweat glistened on their hides. They bayed while their clawed feet dug into the terrain. The two firehounds on either side had short, pointed horns, but the one in the middle, the largest, had a pair of sharp horns twisted into a spiral shape.

"Stay back!" Taimin called to Ingren without looking at her.

He hoped she had listened to him as he turned his body at an angle. Three firehounds would be more than a match for a human, and there was no time for his bow. The big firehound in front was the most dangerous. He would need to weave and strike when it lowered its horns.

The big firehound outdistanced its companions as it snarled. Saliva dripped between its teeth. Taimin waited for the right moment. He stood ready, with the point of his sword slightly raised. The firehound fixed him with its deep-set eyes, and then dropped its head to charge.

Taimin's instincts took over. He stepped to the side, hacked down with the sword, and felt the blade bite deep into the fire-hound's back, just behind the thick neck. The creature yelped and collapsed onto the blackened ground.

As the next pair charged, Taimin knew he couldn't repeat the same maneuver. If he dodged again, whichever creature he didn't strike would continue past him to gore Ingren. He loosened his grip on his sword, but kept the blade steady. He had one chance, and one chance only.

The firehounds lowered their horns. Swift as a snake, Taimin cut twice in quick succession. His blade slashed one firehound's flank, and then he brought his sword across the second creature's legs. They weren't killing blows, but they were the best he could manage to disable them and save Ingren from attack.

Both tossed their heads. Taimin's years of training and experience told him to dodge, but he slipped in the mud and a sharp horn collided with his knee. He resisted the urge to stagger, even as pain spiked through his leg. Instead he sank to the ground and thrust his sword into the nearest firehound's chest. He withdrew the sword and the creature crumpled without a sound.

The last of the firehounds looked like it was wounded, with its front legs moving awkwardly, but it continued to lunge in one direction and then another, throwing up its horns as it searched for something to gouge. Ingren stood frozen with fear as the creature's frantic movements brought it toward her. Taimin judged his moment, and when its head turned away from him he stabbed the creature between the shoulders. It was a swift and deep blow, straight into the heart. But there was fight left in it, and he wasn't prepared for the savage jerk of its head as its huge jaws snapped inches from his hand. He jumped out of reach and watched warily.

The firehound sank to the ground as it died.

Taimin kept his sword up and scanned in all directions, searching for anything else coming out of the haze. He remained wary as he wiped his blade on the flank of the nearest dead firehound.

He glanced at Ingren. She stood still and silent, casting her eyes over the three firehounds, and then she looked at him. It was a while before she spoke. "Thank you, Taimin. This is the second time you have saved me."

He cast her a quizzical look, but then realized she was referring to her escape from the tower. "I wasn't expecting to come across firehounds."

He knew he would now feel dread every time a new shape appeared through the haze. He told himself that firehounds wouldn't like the foul air any more than he did. And he had yet to see a single lizard or snake. It was irrational to expect another attack.

"You must be worried that firehounds are leaving the wasteland." Taimin still had his sword drawn, and didn't look at Ingren as he spoke.

Ingren paused for a moment. "Not particularly. The animals you call firehounds do not belong exclusively to the wasteland. Even if large numbers reached our fields, there would be little to fear. We have complete control of our world."

"Then why worry about us?"

Ingren harrumphed. "Because as I have already told you, unlike animals, you are intelligent. You might hurt our supplies or our important infrastructure."

Taimin shook his head. All he wanted was to find a path to peace. "We wouldn't do that."

Ingren's eyes remained on him. "Yes, Taimin, you would."

12

Selena and Dale stood together at the top of a mountain, in a patch of rocky ground that fell away in a precipitous drop. Bright afternoon sunlight shone down on the summit, which was just big enough to contain Selena, Dale, and the two wyverns that snorted a few paces away, pawing at the ground and straining at the ropes that led to Dale's hand.

Selena's eyes were unfocused, but then clarity returned. When she saw the view, she suddenly felt giddy. It was one thing to be disconnected from her body as she flew high above the clouds, but another thing altogether to realize that if she took a few steps she would plummet down the sheer face of the mountain.

"Any luck?" Dale asked.

"I managed to reach another skalen mystic."

"That makes three?"

She nodded. "They've promised to contact others. Word will spread."

"And they have aurelium?"

"They'll bring what they can to the city."

Dale let out a breath. "Let's just hope they come soon." He stared directly into her eyes. "Thank you, Selena. I mean it."

The way he was looking at her made color come to her cheeks. A stiff breeze blew hard against the mountaintop but, where it tangled Selena's long hair over her face, it only served to ruffle Dale's hair. His blue eyes had depth, as if she were staring into the sky.

Taimin's face came to her. His brown eyes were serious; they didn't sparkle in the same way as Dale's. But there was a steadiness, a depth of character that came from Taimin that made her feel a strong connection whenever she was with him. They had been through so much together.

The two men were different. Yet Dale was here. Taimin had gone.

"You've become serious again," Dale said. He gave her an impish smile. "Well? What are you thinking?"

Taimin's face vanished. Selena tried to think of something to say. "Just about the mantoreans. Rei-kika said we'll soon have a number of their archers heading to Zorn." She remembered the devastation caused by the three strikers. "I'm wondering if everything we're doing will be enough."

"It depends on what comes," Dale said. "If we have aurelium in quantity, as well as a large contingent of archers, we have a chance."

He turned his head, and Selena followed his eyes to gaze from the summit of the mountain. They looked past the Rift Valley, across the rugged plain, to where the city of Zorn could barely be made out as a white circle of stone with a tall tower in the center.

With a nod to himself, Dale moved over to the wyverns and scratched behind one of the winged creature's pointed ears. The wyvern's jaws parted in a toothsome grin.

"That's our home, over there," he said to Selena. "I know you're not from Zorn, but it's your home as much as mine. Together we'll defend it to the last."

"I've never had a home," she said.

"A person without a home is like a tree without roots. There's nothing we need more." As he continued to scratch the wyvern,

Dale's eyes again met hers. For a time they simply looked into each other's faces, and then he smiled down at the wyvern. "Even this fellow fights to protect his home." He sobered. "In truth, when one of my wyverns dies, it hurts as badly as when I lose one of my men. More, sometimes. I've known them since they were pups. Is that bad?"

"It's understandable," Selena said.

"What about you?"

She tilted her head. "What about me?"

"Your friend, Taimin. If the attacks continue, we'll know that his plan failed and he won't be coming back. I don't want to cause you pain. I'm just trying to prepare you. It hurts to lose someone you love." When she didn't answer, he spoke again. "I'm here for you. Anytime you need me."

Selena cleared her throat. "I should get back to the tower," she said.

———

Vance scratched his beard and moustache as he stared at the fallen striker. The winged machine had made a hollow after it came crashing down with enough force to buckle the street. Without doubt, it was heavy. He was in a quiet part of the city, but a few passersby gave the striker apprehensive looks. Vance ignored them. Instead, his eyes roved over the strange contraption as he examined it, fascinated by what he was seeing.

The striker, shaped like an arrowhead, was perhaps forty feet from nose to tail and the same width between the tips of its wings. Its lines were sleek and streamlined, and its silver skin reflected the low afternoon light. Vance cast his mind back to his glimpses of the machine they had found buried under the desert, and the exposed sections where panels had opened and closed despite the fact that no seams were visible. This smaller machine's surface was made of a different substance, glossy rather than dull.

Under the striker's wings he saw rows of black metal cylinders. These weapons had fired on defenseless people and destroyed entire houses while their occupants slept. One of the wings was charred by fire and positioned at an odd angle, torn away from the body to reveal the bizarre interior. The initial impression of smooth skin was betrayed by sections that hid the striker's inner workings. Inside its belly was wire, banks of tiny glass beads, and broken pipes that gave off a sharp, sour odor. There was no cavity, no occupant. The striker appeared to operate under its own soulless initiative.

Vance had no idea how the contraption flew, nor how its weapons functioned. All he needed to know was how to destroy it. He warily laid a hand on its metallic carapace. He bent to look inside again, and then ran a hand along the scorched seam at the broken wing.

He straightened and glanced at Ruth, who stood a short distance away and watched him askance, reluctant to come closer.

"Do you see?" he asked. "The metal skin is as thick as my finger." He wished she would approach, but he knew he couldn't make her. "Aurelium damages it, but in my view we need something better than bows and arrows if we want to reliably punch through it. Something that will deliver more aurelium in a single blow."

Ruth gave him a tight-lipped nod. "Weapons aren't something I know much about," she said. "I'm a healer."

Vance had insisted she come, thinking that once she saw the striker her interest would be sparked, but so far his plan hadn't worked at all. "You're clever, though. Surely you can take some time away to help me?"

"Can't you see how tired I am?"

"If we destroy these things we can save lives. People don't need healing if they haven't been hurt in the first place."

Ruth looked over her shoulder. "I have to go."

"Now?"

"Yes, Vance," she said in a voice of strained patience. "Now."

Vance frowned. "To work with that man, the one with the white hair? What's his name?"

"You mean Jerome?" Her expression became puzzled. "He's a good man. I'm learning a lot from him." She tilted her head. "Why do you ask?"

"You spend a lot of time with him."

Ruth let out a breath. "I'm tired, Vance. I can barely think. People need my help. I'll see you back at home."

"When?"

"I don't know. It depends on what's waiting for me." Her tone softened. "It's good that you're trying to find a way to help. I'm just not the person to do it with you."

Vance watched her leave before he sighed and returned his attention to the striker. Even as he poked and probed, he scowled and muttered to himself. He pictured Ruth and Jerome together, touching each other's hands and sharing meaningful looks that they seemed to think no one else could see.

But as time passed he became consumed with his task and forgot about Ruth. He had a unique problem: to destroy something that commanded the sky and protected itself with a range of weapons and a skin of tough steel. Some animals had soft bellies, weak spots, or tender places. Perhaps the wings might be the best place to focus. This striker had lost its ability to stay in the sky with an injured wing.

Vance walked away from the sleek machine and picked up the bow he had left on the side of the street. He grabbed an arrow and moved to a position twenty paces from the striker. As he prepared himself, he glanced at the arrow. The shaft was as long as his arm and the sharp head was made of fine steel.

He lifted the bow, nocked the arrow, and pulled the string to his cheek. The muscles in his arms groaned as the composite bow made a creaking sound. He sighted along the shaft and took aim at an undamaged wing.

He let fly.

The string thrummed. The arrow flashed through the air. He heard a sharp metallic clang.

He set the bow back down on the ground and approached the striker once more. At first, he couldn't see his arrow, but then he saw it lying on the ground near the wing he had aimed for. He cursed under his breath. The wood had splintered, and the arrow's head had almost broken away from the rest of the shaft. He intently scanned the silver surface of the wing until he found the slight scratch the arrow had left.

He picked up the broken arrow and scowled at it.

"From where I'm standing, that was a waste of a perfectly good arrow," a gravelly voice called. "What did you expect?"

Vance looked up to see Lars watching him. As always, Gretel was with the bald, bearded skinner, her tiny hand in his. She was old enough to talk, but Vance had yet to hear a word pass her lips. Nevertheless, she followed Lars wherever he went. Vance was even getting used to the idea that the self-centered skinner might actually care about someone other than himself.

"What are you doing here?" Vance asked with a frown. The last thing he wanted was Lars mocking his every move.

"I ran into Ruth. She told me you could use some help."

"I'm sure you have other things to do."

"Stay here and watch," Lars said to Gretel. "Understood?"

Gretel gave him a silent nod, and sat down on the street, looking on as Lars joined Vance beside the fallen flying machine.

"I'm good with my hands and I've learned a few things in my time." Even as he spoke, Lars bent down to poke his head into the winged machine's interior. He cast his eyes over the bizarre confusion of beads and wires, and then glanced at Vance. "What is it you're trying to do?"

Still wary of Lars, Vance rapped his knuckles on the striker's thick steel skin. "I need to find a weapon that can damage this."

Lars frowned. "The city guard's already using aurelium arrows."

"I realize that." Vance displayed the broken arrow shaft. "They use arrows like this, with the metal head instead made of aurelium. But if you look at it, the head is barely the size of my thumb."

Lars gave the arrowhead a quick look. "I get your point, but anything heavier would be too much for a standard bow. And a big bow would be unwieldy."

"I know," Vance said. "So I thought javelins might be the key, like skalen use."

Lars shook his head. "Not enough range. And throwing a javelin takes skill."

"Exactly." Vance found himself warming to his topic; Lars was more astute than he had given the old man credit for. "I'm thinking the entire arrow needs to be made out of metal, which we then transform into aurelium."

Lars scratched at his beard as he considered the idea. "Can I hold it?" Vance passed the arrow over, and the older man weighed it in his hands. "Wooden shafts make sense," he said. "Keeps the arrow light enough to travel a long distance. Change that to metal and it's too heavy."

Vance knew weapons, and Lars was right. "So we can't have bigger arrowheads, and we can't make shafts out of aurelium." He gnawed at his lip as he stared at the sinister machine that had killed so many. "There must be a way."

Lars's brow furrowed. "What about crossbows?"

Vance shot a glance at the older man. "I hadn't thought of that." He smoothed his moustache. "Crossbow bolts can be made entirely out of metal. And they're shorter than arrows."

"They're easy to forge." Enthusiasm entered Lars's voice. "They can be heavier too. A little less range, but more power."

Vance worked it through in his mind. "Think about it. You're riding a wyvern. You have to keep moving. What's easier? To close in on an enemy and draw a bow while trying not to be killed? Or to concentrate on your flying, lift your crossbow, and press a lever?"

"One problem, though," Lars grunted. "I've only seen a handful of crossbows in all my time."

Vance became excited. "You're talking to the right man. I know the people to ask. Selena's already helped me get some aurelium. Not much, but enough to experiment with."

Lars headed over to Gretel and picked her up in his arms. He gave Vance a grin. "Then let's get to it."

13

Taimin watched Ingren as they trudged over the blackened ground. Her shoulders were slumped as she walked directly ahead of him. Strong as she was, even she looked exhausted. She no longer checked to see that he was keeping up with her. There had been no rest, no respite, for hour after weary hour.

Then Taimin lifted his gaze. He saw something that made hope stir in his heart.

The haze was clearing. Ahead of him, there was definitely a patch of blue.

The sight fired his blood. With renewed vigor he increased his stride. He was leaving the foul air behind. He was leaving the wasteland. Soon he would see the paradise he had only glimpsed before with Selena, when they had both left their bodies and traveled high into the sky.

Ingren also picked up speed. She glanced at him, her expression eager. More blue appeared in the sky. The air began to taste sweeter. Taimin looked down at his feet and saw that the ground was no longer the color of charcoal. He was walking on the same red dirt he had left behind at the beginning of the day. The golden sun Dex burst through the haze, casting a warm glow on the terrain. The air was clearing with every step forward. Taimin turned and saw that he was leaving the wall of haze behind.

Ingren's rows of sharp teeth parted in a smile. She had been an indistinct figure as he followed her, but now he could see her clearly. The grooves that began above her eyes and swept down her face no longer looked menacing; she was his companion, and they had achieved something together.

They now walked side by side. Blue sky stretched above their heads and the ground was barren, strewn with boulders and gravel. Undulating like a blanket, the landscape rose and fell, but still looked similar to the region where Taimin grew up.

Then, as he and Ingren ascended a long slope, he saw gnarled trees and bushes up ahead. Soon he was walking through a thin screen of dry plant life that followed the crest of a hill. He reached the downward slope on the thicket's other side.

He gasped.

The landscape fell away before forming a hill even taller than the last. A long line of trees stood like a fence along the ridge. But these trees were different, unlike anything Taimin had seen before. Their trunks were straighter and thicker; their branches were heavy with dark green foliage.

Taimin's eyes were wide. "We've made it, haven't we?"

"We have."

Taimin stood for a moment and took in the view. "Do you know where we are?"

"Roughly," Ingren said. "Well enough to find our way."

They traveled up the next slope together. Taimin was surprised to see that the hillside was covered in a carpet of tiny green plants, like soft, miniature versions of the hardy grasses of the wasteland. A warm breeze blew against his skin. He inhaled; the air smelled fresh and fragrant. The towering trees rustled and nudged against one another as if sharing a joke.

When Taimin stepped into the shade cast by the trees' broad branches, he found himself walking on a soft bed of spindly leaves.

Shrubs covered the ground. A flying insect with colorful wings made gentle arcs in the air as it flew by. He touched a tree's trunk as he walked past; it felt smooth and warm. None of these plants even had thorns.

He looked around him in wonder as he walked through the trees. He was awestruck by the brilliant shades of green, his eyes round as he took it all in.

Then he cocked his head when he heard a splashing, tinkling music. It was as if someone was out there, emptying a huge barrel of water onto a hard surface.

He turned to Ingren. "What's that sound?"

Ingren gave him an amused smile but didn't reply. Together they navigated through the thin forest that followed the ridge. As they emerged into the open once more, Taimin stopped and stared.

The hill dropped away until it formed a long gully that stretched across Taimin's vision. Unbelievably, the gully was filled with water that rushed along a bed of smooth stones. Past the river, in all directions, thick forests decorated the vista. Green grass covered the landscape, thick and vibrant along both banks of the gushing stream. Insects buzzed at Taimin's feet. Bright yellow flowers dotted the fields.

Taimin struggled to take it all in. He wished Selena was with him. The world outside the wasteland, which he had seen so long ago, truly was a paradise.

With his mouth open, he turned to stare at Ingren.

There was warmth in her eyes as she looked back at him. "Tell me, Taimin. What is the word for 'river'?"

The need to think broke through his reverie. He summoned the word and replied in the bonded language. He was reminded that he didn't belong here. This was her place.

"Sky?" Ingren asked. "Grass? Tree?" Each time, he gave the name in her language. "Good," she said approvingly.

Taimin turned away from her to again face the rushing water that danced as it carved a path through the landscape. Then, without a word, he started to walk, quickly this time. He took swift steps until he reached the riverbank and stopped to gaze down into the water.

Rain was one thing, but this was more water than he had ever seen in one place.

Taimin slipped his pack off his shoulder. It fell to the ground with a muffled thud, cushioned by the grass. He unbuckled his sword belt and it followed the pack. Then he fell to his knees beside the stream, at the very edge of the water. He cupped his hands and sank them below the water's surface, watching for a moment before he brought his hands up to his nose. He smelled the water, inhaling deeply.

A strong urge overtook him. Without another thought he plunged his head into the river. Cold water enveloped his senses. It swirled around his ears, and wet his hair and scalp. Sweet water entered his mouth.

He raised his head when he couldn't take it anymore. As he shook droplets from his hair, he heard Ingren's chortling laughter.

⁓

Taimin and Ingren followed the river, marching hard until they made a camp in a flat area by its bank. Even with the fast pace he was setting, Taimin was utterly captivated by the world around him. He could drink fresh water whenever he liked and gather enough wood for a fire in no time at all. Ingren said he had nothing to fear from predators, and he slept beside a blazing fire. The grass beneath his blanket was as soft as any bed.

The next day's travel took them far from the edge of the wasteland, and then the landscape became less wild, and Taimin began to see forests replaced with immense fields. Another day found Taimin and Ingren passing through a region of farmland, with broad, straight roads dividing one section from another. Tall green plants stood in orderly rows in one field, while yellow grasses ripened in the sun in the next. As the golden sun fell toward the horizon, they decided to complete their day's journey when they came to a small wood with a thin stream trickling through its heart.

The red sun Lux had already set and soon Dex would join its smaller companion. Taimin stood on the edge of the tree line and gazed out at the fields of crops. This was the kind of world he had imagined when he had searched for a way to destroy the firewall. It felt so safe, so easy. Clouds moistened the fields with rain. Sunlight helped the plants to grow. Food wasn't scarce. Nor was water. There was timber for houses and space for all.

The descending sun made the crops glow. Some fields were golden, others red, purple, white, or green. In the distance, machines trundled through the fields, rolling on immense wheels of metal. Harvesters, Ingren had called them when she pointed them out earlier in the day. This was the first time Taimin had been close enough to see them properly.

There was something captivating about the harvesters that made a swishing sound as they moved amongst the crops, metal arms thrust out at their sides. The last rays of sunlight marked out a solitary machine, motionless and separate from the others, located in a lane where Taimin had a clear view. He shaded his eyes when he saw two tall figures appear from behind it. They were bonded, dressed in drab tan clothing. He could just make out their horns.

He watched the pair of bonded tend to the much larger harvester. One climbed into the contraption's belly and reached out, while the other handed over a rectangular box. Taimin saw that their horns were brown, rather than the fiery red of Ungar's.

Ingren came up to join Taimin and they watched together for a time.

"Workers," she said, nodding at the two bonded. "They will have lost their advisors to sickness, injury, or old age."

"They operate the machines that work in the fields?"

"The harvesters are controlled by an advanced system. Our workers only intervene when something goes wrong. Do you see the buildings, at the intersection between the fields? The workers live in the houses. The bigger structures are barns, containing seeds, tools, and machine parts."

"They were once warriors?"

"Yes."

Taimin remembered Ungar, the warrior who had sought trophies in the wasteland. "They must hate not being warriors anymore."

Ingren glanced at him. "It does not work like that. Our roles are in our bones. As soon as warriors' bonds are broken, they change and become submissive, eager to live the rest of their lives as workers. When Ungar died I also changed. I was filled with a desire to serve and share my wisdom by joining the council of elders."

Taimin continued to watch the two workers. He noticed that one of them had short, pointed horns, like Ingren's, whereas the other had curling horns.

"And not all warriors and workers are male?"

"You have a keen eye," Ingren said. "One of those workers is a female, which answers your question. Sometimes a female becomes a warrior, and she finds a male or female to be her advisor. If the bond is broken, they then follow the usual path of warrior to worker, or advisor to elder. It is not as common, but it happens."

The approach of nightfall robbed the fields of their warm glow. Taimin experienced a strange sense of sadness, combined with longing. He again wondered what life in the wasteland would be like if he could grow crops that ripened in the suns—not cactuses or razorgrass, but proud crops like these. He had never had such a clear vision before, but now it seemed possible. He had seen rain fall on the wasteland. Ingren had said that the weather would eventually change the landscape he had left behind beyond recognition.

If only there could be peace.

He focused on Ingren. "How do you feel, being here?"

She thought for a moment. "Happy to be back."

"Are you sad that Ungar isn't with you?"

"Yes," she said. "I am."

A flash of memory appeared in Taimin's mind. He saw Ingren, kneeling by the side of her dead bondmate, whose body was charred almost beyond recognition. There was something that had occurred to him many times but he had never voiced.

"We had to kill Ungar or he would have killed us," he said slowly. "Even so, why don't you hate me?"

Ingren shook her head. "That is not how a bond works. Ungar was in charge. He made the decisions. My role was to serve. I cannot regret what he chose to do."

"So you don't hate me?"

"No, Taimin. I do not."

Despite his initial misgivings, Taimin realized that without knowing it was happening, he had come to trust Ingren. He also knew that in this strange world he would need her. Back in the wasteland, he could hunt for food, find water, and protect her from dangerous beasts. Here their roles were reversed. He needed her.

"Ingren, can I call you a friend?" He frowned. "Do bonded have friends?"

She chuckled. "Yes, we have friends. Come. Let us finish the last of our supplies, little human."

Taimin stayed in the barn as Ingren had instructed. The pair of tall wooden doors were open a crack and he looked through the gap as he waited for her return.

It was dark outside. He was glad to be indoors, away from the heavy raindrops that fell in a steady patter on the barn's roof, yet the sound wasn't jarring; in fact, it was strangely soothing. He was dry and warm. This would be his second night in a barn, for the previous night had been just as wet.

After their supplies ran out, Taimin had been worried—there wasn't much to hunt that he could see—but then Ingren had simply walked up to a worker and asked for food. Now she was doing the same again. She had always told him that as an elder, her status was high in bonded society. Still, as he watched the circular farmhouse a stone's throw from the barn, it made him uncomfortable to know that there was a bonded inside who had once been a warrior.

With no choice but to wait, Taimin looked past the farmhouse, through the rain, until he focused on a distant valley where he could just make out a low rectangular outline in the darkness. Ingren had pointed out the quadrail, and in daylight Taimin had been able to see the four glistening rails: one pair raised above a second, which ran along the ground. The rails stretched toward the far end of the valley, on and on, until they disappeared at the limits of vision.

The station wasn't much to look at—just a few storage buildings where the rails terminated—but the quadrail itself was fascinating. It was a long, sleek machine, made up of several connected compartments, sectioned like a centipede. Ingren had said that the quadrail would depart in the morning, as it did every morning.

Taimin's eyes moved when the farmhouse door opened to reveal warm yellow light from the interior. Ingren stepped out alone with a basket in her arms. Some property of the gray robe she wore seemed to repel the raindrops so that she stayed dry. She didn't seem to mind her head getting wet as she crossed the short distance to the barn. Taimin stepped back from the doors as she entered.

She set the basket down on the rough stone floor. A few wipes of her face removed the water from the grooves in her cheeks.

"There," she said. "I hope you do not mind if we eat immediately. It has been a long day."

"Are you sure you don't want to stay in the house?" Taimin asked.

"I was invited, of course, but I declined." She shrugged. "I was not questioned. As I said, workers are naturally submissive."

Taimin cast a last look through the gap between the barn's huge doors. He then turned away to examine the barn's interior. It was dry and there was plenty of space. Piled up mats would provide bedding. Crates gave them something to sit on. But he was sure that Ingren was used to better.

"Why stay here with me?" he asked.

She grabbed two of the crates, placing them across from each other. "You need to continue your lessons," she said. She looked his way and smiled. "And after the wasteland, this is pleasant indeed."

He still didn't leave his position. "Ingren, can I ask you something?"

Hearing his tone of voice, she tilted her head. "What is it?"

"What is that?"

He stood back from the gap in the doors so that she could see. He pointed to a vertical line in the distance; with the rain and the deepening darkness, it was only sometimes visible. The pale line climbed the sky in the distant horizon. It rose up and up until it vanished into the clouds.

"Ah, yes. That is the stalk," Ingren said. "It is what makes Agravida such an important city." She gazed toward the stalk as she spoke. "I have already explained elevators, which we use to move vertically between different levels of a building, rather than stairs.

The stalk applies the same concept, but on a much larger scale. It is an elevator to the void." She considered her words. "It is difficult to get ships off the ground, so we assemble them in space. The stalk helps us to take up heavy items, as well as groups of bonded."

"Take them where?"

"To our stations in the void, above this world."

"The stalk . . . It's something you built?"

"Of course."

As Taimin stared at the vertical line that looked so thin he wondered how it stayed aloft, and he suddenly felt frightened. Ingren had tried to prepare him, but the bonded were simply so powerful.

Why would they listen to him?

14

Farmland passed by in a blur. Taimin saw fields of green and gold as well as the occasional harvester. Then forests swept past before the vista returned to cultivated pasture. He could never focus on one scene for long; his passage was too swift to take in anything more than a general impression of rolling countryside and placid rivers. A low hiss came from all directions as he looked through the gaps in the window's horizontal bars.

In the near-darkness before dawn, Ingren had taken Taimin to the quadrail, where she had touched a panel that opened a pair of glass doors. After telling Taimin to get in, she had instructed him to wait while she found him a place to travel. Eventually she had instructed him to hide in this small closet—used for private refreshment, she said—while she found a more comfortable seat for herself.

The temperature was steady and felt different from the fresh air outside, but it was comfortable enough. Taimin watched as the farmland whisked past faster and faster. Then he gasped when the quadrail passed a dense block of buildings. All he could make out was a flash of metal and glass, and structures ten times the height of a tree, before once more he was looking at patchworks of fields.

All of a sudden the vista changed again. Taimin's breath caught when he saw water spread out in front of him in a vast expanse of blue. He wondered for a moment how the quadrail was able to travel over it, until he realized it was still on the rails. The water stretched on and on, as far as the eye could see.

Then once again Taimin was looking at solid land. He sped past dark forests, fluttering by so that individual trees merged together. More farmland followed. Then the quadrail shot through a town, or at least that was what he thought it might be. Cube-shaped buildings filled his vision. He saw roads. Machines traveled over the ground but were much smaller than the harvesters working the fields. Daylight shone through clouds. Then he hurtled through a section of pounding rain. The quadrail was so swift that even the weather came and went.

He was finally appreciating the scale of the world beyond the firewall, and of the bonded civilization whose world it was. After the things he had seen, he knew he would never be the same again.

He wondered what would happen in Agravida. His plan was to talk to the bonded assembly, and the sky marshal, Jakkar. What could he say in the wasteland's defense? How could he explain to a race led by bloodthirsty warriors that there was another option than to take so many lives? How could he convince them to agree to a peaceful solution?

Would he even get his chance? Ingren had remained true to her word; she was taking him to Agravida. They would reach her city before the day's end. But what was going to happen next?

She had told him to stay hidden, but he had to talk to her.

Making a decision, he opened the closet door to peer in all directions. There was nobody around, and he could only follow the corridor in one direction. The quadrail glided along with barely any sense of movement. A pair of glass panels opened when he approached them, somehow aware that he was near. Warily he walked through, prepared to jump if they closed again while he was between them. He reached the compartment beyond, which was filled with row after row of chairs and tables.

There were plenty of seats available, but Ingren was the only occupant; she had explained to Taimin that bonded didn't travel this route often. She had been staring out the window, but when she saw Taimin her eyes widened with surprise. She half stood and then sank back down again.

"I told you to stay where you were," she said. She sighed as Taimin reached her table and took a seat opposite her. "I should have explained. There are places where our administrators keep an eye on things as a matter of course. This is one of them. It is highly likely that when we arrive in Agravida, warriors will now be waiting for us."

Taimin felt foolish. He was still trying to understand so many strange ideas—like the notion of being watched from afar—but Ingren's instructions had been clear, and he had ignored her.

Ingren noticed his expression. "I suppose it does not matter," she said. "I was going to announce our presence as soon as we arrived at the terminus. My status as an elder will count for something."

Taimin's apprehension grew at the knowledge that he would soon be in Agravida, about to meet more warriors like Ungar. But then he reminded himself why he was making this journey. Time was against him. He was going to have to meet his enemies at some point.

"I want your promise," he said. "I have to talk to your assembly."

Ingren glanced around her, looking back over her shoulder as well as in the direction Taimin had come from. Satisfied, but still slightly irritated, she met his eyes. "I will do my best."

Taimin lifted his chin. "Say it in your language," he said. "Say it in Ravange."

She repeated the phrase.

"Thank you," Taimin said.

She was silent for a moment, pensive as she glanced at the vista outside, but then she focused her attention on him once more. "What is it you will ask for?"

Taimin had been given plenty of opportunity to think. "We will agree not to leave the wasteland, provided we're left in peace."

"Can you speak for all five races? Can you even speak for all humans?" When he didn't reply, she shook her head. "Remember, the war council will not agree to rebuild the barrier. The time of the firewall is over."

"I understand that," Taimin said. "But you are far more powerful than we are. Don't you agree that we can find a solution if we work together?"

"I will support your cause, but . . ." She hesitated. "I also must warn you that Sky Marshal Jakkar may not let you live. As an elder, I will be listened to, but that is all." Her mouth drooped at the corners. "I will feel regret if you die. Are you certain that you want to do this?"

"I have to try."

After a long silence, Ingren glanced out the window. Taimin followed her gaze and saw a continuous gray wall. The dull color reminded him of the strange machine buried underneath the desert. He saw a large angular symbol on the wall as it slid past. The quadrail was slowing.

"Taimin," Ingren said. He returned his attention to her. "Your Ravange is better than I could have expected. I will help you, but you must also help yourself. Listen. Pay attention. There is more to our society than our language." The underlying hiss faded away and

Taimin felt the quadrail come to a halt with the slightest of jolts. "Welcome to Agravida," she said, standing.

Taimin cautiously followed suit.

He wondered how he would appear to the bonded he was about to meet. He was tall, by human standards, but to them he would be small. He hadn't shaved in days, and a coating of brown stubble covered the lower half of his face. He still carried his sword in a scabbard at his waist. His bow was strapped to his pack, along with a bundle of arrows. He would no doubt be seen as barbaric, a savage version of the humans the bonded fought between the stars.

"Come," Ingren said.

She led him through the glass panels that slid open as soon as they neared. Approaching the pair of sturdy metal doors that had remained sealed throughout the journey, she touched a blinking blue light. The light flashed red. The metal doors peeled open.

With Ingren's large body blocking his view, Taimin couldn't initially see what might be waiting for him as he stepped out of the quadrail. Surrounding him was a vast, cavernous space, with a ceiling high overhead. Even the long quadrail was swallowed easily. The terminus, as Ingren had called it, was so big that he felt giddy, as tiny as an ant. He descended two steps and then he was on solid ground.

He came to a sudden halt. His stomach clenched with fear. Ingren stood facing six tall bonded warriors with curling red horns, their fiery eyes switching between Ingren and Taimin. Where Ungar's clothing had been supple, these warriors' uniforms were crisp, patterned with black and crimson, and glistened as if wet. But their features were the same. All had wedge-shaped heads that bore angry grooves descending from their brows to below their noses. Leathery visages looked as flat and hard as cut stone. Flared nostrils gave way to wide mouths that were caverns of jagged yellow spikes.

Now that Taimin knew Ingren well, the difference between her and them was pronounced.

The warriors clutched cylindrical black weapons: the field lasers Ingren had described. Taimin's dread became sharp, rising terror. His heart began to pound. He cast a swift glance at Ingren. All it would take was a word from her and he would die.

He kept his hands visible.

As time dragged out, beyond the warriors he saw another half-dozen bonded. Their horns were short and pointed like Ingren's, but lighter in color, and he realized they were the warriors' advisors. All wore pale yellow robes.

Ingren spoke to a warrior with a single star on the breast of his uniform. Taimin listened intently for words he could understand.

"You . . . elder?" the warrior asked her.

Ingren replied with an affirmative. "Great Ungar . . . dead."

The warrior shook his head. "Respectfully, Elder, why . . . human?"

"The barrier is gone," Ingren replied. After spending so much time with her, Taimin found her easier to understand.

"We know this, Elder," the warrior said.

Ingren continued, "The human wishes to discuss our problem."

One of the bonded warriors, a male with deep brow ridges, called out. "The wasteland will be swiftly . . ." He finished with a few words that Taimin couldn't understand.

"However, he is here," Ingren said.

The warrior with the star on his uniform called out to the group. "Take . . . human."

With long strides, the menacing warriors came forward. Taimin was briskly spun around. Despite every sense telling him to flee, he didn't resist as his pack was taken from him. Holding him fast, the warriors removed his sword belt and efficiently ran their talon-like fingers over his body.

"Move," a warrior grunted in the bonded language. Taimin pretended not to understand. "I said move." The rasping voice became an irritated growl. Strong hands shoved Taimin from behind. He stumbled and began to walk.

As he was marched away, he looked back at Ingren. At first he thought she wouldn't meet his eyes. His heart sank.

But then her head turned. She gave him a nod of encouragement.

15

Taimin's escort of five tall warriors took him away from the quadrail, and past several more parallel to the one he had just left. Reaching a row of metal doors, he saw one set parted in the middle to reveal a box-shaped compartment. The warriors herded him inside and then surrounded him as the doors snapped closed.

All of a sudden the compartment whisked Taimin upwards so swiftly that he felt his feet press into the floor. He now understood what Ingren had described to him: he was in an elevator.

Hemmed in by creatures who were so much bigger, Taimin tried to remain calm, but it was difficult. He had no idea what was about to happen to him.

The elevator slowed to a stop and the doors opened once more. Taimin's escort marched him along corridors, through metal doors that slid open on their approach, and traveled on a series of moving walkways. Everywhere he saw the same dull material. The gray stone—or whatever it was—formed floors, walls and ceilings. The journey would have been monotonous if it weren't for the angular symbols, blinking lights, and the occasional transparent window.

As each walkway hurled him along and wind buffeted his body, Taimin tried to ignore his anxiety and take notice of his surroundings. He saw glowing arrows that shifted from blue to red when touched, and diagrams that looked like maps. The symbols on the walls meant nothing to him, but they were all different. Wherever he was being taken, he never had to climb steps or walk until his legs tired—the bonded were able to travel across their city with speed.

He was on a walkway when the long wall changed; in the blink of an eye it became transparent. He glanced through the glass wall and his mouth dropped open.

Two suns shone evening rays on an immense city filled with tall rectangular buildings. The structures were colossal, beyond anything he could have imagined. Bridges connected the buildings at a variety of heights. Flying machines buzzed through the sky, high above curling roads and rails, where quadrails and smaller vehicles created trails of light as they traveled. Right now he was in an edifice that might be just like the ones he was looking at. Soon he would be in another building altogether.

The walkway slowed as it came to an end. Taimin stepped off, and now the transparent wall was gray once more. Three warriors led the way, while a pair followed behind. Taimin glanced over his shoulder. Trailing the group, the advisors in pale yellow walked together. They talked in low tones, most likely about him.

Taimin had only seen Ingren and Ungar before, and noticed that despite the bonded having such strictly defined roles, they were recognizably individuals. Some had wider mouths, others higher foreheads. One warrior had far deeper brow ridges than his companions.

In all cases, warriors and advisors alike wore bands of fabric that were like collars around their necks, matched to their clothes. Taimin had no doubt what the tiny green beads encircling the collars were. The aurelium beads meant that every bonded's mind was protected from mystics. Ingren had told him that there were mystics among the bonded; the ability wasn't unique to the wasteland.

Another elevator took Taimin higher, and then, after traveling a long corridor with dozens of identical metal doors, his escort came to a halt. Other than the small symbol displayed on the wall near the frame, there was nothing to mark this door out as different.

The warrior with the deep ridges below his eyes pressed his palm against the blue light under the symbol. The light shifted color from blue to red. The door slid open with a soft hiss.

The warrior turned to Taimin and motioned; his intent was clear. Taimin cautiously walked alone through the doorway. He felt the warriors' eyes on his back.

The door snapped closed behind him.

Taimin let out a breath to release the tension that had spread throughout his body. He had done it.

He was in Agravida, and alive.

Both curious and wary, he examined his new quarters. The room was basic but a comfortable size, twenty or thirty paces to a side, with a high ceiling and a few sparse items of furniture. A bed occupied one corner, and a table with two chairs filled another. A chest and cupboard lined one of the walls.

All of the furniture was made to human dimensions, which was surprising, but he had already learned that there was little the bonded couldn't accomplish. He walked to a door at the rear, smaller than the room's main entrance.

As he wondered how the door functioned, he saw a blue light. He touched the light and the door glided open with a whisper of sound.

He stepped warily into a strange room with smooth walls and floor, glossy rather than dull, but still the same shade of gray he had seen throughout the bonded city. Levers and pipes jutted out from the wall, but he couldn't understand what it was he was looking at. He walked up to a lever; an arrow indicated he was supposed to turn it.

He turned the lever, and yelped as water shot out from the walls and ceiling. A yank on the lever stopped the flow, but it had been more of a spray than a torrent, and he had moved quickly enough to prevent himself being soaked through. He stood shocked for a moment. This smaller room must be for his personal hygiene. Perhaps he would get used to it.

He returned to the main room and opened the cupboard and chest, which were both filled with plain clothing. Then, with his inspection of his quarters complete, he headed to the sole window, which was oval-shaped, just like the windows in the tower in Zorn.

With wide eyes, he took in the view.

Night had descended on Agravida, but lights were everywhere, outshining the cratered moon. Some of the lights were stationary, while others traveled at speed, attached to moving vehicles that looked like sparks as they curled around the roads. Machines on wings sped through the sky. Some of the windows in the tall buildings revealed bright interiors, while other sections were completely dark. The sight of the city at night was dazzling, but there was one structure that utterly dominated everything around it.

Taimin stared at the stalk in awe.

The stalk lay right in front of him, revealed in all its glory, with its own vertical lights, one on top of the other. Despite its incredible height, it wasn't thick; in fact, from where he was standing, it looked eerily thin. Rather than a solid structure like the tower in Zorn, it was built like a lattice, a rope-like configuration of metal that resembled a braid as it climbed up and up, soaring into the sky.

Taimin tilted his head back and looked as high as he could. It rose into the heavens until it vanished.

His gaze then traveled back down its length toward the ground. Every sense told him that the stalk should get wide toward its base, but it never changed in diameter. He saw structures around its base:

large box-shaped containers and buildings that were low enough for him to look down on their roofs.

The stalk appeared to have four separate rails that enabled multiple compartments to travel up and down. He watched as one of the compartments left the ground. It moved swiftly as it traveled higher, picking up speed until it became a tiny speck in the sky.

He wondered what Selena would make of this place.

The thought of her made his heart ache. She was far away, and he knew he might never see her again. He missed her touch and her smile. After seeing the three strikers fly directly toward Zorn, he had no way of knowing if she was alive or dead.

There was a hiss, and he turned when the door to his quarters opened.

A bonded warrior stood looking at him, his curling red horns matching the trim on his uniform. He looked angry, but Taimin now understood that what he thought was menace was merely the impression created by his face. The warrior crouched and set down a tray, just inside the doorway. Rising steam indicated something hot, and Taimin's stomach rumbled when he smelled the savory odor.

"Food," the warrior grunted in the bonded language.

Taimin was grateful to Ingren for her lessons. He waited for the warrior to leave so that the door could close again, but the warrior didn't move. Soon Taimin heard another voice and the warrior stepped aside for his advisor. Another male, the adviser had curling horns, but his horns were pale yellow and matched the color of his robes.

"Why feed him?" the warrior said in a harsh voice that sounded like stones rubbing together. "All of them . . . soon be dead."

The advisor gave Taimin a look of appraisal and then glanced at his bondmate. "Elder Ingren . . . plan for him."

"To help with the war?" The warrior frowned. "He is . . . human from the wasteland. What could he do?"

"Perhaps something to do with the . . . of the wasteland," the advisor mused.

"Bah," the warrior said. "I do not understand it."

As the bonded pair turned and departed, the door closed behind them.

Taimin approached the tray on the ground. He saw razorgrass bread and roasted tubers, food that wouldn't have been out of place in any settler's homestead. With thoughts whirling through his mind, he took the tray to the table and sat down.

The task ahead of him was both desperate and daunting. All he could hope was that Ingren would keep her word, and that soon he would be able to address the bonded assembly, and the sky marshal who ruled over this strange civilization. The conversation he had just overheard reminded him that if Ingren failed, he was probably going to die.

16

Vance's workshop was little more than an abandoned house he had repurposed. There had been several to choose from—people had been leaving Zorn even before the aerial attack—and he had selected a house with a large central courtyard surrounded by tall columns. The previous residents had sold all their furniture, so he had plenty of space to work.

The heart of his workshop might have contained gardens long ago, but now the ground was bare, revealing the same red-colored dirt found all over the wasteland. Near the edge of the courtyard, a long, sturdy workbench stood beside a rack of tall spears. Baskets contained bundles of arrows. A pair of wooden swords and a javelin sprawled on a table.

Vance glanced at Lars and raised an eyebrow. Lars nodded. Vance let out a slow, steadying breath. In their search for an improved weapon for the city guard to fight with, Vance had been feeling a rising sense of urgency. The next attack could come at any moment.

But now they were ready. The two men had been working hard, and Vance was proud of what they had done.

As they stood at the largest workbench, Vance and Lars peered down into a large ceramic vessel. At the bottom of the container rested a pile of aurelium shards, a large enough quantity to become agitated and seek out metal to devour. On top of the shards lay a solitary crossbow bolt.

The crossbow bolt had once been made of iron. But given time, the bolt had transformed, until it was entirely made of aurelium. The process of transformation was complete.

"Here goes," Vance said.

He reached into the jug, carefully withdrew the glowing bolt, and set it down on a sheet of heavy cloth. He then bent down and inspected the bolt, checking that it still retained the shape and design that would enable it to fit into the groove of a crossbow's firing channel. Once aurelium had eaten a metal object, the object was fixed in that form, and couldn't be melted or reshaped. The reason was simple. A hard blow in warm conditions caused aurelium to explode with force.

"Looks good to me," Lars said.

Little Gretel stood beside the workbench and watched curiously. She reached up to touch the bolt and Lars grabbed her hand.

"No," he said with a stern shake of his head.

"What now?" Vance asked.

Lars gave Vance an enigmatic look and headed to a corner, where a wooden crossbow leaned against the wall. Picking it up, the skinner held the string and put his foot inside the hoop at the top of the crossbow. He pulled hard, until with a final grunt, he managed to pin the string behind the lever. He then hefted the crossbow and walked over to rejoin Vance.

"Time to try it," Lars said.

"Now?" Vance looked askance at the green bolt resting on the cloth.

"You keep saying we have to get the city guard using crossbows before it's too late. There's no time for caution. Either it works or it doesn't. Want to do the honors?"

Vance stepped back from the bench and spread his hands. With a rueful grin, Lars reached out and picked up the explosive bolt. With a deft movement, he slotted it into the groove. He then glanced at Gretel.

"Gretel, go and wait outside," Lars said. He watched as she left the workshop, following her with his eyes until she had left the house completely. Then he turned back to Vance. "Get ready."

Lars pointed the weapon at one of the stone columns that girded the perimeter of Vance's workshop. The house was big, and the column was forty paces away or more. Lars closed one eye as he took aim.

Vance was incredulous. "You're doing it here?"

Lars fired.

The string gave a sharp crack, the crossbow's arms shuddered, and the green bolt shot through the air. A loud detonation made both men duck, and bright flame burst from the opposite wall. Dust and smoke clouded the area.

Lars set the crossbow down on the bench. He waited until the dust settled and then strode over to the far wall. Vance scowled at the older man as he reluctantly followed.

Lars came to a halt at what was left of the wall. "I missed the column."

The wall was three feet thick and made of solid stone, yet the explosive bolt had made a wide hole clean through it. Vance pictured the look Ruth would give him when she saw the damage.

Lars noticed the expression on Vance's face. He shrugged. "At least it worked. What now?"

"Now?" Vance rubbed his chin. "Now we need a hundred crossbows, and a thousand bolts just like that one."

Selena was high in the sky, well above a bank of thick clouds that drifted in the wind. The clouds occasionally drew together and made it difficult for her to make out the tiny city below her.

As she searched for anything that might draw her attention, she knew that her body would be tense as she sat in the tower's observation room. Scanning for threats, she had been farcasting for hours and fatigue constantly sought to drag her back down. She had to fight her exhaustion. She had to remain vigilant. The city guard needed time to prepare, and every moment of advance warning she gave Dale could make all the difference when it came to the survival of the people of Zorn.

The city guard had repelled the last assault and they had to do the same thing again. Elsa needed time: time for the skalen to bring aurelium to the city, time for the mantorean archers to arrive, time for new weapons to be developed, time to prepare to fight back.

Selena froze when she spotted a group of tiny specks in the distance. She swiftly flew toward them. As she sped through the sky, she traveled faster than thought to cross the distance in a heartbeat. Relief flooded through her when she neared and could make out the shapes of birds. She swiftly returned to her position above the city.

Time passed. Dull pain formed a familiar sensation—the pain of farcasting for longer than she should. She swept her gaze from one part of the sky to another. Clouds came and went.

A scatter of bright lights burst into existence. Dread struck Selena with the force of a hammer blow.

Each speck was a silver triangle that twinkled like a star as it reflected the sunlight. The group emerged from a bank of clouds, moving in a straight line, heading toward the city of Zorn.

Selena launched herself toward them. She put on more speed than she ever had before. The triangles grew in size until she clearly saw the group of flying machines with rigid wings and white plumes trailing behind them. She swiftly counted. Her dread became horror.

Twenty strikers.

She turned and pulled hard on her lifeline.

The reconnection with her body was abrupt. She couldn't allow herself time to adjust. She leaped out of the chair in the middle of the observation room and grabbed the rope connected to the bell.

Fear washed away her fatigue. She gave hard, savage yanks of the rope. The loud peals jangled away. The sound pounded at her senses along with every beat of her heart. She pulled again and again and then her arms fell flat at her sides.

Her eyes glazed.

She found Dale at the rectangular collection of buildings that was the city's barracks. The commander of the city guard was close to the center of a flurry of action; she had no doubt that he had heard the peals of the bell. Dale waved his arms and bellowed at his soldiers as they ripped open the bars at the wyvern huts. Blue-uniformed soldiers dragged their wyverns out, hauling hard on the ropes fastened to collars around the creature's necks. Already, each soldier had a bow in his hand and a quiver of green-tipped arrows on his shoulder. One after another they threw themselves onto the saddles on the wyvern's backs.

Dale, Selena spoke into his mind.

His blue eyes widened. *Selena?*

More strikers are coming. She tried not to convey her fear, but she was almost certain he would hear it in her voice.

How many?

Twenty.

As soon as she replied his face looked stricken. Despite the fact that she wasn't visible to him, Selena could make out every freckle on his face. She wished she couldn't see how afraid he was.

By the rains. Twenty. He let out a breath. *Where are you?*

At the tower.

Get to safety.

Good luck. She wished she could tell him how brave he was, but every second counted. She broke off contact and again pulled hard on her lifeline to return to her body and refocus on what she was doing.

The sensation of reconnection gave her another sharp jolt. For a heartbeat she looked at the rope in her hand and wondered where all the soldiers and wyverns had gone. Then she shook herself and hauled on the rope to resume the alarm.

Keeping the rope in her hand, she moved to the edge of the floor to peer down at the city streets, lit up in afternoon sunlight. Crowds of people filled the avenue below. In between the clangs of the bell she heard screaming. Already a stream of city folk raced toward the shelters.

Selena continued to pull on the rope. The peals were so loud that her ears were hurting.

Spying movement, she watched as the wyverns rose into the sky, one after the other. Dozens of winged creatures formed up as they flew away from the barracks, and when she saw their direction of travel she realized that they planned to meet the strikers past the tall white wall. If the city guard could repel the attack farther from Zorn, the strikers wouldn't be able to fire on the houses. Her warning had given the city guard crucial time. She hoped it would be enough. As the wyverns traveled with speed, she knew that Dale would be in the lead.

Selena stopped pulling on the rope.

She now heard a mechanical whining sound that grew louder. A moment later she saw the twenty strikers, roaring toward the city, each spaced equidistant from the other.

The two forces would clash at any moment, over the plain beyond the city wall. There was no better vantage point than the top of the tower. Selena couldn't look away as the wyverns drew closer and closer to the winged machines.

She gave a sudden cry as streams of fiery sparks erupted from the strikers. Flashes of light enveloped wyvern after wyvern. Zorn's soldiers flew skillfully, and used their experience to duck and weave, to plummet or climb the sky. But nonetheless she saw the torrent of sparks rip through a horrifying number of wyverns and their riders.

The distance between the groups narrowed, and then tiny green lights arced through the sky as the soldiers returned fire with their bows and aurelium-tipped arrows.

A striker burst into a cloud of flame, then a second, and a third. Powerful reverberations filled the air. Yet there were far too many enemies for humans armed with bows, even if they were on the backs of agile creatures.

Selena could only watch in horror as the strikers shredded wyvern after wyvern with the red and yellow sparks that darted through the sky. Soon just a third of the city guard remained.

"No," she whispered. She felt sick. She had just spoken to Dale. He couldn't be gone.

A cluster of wyverns broke away from the battle in the sky. Wings beat furiously as the last survivors tried to lure the strikers away from the city.

But with their group mostly intact, the strikers didn't give chase. Instead, now in command of the sky, they reformed their line and advanced over the city wall.

Selena stood frozen in place. It had all happened so quickly. Zorn was exposed and defenseless.

The strikers changed the nature of their attack. Rather than launch volumes of tiny sparks they released projectiles that shrieked as they left each wing to descend toward the ground. Selena's head jerked to the side as a building of white stone detonated into oblivion. The next three in the row exploded a moment later. An entire block shattered in a heartbeat. The strikers continued to advance, firing on the structures and the screaming people as they glided over the city.

The winged machines became larger and larger in Selena's vision. Then her heart beat out of time.

One of the strikers peeled away from the group to approach the tower.

17

Selena sprinted to the stairway. She threw herself down the steps that curled inside the tower's circumference, bracing herself against the wall whenever she was close to stumbling.

Her breath ran ragged as she descended level after level, but the tower was tall, and there were many floors below her.

Something slammed into the tower.

Her ears felt the concussive blast first. Then her skin tingled as a rush of hot air smashed into her back, launching her forward.

With a loud roar and a crash of stone, the top half of the tower sheared off above her. She found herself lying face down, sprawled on the stairway. Smoke and dust clouded her vision.

She coughed and picked herself up. Fear spurred her on. She continued her descent, recklessly racing down the stairway, heedless of falling. Time and again she crashed into the tower's inner wall. Stone particles filled the air and entered her lungs.

Every thought became focused on reaching the bottom. Desperate to escape the tower's confines, she was nearly there when another blow struck the tower. Her entire world shook from side to side.

She reached the wide circular space at ground level. Racing for the doorway, she wrestled with the handle and hauled the heavy door open.

The plaza surrounding the tower's base was thick with fine powder that swirled and obscured everything. She left the tower, bursting into a sprint.

A bright light streaked from the sky. The base of the tower exploded. As the last remnants of the stone structure shattered into a million pieces, a great cloud enveloped Selena. The force of the detonation punched into her back. For a moment she was in the air. Then her head struck the ground.

Everything went black.

———

Vance felt fear race up and down his spine. The warning bell had been pealing, but then it stopped. It took barely any time at all for the terrible sound of exploding buildings to fill the air. Then came a roar, far louder than anything before it.

Lars looked down at the crossbow in his hands.

"Leave it!" Vance shouted. "We know what to do. We can always do it again."

Lars threw down the crossbow. "Blast it," he said as he began to run. "We're too late."

Lars raced through the doorway that led onto the street. Vance followed close behind.

Vance found Lars in the process of hoisting Gretel tight to his shoulder. The suns cast long shadows from the surrounding terraces. Vance looked at the sky. There were other people on the street, and everyone was staring in the same direction.

As soon as he had heard the warning bell, Vance's pulse had raced as he imagined Selena, high at the top of the tower as she alerted the city of approaching danger.

The tower usually dominated the city, far taller than the structures around it.

But now the tower was gone.

Plumes of smoke rose from all quarters. Sinister machines were in the sky, coasting over the city of Zorn. Bright lights streaked down from each of the strikers. Powerful explosions followed.

The color drained from Vance's face. He glanced at Lars.

"Come on!" he cried.

Vance began to run.

———

Selena coughed. Pain throbbed somewhere above her forehead. Her thoughts were confused and her ears were ringing. She realized that her body was in an awkward, sprawled position. A great weight on her back was crushing her down and made it difficult to breathe. Bits of grit in her lungs burned like a fire within her chest.

But it was her head that hurt worst of all. She wanted to reach up and touch her crown to find the place where the pain was coming from, but her limbs were trapped. She couldn't move. Panic threatened to overwhelm her.

She couldn't see through the dust that filled her vision. She heard a distant whoosh and then a powerful detonation made the ground shake. A series of crashes followed soon after.

As she realized she was buried in rubble, remembrance came flooding back. She had fled the tower, which had exploded behind her. She was flung forward and smashed her head on the ground.

She peered into the dust and could now make out the field of debris that coated the ground, so deep in places that she couldn't see the paved floor of the plaza. If she had been closer to the tower, and it had toppled down around her, she might be buried so deep she would never make it out.

Her eyes roved wildly. She wriggled her body, trying to get free, but then the weight on her back shifted. As the pile of stone pressed at her body, terror gripped her heart. She was faced with an impossible choice. If she tried to free herself, she might make things worse. The rubble could reshuffle. A big block could crush her. But she also couldn't do nothing.

Would anyone think to look for her?

Staring into the cloud of fine particles, she listened to the distant screams and explosions, the sound of the city's destruction as building after building, block after block, was reduced to dust. People's cries of fear were abruptly silenced when loud detonations cut them short. She wondered if she should try to move again. Her limbs were trapped, but she didn't think anything was broken. What choice did she have? She had to free herself. Even so, she swallowed. What she was about to do required courage. If things went wrong, she might die here in this pile of rubble.

Selena was preparing to shift her body when she heard shouts. The voices sounded familiar, but her head hurt and her ears were ringing. Shapes moved, growing bigger, until she realized that two men were running toward her out of the dust.

She tried to call out, but broke into a series of coughs. Nonetheless, the big man in front became clearer. His head was completely bald, but it was made up for by his thick black beard.

"I need help!" Lars bellowed over his shoulder.

Selena saw Vance just behind Lars. They had come for her. The two men clambered over the rubble until they were right beside her.

"Don't move," Vance ordered. "Stay completely still. There's a big block on your back."

Lars crouched, and he and Vance grunted as they lifted something away from Selena's body. She felt the pressure ease immediately.

Lars heaved another block away and then started on the next. Sweat beaded on his forehead and dust coated his beard. Vance's expression was grim as he worked with him to clear the rubble.

Vance then grabbed Selena under the armpits and grunted as he pulled her out. She knew it was now safe to move, and kicked her legs. Relief flooded through her. She was free.

She continued to cough as Lars and Vance helped her away from the debris. The spiky pain in her chest began to feel better as she cleared her airways. She reached up and felt just above her forehead; it was sore enough to make her gasp.

As she clambered, she looked back to see that the debris that had buried her wasn't deep at all. She had been lucky. A stone's throw away was a mountain of rubble—all that was left of the white tower.

She blinked in the dust and hazy sunlight. She realized that only a short time had passed since the tower's destruction. White stone littered the plaza. She was able to see more with every passing moment. Screams and wails came from all directions.

"Can you walk?" Vance asked urgently.

Selena nodded and opened her mouth to reply when she heard a high-pitched whine. A striker passed directly overhead. Bright lights left each of its wings and two projectiles arced toward the ground. The resulting explosion made the ground shake. In the distance, a cloud of flame rose from a city block.

More strikers hovered over the city as they fired on the structures below. Rumbles filled the heavens. The ground barely stopped trembling before another explosion followed.

Selena saw Ruth, standing at the edge of the broad avenue that led to the gates. Ruth crouched beside Gretel as she dabbed a cut on the girl's arm. Gretel looked terrified, and jumped when a loud splintering of stone filled the air.

The city had fallen, Selena knew. It was over. The strikers were reducing Zorn to dust, one building at a time.

Selena ignored the pain all over her body and tried to pick up her pace. Her voice was hoarse as she spoke to Vance. "Elsa?"

His expression was grave. "I heard she was wounded, but she made it out."

"We have to run. There's no other option."

"I know." He waved at Ruth. "Ruth! Come on."

Ruth gathered Gretel and hurried over to join them. Selena took a deep breath and moved into a run; she saw Lars cast her a worried look, but he and Vance followed suit. Soon their group had joined the torrent of people rushing toward the gates. Hundreds of frightened faces surrounded them. Field workers and laborers ran side by side with merchants and craftsmen. The strong helped the weak. Parents carried young children in their arms. The occasional bax or skalen mingled with citizens who had lived in Zorn their entire lives.

Selena heard a whoosh behind her and glanced over her shoulder. She cried out as a streak of light flew down toward the street. In an instant dozens of figures farther back vanished in flame and dust.

The crowd screamed. Selena fixed her attention ahead. Everyone around her was fleeing, their eyes wide with terror. Lars's face was red as he held Gretel to his shoulder. Vance gripped Ruth's hand tightly.

They passed rubble on both sides that had once been buildings. Then Selena saw a wide gap in the broken wall where the gates had been. The white stone nearby was burned black. Stones and debris littered the ground, making the footing treacherous. The crowd slowed as people were forced to climb over the remnants of the gates and the surrounding wall.

A striker glistened like a knife blade as it sped overhead and performed a tight turn. Even as Selena reached the gap in the city wall, at any moment she expected to have her vision washed with fire as searing heat enveloped her. She clambered from one stone to the next.

Dry, dusty terrain opened up ahead. The fleeing people dispersed. Selena left what remained of Zorn behind, together with Ruth, Vance, Lars, and Gretel.

She risked a last look back. The flying machines made sweeping passes and continued to launch their destructive fire onto the structures below. It was an image that she knew would always stay with her—the last she would see of Zorn before the white city was gone forever.

18

Ingren's transition to life back home was not as smooth as she had thought it would be.

She was following one of Agravida's long corridors, where Elder Vey walked ahead of her with bowed shoulders and shuffling steps. In her previous role as advisor, Ingren had never spent much time with elders. She now wondered if Elder Vey was always the one who helped new elders adjust to their changed circumstances.

Vey stopped outside a door. Ancient even when Ingren was young, her skin was like old leather and her voice was so soft that, when she spoke, Ingren had to move close and listen carefully.

"My hearing is not as it should be . . . What did you say, Elder Vey?"

"Your hearing is not the problem," Elder Vey whispered. "I am old, but it has not affected my wits. I know how I sound." She put her mouth close to Ingren's ear. "I said that beyond are your temporary quarters until we find something better for you." She gave a shrug. "We all thought you were dead, Ingren, you and Ungar both." She cleared her throat. "Apologies, I did not use your title, Elder Ingren."

"No need to apologize," Ingren said. "When I left I was an advisor. I am expecting a period of settling in."

"I remember when my bondmate died." Vey gazed into the distance. "He was good to me. It was an interesting life."

"The war?"

"Yes, the war, of course." The elder who had seen many sky marshals come and go shook herself. "You have made a long and difficult journey. I am sure you wish to rest. I will see you at council."

Ingren gave her thanks and watched Elder Vey depart, before turning toward her new quarters. As Ingren opened the door, the familiar gesture felt strange, as if someone else was in control of her hand. The door glided open with an accompanying hiss.

She entered the room beyond.

Her eyes widened as she took in her new quarters, which were far more luxurious than the apartments she had occupied with Ungar. As soon as the door closed, soft music began to play. Along with the gentle melody of tinkling chimes, a variety of moving images decorated the walls: a flowing river, swaying trees, a white sandy beach with rivulets lapping at the sand. The wall at the rear showed a view of Agravida at night, something that Ungar had always mocked Ingren for liking.

Ingren's gaze moved to a divan that looked so comfortable she longed to lie on it. Pink lamps, arched into graceful shapes, sat on low tables alongside decorative crystal urns. A glossy black palm reader rested on a table, and a medical array, akin to the device she had taken to the wasteland, filled a slot at the back of the door. Two more doors, one gray, the other gold, would lead to the wet room and sleeping quarters.

Ingren wondered what her bondmate would have made of her change in circumstances. But Ungar was gone. She was now an elder, and could do almost anything she liked.

Her thoughts turned to Taimin in his cell, and she felt strange. She had been away from Agravida for a long time. As much as she had wanted to return home, Ungar's quest, and its outcome, had changed her.

She issued a command: "Show me the wasteland." A gesture accompanied the instruction.

All four walls changed simultaneously. Ingren found herself staring into a landscape, and if she turned, she could see in a different direction, as if she were in the middle of a sunburned plain filled with green cactuses. Two suns shone from the sky. Scrub grass rustled in the breeze. A distant sand lizard tore berries from a pricklethorn bush.

Ingren gave another command and the music stopped, to be replaced with the howl of a dry wind.

She smiled.

Focusing on herself, she realized that she still wore her dusty traveling clothes. No wonder some of the other elders had given her strange looks. She strode to the tall wardrobe and parted the doors. When she saw what lay within, she wasn't surprised, but it was yet another reminder of her changed status. Golden robes filled the wardrobe, all identical, with long hems that would trail when she walked. A rack displayed matching collars encircled with aurelium beads.

For a time she stared at the array of clothing, before taking one of the robes and heading for the wet room. Once inside the plain gray interior, she hung the fresh robe on a rail and prepared to remove her old clothing, which she was looking forward to sending to the incinerator. Her plan was to cleanse herself with water as hot as she could bear, before enjoying a proper meal.

Food was the one thing she was looking forward to more than any other. Of all the comforts of home, it was what she had missed most of all. The tube rations she and Ungar had taken with them were bad enough, but not nearly as foul as the stuff the wastelanders subsisted on.

She stopped in mid-movement when she heard the hiss of parting metal. A frown creased her face. She couldn't mistake the sound of the door to her quarters opening and then closing again. Ingren's status was clear. To enter without forewarning, whoever it was had to rank even higher than her.

Still in her old robe, drab and dusty as it was, she opened the wet room door and saw a bonded advisor waiting for her just inside the main room.

For a brief moment, when Ingren saw the pale yellow robes, she was surprised and confused. Then her initial confusion melted away when she recognized the advisor's face. Yes, there was one advisor—the only one—who outranked her.

"Elder Ingren," Astrin said with a smile and her arms spread wide. "Welcome home." The grooves in her face were gentle and her eyes were warm. Ingren had never heard Astrin raise her voice and, despite her lofty position, she was someone liked by everyone who met her. Ingren didn't know her well, but they had spoken several times.

"Astrin." Ingren initiated a bow. "This is an honor."

In a kind gesture, Astrin reached out to prevent Ingren's bow. "You no longer bow to me, Elder Ingren." She smiled again. "It is good to see you well after we all thought you were lost to us. And now, you are an elder. To be truthful, your new status brings me pleasure. I have always liked you, and I find elders easier to be friends with."

Ingren felt a flush of pleasure.

"I regret disturbing you, and so soon after your return. But Jakkar wishes to see you and you know how he can be. We cannot keep him waiting."

Ingren's face gave nothing away, but she realized that the time to rest had not yet come. Her promise to Taimin was fresh in her mind. What happened next would determine his fate. She only wished she were able to meet the sky marshal in the golden robes of an elder.

Astrin looked her up and down, and spoke as if reading her thoughts. "Perhaps my bondmate can wait." She smiled. "Just a little. It might be best if you finish what you were doing."

Ingren and Astrin approached the base of the towering stalk. They walked through a broad, clear area, where dozens of immense cube-shaped storage containers stood in orderly rows. Everything was spaced far apart, and the path between the containers was wide enough for Ingren's view of the stalk to be unobstructed.

A cool breeze blew against her face. The day was bright, and plump white clouds drifted through the blue sky. The golden sun shone from high above, while a glint of the crimson sun peeked from between two buildings. Agravida's rectangular structures were tall, but nothing could compare to the stalk.

"I realize you must be tired," Astrin said. The gaze she turned on Ingren was sympathetic. "You have had quite an ordeal. If you like, I can arrange quarters for you up above."

"No, but thank you," Ingren said. "I prefer to get reacquainted with Agravida."

"I completely understand. I spend so much time up above that I barely see my home in the city."

As Ingren and Astrin approached their destination, the stalk reflected the bright daylight. It was a crucial aspect of bonded civilization. Everything that enabled a war to be conducted in space went up there via this one all-important mechanism.

A haulage vehicle trundled past, heading to one of the storage containers. Workers in tan clothing moved about with purpose; the flow of supplies between Agravida and the stations and ships in the void was constant.

Viewed up close, the stalk wasn't as thin as it appeared to be from a distance. The twisting lattice, made of a unique material paler than steel, comprised of multiple bars fixed to one another in a series of spirals. The four vertical rails, however, were perfectly straight.

Ingren heard an ear-splitting sound and grimaced as the screech became louder. All of a sudden a compartment came into view, a tiny speck high on the stalk that plummeted toward the ground with incredible speed. It was only as it passed the golden sun that its rate of approach slowed. The high-pitched sound softened until it faded altogether. The compartment—big enough to lift the largest ship components, hundreds of bonded, or thousands of crates, vats, and barrels—came to a gentle rest on the ground.

The compartment doors parted. Ingren glanced at her companion. Astrin was only an advisor, but Ingren knew that the compartment would have been called just for her.

True enough, when Ingren entered, she saw that the multitude of seats inside were empty. The compartment's walls and floor were transparent, with each section fixed in place with strong bars. Symbols traveled along the clear panels at eye height, providing information on the internal and external environment.

"Sit anywhere you like," Astrin said.

Ingren settled herself in one of the seats and pulled the straps down over her shoulders, before fiddling with the waist and leg buckles until she was firmly bound in place.

The compartment doors snapped closed.

"I always hate this part," Ingren muttered.

A sharp hiss told her what was coming. Then she gritted her teeth as a heavy weight pressed her down in her seat. Glancing through the transparent floor, she saw the ground below drop away. The city of Agravida shrank and was swallowed up by the industrial areas on the outskirts, like organs connected by blood vessels to a beating heart.

Ingren returned her attention to the environment display. The readouts told her she was traveling at a formidable speed. Then the compartment began to slow, and she swallowed as the tension in her body relaxed.

The journey would continue for a while longer. Ingren glanced at Astrin, seated beside her.

"What is it like, to be bonded to the sky marshal?" Ingren asked.

Astrin gave Ingren a slight smile. "What was it like to be the bondmate of Sub-marshal Ungar?"

Ingren gathered her thoughts. "I advised him. Sometimes he listened. Many times he did not."

"Then you already know the answer." Astrin looked away. "Between us, Elder Ingren, after two decades bonded to Jakkar, it still does not get any easier. The bond makes me submit to him, even when I disagree. Of course, you understand what I mean. Jakkar is stubborn. Before he became sky marshal, it was irritating, now . . ."

"He appears to enjoy his role," Ingren said, choosing her words carefully.

Astrin gave a soft snort. "He does indeed. Nine years, it has been. Ever since Sky Marshal Malik was killed at Syleth." Her gentle eyes became sad. "This endless war. There are so many other things we could be doing."

"Warriors live for fighting," Ingren agreed.

"Tell me something, Elder Ingren. Did Ungar's decisions lead to his death? Could it have been avoided?"

Ingren nodded. "Yes."

"If the stars shine upon us, Elder Ingren, one day soon this war will be over. Then there will be a reversal. And we will be the ones in charge."

———

Ingren was in Nashar Station. Through the glass that surrounded her, she saw swathes of stars, spread across the black expanse of space. She could look down at the stalk below, and her eyes traveled down its length to the world of her birth, Lumea, a beautiful sphere full of swirling clouds, blue oceans, and verdant landscapes.

She stood alone. Astrin had left her to return to her bondmate's side, and now Ingren waited to be summoned. She watched Sky Marshal Jakkar from a short distance away. A tall, powerful warrior with curling horns and strong brow ridges, he wore red armor with a high collar and a trim of black and silver. Half a dozen of his marshals clustered around him, and they were all focused on dozens of departing warships. Green lights shone at the ships' tails. The fleet appeared to grow smaller and smaller as it left Lumea behind.

Ingren heard voices and turned to see two mystics talking. Both were elders, like her, but their golden robes were also hemmed with blue to mark out their status. If Ingren had been born with the talent, she might be among them. One of the mystics glanced her way with a smile and a nod. Ingren gave a slight bow. Elders had high status, yet elders who were also mystics were among the most respected members of bonded society.

Sky Marshal Jakkar's conversation with his marshals came to an end, and he dismissed them with a few curt words. Ingren's apprehension grew.

She had been in the sky marshal's company only once before, and then Ungar had been at her side; she had only been an advisor, and the sky marshal had ignored her.

Now she would be directly under his scrutiny. She was glad that Astrin had given her a chance to change into her glistening golden robe.

Astrin said something to the sky marshal and he turned his red eyes on Ingren. He waved at her to approach. Taimin's fate was on her mind as she held her head high and walked over.

"Your Eminence," she said. She gave him the appropriate bow from an elder to the leader of the entire bonded civilization.

"Elder Ingren," Jakkar said. He took in her robe and her bright horns. "Your new status tells me that Sub-marshal Ungar is dead. I had great plans for him."

"He died as he lived, Your Eminence. He was a true warrior."

"Yet his quest killed him."

"He entered the barrier generator. The aurelium ignited. I also would have died if he had not thrown me clear."

Sky Marshal Jakkar shook his head, evidently considering the end of the barrier. "If there is one thing I will say about Ungar, it is that he was always rash. Now my son will never make a quest." He watched the departing spaceships for a moment. "I suppose the old ways must pass at some point. I remember my own quest. As primitive as they are, those creatures in the wasteland have been tested by their environment. There are fighters among them." He spent some more time reminiscing, and then turned the full force of his gaze on Ingren. When he spoke, it was in a brisk growl. "I hear you brought a human here, a savage. It was strange enough to arouse my curiosity. Why?"

Ingren chose her words carefully. "He wants to address the assembly."

Sky Marshal Jakkar became puzzled. "To what end?"

"The wasteland's inhabitants have learned the truth. He wants to come to an agreement."

The sky marshal's lips parted in a smile as he revealed row after row of sharp teeth. He glanced at his bondmate. "Did you hear that, Astrin? The savages think they are our equals." He snorted. "If we will not heed the overtures of our enemies out there"—he nodded toward the stars—"why would we listen to a human from the wasteland? Elder Ingren, you do realize I have a war to win?"

Astrin spoke up. "Bondmate," she said. She employed a patient tone of voice that Ingren remembered using with Ungar. "How long will it take that battle fleet to reach its destination? Years? This constant fighting has been the state of affairs for a long time. Perhaps a little talk would not be amiss."

Sky Marshal Jakkar glanced at Astrin but ignored her. "Elder Ingren, speak with one of my officers on your return to Agravida. See to it that the human is killed."

Ingren knew when she was being dismissed, but she didn't move. "Eminence, he is the human who defeated Ungar."

Jakkar's head jerked round; he focused on Ingren as the burning coals of his eyes registered surprise.

"He is a notable warrior," Ingren continued. "In the wasteland, thousands of humans know his name. He is spoken of among all five races."

Sky Marshal Jakkar thought for a moment. "Can he speak Ravange?"

"Relatively well," Ingren said.

The seconds trickled past. As Ingren waited for the sky marshal's next words, her shoulders were tense.

"Very well," he said at last. "Let him make his address. And, Ingren, the speech of our enemies should never be heard in Agravida. Ensure he does not make a mockery of our language."

Ingren bowed. "Your will, Eminence." She glanced at the cluster of green glowing circles—all that was to be seen now of the departing fleet. "Where are they going?"

"To war," Jakkar said flatly. "That is all you need to know."

Taimin stood at the window in his quarters and watched the stalk.

The two suns lit up the surrounding city of metal, glass, and stone. Tall buildings and the bridges between them formed a dizzying array of structures. The quadrails glided and the flying machines buzzed like insects, but it was the stalk that he found most captivating. It was so thin, so delicate, but it soared above its surroundings, climbing to eternity, so tall that he couldn't see the top. He was mesmerized by the speed of the compartments that shot up into the sky or plummeted like stones.

He heard a whisper of sound behind him and turned away from the window.

The door to his quarters had opened.

Taimin wondered who was about to come in; he wasn't due for a meal. Most likely it would be a bonded warrior, but he was desperate to see Ingren, who he hadn't spoken to since his arrival in Agravida. He needed to do something, to make some sort of peace with his enemies before it was too late for Zorn—and Selena.

As a figure stepped into view, Taimin's eyes widened. He couldn't believe what he was seeing.

A young woman—a human—stood framed in the doorway. Her lips were pursed as she gave Taimin a careful appraisal. A few moments passed and then, as she entered his quarters, the door closed behind her.

Briefly Taimin thought that the bonded might have found another human prisoner to share his quarters, but then he saw from her manner and the way she was dressed that she was no captive. She was clad in a garment that looked like it was all of one piece, with long sleeves that stretched to her wrists and wrapped around her narrow waist and legs just as snugly. The fabric was the whitest thing Taimin had ever seen, and glossy, so that it reflected the daylight pouring through the window.

Straight blonde hair fell past her shoulders and her eyes were a pale shade of blue that was almost gray. Her face was heart-shaped, with a small chin and an upturned nose. She was pretty, but she had a serious, almost solemn, demeanor. She approached slowly and then came to a halt, still inspecting Taimin with quiet curiosity.

"Who are you?" Taimin asked incredulously.

"My name is Hannah. And you are Taimin." She uttered each syllable slowly, as if unused to forming the words she was speaking. She glanced at the table and the two chairs that faced each other across it. "May I sit?"

Without waiting for a reply she took a seat at the table. She indicated the chair opposite, and Taimin hesitated before joining her.

"Sky Marshal Jakkar has agreed to let you make an address to the assembly," she began.

"When?" Taimin asked impatiently. "Today?"

Hannah gave him a perplexed look. "No, of course not. The assembly is made up of all of the marshals and sub-marshals, as well as the council of elders, and of course, the sky marshal himself. The next convening is in three days."

Taimin shook his head. "That's too long," he said.

Hannah frowned. "The sky marshal is busy. Do you believe that he often thinks about the place you come from? He has a civilization to lead, and a war to win. Count yourself fortunate that you have been granted your opportunity at all."

"There must be some way to talk to him sooner."

"There is not," she said flatly.

Taimin saw that she was becoming irritated. His heart sank as he thought furiously. Selena had said that Zorn had only a matter of weeks. Three days. He might still accomplish his goal in time.

"Now," Hannah continued. "The sky marshal would like you to deliver the speech yourself. I understand you speak some Ravange, but I expect some help may be required. I am here to assist you." She met his gaze. "Otherwise your address will be without meaning, for the bonded will never understand you. I can also answer any questions you might have."

There was one question Taimin was burning to have answered. "How did you come to be here?"

Hannah considered her words before replying. "You know about the war?" She waited until he nodded. "I was on a human warship the bonded captured. The one who found me was an elder, which is unusual—it is rare for elders to leave Agravida. Elder Vey decided she wanted me to live. The warriors had to agree with her demand. A warrior is strong, and strength demands honor." The last statement sounded like something that had been drilled into her.

Taimin felt a surge of sympathy. "How old were you when you were captured?"

"I was seven."

"And the bonded killed your parents?"

"That is the usual practice in war."

Taimin tried not to show his surprise at her matter-of-fact tone. "Are you the only human here?"

"Aside from you," she said.

"And you've lived here all this time?" Taimin couldn't imagine what her life must have been like. "Did you ever think someone might rescue you?"

"Lumea's location is a secret," she said. "No one is coming. And why would I want them to?"

Taimin knew in his heart that at some stage, long ago, Hannah had cried tears at the death of her parents and trembled with fear of the strange creatures who had captured her. "Why—?"

Hannah's eyes narrowed as she cut him off. "When I said you could ask questions, I did not expect a series of questions about me." Her mouth tightened and she gave him a firm look. "Now," she said, "why don't you speak some Ravange to me?"

Taimin leaned back, despite the fact that there were so many things he wanted to ask her. He thought for a time, and then cleared his throat. He met Hannah's eyes. "I am sorry your parents are dead," he said, making the guttural sounds of the language that Ingren had taught him.

Hannah scowled. "Close," she said. "But not good enough." She tapped her fingertips one by one on the table. "What is it you wish to say in your address? Perhaps we should start there." When Taimin didn't reply straight away, she raised her voice. "Begin, Taimin."

Despite her curt command, Taimin realized that he needed to change his approach. Another human might become an ally in this strange place.

He softened his tone. "Before we start, why don't we get to know each other first? This will work better if we can be friends."

"Friends?" She raised an eyebrow.

"Yes, friends," he said with a smile. "What do you normally do here?"

"My role is to translate the communications that we intercept."

"On behalf of the bonded?"

She tilted her head and spoke to him as if he were a child. "Of course."

"How does that make you feel?" he asked.

"Useful," Hannah said. "The marshals appreciate my work."

Taimin kept his expression smooth. "That's a good thing."

Hannah glanced toward the window. "Once, they even let me travel up the stalk." A dreamy cast came over her eyes. "The view from up there is incredible."

"You appreciate beauty."

"Don't we all?" She gave him a look of disdain. "I have heard that the wasteland is ugly."

"It's dry and hot. There aren't many trees. But I suppose it's beautiful in its own way." He smiled without humor. "I've always wanted nothing more than to find somewhere better, somewhere safe."

"You must be glad that you're not there now. Life in Agravida provides many comforts. There is no danger here."

He kept his tone light. "Perhaps not for you."

All of a sudden, she leaned forward and stared into his eyes. Behind her serious facade, there was a young woman filled with life. "Believe me, Taimin. You have come to a better place."

Taimin didn't share his true thoughts. "I hope so," he said.

He decided to give her time. At any rate, the reason he was in Agravida was more important than either of them. He wasn't in control of events. They wanted him to learn their language, so he would learn. But if a chance came to speak to the sky marshal sooner, he would take it.

"Shall we begin?" he asked.

She nodded, and Taimin turned his mind to the things he wanted to say in the wasteland's defense.

19

Shock was the most common expression of all. Selena saw it on the faces of the people huddling on the floor of the ravine. It was in the glazed eyes of former city folk who shrank into the steep rock walls. Shock was in the stories people told.

Selena navigated a path through the mass of refugees. This was just one gorge in the Rift Valley, but it was filled from beginning to end. As she glanced grimly from one group to another, she was thankful for every man, woman, and child who had escaped the fall of Zorn. These people had made it out. Many hadn't.

Selena passed a snub-nosed trull talking with two humans; all shared the same low tones and worried faces. She saw a group of newly arrived mantoreans in the distance, lean and insect-like, with long bows on their shoulders. Bax traveled the area, some guiding groups of humans to caves, others passing around food or water.

Someone tugged on Selena's sleeve and she turned to see a thin woman with a child in her arms. "Mystic, did . . . did Elsa make it?"

"I'm sorry," Selena said. "I don't know. I'm looking for her now."

"Can't you"—the woman waved a hand—"find her?"

Selena wished she could. She shook her head. "Not one person among so many." She clasped the woman's arm. "Last I heard, she made it out of the city."

She continued to walk and scan the crowd. This gorge was one of the deepest she had seen yet, with walls that climbed to a soaring height and the sky just a thin swathe of blue high above. Dirt made up the floor and the shade banished most of the heat. Chaos had ensued after the fall of Zorn, but the city's surviving populace was now finally in one place. Elsa was missing, but Blixen had taken charge. The refugees would be housed in caves. Humans would sleep beside bax, trulls, skalen, and mantoreans. No one would complain.

As she made it through the most crowded section, Selena saw Ruth crouched next to an old man dressed in the remnant of a laborer's smock. The old laborer glanced Selena's way and gave her a nod. Ruth smiled at something the old man said to her.

The refugees in the Rift Valley had heard Selena's warning bell, and her talent had saved their lives. Many had seen the tower destroyed in front of their eyes, yet she had miraculously survived. It seemed that everywhere she went, people knew her.

As the vista opened up, Selena saw a group of skalen heading her way. They wore tight vests tucked into trousers, along with high leather boots, and most had a bundle of javelins strapped to their back. Their dark, diamond-patterned skin, sinuous walk, and tilted reptilian eyes marked them out among so many humans.

The skalen in front was young, with glossy skin and a mouth full of sharp white teeth. He looked familiar, and when he saw Selena his eyes lit up. "Selena," he said, placing a hand on his chest. "My name is Wielan. You visited my home."

Selena suddenly remembered entering the mine in the mountain, and following the toothsome skalen as he guided them deep into the interior.

"Recently you contacted Treel," he continued, "and Treel contacted us. We have brought the aurelium you asked for." He swept his gaze over the gorge, before returning his attention to her. "Who is in command here?"

Selena turned. She couldn't see Blixen and didn't know if he was anywhere nearby. Elsa was missing. No one had heard from Dale.

Back the way she had come, Selena saw an old skalen deep in conversation with a wart-faced bax. Relief flooded through her.

"Rathis!" she called. She waved her arm. With a parting word to the bax, Rathis came over. "This is Wielan. He's brought aurelium."

"Clan Leader Rathis?" Wielan bobbed his head. "I know your name. I am merely a watch leader. But my clan leader will be honored to meet you." He glanced over his shoulder and Selena saw that while the skalen in front carried javelins, the larger number at the back were all burdened with packs. "There are more of us coming. Where shall we store the aurelium? Are any of these caves empty?"

"Wait here, Watch Leader," Rathis said. "I will speak with Blixen. He is the bax who rules over this region."

"Rathis," Selena asked, "have you seen Elsa?"

Rathis gave Selena an inscrutable look and pointed farther along the ravine, in the direction she had been walking. "Do you see that cave, where the gorge narrows? You will find her there."

———

Selena stooped as she entered the cave, but the ceiling opened up after the low entrance and she was able to straighten. The cavern's interior was shadowed. It would have been difficult to see if it weren't for the flickering light cast by a torch on a pole.

The cave wasn't deep and even as she walked, the bed pallet at the back drew her attention. The white-haired healer with the kind face, Jerome, leaned over the pallet. But then he moved to reveal the woman he was tending.

Selena swallowed. Elsa was covered with a blanket. Her eyes were closed and her face was gray. As Selena neared, she heard the sound of Elsa's labored breathing. The leader of Zorn had always seemed indomitable, filled with boundless energy despite the gray streaks in her hair and her slight frame. Now she looked old and frail.

Harvin, a round-faced man a decade or so older than Selena, sat on a rock by Elsa's bedside. He cast a quick glance at Selena but didn't offer a greeting. An aloof man with a head for numbers, he had been one of Elsa's senior administrators, in charge of the city's supplies of food and water.

"How bad is it?" Selena asked softly.

Jerome looked up at her. "A shard of stone pierced her abdomen. It is difficult to say how much it damaged her internal organs."

Selena turned her head when a newcomer entered the cave. She recognized another of Ruth's colleagues from the infirmary, a plump woman with a curt manner.

"Is she awake?" the woman asked briskly. "Someone needs to take charge out here. People are frightened. They need leadership."

"Shh." Jerome cut the air with his hand and scowled. It was the angriest Selena had seen the mild-mannered healer. The woman glared back at him and then turned on her heel and left.

Elsa's eyes fluttered open. She tried to lift her head.

"Don't try to move," Jerome said to her.

Elsa coughed and followed it with a wince as she placed a hand on her stomach. Her face contorted with pain. Jerome offered her a water flask and she took a few sips. She pushed the flask away to look up at the faces surrounding her.

"Zorn is gone," Elsa said. She rested her penetrating eyes on Selena. "We are all wastelanders now." She sucked in a breath. "Dale?" Her gaze moved around. "Where is he?"

"I'm here, Mother."

Selena turned and her breath caught.

Dale's uniform was torn, his face was dirty, and his red hair was in disarray. He looked both fatigued and scarred by suffering as he hurried to Elsa's bedside.

"Good," Elsa said in a hoarse voice. "Dale, your task is to keep the people safe. I'm in no position to lead."

"You'll be fine," Dale said. Selena saw that his lips were set in a thin line. "You just need rest."

Elsa gave a soft snort. "We both know better than that."

Dale cast Selena an anxious glance. "But what should we do?"

"Let Selena guide you." Elsa's eyes closed once more and she became still. Only the slight rise and fall of her chest revealed she was still alive. Everyone watched and waited, but soon it was clear she wouldn't say anything more.

Dale sank to a crouch by his mother's side. He took her hand in his and stared into her face. Selena's heart went out to him as she gave him the space he needed. He leaned forward to kiss Elsa on the forehead.

When he was done, Dale straightened. He looked down at his mother for a little while longer.

Selena spoke in a low murmur. "What happened?"

Dale didn't meet her eyes. "We tried to lead them away. We failed. A few of us were injured, so we had to land. By then . . ." He trailed off. "By then it was over. I'm sorry it took us so long to get here. I couldn't leave anyone behind." He watched Elsa again and then turned to Jerome. "Will she live?"

"The healer can't tell us," Harvin said curtly. "Did Elsa just say what I thought she said? She wants the mystic to decide our next move?" He nodded in Selena's direction.

"I believe she did," Dale said. "I don't know the wasteland." He raised an eyebrow at Harvin. "Do you?"

It took Selena a moment to understand what was being asked of her. All of a sudden Jerome, Harvin, and Dale were looking at her expectantly.

"We need to take care of the people here and then we need to move on," Selena said.

"Move on?" Harvin frowned. "We should stay here."

"We can't." Now that she was thinking ahead, Selena's voice firmed. "They'll find us here. We have to leave the wasteland altogether."

"Commander?" Harvin asked Dale.

"She's right," Dale said. "We can't stay here. But as for where to go . . ."

"I have an idea," Selena said. "Commander, let's get things organized outside. Then, I suggest we go and find Blixen."

⌣‾‾⌣

Between Dale's soldiers and the contingent of healers, soon the anxious refugees had someone to turn to for their needs.

Rather than ignore Harvin, Dale asked him what he wanted to do, and he surprised Selena by volunteering to ensure everyone had food, water, and a place to sleep for the night. Harvin even found some members of Elsa's former leadership structure and set them tasks. Elsa's style had been to give her administrators big problems to solve independently, only letting them turn to her when faced with a difficult choice. It seemed that all they wanted was to know someone was in charge.

Later in the day, Selena and Dale found Rathis and Blixen coordinating the efforts of a group of skalen as they stacked jars of aurelium against the wall of a large cave. With his intimidating size and necklace of bones, Blixen was clearly in charge. The skalen made short work of emptying their packs. Selena was stunned to see how many jars there were.

"Never fear," Rathis said, noting her stare. "A skalen knows how to store aurelium properly." He tilted his head in Dale's direction. "Is there news of Elsa?"

"Still the same," Dale said soberly.

Selena's gaze took in both Rathis and Blixen. "We've found you because we need to talk and make plans. Together we can speak for the humans here."

She heard approaching footsteps and saw Rei-kika. The mantorean walked with her strange, double-jointed gait, and regarded them all with her multifaceted black eyes.

"Apologies I could not come sooner," Rei-kika said. "There are many newcomers who need settling."

With the jars now arrayed by the walls, Blixen glared at the skalen. "All of you. Out."

Soon there was just Selena, Dale, Blixen, Rathis, and Rei-kika in the cave; of the five races, only a trull wasn't represented.

Selena gathered her thoughts. Dale had asked her to speak first. "Zorn is gone," she said, "reduced to dust." She met the eyes of each of her companions as she spoke. "We're not safe here. Leaving is dangerous, but it is our best option. If we stay, it will only be a matter of time before we are attacked again."

"So much devastation," Rathis said, shaking his head. "I was there. I barely made it out alive. I have to constantly remind myself that this is only the beginning."

Blixen grunted. "I accept that we are not safe here. Not once they find us, and then we would never get away. So we leave. There is no firewall to prevent us doing so. But what then?"

"Isn't it clear?" Dale spoke in a voice filled with both anger and determination. "We have to take the battle to the lands of our enemy."

Selena watched Dale. Recent events had changed him. He had been brave, and fought with everything he had, and he had lost.

"What do you say, Selena?" Rei-kika's antennae swished from side to side.

"There are many of us here in the Rift Valley, from all races, working together for the first time. Survival has to take priority." Selena tried not to look at Dale. "We do have a large quantity of aurelium, but I don't know if we have the strength to fight the bonded in their own lands." She paused. "What I do know is that everyone has to get moving, and fast."

"I know what I think," Blixen said. "There is a huge world out there. They will never find us all."

"Respectfully, I disagree," Rathis said. "Wherever we go, they will hunt us down."

"My point exactly," Dale said forcefully. "Yes, we could disperse. Yes, it would make it harder for them to destroy us. But there would be one result. Eventually they would slaughter us all. Unless we stay organized and united, we lose any chance to strike back. We should spread the word that this is a war, and that we plan to make them pay dearly for every life they take. We should gather every settler and rover, and every bax, trull, skalen, and mantorean. There is power in numbers. Let us show them what we are capable of."

Blixen looked uncertain, but Rathis slowly nodded as a fierce gleam came to his eyes. Rei-kika's face was as inscrutable as ever, but Selena knew from her posture that she was tense, even afraid.

"For now, let's focus on our immediate future," Selena said. "I agree that we should stay together. We can take care of the weaker among us, and Dale is right: there is strength in unity. We have learned that their machines can be destroyed. We have aurelium. Our numbers are growing. We need to apply our hearts and minds to whatever comes our way. We can't just think about survival. We have to think about how to defeat them."

"What if they cannot be beaten?" Blixen asked. "Hiding might be all we have."

When Dale scowled, Selena held up a hand. "It doesn't matter," she said. "This isn't a choice we have to make today. Whether we fight them in battle or flee the wasteland, what we need is a place to journey to, a place of refuge, and"—she glanced at Dale—"a place where we can tell others to gather."

Selena waited. All eyes were on her. She had their attention.

She nodded at Blixen. "I acknowledge your point about the wider world outside. I know somewhere, close to where the firewall once was. A sheltered place, below a cliff, with hundreds of caves and fresh water. It's a good destination while we plan our next move."

Blixen shook his head, still uncertain.

"Warden," Selena said to him. "No matter what happens afterwards, you have to get every bax in the Rift Valley safely to the edge of the wasteland."

"Fine," he said. "I agree to it."

"Rei-kika?" Selena asked.

"We are stronger together," she said in her clicking voice.

"Rathis?"

"More skalen are coming," he said. "If you share our destination, our mystics can tell them where to go."

Selena turned. "Dale?"

"We'll put out the word and gather numbers as we go," he said. "You know the wasteland better than any of us. Lead the way."

20

As he often did, Taimin stood at the window and gazed at the stalk. He watched the mesmerizing sight of the individual compartments going up and down with daunting speed. Pent up in his quarters—his cell—he was always tense, wanting to do something, to take action. This was how he distracted himself.

He had asked Hannah how tall the lattice was. She said that it was difficult to imagine, that it was better to think of it as long, like a rope. Her demeanor was too serious for her to have been jesting when she said that the incredible ladder to the heavens was long enough to wrap around the world three times over.

All Taimin could see with his own eyes was that the stalk didn't look anything like the tall buildings that made up the city of Agravida. He had no idea what enabled it to climb all the way to the void where the layer of sky ended altogether.

It was morning, and the city's streets and structures glowed with a yellow sheen. The golden sun Dex was low, glistening from a gap between two buildings. Taimin regularly glanced at the metal door. He was expecting Hannah to arrive at any time.

Finally the door slid open. Hannah entered; as always she wore the same white costume, and her blonde hair looked so straight she must have brushed it a thousand times. Her brow was creased in a slight frown.

"Hello," she said, giving him the bonded word for a formal greeting.

"Hello," Taimin replied. She nodded, and he continued the conversation. He turned to the window, where the stalk was clearly visible from the room's interior. "What stops it from falling?" he asked in the bonded language.

"It is complicated," she said. "The stalk is supported by a delicate balance of forces."

"So if the ballast changed it could fall?"

"Balance," she corrected. "That will not happen." She hesitated. "Let us switch to the common tongue," she said in the language Taimin was infinitely more comfortable with. "I have something different planned for today." She indicated the door. "Come with me."

Surprised, Taimin watched as she placed her hand against the red light near the door, which flashed to blue before the door slid open. He followed her from the room, leaving his quarters for the first time since his arrival.

The corridor outside was empty. The same gray walls greeted him, and the same row of metal doors stretched in both directions.

As Hannah led Taimin along the corridor, she glanced his way. "You are progressing well enough, but unless you learn some fundamentals you will never understand the bonded, let alone Ravange. So we are going to visit the archive."

The passage terminated at a group of elevator doors. Hannah summoned a compartment, and she and Taimin both stepped inside. She activated an arrow, and in an instant the compartment dropped like a stone. Barely any time passed before the metal box glided to a halt, the doors opened, and Taimin followed Hannah onto another moving walkway.

Taimin tried to take in as much as he could. The ability to navigate the bonded city might save his life one day. He paid attention to every motion Hannah made, every symbol on the walls, and the information conveyed by the arrows and diagrams. Despite the strangeness of the place, a few things were starting to make sense to him.

While the walkway whisked him along, he looked through the transparent glass wall to the city outside. He saw glimpses of bonded on other walkways, and centipede-like quadrails speeding through the city. It was daytime, yet bright lights were everywhere, attached to buildings and the bridges between them, streaking across the sky and circling far below.

"The archive is a place where we can discover an infinite variety of knowledge," Hannah said as they reached another elevator. The cube-shaped room plummeted, the compartment came to a halt, and the doors slid open. "Advisors and elders visit the archive to access the information for pleasure or research."

Soon Taimin and Hannah approached a broad archway up ahead. The corridor was wide, and the entrance it led to was huge, even by the standards of the city. Sharp white symbols, stark against the gray, decorated the top of the arch. It looked like the entrance heralded an important place, but there was no door; anyone could simply step inside.

Taimin followed Hannah through the archway, looking around in wonder.

He was in a vaulted chamber, not as immense as the terminus, but still big enough to make him feel small. The room was empty; he and Hannah were alone. He saw an array of large drawings spread across the four walls, but the rest of the archive was confusing.

Rows of panels filled the interior, forming long corridors between them, and all of the panels were white. The corridors led nowhere, simply to the back of the space. A handful of tall, circular tables stood in the far corner, along with oversized gray chairs.

Glossy black boxes rested on the tables, similar to the healing array that Ingren had carried around with her.

Taimin peered along one of the corridors. He started as something colorful appeared on several of the white panels. Moving images flashed up and then disappeared, to be replaced with other dancing lights and sliding pictures.

"This is the archive," Hannah said. "There are maps here, as well as written texts and moving pictures with sound. The knowledge can be accessed in a variety of forms."

Taimin spent a few moments adjusting to the strange room, and then walked up to one of the large drawings on the wall. "This is a map, isn't it?"

"Correct. That is a map of Garvalan, a town far from here."

He continued and passed several more maps, before stopping at the largest of all. It was so big that it covered a sizeable portion of the wall, and as he examined it in detail he began to make sense of it.

"What about this one?" he asked.

Hannah came over to join him. "That is Agravida."

"Where are we?"

She pointed. "The archive, where we are, is here." Her finger then moved to indicate another place. "Your quarters are here."

"Where do you live?" he asked curiously.

"Here." She showed him another part of the city. "This is the stalk. This is the auditorium, where you will give your speech to the assembly."

"What about Ingren? Where does she live?"

Hannah inspected the map for a moment before giving a slight shrug. "That is not something I would know. Come, let me show you some more."

She led Taimin away from the wall and over to the nearest of the vertical panels. Taimin and Hannah faced it together, and with practiced ease she wiped her hand across the surface. The moving images disappeared, and now it was pure white.

"We can access information about any topic imaginable," Hannah said. "Although, because the warriors are in ascendancy, much of what has been studied in the last thousand years is about war."

Taimin thought hard. There was one topic that he wanted to know about more than any other. The warriors were in charge. But if the situation were reversed, a bonded like Ingren would be the leader, rather than the sky marshal.

There was a potential solution, he knew, to all of his problems— if he could only understand.

"Tell me more about ascendancy," he said. "Ingren tried to explain it to me."

Hannah rested her fingertips on the white panel. "Key: ascendancy," she said in the guttural syllables of the bonded language. She followed with some more commands, uttering them too swiftly for him to follow.

Taimin's eyes widened when two bonded appeared on the panel's surface. They were life-sized, and for a moment he was stunned as he looked at them. He tilted his head and realized that they were just flat images, displayed in reaction to Hannah's voice.

One of the pair stood tall and wore a glossy crimson-and-black uniform. He had eyes like fiery embers and curling red horns on either side of his crown. The other had a more submissive posture, with short, pointed horns that matched the color of her pale yellow robe.

"Not all bonded pairs are male and female, but you will see many like this in the city. The warriors direct their advisors. Even the council of elders must obey the wishes of the war council." She watched him to make sure she had his attention. "However, the present situation was not always the case."

Hannah touched the panel and spoke again. The image vanished. She muttered a command and the two bonded appeared again. They looked essentially the same, but now there was a subtle difference. The advisor stood in front of the pair and her posture was more erect. It was the warrior who looked submissive.

"In times of peace, it is the warriors who serve and protect their bondmates. With the advent of war, a reversal takes place. Then the warriors are in ascendancy, as they are now."

Taimin tried to understand. Without the war that raged in the void, the bonded would be altogether different. He began to realize how Ingren could be so unlike her bondmate.

"What happens in a reversal?" he asked.

"When the next reversal takes place, the warriors will agree to give up power. The advisors and elders agree to take it. Words are spoken, and it is done."

"What could possibly make the warriors willingly give up power?"

"Victory," Hannah said simply. "When fighting no longer serves a purpose, bonded society changes." Seeing his frown of concentration, she continued. "Let me show you."

She wiped the panel's surface to clear it. The surface remained white until she spoke, "Key: alman."

A new creature appeared. Tall as a bonded, with similar proportions and the same rust-colored skin, it was nonetheless different, with softer features, and no facial ridges or horns at all.

"This is an alman," Hannah said. "Once, long before the stalk, long before Agravida, in another age altogether, the bonded were not the only intelligent race on this world. Bonded and alman lived on different landmasses, separated by oceans. But then each civilization expanded, and when they came into contact they began to fight for resources. The alman lacked unity, and as well as fighting

167

the bonded they also fought each other." She paused and glanced at him. "It was different among the bonded, for the warriors were able to take charge. They became ascendant, and organized themselves into a fighting force. Nothing else took precedence. They fought the alman until they were victorious."

"And then?"

"When the alman were all gone, and there was no more reason to fight, organization for war was no longer needed. There was a reversal. Depending on the circumstances, bonded society is either geared for war or peace."

Taimin took a moment to think about what Hannah had just told him, and then as realization dawned he looked at her in horror. "So the warriors were in charge until their enemies were completely eradicated?"

"That is correct. As long as they are in ascendancy, the warrior's way is to fight until there are no survivors. The last alman was killed long ago."

Taimin let out a breath. "Go on."

"After the reversal, knowledge became the focus of all bonded, and technology flourished. This state endured until the war with the five races began. Humans started it." A look of resolve came over her face. "But we will finish it."

"Hannah," Taimin said. "You are human." When she scowled at him, he decided it best to change the subject. He needed to learn all he could. "You say humans began the war. Why?"

Hannah waited a moment and then returned to the panel. "Perhaps we should start earlier than that." She spoke commands and made gestures while she explained, and new images flashed up on the white surface in front of them. "You understand what space is?"

"I think so."

"Then you know that stars are actually suns, and space is the void between them. Many suns have planets, worlds like this one, and every race uses ships to travel from one world to the next."

She watched his face, and he nodded uncertainly. The panel continued to shift between vistas of suns and spherical worlds with clouds, oceans, and land masses.

"The age of space began in earnest when the bonded received a message from a distant star. They were already building advanced machines, but found space difficult to explore. The message changed everything."

"Who was it from?" Taimin asked.

"We still do not know. What we do know is that the message came in the form of a set of instructions, two sets, to be precise. Today, we think of them as two gifts."

The panel now showed a long sleek cylinder with a tail that glowed green. The ship sped through a void as black as deepest night, past fields of glittering stars.

"One of the gifts was an organism: aurelium. Aurelium is used to power the ships that explore the stars."

Taimin watched the ship for a time. Something occurred to him. "And aurelium also powered the firewall."

"Correct. It has many uses."

He thought about the aurelium mine he had seen with Selena. It was staggering to learn that the strange life form wasn't from this world. "What was the second gift?"

"The second gift was another organism, so tiny that you would never be able to see it unaided. So small, in fact, that it can be considered to be a building block of life itself."

Hannah spoke in the bonded language, and symbols appeared on the panel, but to Taimin they meant nothing at all.

She rubbed her chin. "How do I explain? The second gift enabled us to change the instructions of life that make one creature a human, and another a mantorean. It gives some individuals the ability to communicate across space. The trait can be passed down the generations." She turned and met his eyes. "We call those with this talent mystics."

Taimin's mouth dropped open. He still had so many unanswered questions, but gradually the world he had lived in his entire life was starting to make sense.

"Seeing things on land is useful, but the abilities were designed to be applied to the void. Without mystics, the captains of the ships would not be able to communicate with one another across the vast distances of space. It takes many years for ships to travel from one place to another, which is why the war with the five allies has raged for so long. A mystic's awareness can travel faster than anything else. Mystics make space exploration possible."

Hannah trailed off and glanced past Taimin's shoulder. He turned and was startled to see Ingren approaching. She looked different. She now wore golden robes, and held herself erect, almost loftily. Her bright yellow horns were glossy. She looked well.

Taimin was surprised by the warmth he felt when he saw her. Even though Hannah was human, it was the sight of Ingren that made him feel less alone.

Ingren met Taimin's gaze and gave him a nod of recognition. "It is good to see you, Taimin." She focused her attention on Hannah. "How is the instruction going?"

"I was just telling Taimin about the two gifts, Elder Ingren."

Ingren glanced at the strange symbols littered across the white panel. "Ah, the new sequence." She gave Taimin her familiar expression of amusement. "Are you managing to understand?"

"I'm trying," he said honestly.

"Go on, Hannah," Ingren said with a nod.

Hannah cleared her throat, evidently a little self-conscious with Ingren watching. "We know that the same message was also received by the other five races," she said. "For a time there was peace, as civilizations discovered each other and began to trade. It was still a slow process with space as vast as it is, but it is looked back on as a golden age." Her expression darkened. "But then a splinter group of humans raided a bonded ship. Human civilization has always been far from cohesive, with no central authority, and it was only the beginning."

Hannah issued some more commands and Taimin watched as bright flashes of light erupted from different groups of ships. He saw one of the cylinders explode in a burst of fire. The corpses of bonded warriors and their advisors drifted through space.

Hannah continued. "Thinking that the bonded were weak, more humans joined in. The warriors defended those they were bonded to, but lacked direction as a group. There was a clear need for a reversal. The elders and advisers agreed to it, and the warriors took charge. From then on, they were in ascendancy, and still are today."

Taimin looked at the panel as scenes from the ongoing war played out in front of him. "Why did the other races join forces with the humans, rather than the bonded?"

"After the reversal, everything changed," Hannah said. "A bonded warrior, freed from constraint and eager to follow his or her most aggressive instincts, is a fearsome thing indeed. The other races thought the bonded were almost passive before the change, but no more. Bonded society is focused on nothing but war. The other races maintained their ties with humans, even as bonded warriors destroyed humans in great numbers, and many of them died too. The humans were losing and asked for help. The five allies grouped together. Now, total victory for our warriors means an end to all five races."

Taimin glanced at Ingren, whose expression was impassive. He wasn't surprised that she hadn't told him all of these things as they traveled together.

Ingren spoke up, issuing a command that altered the moving images. "Both sides in the war have developed weapons that would chill your blood," she said to Taimin as he saw a spherical world burn. "Radiation devices, we call them, able to destroy all life on the surface of a world." Her distaste was obvious. "There is a reason we keep Lumea's location a secret. Do you understand, now, why the fate of your friends in the wasteland is not a priority? I hope you realize the difficulty of the task ahead of you."

Taimin did, but he still had to try. "You say the warriors don't believe in peace," he said. "But have the five allies tried?"

It was Hannah who replied. "Until the war is won, communication with our enemies is strictly forbidden."

"The two sides don't speak?" Taimin was shocked.

"No," Hannah said. "I have already explained. The war will only end with total victory."

Taimin turned away from the panel. "When was the firewall created?"

Ingren replied, "You already know much about your origins. Your ancestors were captured a very long time ago. Prisoners were taken and abandoned in the wasteland, so that all warriors could prove their mettle, as was a warrior's passion long before we developed civilization."

Taimin stared into the distance. He felt both powerless and incredibly small.

"Taimin . . ." Ingren's hesitant voice made him focus on her. "As you know, you will soon be called up to address the assembly. This may be my last opportunity to get you out of Agravida."

"I want to speak."

Ingren and Hannah exchanged glances; the look they shared was filled with import.

"There is something you should know," Ingren said. "There may no longer be much purpose in what you are trying to do. The city you call Zorn is gone."

It took Taimin a moment to comprehend. Then, when he did, Ingren's voice sounded like it was distant. Blood roared in his ears.

"It is now nothing but dust and rubble. Some escaped, but soon the sky marshal will be sending ground forces to kill anything still living."

Taimin's heart thumped once, twice, so slowly he could count the beats. Selena had to be alive. She was a mystic. She could see danger coming.

With a supreme effort he clenched his jaw and took hold of himself. "I still have to find a way to end this." He turned to Hannah. "I know what I want to say, but there are words you will have to teach me, even if I don't understand them myself."

Hannah opened her mouth, but Ingren forestalled her. "I would like to talk to Taimin alone, Hannah. Thank you. You may go."

Soon Taimin and Ingren were alone in the archive. He looked up at her, wondering what would happen now.

Ingren surprised him by reaching out and gripping his shoulder. "I would not be here without your help. For what it is worth, I will teach you."

21

Fiery heat seared the wasteland. Both suns were high in the sky and poured terrible brightness onto the plain below, where an immense column made up of all five races stretched for so long that its tail plunged between two cliffs and on to another plain altogether. To some it was an exodus; to others it was the birth of an army.

Selena blinked sweat out of her eyes. She was close to the head of the column, walking on dry red dirt that crunched beneath her boots. She passed cactuses on both sides, green and spiky with limbs arranged in a variety of poses. Boulders lay strewn over the landscape. Lizards scurried off when they sensed the approach of marching feet. Tall cliffs loomed in the distance.

She glanced at Dale, walking by her side. A sheet of moisture coated his forehead, but his expression was determined. Behind Dale she saw more humans, but also the stooped forms of bax in leather armor. Turning her head in the other direction she saw a powerfully built trull grumble something to a man nearby. Farther back, a group of mantoreans mingled with skalen, while more bax followed behind, and then a large number of marching humans.

As far as she could see, it was the same all the way to the column's end. It was simply too difficult to stay in separate groups according to attributes like race or clan, settler or rover. Instead those up front were the strongest and fastest. The skalen hated bright sunlight and yet here they were, ready to throw their aurelium-tipped javelins at a moment's notice. The mantoreans were renowned archers, nomadic by disposition, and more arrived as word of the column's existence rippled throughout the wasteland. Most of the bax were from the Rift Valley, just as a great number of humans were from Zorn, but every day a band of human rovers or bax villagers joined the immense group, until Selena imagined that the entire population of the wasteland must be filling the plain.

"Do you think they know we're here?" Dale watched the sky before he turned his attention to Selena. "I want us to survive long enough to build this," he indicated the mass of figures, "into an army."

"All I can promise is that we'll have warning," Selena said. "I know where I'm taking us. And we've made it this far."

"Then lead on," he said. The tension in his eyes relaxed; she liked it that she had reassured him.

Selena also took comfort from the fact that she wasn't the only mystic looking out for danger. Among so many, there were inevitably dozens of mystics, with mantoreans like Rei-kika the most skilled of all. A voice sometimes spoke into Selena's mind, telling her about what lay ahead. She returned the favor in turn. At any time she could farcast to the rear of the column and check on the wherries that trudged along, their sturdy backs packed high with supplies. The ability to communicate over distances meant that the column's movements could be coordinated. Problems were tended to swiftly, and no straggler was left behind. Both she and Dale would know the moment anything was sighted in the clear blue sky.

She heard a piercing shriek and looked up as a wyvern flew overhead. She followed it for a time, tracking its passage with her eyes. There were just ten wyverns in the column, flown by the surviving members of the city guard.

Even as Selena watched the wyvern, she heard a sibilant voice speaking in her mind. She turned to Dale a moment later. "Another group of rovers. A dozen men." The skalen mystic who had contacted her had also gifted her an image. "They're a rough-looking bunch," she added.

"Good," Dale said, pleased. "You wastelanders aren't like people from the city." He glanced back again. "We've got a strong group here. A lot of fighters. Not just humans but bax, mantoreans, trulls, skalen . . ." Whatever he was thinking, a fierce look came to Dale's eyes.

Selena reflected. Even after the fall of Zorn, most members of the column were like Dale, and wanted to fight back. After this journey, when they reached the edge of the wasteland, Dale planned to take charge, fashion weapons, and build an army. They would leave the wasteland, ready to fight anyone who tried to stop them. They would have the opportunity to challenge the bonded on their own ground.

The newcomers Selena had spoken with brought tales from afar. The strikers had destroyed countless homesteads and villages. Fear came to be replaced with anger. Everyone heading to the edge of the wasteland shared a desire for vengeance.

Selena thought about Taimin. He had been so convinced that it was futile to try to fight the bonded. She wondered what he would say about Dale's plan to take an army to the heartland of the enemy.

She heard a voice behind her, calling her name, and saw Ruth navigating through the column to reach her. The moment she saw her expression, she knew it couldn't be good news.

Ruth was panting by the time she reached Selena and Dale, her forehead beaded with sweat. "I've come to tell you . . ." she said. She then glanced at Dale.

"What is it?" Dale said.

"I'm sorry. Your mother . . . She's gone."

Selena put a hand over her mouth. She felt a strong sense of sorrow, along with a heavier weight of responsibility now that Elsa was gone.

Dale's face was like stone. "Did she say anything, at the end?" he asked.

"Just the one word," Ruth said. "Survive."

———

Vance trudged alongside Lars. The big skinner was red-faced and a sheen of moisture covered his bald head. Vance was glad he didn't have such a thick beard in this heat; even his own trimmed beard and moustache felt wet with sweat.

They were about halfway down the column and surrounded on all sides by panting humans, grunting bax, sleek skalen, stick-thin mantoreans, and a handful of angry-looking trulls. Hoarse breath came from all directions, and every back was burdened with a heavy pack. Lars guided a wherry that plodded along next to him, and Gretel perched precariously on top of the wherry's high load.

Vance lifted his flask and took a mouthful of warm water, before reaching out to hand it over to Lars. The skinner shook his head, and Vance felt a spike of irritation. Lars was always trying to prove that he could handle himself better in the wasteland than Vance could. He had another sip before returning the flask to his hip. When he drank his flask empty, Lars wouldn't say anything, but his dark eyes would rest on the flask for the briefest instant and he would give a subtle shake of his head.

Vance wondered how much longer the journey would take. He was hot and the suns were blinding his eyes. His legs were tired and he was desperate to throw his pack off his back and stretch his sore muscles. But it was barely noon. He wouldn't rest until everyone else did.

A group of humans had been approaching the column for some time, and Vance shielded his eyes when he saw they were close enough to make out their faces. They were all men, coarsely dressed, armed with hardwood swords and bows on their shoulders. A few had scars on their faces, and most were bearded.

"Rovers, by the look of them," Vance said. Not long ago he would have steered clear as soon as he saw them. They looked like younger versions of Lars. He watched them until they merged with the column up ahead. "Still they come."

"This is foolish," Lars growled. "We're impossible to miss. We shouldn't stay together, we should separate."

"So you want to give up?" Vance asked.

"I don't care what you call it. I want to live."

"The first time the strikers came we drove them away. We have bigger numbers now and plenty of aurelium. You heard Dale. He's keen to get to work making crossbows. The only way to fight back is to work together."

"Dale is wrong," Lars said. "I know it, and you should know it too. Marching as a group like this, all we're doing is making things easy for them."

"What's your plan, then?" Vance asked. "Find some hidden corner of the world? Live out your days as a hermit?"

"At least I'd be alive."

"It's giving up. You'd spend the rest of your short life in hiding. Is that what's right for Gretel?" Vance indicated the little girl sitting high on the wherry's back.

Lars scowled. "What do you suggest?"

"We have to keep adapting until we find a way to beat them. The crossbow idea is good. We'll soon get to try it out."

"I'm telling you, Vance, we should run while we still can."

Vance shook his head and looked away. He didn't want to reveal it, but Lars's talk of doom was beginning to affect him. "I wish Taimin was here," he muttered.

"Well, he's not. He's probably dead."

"And you don't even care?"

"Of course I do." Lars gave a rare glimpse of emotion. He paused, and then continued in a lower voice. "Remember: he said all along that we can't fight on even terms."

Vance met the older man's eyes. "He wouldn't run away."

"What would he do then?"

"I don't know." Vance scratched his chin. "It's Taimin. He always has a plan."

They both marched in silence for a time. Flies buzzed around Vance's face and he swiped them away. The two suns blazed down. The air was utterly still. Vance wished there were some breeze, anything to dispel the heat. As Lars watched Vance take another big swallow of water, the skinner shook his head disapprovingly.

Vance decided that he was definitely tired of Lars's company. "I'm going to find Ruth," he said.

"Looks like she's busy," Lars said.

The skinner nodded and Vance followed his gaze to see Ruth in the distance up ahead. She was standing off to the side of the column and talking with her white-haired colleague, Jerome. Vance watched as Jerome reached out and gave her shoulders a squeeze.

"I don't care if she's busy," Vance said.

He left Lars behind and walked quickly, weaving through a group of bax. It took him some time to navigate the crowd and approach Ruth and Jerome.

"Ruth," Vance said as he approached. He was grim-faced as he raised his voice to cut through whatever she and Jerome were talking about. "We need to talk."

Vance's worry weighed him down . . . that, and the heat and his fatigue. Was hope truly lost? Should they go their own way?

Ruth looked over. "Not now," she said. Frown lines creased her forehead.

Jerome offered his hand. "Vance, isn't it? We haven't properly met."

"I don't care." Ignoring Jerome, Vance turned his full attention on the woman he loved. "We used to be able to talk about the future, Ruth. Our future."

"Vance," she said wearily, "this isn't the time."

Vance scowled. Ruth at least owed it to him to have a conversation. He was afraid, not just for himself, but for her. If Lars was right, they were all marching to their deaths. Yet even if something terrible happened, Ruth would stay with the group. She was a healer to her core. There were too many people who needed her.

"If not now, then when?" Vance demanded.

"Vance. Please. Just go away," Ruth said harshly.

Vance's eyes shot open. Her tone struck him like a knife to the heart. He opened his mouth, searching for something to say. Jerome was looking at him with something approaching pity. After glaring at both Ruth and Jerome, Vance stormed back to Lars.

Lars was shaking his head. "Lad, listen to some advice."

"I don't want your advice."

"Fine." Lars gave a shrug. "Up to you."

Vance sealed his lips and fixed his gaze ahead. He forced himself not to look at Ruth again.

The march in the heat continued.

22

Taimin practiced his speech. He paced the length of his quarters and tried to move his mouth around the strange syllables of the bonded language. He spoke with conviction, as Ingren had taught him. He knew he needed to convey both sincerity and determination.

Tension filled his body. He walked back and forth, his pulse already racing. A whisper of sound made him look up sharply.

The metal door slid open. He saw Ingren standing in the doorway, tall and imposing in her golden robes. His heart pounded in his chest.

Ingren's expression was grave. "It is time," she said.

Taimin nodded. He took a deep breath. This was going to be the most important speech of his life. He had to save a multitude from extinction. He had to convince the warriors of the assembly—who lived to spill the blood of their enemies and despised every creature in the wasteland—to think again and spare their lives.

He would be addressing a group that was just a small portion of Agravida's population, only those who made key decisions, yet he would be speaking to thousands of bonded warriors and their advisors, as well as the council of elders. From the map he had seen in the archive, the auditorium was huge. Now he was about to go there.

Thinking about his objective made him remember that Zorn had been reduced to dust. The arena, the tower, the barracks, the houses . . . all destroyed. Ingren had said that soon ground forces would be unleashed to scour the wasteland for anything left living. If Selena had made it out of the city alive, he only hoped she had the sense to hide.

He focused on the task before him. Ingren had impressed on him that Sky Marshal Jakkar was the one to convince. He could do this. He had to.

"Are you ready, Taimin?" Ingren asked.

He met her gaze. "I am."

———

Ingren walked by Taimin's side. They traveled a long corridor alone, and neither of them spoke. Taimin's lips moved as he silently rehearsed his speech. His thoughts whirled. He knew he was breathing hard, and his heart was beating too fast, but there was nothing he could do to calm himself.

Already he could see an immense archway at the end of the corridor, where two brightly colored doors met in the middle, one gold and the other crimson. The doors loomed, three times as tall as Taimin was himself. It was a special entrance to the auditorium, which Ingren explained was just for him to walk through alone. Taimin's tension grew with every step closer.

Ingren came to a halt. She stared at Taimin for a time, and he knew her well enough to guess that she was searching for the right words to say. She looked anxious, which didn't make him feel any better.

"I wish you well," she said finally.

Taimin gave her a nod in reply. He knew her eyes were fixed on his back as he took the last few steps toward the arch. The churning in his stomach was familiar. He felt as if he were about to fight for his life in the arena.

The gold and crimson doors parted as soon as he neared them. He entered the auditorium.

As soon as he was through the entrance, the doors closed behind him. He experienced the overwhelming sensation of being a tiny creature in a gigantic space. The auditorium was immense, a huge bowl with a domed ceiling high overhead. Artificial stars in the dome created an impression of the night sky. Thousands of bonded filled the tiered seating. The alternating pattern of costumes—red, yellow, red, yellow, over and over again—was dizzying. They all faced the long walkway, supported above a void, where Taimin now found himself.

He kept moving. Some of the bonded were at eye level, but most were on the lower tiers, heads tilted back as they looked up at him. He saw that the walkway led to a raised podium that stood at the epicenter of the auditorium.

Taimin clenched his jaw and focused on the podium. Yet as he approached he couldn't help looking past it, to a warrior seated at eye level on the auditorium's far side. He was one of the most imposing bonded that Taimin had ever seen. Despite the distance between them, he dominated Taimin's vision. The warrior's twisting horns and sharp brow ridges gave him a haughty look, heightened by his high collar and red armor trimmed with black and silver. From Ingren's earlier explanations, Taimin knew that he was looking at Sky Marshal Jakkar.

The sky marshal's advisor sat beside him, dressed in a pale yellow robe with gold bands on the sleeves. Her features were softer than her bondmate's and there was something kind about her face. Her name was Astrin, Taimin knew, and Ingren liked and respected her, although of course Astrin had no power over her bondmate.

Arrayed behind Jakkar and Astrin, Taimin saw a group of bonded in golden robes: the council of elders. From their positioning it was clear that the sky marshal was the head of the beast, while they were merely part of its body.

There were so many strange staring faces. Taimin felt exposed, with thousands of fiery eyes directed his way. Part of him wanted to find a dark place to hide in. The warriors all resembled Ungar, who had been frightening enough when there was just one of him.

He tried to calm his nerves. What happened now would determine the fate of the wasteland.

A low murmur of conversation filled the air, but it died down as Taimin took his final steps to the podium. There was nothing for him to rest his hands on. He was on display.

He sucked in a deep breath.

Ingren had said there would be no preamble, no call on him to begin. Taimin told himself to remember to sweep his gaze now and then around the auditorium, but most of all to direct his words at Sky Marshal Jakkar.

He opened his arms and began to speak the bonded language, uttering words he didn't understand but had memorized with Ingren's help. As expected, a hidden mechanism projected his voice.

"Bonded warriors have a reputation for honor, and that is how it should be," he said. "Honor is important. Without honor, civilization is lost."

He paused. He was quite certain that he had delivered his words correctly. There was no reaction from the sky marshal, who just stared directly at him.

"We of the wasteland were put there long ago," Taimin continued. "We were imprisoned so that you could satisfy your urge to fight and hunt. But that is in the past now. The hunts all but finished when the barrier began to behave erratically. Most of your society lost interest. Yet we remained."

He turned slowly and took in the multitude of bonded staring at him. He knew he had to convince the warriors—even if every elder and advisor supported him, any change had to come from the dominant half of the bond. But the faces he saw were stony. It was impossible to tell what effect his words were having.

"You abandoned your outpost," he said. "You left us to our own devices. Only a few members of your higher ranks still followed the old traditions, and one of them was the warrior Ungar. He embarked on a quest. I was one of his targets."

A ripple of interest spread throughout the assembly. Ingren had explained to Taimin that Ungar had been a sub-marshal—a well-known and respected warrior.

Taimin tried to ignore the crowd and focus on the sky marshal. "We fought in the belly of the machine that powered the barrier. The machine was destroyed. Ungar died in the explosion, and his former bondmate, Ingren, is now an elder. An elder needs protection. I brought Elder Ingren safely through the wasteland. She is only home, and alive, because of me."

Taimin had to wait for the loud murmurs to die down in the audience. As soon as there was silence, he put conviction into his voice. "The barrier is gone. You worry that we are now free. Yet you also claim to have nothing to fear from us."

Taimin's eyes narrowed. "Which is it? I doubt you are afraid. Am I right? And, if you are not afraid, does your honor not demand that you treat us as you would children—like the human girl, Hannah, who has been teaching me your language? You granted her leniency—why not us? I acknowledge that you may think it simpler to destroy us, but we are many, and we are determined to survive. If you offer to take us away in your ships, we will go. If you want us to come to an agreement about borders we must not cross, we will honor it."

Taimin had been struggling the entire time to make the strange sounds of the bonded language. He had worked hard, not only with help, but also alone, from before dawn until late into the night. It had taken him a great effort to make it this far.

He now said his final sentence. "We deserve to live."

There. It was done.

Silence ensued.

Taimin scanned from one side of the auditorium to the other in a vain attempt to gauge the reaction of so many bonded warriors. No one moved. Everyone stayed where they were. Then, slowly, multiple heads turned. The bonded all looked in the direction of the sky marshal.

Legs apart, Taimin lifted his chin. He kept his face impassive as he stared directly at the imposing warrior in the crimson armor. No doubt it was the sky marshal who had ordered the destruction of Zorn. He was responsible for everyone who had died. Part of Taimin screamed at him, telling him that the sky marshal was his enemy. He should be fighting with all his heart. Yet his head knew better, and here he was, pleading for leniency.

After a few moments, Taimin's brow furrowed. The sky marshal was emitting a growling noise and his shoulders were shaking. Taimin wondered what the sound was before he realized.

The sky marshal was laughing.

Jakkar slowly raised his bulk until he was standing. His bondmate beside him looked as if she knew what was coming. Despite the many faces turned his way, the sky marshal addressed his words to Taimin.

"We allowed you to address this assembly because you are a notable human warrior, who defeated the mighty Ungar." The sky marshal lifted his hand and stared at the claw-like fingers for a moment before clenching his hand into a fist. His malicious stare returned to Taimin. "Yet surely you, as a warrior yourself, must know that what you ask for is so impossible as to be ridiculous." He pounded his fist on his chest. "We are the strong, and those you speak for are the weak. There is no peace now. There can be no peace in the future."

Despair sank into Taimin's guts like a heavy stone.

But he summoned one last effort. "Listen to your elders," Taimin said. He indicated the group in golden robes arrayed behind the sky marshal. If Ingren was with them, he couldn't make her out from the rest. "Conflict is not the only path to harmony."

The sky marshal snarled. As Taimin watched the leader of the bonded, who was strong enough to tear Taimin's arms from his body, he tried not to show his fear.

The sky marshal made a slicing motion with his hand. "This is over. I let you speak, human. It was my decision, just as your life is mine to do with as I please. I may choose for you to meet an interesting end. Or I may think of an amusing use for you. Either way, we are done here. Never forget that your race and mine are at war."

Taimin's shoulders slumped. The sky marshal continued to stare at him with nothing but contempt. No one in the auditorium spoke up for him. He knew he had failed.

And there would be no second chance.

23

"I'm sorry," Hannah said as she entered Taimin's quarters.

He stopped pacing the room and hurried over to her. She took a step back when she saw how frantic he was. He couldn't help his tight expression. Urgency fired his blood.

"You have to take me to the archive," he said. "You can get me there. They know you."

Taimin had only just finished making his appeal to the assembly. He knew he didn't have much time before new orders were given, and that the most likely outcome was for Sky Marshal Jakkar to think of some novel way for him to die. Hannah was here now, but she might never return.

"Why do you want to go there?" Hannah asked.

"Please, Hannah. If you care about me at all, you have to take me."

Her frown was familiar. "You won't be able to escape," she said.

"I'm not trying to escape."

"I can see that you're upset—"

"Please, Hannah. Will you take me there or not?"

She gave him a perplexed look. "What is it you're trying to do?"

Taimin took a deep breath and then let it out. When he spoke again, he used a softer tone. "I'm trying to get you to help me."

"Why would I help you?"

Even now, he still felt sympathy for her situation. "Because the more I learn about the bonded, the more I might be able to become like you . . . A friend of the bonded. Happy."

A change came over her. For a very brief moment, so quick he almost missed it, her eyes sparkled. "Follow me," she said.

———

Hannah led Taimin through the city, along the moving walkways and in and out of the elevators, until they reached the broad corridor and passed through the archway with angular symbols.

Taimin rushed into the archive, while Hannah trailed behind him. He scanned the room, looking from the maps spread on the walls to the white panels that formed long corridors.

Faltering, he came to a halt. He didn't know what to do. His speech had failed. He hadn't been able to make an accord with the bonded. There must be something here that could help him find a way forward.

"What are you looking for?" Hannah asked.

He ignored her. With swift strides he walked to the nearest corridor and looked at the tall panel. He slapped his palm against it, but couldn't decipher the strange symbols that floated across the surface. Frustration coursed through him. He knew what he wanted: something . . . anything. A solution.

"Taimin, stop." He turned and saw Hannah beside him. "I thought you said you wanted to come here to learn."

"I do," he said absently.

"This is about what happened today, isn't it? Just let it be. You tried. It's time for you to think about yourself."

Rather than respond, Taimin looked wildly around the room. There was information here, but he didn't even know what he was looking for.

"Please. Just give up." Hannah implored. "Forget the wasteland."

"You don't know what it is you're asking," he said. "I have to do something."

Turning away from the row of panels, he once more scanned the walls. His eyes moved past the maps of towns and cities, and to the far wall. His frantic steps took him away from the panels, past the maps, and over to the images he hadn't inspected before.

He was standing in front of a map—if that was what it was— utterly unlike the others. His head tilted back as he stared up at a collection of stars. Pale dots lay sprinkled over a coal-black surface, like a frozen image of the night sky. The dots were a variety of colors, some red or blue, others white or gold. They were suns, each and every one of them, and so far away that it took years to travel between them.

Unless that person was a mystic.

Excitement made his heart beat faster. He saw Hannah watching him. "You said that the reason we have mystics is so that ships and worlds can communicate?"

"Yes," she said uncertainly. Her manner was cautious, as if he were a beast that might attack her. "And to scout and warn ships of dangers. What of it?"

"So a mystic on this world might be able to communicate with someone out in space." He pointed upward. "Perhaps to ask for help?"

"I . . ." She hesitated. "Yes . . . It's possible."

"How does it work?" He frowned. "Do you just . . . go out there and call?"

"Taimin." Hannah approached him again and now her voice was pleading. "Stop it. Just stop trying."

Taimin thought furiously. He needed to get back to the wasteland as quickly as possible. He had to find Selena. Zorn had fallen, but she was still alive. She had to be. He knew that farcasting had limits, but everyone always said that Selena's strength as a mystic was beyond what they were used to. Together they would try to contact the five allies—and ask for help.

He met Hannah's eyes. "Hannah, will you help me escape?"

Her mouth tightened. "I knew it," she said. "Don't you understand? They're sending ground forces to the wasteland. Why would you go back there?"

"I've told you. I have people I care about. Please. You're human. You can come with me."

"Leave Agravida?" she asked incredulously. "Why would I want to do that? You want me to live like a savage?"

"Don't you want to meet other humans? Be part of a community? They'll welcome you."

"I'm already part of a community," she said. "This is my home."

"You're all alone. This isn't a good life—"

He knew he had gone too far when she scowled, turned on her heel, and strode toward the archway. Searching for something to say, he hurried after her and grabbed her hand. He needed her help. He had to make her understand what she was missing. She struggled and tried to pull away. "Let me go!"

Startled, Taimin released Hannah when he saw a newcomer.

Ingren stood at the archive's entrance. Tall and stately, she had stopped to stare.

Hannah lifted her chin. "He wants to escape," she said to Ingren. "He is a human, and humans are our enemies."

Ingren's eyes traveled from Taimin to Hannah and back again. "I see," she said. Her face was blank, but she gave a sharp nod. "I will deal with him. You may go, Hannah."

Ingren moved to allow Hannah to pass her, and the young woman turned to curl her lip at Taimin before leaving through the archway.

Taimin wondered what was about to happen. Ingren watched and waited until Hannah was gone, and then she returned her attention to him.

"Quickly," Ingren said. "No orders have yet been given for your death. If you want to make it out of here alive, you must come with me now."

24

Selena gazed up at the long series of cliffs that towered above her for at least a thousand feet. It was early afternoon and the sky was strangely hazy, blurring the outlines of the two suns. As she peered up at the heights, she shielded her eyes, and followed one of the seams that traveled down from the tall escarpment to the bottom of the cliffs. She had come this way with Taimin, after he showed her his homestead, and she remembered descending the trail. Together with Vance, Ruth, and Lars, she and Taimin had sheltered in the caves that peppered the bottom of the cliffs. This was Taimin's place. It was as rugged as he was . . . With sadness, she changed the thought. As he had been when he was alive.

The immense column, made up of all five races, had reached its destination.

"So this is it," Dale said beside her. "This is where you've been leading us."

Selena cast a swift look over her shoulder. A cloud of dust clung to the plain and marked out the approaching column. She and Dale had gone ahead so they could begin to make plans. Soon the deserted area in front of her, where rocky ground spread out along the base of the cliffs, would be filled with humans, bax, skalen, trulls, and mantoreans.

"Why here?" Dale asked.

"If you want to make plans, this is the place to do it." Selena nodded up at the escarpment. "The wasteland's boundary isn't far from the top of the cliffs. There's a trail to the top—it's steep but not as bad as it looks. There's fresh water and hunting. The cliffs will help hide us, and there are plenty of caves. Finally . . ." She scanned the cliffs that stretched in both directions as far as the eye could see. "Do you see them?"

Dale frowned. "See what—?" He broke off.

The winged creatures were a similar color to the cliffs, but now and then they wheeled above the escarpment or soared away from their nests. Dale's eyes widened.

Selena glanced at him and smiled. "Wyverns."

"Ah," Dale said slowly, and he grinned along with her. His spirits had improved since the fall of Zorn. Some of the former light had returned to his blue eyes. "My mother chose well. You are clever, Selena. No one from the city could have brought us here." He began to make plans. "I'll house the weakest first, but then I want us making weapons as soon as possible. We'll spread the word. I'll have my men start taming wyverns right away. We'll leave this place not as refugees, but as an army. Anyone who travels with us must be willing to fight."

As always, the talk of fighting made Selena worried, but she was pleased to see him excited. "We should probably go and check on the spring. I doubt it's dried up, but it's best to be sure."

He looked back at the dust cloud and nodded. "Lead the way."

Together they crossed the rocky ground and headed closer to the base of the cliffs. They walked in silence, hopping from rock to rock, each lost in thought. No doubt Dale was thinking of the army he planned to lead out of the wasteland. Selena was just glad that they had made it this far. The old, weak, and injured would be able to rest in the shelter of the caves. Ruth and the other healers among them could set up a proper infirmary. They could take stock of their supplies of food and water. Everyone would get a chance to rest and recover from the journey.

Selena set her sights on the cave with the jagged entrance shaped like a hand, ignoring all the others. Now that she and Dale were nearer, the going was easier. The rock rippled where the steep cliffs met the ground below, smooth and wide enough that even with their numbers they wouldn't all be on top of each other. The cliffs provided shade, and there would be space to work outside at all manner of tasks. Ideally everyone would be housed with rock overhead, but if not there was plenty of room to camp in the open.

Dale gave a shout.

The sound jolted Selena out of her reverie. Dale's eyes were narrowed as he peered up at the sky. With a swift movement he yanked his bow off his shoulder and an arrow was in his hand. He fitted his arrow to the string, tracking his target as he prepared to shoot.

Selena's heart thumped as she saw the danger. A wyvern had left the sky to plummet toward the base of the cliffs. The wyvern's wings swept down and then tucked in as it swooped in a direct line for the two humans. With rust-colored skin and a lean body, it wasn't a big wyvern but was clearly bold enough to consider them prey. As the wyvern's mouth parted to reveal sharp teeth, a piercing shriek split the air, loud enough to jar Selena's nerves.

Dale's bow creaked as he sighted along his arrow.

Selena gasped.

She threw herself at the man beside her, crashing her shoulder into his. At the same time, she grabbed Dale's arm and pulled. The bowstring thrummed, knocked out of his fingers. Dale's arrow shot wildly and vanished into the distance.

Meanwhile the wyvern continued to descend.

"Stop!" Selena cried. She gripped Dale's arm and held his gaze.

His expression was bemused. He tried to free himself but she held fast. Then a look of puzzlement crossed his face. He saw the wyvern slow its rate of flight, still a short distance away. Its wings beat down at the ground, and then it settled itself as it landed.

The tapered head tilted. The wyvern didn't approach, but its inquiring eyes glanced at Dale, before alighting on Selena.

Selena relaxed her grip and let go of Dale's arm.

The wyvern was a male. His wings fluttered and his claws stretched in and out as they dug at the ground. The eyes that regarded Selena were warm, brown, and a little sorrowful. She knew those eyes.

"Griff?" she asked. A warm feeling welled up within her. The sensation grew until she was smiling. "Is that you?"

Selena left Dale behind, and the nearer she came, the more certain she was. Griff bobbed his head and gave a rumbling whine.

"Selena, be careful," Dale called from behind her.

She continued her approach, and then Griff nuzzled her and she reached out to wrap her arms around him. "I missed you," she whispered as moisture welled in her eyes.

She stroked Griff's head. He gave her another inquiring look.

"I'm sorry," she murmured. "Taimin's gone." She then spoke over her shoulder, loud enough for Dale to hear, "Griff and I have known each other for a long time."

Dale came over to join her. "I still think you should be careful, Selena," he said. "He's clearly wild."

Griff glared at Dale. He gave a shriek, making Dale step back, and then his wings opened as his feet pushed down at the ground. He rose into the air and gave Selena a last look before turning away.

Happy to see Griff alive and well, Selena only wished that Taimin was with her. As she watched Griff fly up toward the cliffs, she remembered when she had first met Taimin, riding his wherry, brave to the point of recklessness as he saved her and Lars from a group of marauding bax. She missed Taimin desperately.

She waited until she couldn't see Griff anymore and then turned to Dale. "Do you know how I know this place?" she asked. "This is where Taimin grew up. He showed me the ruins of the homestead he lived in, past the top of the cliff."

Dale took a moment to reply. "He did something brave. I wish he had succeeded. We all do." Despite his blunt words, his tone was gentle. "But he didn't, and he's gone now." He reached out to take her hand. "Come on, we've got a lot of work to do." Before she knew it he had taken her hand and brought it to his lips, surprising her. "It's you and me now. We have to find a way to survive together."

25

Hidden in the quadrail, Taimin was again confined to a closet, but this time he was making the journey to the distant farmland alone.

He peered through the slits in the window and watched the world rush by. After gazing up at the tall gray buildings of Agravida, he took in the machines on the ground and in the sky. The bright lights of the city gave way to sparser districts where cube-shaped structures sprawled for mile after mile. Forests flashed by; the expanse of water spread out to fill his vision. More forests thinned until he saw farmland. He sped through smaller towns without stopping. Time passed, and then there were no more towns, just fields colored red and gold and green.

With a lot to think about, he pondered his time in Agravida. His plan for peace had failed and Ingren had helped him to escape before it was too late. Yet he hadn't come away with nothing. While he had been among the bonded, he had learned, and he now had a new goal.

There were members of the five allied races out in the void, traveling between the stars on their ships. Taimin would find Selena. She would contact them and ask for help.

Selena had to be alive. Zorn was gone, but she was out there, somewhere. He clung to the only hope he had, for without it, he didn't think he could go on.

He knew he loved her. He had known it since he met her and stood transfixed, momentarily at a loss for words as he drank in the sight of her. Their friendship had developed, and then it became something more. He wanted to protect her and care for her. They were meant to be together.

"She is alive," he muttered, as if voicing it aloud would lend strength to his desperate hope.

He had made what he believed was the right decision, and traveled with Ingren to her city, but he knew Selena might not forgive him for leaving her. All he wanted, more than anything else, was to find a way to solve this conflict so they could build lives together—real lives.

He pictured her face. She was smiling in the image he built of her, smiling as she danced in the rain.

For a time the quadrail sped through a region of empty terrain. The ground was barren, devoid of life, reminding him of the wasteland. Rather than vibrant green grass or tall crops that glowed in the sun and swayed from side to side in the wind, he was greeted with red dirt that stretched all the way to distant hills.

The quadrail slowed, and he wondered why; this land was nothing like the surrounds of the station he was traveling to.

He drew in a sharp breath. The vista wasn't empty anymore.

He saw armored war machines—devastators, Ingren had called them—row after row of them, huge hulking vehicles that were perfectly lined up as they hugged the ground. The devastators were squat and black, similar to the harvesters that he saw working in the fields, but bigger and made for a different purpose. The size of houses, they rested on multiple huge wheels joined by grooved belts. Long cylinders pointed from their domes. And here they were, close to where the quadrail would bring him to his destination, a few days' travel from the wasteland.

The quadrail continued to slow and came to an unexpected halt. Taimin heard a series of clangs and then a vibration shook the walls, along with an accompanying groan. Through the window, he saw a bonded warrior in uniform, walking beside his advisor as he directed a devastator off the quadrail and into a row. If the war machine had occupants, they were well hidden.

More bonded appeared. More devastators left the quadrail to join the rows. Taimin watched them pass, one after the other. There were already so many, even before the quadrail's arrival, yet still they kept coming.

Another clang came from somewhere farther along the quadrail's trail of compartments. A moment later the view started to slide past. He saw bonded striding outside, pointing things out to each other.

Then, as the quadrail began to increase speed again, he saw the strikers.

They were just like the winged machines he had seen in the sky as they streaked toward Zorn: silver in color, with narrow noses that tapered out to fixed wings. They rested in rows on the ground. He swiftly counted. The first row contained a dozen. He saw a second row. The quadrail picked up speed. It became difficult to count, but the bonded clearly liked order, and the rows were all the same length.

As the terrain became empty once more, Taimin clenched his jaw as he thought about the size of the force he had just seen, which would enable the bonded to sweep across the wasteland like a scouring wind.

There was no doubt left in his mind: the wasteland was doomed.

He felt a chill. The quadrail glided along, faster and faster. Once more he was looking out at a blur of fields.

There was no chance for survival, none that he could see, other than to find the enemies of the bonded and ask for help.

26

Vance carried a bundle of sticks and dried cactus into the cave that was his new, temporary home. His back was sore and he was eager to set down his load. It was a false night, with just Lux in the sky, and the softer rays of the crimson sun shone on his back and lit up the cavern's interior.

He was exhausted after working since before dawn. He had spent hour after hour fitting arms to crossbows, attaching levers, and instructing the smiths on the fashioning of bolts to go with them. Everything made of metal was being melted down. Meanwhile the skalen worked to transform the bolts they made into aurelium. Human and mantorean archers converted their metal arrowheads. Bax replaced the points of their spears. It was dangerous work, and the frantic pace could cause mistakes, but the skalen among them were experienced at handling the explosive substance.

Vance's work still wasn't done, for he wanted to do something to make his new home a little more habitable. Everything had been frantic since his arrival. By the time he came back each night it was too dark to make up a decent bed and he was too tired to light a fire. He had barely seen anything of the people he was sharing his quarters with: Ruth, Lars, and Gretel. The false night would provide the opportunity he needed.

He set down the bundle of kindling in the middle of the cave and then glanced around. The space was misshapen, with plenty of nooks and alcoves, and sharp stones littered the ground. He knew the stones well: even after a long day he could still feel the imprint they had made on his back the previous night. A few packs lay in different corners, alongside blankets, water flasks, and weapons.

First of all he assembled the kindling into the makings of a fire. Down on his knees, he used his knife to tear away the skin from the lump of dried cactus. He tore the skin into thin shavings, and then built them up into a pyramid with smaller twigs and thicker sticks. He kept the trunk of the cactus for later; it would burn slowly and enable the fire to last.

Next he returned to the entrance, where he had left four flat rocks. One by one, he groaned and lifted them up, struggling with their weight, until he set them down in a circle surrounding the pile of kindling. He then moved to the corner where Lars had slept the previous night. He removed the big man's blanket and smoothed the ground. Every time he found a stone he tossed it inside the circle of big rocks.

He repeated the process with Gretel's blanket, located in a separate alcove near the back of the cave, and then came to the place that he and Ruth had claimed.

For a moment he looked at the two blankets and didn't move. They were a reasonable distance apart, at an angle to each other: together but also distant. With a sigh, he crouched and his back gave a crack like the sound of a whip. He moved the two blankets away, and then with long sweeps of his arm he found stone after stone until he was certain that there weren't any more. He lay down his own blanket and then picked up Ruth's.

Holding her blanket in his arms, he hesitated, but then he spread out her blanket right next to his. He went to his pack and emptied out everything except for his clothing, and then set his pack at one end of the blanket to make a pillow. Ruth's pack soon marked out where she would be resting her head. He patted Ruth's section down until he was certain she had a comfortable place to spend the night.

With his task complete, he stood and stared at Ruth's empty blanket. Without fail, she always came back from the new infirmary in the early hours of the morning. They barely saw or spoke to each other.

His brow creased. He had to do something about it.

With long strides he left the cavern. Out in the open, the air was warm and a steady breeze blew against his skin. As he walked, he followed the row of caves that stretched along the bottom of the cliffs. Hundreds of tents filled his vision. Smoke rose from both cookfires and makeshift forges. He threw a quick glance at the red sun, which only just managed to hold itself above the horizon.

The encampment wasn't as busy as it could sometimes be, but many were taking advantage of Lux's fading light. Members of all races moved about as they worked at one task or another. Humans and bax were the most numerous, but Vance caught sight of a group of skalen carrying poles on their shoulders; the dangling rock lizards and raptors made his stomach rumble. Farther away some bax fired crossbows at a row of cactuses. A pair of trulls grunted to each other as they walked past with water sacks on their shoulders. Humans weren't the only ones to operate bellows at the forges; the skalen were equally skilled at metalwork.

Vance knew where to find the infirmary and set his sights on the entrance to one of the largest caves. A dark-haired youth limped out of the cave's wide mouth, supported by two companions.

He saw Ruth.

She was also outside, crouched on the rocky ground as she washed her hands. She didn't lift her head and it wasn't until he stood directly above her that she saw him.

"Ruth . . ." he said hesitantly.

She splashed some more water from the flask onto her hands and then scrubbed at them with a chunk of caustic soap. "It's been a long day," she said. "I don't have the strength to argue."

"I know. I haven't come to argue."

She finished up by wiping her hands with a clean white cloth and then straightened. "Then what is it?" she asked, meeting his eyes.

"I've come to say I'm sorry." He let out a breath. "Look. I've been a fool. You're helping people. I realize that. I've always realized that. I've been trying to think about what I can say to make up for my behavior but that's all I've come up with." Ruth's brow furrowed as he continued. "If you want to be with Jerome, that's your right. I love you, and I'll be devastated, but the choice is yours."

Her eyes widened and then her frown softened. All of a sudden, she surprised him by giving a short laugh. "That's what this is about?" Mirth formed creases at the corners of her mouth. "You're right, Vance. You are a fool." She shook her head wryly. "Jerome is married. His wife is very sweet. He dotes on her." As Vance's mouth dropped open, she came closer, until she was looking up into his face. "But of course, they argue. It's the healer's life. The calling gets in the way of everything else. There's always more to be done, and when lives are at stake, the ones we love get pushed to the side. And that," she reached out and took his hand, "means you."

"Jerome has a wife?"

"Yes." Ruth's expression was still amused. "He's also twice my age. He's more like a father to me than anything else. And I've learned a lot from him." She hesitated. "Look . . . I know we've barely seen each other—"

Vance felt color come to his cheeks as he interrupted her. "By the rains . . ." he muttered. He trailed off and then gave a firm nod to himself. "I'll talk to Jerome and apologize."

"Don't worry, he understands."

Ruth leaned in, and Vance opened his arms to pull her into an embrace. For a long time he simply held her. He sank his face into her hair and inhaled. He couldn't remember the last time he had held her warm body so close to his.

"Perhaps you could come to bed tonight, just this once?" he asked.

"I'd like that," she said.

Vance and Ruth broke their embrace when they turned and saw Lars heading their way with Gretel by his side. Beads of sweat covered the old skinner's bald head, and he was dirty, with dark green plant matter on his arms and hands. The little curly-haired girl was just as filthy as he was, with her tunic in desperate need of a wash.

Ruth shook her head. "You haven't been getting her to work, have you?"

"Why wouldn't I?" Lars ruffled Gretel's hair.

"I've been cutting up cactus," she said proudly.

A sudden silence descended on the group. Everyone stared at Gretel. It was the first time any of them had heard her speak.

"Well, that's something, then," Lars said. He spoke gruffly, but his voice had a catch at the end. He glanced over his shoulder, farther along the row of caves. "I came to tell you that the meeting is taking place right now." He scratched at his thick black beard. He looked worried. "There are no good options. Sure, we've got bigger numbers and new weapons. But none of us should forget what happened at Zorn."

Selena's heart sank as she entered the cave. It was good that representatives from all five races were present. But clearly their arguments were getting them nowhere.

She was in the biggest of the many caves, a designated meeting area for the leaders from the different groups. A rocky, dome-shaped ceiling stretched overhead. Veins of some mineral in the walls reflected the green light of the aurelium lamps that rested in a handful of niches. There were a few flat rocks for stools, but everyone present was standing.

Blixen was growling something at the skalen clan leader Rathis and two other bax wardens. But even Blixen couldn't be heard over the humans who were close to shouting as they debated their options nearby. Rei-kika's antennae twitched in agitation as she looked at Selena, but she was trapped in conversation with a snub-nosed trull who made points with jabs of her meaty finger. Another trio of mantoreans stood in a circle, their clicking voices bouncing around the cave.

Selena wondered where Dale was. He had called the meeting, and already any sense of purpose was steadily draining away. She opened her mouth to try to establish order, but then Dale entered the cavern behind her.

He had somehow procured the clean uniform of a soldier in Zorn's city guard. With his striking appearance, he drew attention and nodded to every face that turned his way. He glanced at Selena and then headed directly into the center of the cavern. The leaders made space for him and formed a circle. Dale spread his arms, waiting as he held himself tall.

The din faded, and gradually the cavern fell silent. Selena joined Rei-kika's side and waited for the commander to speak.

He lowered his arms. "I know you are all afraid," he said, meeting as many eyes as possible. "But think about how far we have come. For the first time, all five races are united. Our numbers grow as more come to join our cause. We are learning not only to work together, but also to fight together. We have mystics who will see our enemies before they come."

"So why not stay here?" one of the humans asked.

"We can't," Dale said firmly. "This is a good place, but you all know as well as I do that we will never hurt our enemies as long as we stay here. We have to seize the initiative. We need to leave the wasteland behind and reach the wider world outside." His expression became dark. "And if anything tries to stop us, we must fight. The firewall is gone. There is nothing preventing us from going."

Blixen rubbed his meaty chin. "I still say we should split into smaller groups." He addressed the assembled leaders. "Surely you can all see that we would be safer?"

A murmur filled the cavern, but Dale raised his voice above it. "We have a large number gathered here, which will make us the focus of our enemies, it is true. Splitting up would give us the advantage of providing more targets. Some might make it through." His voice turned ominous. "But then what? They would hunt us down, slowly but surely. It might take months or years, but eventually we would all be killed. If we remain united, we are a force to be reckoned with. After leaving the wasteland we can keep going. We can take the fight to our enemy's heartland."

Without meaning to, Selena shook her head. She had been thinking hard, since coming to this place, and she knew what Taimin would say. In order to retain the option of fighting back, Dale was prepared to risk thousands of lives. What if he was wrong? Of all of them, Taimin had spent the most time with Ingren, even before they left together. Dale had never met Ingren, let alone spoken to her. He had never seen the vast machine buried under the desert.

Selena had described the things she had witnessed. But there was a difference between learning about a structure under the sand,

and the actual experience of entering its belly, visiting its heart, knowing it was so vast that to travel its breadth over the surface had taken days. How was it possible that a moving floor could propel her to the machine's center in moments? How was it possible to enclose the wasteland in a wall of fire?

She could see many in the cavern nodding along with the things Dale was saying. He had a point, that if they lost the option of fighting as one, it would never come back. She couldn't come up with an alternative proposal. Yet there were so many lives to think about.

"Now," Dale said, "I have fought these machines in the sky. We have a weapon that we know works: aurelium. And thanks to the skalen"—he nodded at Rathis and some of the skalen with him—"we have a vast quantity. We now have many crossbows and more of these new bolts. We are ready to take action."

He paused to let his words sink in. Scanning the faces of all the leaders, Selena saw determination in their eyes as Dale continued.

"I suggest that soon all of our fighters should ascend the trail to the top of the cliffs. Once we are at the escarpment, we will form up, as an army this time. We will then begin our march, and our crossing to the world outside. If our enemies come, we will be ready. Once we have achieved victory, we can come back for those we have left behind. It is time for us to invade their cities." His tone became low and ominous. "We will see how they like it."

27

A burst of fresh air greeted Taimin as he emerged from the region of gray haze where the firewall had once been. He had retraced the journey he had made with Ingren, but this time he missed her company. Once more the familiar landscape of the wasteland opened up in front of him. He grimaced at the foul taste that remained in his mouth. His legs were tired as he focused on putting one foot in front of the other.

The sky was the same shade of blue as it was outside the wasteland, but now the difference in environments was stark. There was no green grass covering the hills in a soft carpet, no thick forest hugging rivers where water flowed. The raptors that clung to the branches of the withered trees were hardy, leathery creatures, rather than the flitting, colorful birds he had seen. The dirt was the same red color, but he was walking through an empty expanse, decorated with sharp-edged boulders and spiky cactuses.

He wearily trudged through a field of gravel that crunched beneath his boots. Lizards watched him from under nearby boulders. As he pushed on, he scanned the terrain for snakes and scorpions, and kept his ears pricked for signs of danger: a firehound's howl or a wyvern's shriek. The bonded had confiscated his sword on his arrival in Agravida. He had some provisions in his pack, but he was alone and unarmed in the wasteland. He looked around for a piece of wood he could use as a club. Traveling without a weapon felt wrong. He had to hope that danger wouldn't find him.

Soon he would be approaching the region of cliffs where as a young boy he had hunted for wyvern's eggs with his parents. The golden sun had set, leaving the crimson sun Lux to sink toward the horizon up ahead. False night was always unnerving, when the low rays cast long shadows and washed everything the color of blood. The escarpment was just up ahead, but soon the crimson orb would fall below the world's edge.

He began to get worried. When darkness came he would need to find somewhere safe to rest. He would have to wait for dawn before following the trail down to the bottom of the cliffs.

He reached the place where the landscape dropped away, and in the fading light he took his final steps to the cliff edge. As he gazed down at the plain far below, he decided to follow the escarpment for a time. Perhaps he could find an old wyvern's nest to sleep in. He watched the winged creatures warily as they flew about the cliff below, making slow circles. The red sun would be gone in moments.

The top of the cliff was broken in the region where he was walking. Occasionally it created a slope gentle enough that he might be able to find a nook to shelter in. Spying a promising place, he came to a halt and peered down, searching in the last of the crimson sunlight.

He didn't hear the scuffle behind him until it was too late.

Something big made a snapping sound in the sky, right at his back. Wings fluttered, and then a piercing shriek split the air. A chill ran through his blood.

He whirled.

The wyvern landed just a stone's throw away, wings giving a last few sweeps. Long jaws parted to reveal sharp teeth. The moment it settled on its clawed feet the wyvern began to close the distance. The wyvern rushed toward him. Fast.

Taimin's heart thudded in his chest. Facing the menacing creature, he kept his arms spread, keenly aware that he had no weapon at all. The wyvern fixed its dark eyes on him. A low, rasping sound came from somewhere deep within its chest.

But then Taimin's tension eased. He tilted his head. The wyvern was a mid-sized male, and his eyes . . . they were soft, brown, and had a gentle, almost mournful, cast to them.

"Griff?" Taimin asked in wonder.

The wyvern gave a snort and flashed more teeth in what was steadily becoming a grin. He didn't slow, and Taimin didn't have a chance to dodge as a strong head butted into his chest. Taimin laid a hand on the wyvern's flank, and knew for certain it was his old companion when, without warning, he was forced to the ground as Griff sank down on his haunches, with his abdomen resting on Taimin's knees, the way he used to when he was a wherry. Taimin reached forward and scratched behind Griff's ears, which were pricked and upright where once they had been floppy.

He remembered finding Griff in one of the caves far below. Raptors had tormented him until blood ran in rivulets down his flanks. Taimin had nursed him back to health, and they had built a friendship. His aunt Abi had always called Griff a runt, but then Griff had transformed. He was now a strong, proud wyvern. And he was free.

"It's so good to see you," Taimin murmured.

The rumbling in Griff's chest continued as Taimin scratched his old companion. He hugged the wyvern tightly while Griff nuzzled into him, and then Griff's head turned. Griff looked into Taimin's eyes, and Taimin reached out to stroke his face.

"You were born here," Taimin said softly. "You've found your way home."

211

Griff tossed his head and pulled himself away, becoming animated and filled with energy. The change was as swift and sudden as it had been when he was a wherry. His wings gave a few sweeps and his powerful hind legs kicked forward. He put some distance between himself and Taimin, and then looked back and dipped his shoulder.

Taimin knew what Griff was suggesting, but he had no idea what his old friend intended. Nonetheless, as a warm wind blew over the top of the cliffs, and the red sun became just a glimmer of light on the distant horizon, he walked up to the winged creature. For only the second time in his life, he climbed onto Griff's back.

Griff barely waited for Taimin to settle before he pushed with his back legs and opened up his wings. He propelled his body forward, and his wings beat down hard at the same time. As the wyvern shot up into the sky, Taimin's stomach plummeted in his body.

The creature under him tilted forward, and Griff dropped like a stone. Taimin saw the plain a thousand feet below rush toward him. His eyes watered. Everything in his vision was a blur. He gripped hard with his knees and hugged the wyvern's body, and then the pressure changed again. Griff turned sharply, circling back toward the cliff. At any moment Taimin expected to smash into the sheer rock face.

But Griff knew what he was doing, and slowed as he approached a wide ledge. Partway down the tall cliff, the ledge was inset into the rock so that an overhang protected it from above. Griff was now far more careful as he soared toward it, and when he saw the desert grasses covering the ledge, Taimin knew he was looking at a wyvern's nest.

Griff judged his approach well, and after a few more sweeps of his wings he settled down in the middle of the ledge. Taimin slipped off his back and found himself on solid ground, but with a precipitous edge far too close for comfort. Shaken by the flight, he took a few steps closer to the wall. He put his back to the cliff face and fixed his gaze on the abrupt drop where the nest ended, just a dozen paces away.

Then he heard a growl, followed by a high-pitched mewling.

Taimin's head jerked to the side and he looked past Griff to see a clutch of little wherry pups clustered around another wyvern—a female. She watched Taimin for a moment, her eyes considering him carefully. But Griff was between them, and Taimin showed her his empty hands. She soon went back to tearing at a rock lizard with her teeth and feeding strips of red flesh to her young.

Taimin returned his attention to Griff, who was grinning again. "This is your family?" Taimin asked.

Rather than answer, Griff sprawled out and rested his head on the ground. With another glance at the female and little wherry pups, Taimin decided to slip his pack from his shoulder. He moved closer to Griff, and sank to the ground so that he was propped against the wyvern with his back against the wall.

As night settled on the wasteland, fatigue dragged at his eyelids.

Taimin woke to a strange sound. He thought at first that he had dreamed it, but then it came again. He was lying on his side, supported by a padding of grass, with his back against a hard surface. As he blinked, he found himself looking into a pair of shining eyes.

A soft mewl came from the direction of the eyes, barely a few inches from his face. The night was dark and he couldn't see much more.

Remembrance came flooding back. Past the small creature crawling toward him he saw a wide expanse of glittering stars. He was on a ledge that precariously jutted from the sheer cliff. One of Griff's curious pups had wandered over to him.

Wings fluttered. A big shape moved behind the little wherry. All of a sudden Griff's mate loomed overhead. She craned her neck and opened her jaws as she bent down. Taimin froze. With a swift movement of her head she plucked her pup up by the scruff of its neck. Her body turned; her wings crackled again, and then she carried the small creature back to where Griff lay sprawled beside the rest of his young.

Taimin's heart was still racing as he watched the wyvern resettle herself. He shook his head and chuckled.

He was now wide awake. As a warm breeze blew against his face, he leaned with his back against the rock and gazed out at the night, where a scatter of distant suns glimmered back at him. His eyes followed one of the stars as it slid ponderously across the heavens. What he was looking at was too slow to be a shooting star, he knew that now. It might be a bonded ship, or some other artifact of theirs with a purpose he would never understand.

The silver moon, huge and glowing, hung motionless in the night sky. He watched it for a time and wondered if Selena was out there, somewhere in the wasteland, under the same moon.

His gaze left the moon and traveled downward, to the plain far below. It was an area he knew well. It looked different in the pale combination of starlight and moonlight. When dawn came the terrain would display its true colors of fire and blood. The apparently flat expanse would reveal its rugged nature, with narrow ravines, rocky knolls, and rust-colored boulders strewn across the landscape. He would be able to see the distant fields of cactus at the limits of vision.

A flickering red light caught his eye. He frowned. The light was somewhere near the bottom of the cliffs.

He inched forward. The sensation of approaching the precipice wasn't pleasant, but he was rewarded when he saw more lights. The closer he came to the edge, looking directly down, the more flickering lights he saw.

There were fires far below. Not just one, but dozens and dozens, perhaps even hundreds. His gaze roved over the rocky area where the plain met the cliffs at their base.

Whoever was down there, there was a great many of them.

28

"This one's more spirited," Dale cried.

He had a rope in his hands and sat astride a wyvern's back as it heaved, trying to throw him off. Dale's hair was in disarray and eyes were as wild as the beast he had mounted. The wyvern threw itself in one direction and then another. The creature bucked up and down furiously and gave an ear-splitting shriek. The wyvern would have rolled but its wings were in the way. Every time it tried to fly it was prevented by the long stick on Dale's lap.

Selena was out on the plain but still close to the little black holes that indicated the mouths of caves. Both Dale and the wyvern underneath him cast long dancing shadows; it was early, and a morning wind blew dusty air over the red dirt.

With a roar, the wyvern gave a mighty heave. Selena gasped as Dale lost his grip on the rope. A final buck threw him into the air. The wyvern craned its neck. Jaws snapped at the irritating human, but closed on empty air.

Dale's limbs flailed. His long stick went flying. He struck the ground and rolled over and over. Freed at last, the wyvern spread its wings and kicked its legs to launch itself into the sky. An angry shriek told Dale not to try again.

Dale's pride was all that he had injured, and Selena smiled ruefully as she walked to stand over him. Face down in the dirt, he looked up at her.

"What was it you said?" Selena asked, raising an eyebrow. "You'll show me how it's done?"

Shaking her head, she reached down to help him up. He took the offer, but rather than what she had been expecting, he gave her a hard pull. She fell forward and he rolled with her, until Dale was on top of her, pinning her down.

Selena found herself on her back, looking up into Dale's twinkling eyes. His legs were astride her waist. He brought his face down. She could make out every freckle on either side of his nose.

"Be careful," he said. "Or I'll tame you."

Selena jabbed him hard in the ribs. He gave a grunt of pain and she twisted at the same time. All of a sudden she was the one on top. She threw him a look of triumph and then climbed off him to brush herself down.

"Don't expect me to help you up this time," she said.

Dale chuckled and returned to his feet. He opened his mouth to say something, but then his expression changed completely. His smile fell away as he saw something past Selena's shoulder. Astonishment filled his face.

Selena spun around. "What is it?"

She froze as she stared. Shock hit her with force. She felt as if she had been grabbed and roughly shaken. A mixture of emotions surged through her: relief, joy, guilt, shock.

Taimin stood just a short distance away.

The dawn sky silhouetted his tall figure. The soft wind ruffled his bristling brown hair. As Selena saw Griff behind him, the wyvern snorted at her—as if in disgust—and flew up into the air until he was out of sight.

Selena didn't know how long Taimin had been watching. His eyes moved from her, to Dale, and back again. He wore the exact same linen trousers, leather vest, and high boots she had last seen him in, but his clothing looked worn, and so did he. His brown eyes were shadowed. He didn't carry a weapon.

He looked terrible.

Selena's initial shock became something else. A fist was squeezing her heart, tighter and tighter, even as it beat faster, until it was going to explode.

"Taimin?"

She was barely aware that she was moving as she ran.

His arms opened. He grabbed her and she hugged him harder than she ever had before. He was alive. He had come back to her.

"Taimin? Taimin!"

He held her for a time, but then something changed. He gently took her by the shoulders and pushed her away.

She heard Dale's voice as he came up behind her.

"What happened?" Dale asked. "Did you make it to their city?"

"I did," Taimin said shortly. After a long pause, he continued. "Elsa was right all along. There can be no peace. Ground forces are on their way." He looked over his shoulder. "Where is Elsa? I need to speak with her."

"She's dead, Taimin," Selena said softly.

Taimin's shocked gaze went to Dale. "I'm sorry," he said.

Dale ignored him. His face remained hard as he glanced toward the cliffs. "How soon will they come?"

"I don't know. Soon. I've seen their forces." Taimin rubbed at his temples. "You wouldn't believe the things I've seen." He turned and Selena saw him watch as members of all five races moved about, organizing themselves, fashioning weapons, cooking, training, and packing in preparation for the ascent to higher ground. A cloud of flame appeared near a row of cactuses as crossbows were tested. "They will know about your . . . army."

"If our enemies are coming, then it's clear," Dale said. "We have no choice. We have to fight."

Taimin's eyes rested on Selena. She saw a familiar determination. "There may be another way."

———

"They've been mooning over each other ever since you left," Lars said.

Taimin scowled. He was in the small cavern where Lars and the others had settled; there were flat stones he could have sat on, but he wanted to stand. Nearby, Gretel straddled a rock while Lars wiped dirt from her face. Taimin's initial surprise at seeing the self-centered skinner care for the little girl was already becoming something closer to admiration. It was also another sign of the strange times they were living through.

Lars dipped his cloth in water, gave Gretel's cheek a final wipe, and nodded to himself, satisfied. He pulled Gretel to her feet and then glanced at Taimin. "You may not be happy about it, but pull yourself together, lad. From what you've told me, we've got more important things to worry about."

Hearing voices, Taimin turned to see Vance and Ruth enter the cave. Despite the situation, he couldn't help but smile when he saw them together. Vance's moustache and beard were as well-trimmed as ever, and his hair was neatly combed. He had built up a bit more muscle since Taimin last saw him. Taimin's attention moved to Ruth, whose short, wavy hair was unmistakable. She smiled at something Vance said, and the smile lit up her careworn face.

They were speaking in low tones as they entered, but then Vance stopped in his tracks. Ruth faltered in mid-conversation.

"Taimin?" Vance asked incredulously.

Without another word he raced over and the two men embraced. They slapped each other on the back, and then Vance pushed Taimin away. Taimin opened his arms to pull Ruth into a hug, and she squeezed him back just as tightly.

"When did you get back?" Vance demanded.

"Just today," Taimin said. "I've already seen Selena." He grimaced. "Her and Dale."

Vance and Ruth exchanged glances and then Ruth changed the subject.

"What happened?" she asked. "You went to their city?" She pulled him hard to sit him down on one of the flat rocks. "You have to tell us everything."

While Lars fed Gretel her early dinner, Taimin explained about the city of Agravida, the incredible stalk, and the endless war in the void between the stars. He told them about his speech, the sky marshal's response, and finished with the rows of devastators and strikers he had seen on his return to the wasteland.

"Our only chance is to seek help from the five allies beyond this world," Taimin said. "Dale's idea of some grand, noble, battle against the bonded . . ." He shook his head. "It's not just foolish. It's reckless. Everyone he leads will die."

He broke off when he saw Selena just inside the cave's entrance. She had changed in the time he had been away. There was a weight on her shoulders that hadn't been there before; he could see it in her eyes, and in the tension in her face that she probably thought she was hiding.

Then he remembered seeing her with the red-haired, smooth-cheeked soldier with the bright eyes. He didn't know if they were together—like Vance and Ruth were together—but there was obviously something between them.

"They're ready for you," Selena said.

29

Darkness settled on the plain. Features in the terrain became hard to distinguish and then shrouded until it was as if they had never existed. The world was always smaller under night's grip.

Taimin walked with care. The moon had yet to rise and starlight wasn't strong enough to make out anything but Selena's slender form and the rocky ground a few steps ahead. The fires he had seen the previous night were absent. Vance had said that the army would soon be leaving; everyone was getting what rest they could.

He followed Selena toward another cave, where the leaders representing the various groups were gathered. The stars became brighter as the night deepened. Selena kept glancing back at him, but he kept his face expressionless and his eyes focused straight ahead.

"You left me," she finally said.

His jaw was clenched even as he replied. "I was trying to save you. To save everyone."

Selena stopped outside a large hole in the cliff, where crisp green light poured from the inner depths. She turned to say something, but Taimin kept moving.

He walked into the cavern and saw a wide circular area. A domed ceiling opened up overhead. Mineral veins glistened in the light cast by aurelium lamps.

Taimin was conscious of loud conversation becoming quieter, and then the voices stilled as heads turned and eyes rested on him. The eyes came in different forms: the deep-set eyes of bax, the reptilian eyes of skalen, the multifaceted black eyes of mantoreans, and the round eyes of humans and trulls. He recognized Rei-kika and Blixen, and nodded at Rathis, his fellow prisoner in the arena. But there were many faces he didn't recognize, from all races. Dale was tight-lipped, but Taimin noticed the way he looked at Selena.

"We have gathered, as requested," one of the trulls said. Stocky, with arms as thick as Taimin's legs, his nose was upturned and the incisors outside his mouth bobbed up and down as he talked. "What is this news you have for us?"

The gathered leaders made way as Taimin approached, until he was at the edge of a circle, with everyone else facing him.

"It is good that we have two mystics here, mystics I respect and trust," Taimin said. He indicated Rei-kika and Selena, who stood at his side. "They may be the only chance we have."

"Go on," said Blixen in his rough, booming voice.

"I have been to Agravida, our enemy's most important city." Taimin's voice became grim. "I have seen things and learned things you would not believe, but most importantly, I have seen their forces. I can tell you that the wasteland has only witnessed a tiny fraction of the power the bonded have at their disposal. I believe I was right to go." He was keenly aware of Selena beside him. "But although I tried to make peace, I failed."

An older man dressed in the coarse leathers of a rover called out, "I thought you had news."

"I do," Taimin said. He swept his gaze over the group. "The bonded are our enemies, but while I was in Agravida I learned something." He paused. "Something about *their* enemies."

All eyes were on him; he had their attention.

He continued. "We know that the bonded fight our kin among the stars. They are five allies, as we are. But unlike us, they are able to fight the bonded on equal terms." He took a breath. "I have learned that we might be able to contact them."

A loud murmur broke out as the leaders exchanged glances.

"How?" Dale asked.

Taimin gathered his thoughts, wondering how to explain. "We take it for granted that there are some among us with special abilities. We call them mystics and we all know what a mystic can do. They can speak in our minds and free themselves from the constraints of their bodies to see things far away." Selena stirred as he spoke. "I have learned that these abilities weren't always a part of us. They were given to us, for a specific purpose."

He glanced at Selena. Her expression was startled.

"You all know by now that there are other worlds beyond this one, worlds that circle around stars," Taimin said. "Ships travel through the void, moving from place to place, but the distances are vast. Usually, there would be no way to share information." His next words were filled with import. "But there is."

He thought again about his time in the archive in Agravida.

"It is mystics who make communication possible between the stars. The ability to farcast means that mystics can travel the void faster than the most advanced machines. They can warn of dangers. They can convey important news and knowledge." He gave a wry smile. "At least, that is how it was explained to me."

Rei-kika's antennae twitched. "How can that be? Even Selena cannot farcast to the other side of the wasteland."

"That's not true," Selena corrected. "I just wouldn't be able to rely on my lifeline."

Taimin's brow furrowed. "I don't understand it, but somehow the void is different." He knew that Selena was remembering when she flew so high that she brushed the edge of the sky, while her body lay still and unbreathing. "In any event, we know we have potential allies beyond this world, allies who don't know about our plight. We should make the effort to contact them."

Taimin examined the faces before him. Dale was deep in thought. Others in the room looked uncertain.

Rathis glanced at Blixen and their eyes met for a moment. The old skalen returned his attention to Taimin. "As you said, they share our blood. And we know we share a common enemy. They truly might help us."

"That is my sincere hope," Taimin said.

Everyone started speaking. "We should make the attempt immediately," the old rover said. "Then we will know, one way or the other."

"I agree," Blixen grunted.

"Who is our strongest mystic?" asked the trull who had spoken earlier.

Several heads turned toward Selena.

"More than one should try," Blixen said. He indicated Rei-kika.

"There are others with my strength," Rei-kika said. "But it is true that Selena and I have worked together before."

As events began to move swiftly, Taimin realized something that he hadn't thought of before.

He had been so consumed with the idea of contacting someone from beyond this world, that he hadn't considered the risk to Selena. She would have to break her lifeline, as she had done when she last touched the void. Her body would stop breathing. If she stayed outside her body for too long, she would die.

"Selena . . ." He spoke in a low voice for her alone. "It's going to be dangerous."

She returned his look. "You went to Agravida, and now you're worried about taking risks?"

Taimin opened his mouth, although he didn't know what he was going to say, when a coarse voice interrupted him.

"When are we doing this?" the old rover demanded.

Something passed between Selena and Rei-kika, and then Selena nodded. "Right away," she said.

"It won't help them to have us watch," Blixen growled. "Come on. Everybody out."

Selena waited for the gathered leaders to file out of the cavern. She thought about what she was supposed to do. Her goal was clear: she needed to search the void for help. Taimin had learned that mystics contacted each other all the time. But how did one mystic find another?

A hand gripped her shoulder and she turned to see Dale. "Selena? I need to speak to you alone."

He didn't wait for her reply and pulled her to the side. A few curious glances shot their way, but Taimin was speaking with Rathis and didn't notice.

"What are you going to do now that he's back?" Dale asked without preamble as he stared into her eyes. "You must know how I feel about you. If you don't, I'm telling you now."

Selena saw that Taimin had finally noticed Dale standing close to her. Taimin's expression darkened.

With her attention on Dale, she spoke firmly. "This isn't the time. What I'm about to do could cost me my life."

He drew back from her, startled. "Is that true?"

"Yes."

Dale's face became concerned. He cast a swift glance at Taimin and then nodded. "I understand." His voice softened. "Be careful, Selena. I need you to live. It's because of you that I'm willing to fight and risk my life. I want us to be free, to have a future."

He reached out and took her hand. Giving her palm a squeeze, he walked away without another word.

30

Selena and Rei-kika were soon alone in the cavern. With the highest point of the domed ceiling directly above their heads, they sat on the floor together, facing each other, with their knees almost touching. Green light from the aurelium lamps gave Rei-kika's bone-colored carapace an eerie tinge. Her penetrating black eyes remained fixed on Selena.

"You know what this means," Rei-kika said in her clicking voice. "The void may be easier to travel, but first we have to get there. Our lifelines must be broken. Our bodies will cease to breathe. We will have only a short time."

When she saw how anxious Rei-kika was, Selena's own dread rose. "I understand the danger," she said.

"Are you ready?" Rei-kika asked.

Selena drew in a deep lungful of air and slowly released it. There was no use holding her breath now, her body would do it on its own, as soon as her lifeline was severed. But thinking about what she was about to do frightened her. She wanted to taste the air while she could. As she breathed in and out, she tried to remain calm, but already her heart rate was increasing. It was a warm night, and beads of sweat broke out on her brow.

She nodded, as ready as she would ever be.

Her eyes lost focus. She summoned her symbol—a pure white circle like a featureless moon—and touched the radiance inside her mind. As she allowed imaginary hands to pull her consciousness free from her body, her awareness became liberated, unfastened. Rising up slowly, she found herself still in the cavern, but freed from her physical form.

She floated for a time and looked down at the young woman with the coal-black hair. The woman was her, and something connected them: her lifeline. She watched the woman's chest as it expanded and then contracted with every breath. With a great effort, she clamped down on her fear.

She soon saw a ghostly image, an insect-like silhouette floating in the air. Rei-kika was with her.

Selena was grateful not to be alone.

As soon as they were together, they faced each other and nodded. Without another word, they began their journey.

Traveling upward through the rock above was strange but Selena was through it in moments. She burst free, now in the open, and focused on the night sky. A multitude of glittering stars shone down at her, and she flew directly upward, as swiftly as she could. A brief glance down showed the region of darkened cliffs become smaller and smaller. The wasteland fell away beneath her. A faint white cord connected her to her body far below.

She once more focused on the night sky and climbed at a furious pace. As she kept her attention upward she saw a bank of clouds. A moment later pale mist clouded her vision, but then she was through. The silver moon hung low in the sky but it was the stars she was interested in. The black expanse above her beckoned.

She remembered what her father, Milton, had told her. *You were always fascinated by the stars.*

She understood now why she had always been drawn to the heavens. The stars were a part of who and what she was. They were the guiding lights she had been born to navigate.

She was now well above the clouds and flying ever higher. Her attention was on the night sky, but she knew Rei-kika was with her.

Then the mantorean's ethereal figure was gone.

Selena stopped. She peered down, scanning the wasteland far below. Her position in the sky was so high that the wasteland was a broad, moonlit landscape, filled with plains and deserts, mountains and valleys. As she scanned, she saw Rei-kika far below. The mantorean's wavering image stayed where it was.

Selena descended to join Rei-kika. She saw a hint of black eyes turn to meet her gaze.

Rei-kika? What's wrong?

My lifeline has reached its limit.

Selena glanced down at the white cord that traveled downward, below the place where she was floating. She sensed that she could still cover some distance before her own lifeline would break.

Rei-kika sounded distraught. *I am sorry, Selena. I cannot do it.*

You can.

I cannot. My training prevents me.

Selena looked up at the broad swathe of stars scattered across the darkened sky. Knowing that she would soon confront the same fear Rei-kika was experiencing, she felt panic steadily rise within her.

Please, Rei-kika. I can't do this alone.

Your lifeline is still with you? Rei-kika asked.

Yes.

Wait. I have an idea.

Rei-kika vanished. In an instant, Selena was on her own. To fight her apprehension she returned her attention to the stars. Some were much brighter than others, and there was also a subtle difference in their individual colors: blue, white, yellow, or red. They twinkled merrily.

Time passed as she wondered if she would have the same difficulty as Rei-kika. She knew that if she faltered now, she would be failing every one of the wasteland's inhabitants. If she didn't find help, the bonded would kill everyone she cared about.

All of a sudden, Rei-kika appeared again. *I have someone I can send to you. He wants to do this with you. He can help.*

Who?

You know the answer. The man I know you love. Are you ready? I know how hard this is. But remember, he will have no lifeline at all.

Rei-kika vanished. Selena waited.

And then Taimin was with her, transparent but clear in every detail. She felt a surge of relief to see his square jaw and gentle eyes. She felt stronger with him beside her. Her determination renewed.

But then she remembered. Already, his body below wouldn't be breathing at all.

Taimin, are you sure—?

There's no time to argue. He stared into her face. *Lead the way.*

———

Selena couldn't believe it. She and Taimin were traveling through the void. The spherical world behind her shrank smaller and smaller, until it became a tiny glimmering pinprick and then disappeared from view. When she glanced backward all she could see was a large golden star with a tiny crimson companion.

She realized that Taimin's prediction was true. Traveling the void was utterly different from farcasting across the wasteland— the casting she had done before was like crawling through mud compared to what she was experiencing now. The sensation was extraordinary . . . she was swifter than a ray of light. She sensed that if she hadn't been forced to break it to get to the void, her lifeline would stretch on and on.

Taimin stayed with her at all times, but he let her choose the direction. Darkness surrounded them both, along with more stars than Selena had ever seen. The formations of tiny glittering lights slowly changed as she hurtled through the void; she was moving fast enough to cause the vista to change around her. With a start, she glanced back to keep sight of the pair of stars, one yellow and the other red.

But then she realized something. All she had focused on was creating distance from the world of her birth. She needed to be going somewhere.

Selena slowed until she had stopped completely. She felt dizzy and experienced a surge of vertigo. Twinkling stars, some bright, others dim, filled her vision.

What is it? Taimin asked.

She focused on his shadowy form and it steadied her, despite the fact that she could even see stars through his body.

This is hopeless. I don't even know where we're supposed to be going.

He gave her a look of understanding. *We should return.*

Selena's eyes refocused and she gasped. Her body made great heaves as she sucked air into her chest. She had hurtled so swiftly into her physical form that the jolt of reconnection was painful. Even as she wheezed, bile rose to the back of her throat. She swallowed. She put her fingers to her temples until she managed to steady herself.

Rei-kika and Taimin both sat in front of her, so that they were all in a circle on the floor of the cavern. The green light from the lamps cast strange shadows on Taimin's face. Her intuition told her that they hadn't been traveling the void for long, but his face was red as he struggled for breath. He coughed a few times until the expansion of his chest evened out.

"What happened?" Rei-kika asked, glancing from face to face.

Selena took a few moments to reply. She swallowed again and then cleared her throat. "We made it to the void." She glanced at Taimin. "But we don't know what we're looking for."

Taimin nodded slowly, but his manner was pensive. "I have an idea." He broke off with a ragged cough before speaking again. "Their mystics can only see the same things we do."

Selena's frown deepened. "All I can see are stars."

Rei-kika's antennae twitched. She also looked perplexed.

"Exactly," Taimin said. "Yes there are stars, and around them are worlds like this one. We both know there are too many stars to search them all. But . . ." He hesitated and then his voice firmed. "We might also find something else. We aren't searching for stars. We're trying to find ships."

"Isn't that even more difficult?" Selena asked.

"Not necessarily," Taimin said. "They must make it possible for us to find them. They must use light, like starlight, but easily marked out as different. And remember, we're looking for ships that are close enough to help us."

Selena thought about the man beside her. He had made a great sacrifice, to try to make peace with the bonded. Not only had he risked his life, he had risked her love. It was then that she realized that it was she who had been selfish. He had told her all along, but she had refused to listen. Everything he had done, he had done for her. What use would it be, to remain by her side, if only to die together? He had always accepted her for who she was, what she was, but had she accepted him? He was courageous and noble. He had been willing to die if it meant that she might live.

"We have to keep searching until we find something," she said with determination. She took a deep breath. "Ready to try again?"

31

Selena and Taimin sped through empty darkness—which at the same time was full of light. The golden sun and its red companion grew fainter and fainter behind them. Like sparks from a fire, the shining stars arced slowly across their vision as they searched for any that appeared different.

Each attempt increased the danger, and as fatigue wore at Selena she wondered how Taimin felt; at least farcasting was something she was familiar with. As she scanned the stars that spread out in all directions, her gaze kept traveling from one section of the glittering heavens to another. Almost absently, she noted that one of the stars she had swept past wasn't glowing with a steady fire, it was blinking.

Selena's attention snapped into focus.

As she watched the star, she slowed her rate of travel and then stopped. The moving vista of bright dots shuddered to a halt. The red light kept appearing and then disappearing. The blinking was repetitive but irregular, singling the star out as different from everything around it. Hope rose inside her. There was something special about the star's rhythm. The radiance of her power pulsed with each repetition.

Look, she said to Taimin. A pale presence beside her, Taimin glanced her way and then turned as she pointed. *Above the three stars in a row, do you see?*

Together they watched the blinking red light. It came on and off, again and again. It flickered three times, and then there was a pause. Then it blinked three times more.

Hurry! Taimin said.

The stars surrounding them gave another lurch as they sped toward the blinking red light, moving incredibly swiftly through the void. The light continued to call. It grew steadily brighter.

Selena gasped as something became visible.

At first it was a tiny metallic speck, but it grew bigger as they approached, until its shape was clear.

The light was attached to a sleek metal cylinder.

The cylinder was tapered at one end, giving it a blunt nose and sweeping tail. The metallic skin was black, aside from a pair of long stripes that decorated its sides, one red and the other gold. A steady green glow came from its tail.

Selena and Taimin flew directly toward what was clearly a ship that traveled between worlds. Selena's excitement grew.

But then she came to an abrupt stop. Fear stabbed into her as an apparition appeared in front of her. Taimin gave a cry. She saw a tall creature with curling horns, glaring at them with deep-set eyes beside angry ridges. The ethereal giant wore long robes with a high collar and put out its arms in a clear barring motion. The bonded mystic growled something unintelligible.

Selena fled.

She checked that Taimin was at her side, and there he was, hurtling with her through the void. Stars made long streaks around them as they left the cylinder behind. In moments the blinking light became faint, and then disappeared altogether.

Selena stopped so that she and Taimin could speak. He returned her grim stare. It was time to go. Back in the cavern, their bodies would be screaming for air. She turned toward the golden star. *We need to return.*

I suppose we should have expected it. Taimin shook his head. *Next time—* He broke off.

What is it? She knew they should leave, but also that wherever they were in the limitless void, they might not be able return to this region again.

There. Taimin pointed. *Do you see? To the left of that bright white star.*

This time, the blinking light was green, and the pattern was different. It came on and off rapidly, once, before a pause, and then twice, before another pause. But now that Selena was expecting it, her power responded in the same way that it had with the light from the bonded ship.

She turned to Taimin. *We have to see.*

Urgency fired through her as she and Taimin sped toward the flickering green light. It came to dominate Selena's vision, excluding all of the other glittering points of light around it. Flash. Pause. Two flashes. Pause.

Selena traveled so quickly that it felt as if she was reaching out and grabbing hold of the green light to pull it close. Part of her was frantic to turn around and return to her body. But she was also desperate for the search to meet with success.

A ship bearing a green light grew from an infinitesimal speck to life size, filling her vision in a heartbeat.

The ship was different from the bonded ship, although it also gave off a green glow from the part she thought was the end. It was shaped like an arrowhead, with a sharp nose and angular ridges spreading out to give it a swift, windswept appearance. An immense symbol decorated its side: a five-pointed star, with each point curled like a grasping hand. Its metallic exterior was white and glossy, so pale it was almost silver.

As with the bonded ship, a ghostly figure appeared as soon as they approached.

A human.

The man wore crisp clothing with a stiff collar and symbols on the shoulders: a uniform. His hair was cut short and he had a hard, angular face.

As soon as she saw the man the realization struck Selena with force: what she and Taimin were doing was momentous. Eons ago, their ancestors had been captured and taken away from everything they knew. Now, they had made contact with their long-lost kin. In another life, she would be the mystic keeping watch over the ship she was looking at.

The man frowned as he swiftly took in Selena and Taimin's appearance. He challenged them in a sharp, authoritative tone. *Who are you? Why are you here?*

———

Rei-kika looked at Taimin's motionless body, then at Selena's, and back again. Her antennae twitched; she was becoming increasingly anxious. This period of absence was far longer than anything before. She didn't know how long a human could hold their breath for, but surely not as long as this . . .

Time continued to drag out. Both Taimin and Selena sat cross-legged, their eyes glazed and unseeing. Rei-kika was seated in the same circle, but she was alone. The two humans were so still that anyone entering the cavern would have thought they were already dead.

As the moments trickled past, Rei-kika's unease shifted to panic. She didn't know what to do. She had the skill to free Taimin from his body, but returning was something only he and Selena could do.

Could anyone go so long without breathing and still come back to life?

Taimin and Selena had a future together. They couldn't die here on the floor of this cave. Even if their search failed, at least they would know they had tried their utmost. There was no use sacrificing themselves for a lost cause.

"Please," Rei-kika said aloud, voicing her desperation. "Breathe."

———

Selena spoke quickly. She didn't have long.

We are humans like you, she began. *Captives on a world with two suns. My name is Selena; this is Taimin.*

Who are you? Taimin asked.

I am Specialist Carter, the uniformed man answered. He frowned. *What world? Who is holding you captive?*

The bonded, Taimin said. *Their world.*

Wait. Carter's manner changed. Where before he had been stern and challenging, he was now taken aback. *Let me be clear.* He leaned forward. *Are you telling me that you are on the bonded homeworld right now?*

Yes, Selena said impatiently. *We need help.*

Carter came closer, until he floated directly in front of Taimin and Selena. If Selena had physical form, she had the feeling that he would have taken her by the shoulders. *Lumea's location is a secret*, he said. *We have never found it. Selena, please, where is it? Can you show me?*

Selena turned. It was difficult among so many stars, but she had kept a constant bearing for so long that it didn't take her long to find the twin, distant pinpricks of light. *Do you see that golden star, with the faint red star right beside it?*

Carter looked where she was pointing but became impatient. *If you open your mind and allow me to create a link, I can find your physical location.*

Selena was puzzled, but Carter was a trained mystic; of course he would know how to do things she couldn't. *I don't understand.*

Open your mind, he instructed.

She felt a touch, a caress, and let it in.

We don't have much time, Taimin said. *We need your help. The bonded have held us all prisoner—a vast number of humans, bax, mantoreans, skalen, and trulls. You have to come.*

Of course we can help you, Carter said. He shook his head, as if struck by awe. *You will never understand what this means to us. Now that we have Lumea's location, we have the power to end this war, one way or another.*

We need you to come quickly, Taimin persisted. *We don't have long. I've been to their city, I've come to know them . . . and one of them in particular. I do think that peace is possible. If you come, and they realize they've lost, the bonded may change.*

Change? Carter frowned. *The bonded will never change. Fighting is all they live for.*

All that matters is how fast you can get here, Selena said.

Listen . . . Carter hesitated. *I can promise you that plans will be made immediately, with all five allies involved. I can promise you that we will do everything we can to end this war. However I am afraid I have bad news. My ship is the closest to your location but it would take me two years to get there. We will come. We will help you. But there is nothing I can do about the laws that govern our universe.* He seemed genuinely upset. *I am sorry.*

Selena suddenly felt her world closing in. Her vision blurred and then grew dark at the edges.

Taimin, she said weakly.

I know.

They sped away together, back toward the golden star.

32

It was a windy morning, hot and clear. Dust skittered along the surface of the plain. The wyverns that nested in the cliff took advantage of the updraft to soar high in the sky as they searched for prey.

Selena stood alone and stared up at the sky. In daylight, it was as if there were no stars at all. The solid blue obscured everything behind it. But the memory of her and Taimin's frantic search stayed with her.

Two years. Carter wanted to help, and clearly, now that he had Lumea's location, he thought the five allies could end the war that had endured for centuries.

But he would take far too long to arrive. Her hopes had risen, only to be dashed against the obstacle of time. Despair weighed her down. In finding Carter, she had succeeded, but he was too far away to do anything soon enough for the wasteland.

To Dale, there would only be one remaining option. He would lead his army to battle. But Taimin was no longer alone in saying that further conflict meant certain death. For Selena now agreed with him, without reservation. She had seen the approaching ground forces herself.

After a sleep of utter exhaustion, she had woken to a feeling of hopelessness. Despite knowing what she would find, she had been unable to stop herself from farcasting past the cliffs, toward the region of gray haze. She had severed her lifeline once more. Heedless of the danger, she had flown into the world beyond.

She was horrified at what she had found.

Row after row of hulking machines—Taimin had called them devastators—rumbled slowly but inexorably along a wide road. The grooved belts connected to their immense wheels turned over and over. Long tubular weapons thrust out from their crowns, pointing straight ahead. They formed a winding column that climbed up hills and down valleys, and carved its way through the gaps between fields. It only took her a moment to gauge their direction and rate of travel.

Taimin had been right all along.

Selena's thoughts were in turmoil as she stood alone on the plain and the hot wind blew at her hair. The only option she could see was to find somewhere to hide, along with Taimin, Ruth, Vance, Lars, and Gretel. Perhaps they could remain in the wasteland, and find some dark hole in the belly of a mountain. Or they could escape through the hazy borderland before the bonded closed off the route. What other choice was there?

She turned to watch the commotion at the bottom of the cliffs. Figures scurried about. The army, made up of all five races, was preparing to head up to the escarpment. It would take a long time to get everyone to the top.

Hearing a voice call her name, she turned to see Dale approaching, looking smart in his blue uniform. His eyes were grave, but he walked quickly. He had a busy day ahead of him. She wondered how he felt about the impossible task he had, and whether he ever had second thoughts.

"You said they'll be here in a week?" he asked.

"That's my best guess."

He hesitated. "Are you coming?" When she didn't reply, he continued. "We can beat them, Selena. Have faith. Once we get up there, we have time to prepare." He gazed toward the escarpment at the top of the cliffs. "The haze at the wasteland's boundary will impair their vision. When they emerge, we'll be ready to greet them. We're going to lay mines along the boundary. As soon as they travel out of the haze, we'll ignite it underneath them. That's when we'll counterattack." He paused and then stared directly at her. "So you made your choice, then? You're going to stay with him."

"What makes you say that?"

"You, to be honest."

"I'm just afraid," Selena said. "Aren't you?"

Dale didn't reply, and the ensuing silence dragged out as they both watched the preparations of the great number of humans, bax, trulls, skalen, and mantoreans. Every able-bodied fighter was going to leave the area behind. They would carry food, water, bows and crossbows, javelins, swords, axes, and explosive bolts and arrows. Dale's scouts were already far away on their wyverns, making plans for the preparation of defenses. Selena's worst fears had come true. The army of the wasteland would meet the war machines of the bonded in one final, cataclysmic battle.

She had to speak up. "You're leading them all to their deaths."

The only reaction was a tightening of his mouth and eyes. "What would you have me do?" When she pursed her lips and shook her head, he spoke with force. "If you don't believe in what we're doing, it's best you say nothing at all."

"What I do know is that you can't win," she said. "Yet there might still be a chance to flee. Don't you want to know what you're facing?"

"Machines," he said flatly.

"Do you want to know how many?"

Now that she had begun, she had to convince him to change his plan . . .

———

Sacks, leather bladders, crates, and bulging packs littered the area outside the row of caves. Mantoreans worked beside baskets stuffed full of arrows, bundling them up and handing them to waiting archers. There were no skalen to be seen: they had all climbed up the precarious trail the previous night, when their vision wasn't blinded by the bright suns. Yet the bustling bax and humans, more numerous than the other races, still created a sense of frantic activity that threatened at any moment to descend into chaos.

Vance wiped grit from his eyes. A stiff wind howled from the direction of the plain. Anything loose blew across the ground. He crouched over a thick piece of fabric that ruffled each time a gust came up and kept it pinned down with his foot at an awkward angle. One by one, he fitted crossbow bolts that glowed green into the pouches sown into the material. Beside him, Lars was doing the same thing with his own square of fabric.

Vance slotted his last bolt into a pouch, rolled up the material, and then climbed to his feet. One of Dale's men came over; like his commander, he wore the blue uniform of Zorn's city guard. The soldier collected Vance's bundle and then Lars handed over his.

"That's the last of them?" the soldier asked.

"The very last," Vance said.

The soldier hesitated. "Listen," he said. "I overheard the commander." He focused on Vance. "The crossbows and explosive bolts were your idea?"

Vance and Lars exchanged glances. "My friend here, Lars . . . he thought of it first," Vance said.

The soldier turned toward Lars. "Wish we'd had them back in Zorn. But at any rate . . ." The soldier looked uncomfortable, and then put out his hand. "Thank you."

Lars shook the soldier's hand, and then it was Vance's turn. Vance felt a surge of pride as he had his own handshake and nod of appreciation before the soldier walked away with the two bundles under his arm. Vance watched him go.

"Strange to think that we'll be shooting them soon," Vance said.

"Eh?" Lars gave him a dark look. "I hope the crossbows work, and work well. If a thousand machines go up in flames, I'll cheer. But I don't plan to fight. And you shouldn't either."

"After all this effort, you're not going to see them in action?"

"No," Lars said flatly.

The big, bearded skinner tilted his head back to gaze up the cliffs, following the long column of fighters as they traveled up the seam in the rock to reach the heights above.

"So what are you going to do?" Vance asked.

"Blast it if I know," Lars said. "But I'm not going up there to die."

———

Taimin didn't help with Dale's preparations. Instead he sat on a solitary rock out on the plain. The towering cliffs loomed above him, tall and indomitable. He rubbed his eyes. He was tired. After the previous night, and the realization that no help would be coming, he hadn't been able to sleep at all. He had spent hours pacing under the stars, wondering how he would be able to save the lives of everyone he cared about.

He wasn't a man accustomed to not having a plan. As his dark thoughts turned from one idea to the next, he remembered another time, when he had been close to the place where he was now. He gazed toward the top of the cliffs and cast his mind back to the thunder and lightning that speared down from the sky. The sight had been terrifying. Ingren had laughed at him, but he wondered how she would have felt if she had been standing underneath the fire from the heavens.

He smiled without humor. If only he could harness a power like lightning.

He was afraid. More than at any other time, he wished he could make the sky marshal feel the way he felt now.

The bonded had nothing to fear from the wasteland. Their warriors had no interest in peace. No rescue or help would come from outside. Everyone was going to die.

He frowned. There was something Ingren had said. It tugged at his memory as he tried to recall it. As he squinted up at the sky, it came back to him.

"We have complete control of our world," Ingren had said.

"Then why worry about us?"

"Because, unlike animals, you are intelligent. You might hurt our supplies or our important infrastructure."

"We wouldn't do that."

"Yes, Taimin, you would."

As he recalled the conversation, Taimin's jumbled thoughts took focus. Lightning from the sky. Weaknesses. Important infrastructure. He imagined the towering cliffs he was staring at replaced by something else: a tall lattice that rose higher and higher until it disappeared into the heavens. He pictured the stalk at the center of the bonded city. Hannah had said it was supported by a delicate balance of forces. The concept of fragility led to an idea. There was one weapon that worked against the bonded. Aurelium could damage the strongest steel.

What would happen if he were to detonate a large amount of aurelium at the base of the stalk?

A thrill of excitement crept up his spine. The stalk was crucial to bonded civilization. If Taimin could destroy the stalk it would cause them irreparable harm as it came down.

He continued to follow his idea to its logical conclusion. The bonded would no longer be able to fight their war in the stars if they had no means of travel between space and the ground below. They wouldn't be able to assemble ships in the void, take up supplies, or send up groups of warriors. For them, if the stalk were destroyed, the war with the five allies would effectively be over.

What then?

With their civilization crippled, the bonded would be forced to change their ways, which meant that the warriors would have no choice but to relinquish power. With the elders and advisors dominant, the bonded would become peaceful.

He remembered all of his conversations with Ingren. If she had the power, she would never kill every living creature in the wasteland.

Still seated on the rock, he shot to his feet. Hope stirred in his chest. This wasn't a change that would take two years to bring about.

A plan emerged. He wouldn't need to actually destroy the stalk. He only had to make the threat. If he planted aurelium at the stalk's base, ready to spark, the bonded wouldn't risk killing him. The consequences would be too catastrophic. Taimin could demand an end to the wasteland's destruction. He could make the warriors give up power, or he would lay waste to their city, cripple their civilization, and end their ability to wage war.

The more Taimin thought about it, the more he realized it might work. Scanning the plain and the area at the base of the cliffs, he searched for someone to explain his plan to.

It wasn't long before he saw Selena.

She was with Dale, of course. He started to walk toward her. The rising suns beat down on his head as he opened up his stride.

The two figures grew larger in his vision: a slender woman with coal-black hair and a red-haired soldier in uniform. He soon saw that they were arguing. Whatever Selena was saying to Dale, he had a dark expression on his face.

Dale turned his head and his eyes narrowed. As soon as Taimin was close enough he called out, "Did you hear, wastelander? Selena has scouted their forces. They'll be here in less than a week. And yet I don't see you helping. When we defended Zorn, where were you?" He shook his head. "Still you won't fight."

With a scowl, Dale stalked away.

"Selena," Taimin said. He watched Dale depart and then focused on her. "I know you might feel like we failed, but I don't think that was the case." He paused. "I have an idea."

She looked surprised when she heard the determination in his voice.

"It was meeting Carter that made me think of it." Taimin took a deep breath. "First—think about this. When the five allies come, there will probably be some kind of battle. I learned about the bonded. If they lost their war, they would change their ways. The warriors would have no choice but to give up power in order to make peace. It's inevitable."

She frowned. "But that doesn't help us now," she said. "Help is at least two years away."

"I know. We have to do something ourselves. The warriors are going to have to give up power at some point. We need it to happen now."

"Go on."

"We have to threaten them with something terrible. I know a way to make them afraid, perhaps for the very first time . . ."

———

"The only thing the bonded respect is strength," Taimin said. His gaze traveled from Vance to Lars, Ruth, and Selena.

Lars grunted. "I could have told you that a long time ago."

"Lars," Ruth said. "Let him speak."

"The problem is," Taimin said, "Dale's plan isn't enough. The bonded don't fear an army of wastelanders. This is their world. Compared to us, they have unlimited power. You've heard me describe their ground forces, and now Selena has seen them too. What Dale is planning won't be a battle, it will be a slaughter."

The area outside the caves was much quieter; a few old men and women stood in groups to discuss their plans now that they would be left waiting for news of victory or defeat. Gretel sat on a boulder nearby and plucked a desert flower, following the petals with her eyes as they danced in the wind. An ancient bax with skin like worn leather passed by with a bundle of kindling in his arms. A mantorean stood silhouetted in the mouth of a cave before turning and disappearing from view.

"The bonded have a structure," Taimin said. "It stands tall at the center of Agravida. They call it the stalk. It enables them to transport whatever they want from the ground to their ships in space." When Lars frowned, Taimin opened his arms to indicate height. "It's like an immense ladder, climbing to an incredible height."

"What of it?" Vance asked.

"Think for a moment. What would happen to their city if the stalk came down?"

Lars glanced at Vance and then shrugged. "How would we know?"

"It isn't just long, or tall if you think of it as a kind of ladder. While I was in their city I learned that it's long enough to flatten much of this world if it came down. Believe me, I am speaking the truth. If we destroy just one part of it, the rest will fall. It would do an incalculable amount of damage."

Lars was skeptical. "Even if we strike at their city, they'll still keep fighting."

Taimin shook his head. "There's something you need to understand," he said. "Among the bonded, the warriors are in charge until every enemy is dead. Then the roles change. The advisors take control, and there's peace. They call this a reversal." He paused. "But what if rather than victory, the bonded are faced with destruction— and inevitable defeat? We could force a reversal. If we can do it, we can save everyone."

Lars scratched at his beard. "I think I understand," he said slowly. "So what's your plan?"

"Two packs filled with aurelium would be enough. Dale has a lot more than that. We need a small force to head to their city, plant the aurelium, and make the threat."

"And if they don't listen?" Vance asked.

Taimin spoke grimly. "Then we do what must be done."

Selena met his eyes, and there was a fire there that he hadn't seen for a long time. "How small a force?"

Taimin thought about the journey through the haze and the farmland beyond, the speed of the quadrail, and the layout of Agravida. "Well . . . whoever went would have to remain hidden. The hardest part would be getting to the stalk . . . but there are maps in the archive."

"So two people to carry the aurelium," Selena said. "Then, if you take me to the map, I can give them directions and stop them from being seen, so they can get to where they need to go."

Vance spoke up. "Everyone who plans to fight . . ." he said slowly. "We should tell them what we're planning, shouldn't we?"

Taimin shook his head. "There's no time to lose, not if we want to get to Agravida before it's too late. And the fact is, we might not succeed."

Vance frowned. "But won't we have to ask them for the aurelium?"

"Leave it to me," Taimin said. "I'll get the aurelium, and while they're busy building defenses we can travel to Agravida."

"Count me in," Vance said. "I trust you, Taimin."

Ruth's expression was resolute. "I'm going too," she said.

Vance turned to her. "No, Ruth. Please. Stay here. There are people who need you."

Ruth opened her mouth to protest when Lars interrupted.

"I'm going," he stated, "which means someone has to take care of Gretel for me."

The curly-haired girl's mouth dropped open. "Papa?" she asked. "Where are you going?"

Lars opened his arms and she fell toward him, wrapping her arms around his neck. Taimin was surprised to see moisture in the brawny skinner's eyes.

"I have to do this, my love," he said to her, unmindful of everyone watching him. "It's because of you that I have to go."

"Papa . . ."

Lars's face contorted as he fought to control his expression. He gave Gretel a kiss on the cheek, before carrying her over to Ruth, who opened her arms to take the little girl.

"Stay here," Vance said to Ruth. "Help people."

Taimin turned to face Vance and Lars, and then rested his eyes on Selena.

"Four of us, then," he said. "We'll head up the trail tonight and take the aurelium we need on the way." He let out a breath. "Are you sure you're willing to do this?" he asked Selena, Vance, and Lars.

He waited until they had all nodded. "Good," he said. "Start packing, but don't bring much. We'll travel light. And by nightfall tomorrow, we will have left the wasteland."

33

The four companions traveled across blackened ground covered with a low, foul-smelling haze. After they crossed over to the world of the bonded, Taimin enjoyed the reactions of the others when for the first time they saw fast-flowing rivers, brightly colored flowers, buzzing insects, fields of lush grass, and tall trees that swayed in the fragrant breeze. But there was no time to stop. As the days passed, he kept the group moving from dawn to dusk, through the region of bonded farmland until they came to the quadrail that would take them to the heart of Agravida.

He made a careful inspection and then led his companions toward a waiting quadrail in the black of night. Of the multiple connected compartments, he found a different kind from the one he had traveled in previously. The huge sliding panels that made entry possible weren't locked, so it was easy to get inside. The cavernous metal box was stacked with huge black barrels, almost certainly filled with harvested crops. He had to hope that this storage compartment wouldn't be inspected on their journey to Agravida.

The quadrail started to move in the light of morning.

Even with the sliding doors closed, there was a thin gap between the metal panels. As the quadrail picked up speed, Taimin's companions gathered to stare through the opening and marvel at the world outside the wasteland. A variety of landscapes soon rushed by. Multicolored fields laid out in neat grids flickered past their vision. The morning sun glowed on forests and glistened on silver rivers. Distant hills gave way to a row of mountains that were so far away they were mere silhouettes. Now and then Taimin pointed out a harvesting machine, but the quadrail was moving too fast to make out much detail. Soon they would be leaving the region of farmland altogether.

As the hours passed, first Taimin and then Selena and Vance left the gap in the doors. Lars remained in place, silent as he took in the paradise that he had been desperate to see for so long. Weary after his journey, Taimin found a place to sit at the back of the goods compartment. Selena and Vance clearly had the same idea, and nestled into what space they could find between the towering barrels.

Taimin glanced at Lars and smiled when the older man cried out in astonishment at whatever he was seeing. Then Taimin turned when he heard Vance's voice.

"I hope you're being careful with that," Vance said to Lars. His anxious focus was on the coil of green glowing wire that Lars carried on his shoulder. "One misstep and that fuse could ignite."

"Course I'm being careful," Lars growled. He nodded toward the two packs on the floor by Vance's knees. "You just keep an eye on the aurelium. That's where the danger is."

When Vance opened his mouth to retort, Taimin interjected. "Rathis said it takes a hard impact to spark the wire. He knows what he's talking about."

Lars made a sound of surprise. "So that's how you got the aurelium," he said. "I'd been wondering." He frowned. "Still, it's a lot to take without asking Dale."

Taimin gave a smile and a shrug. "I have my ways."

As Lars returned to watching the view, Taimin again thought about his plan. The stalk was everything to the bonded. Without it, their war amongst the stars would be impossible. But he also knew that if the stalk came crashing down the destruction would be even greater than he had been able to convey to his companions. It wouldn't be just Agravida that was affected; it would be the entire world.

Time passed. The journey was utterly smooth and almost silent aside from a steady hiss. As usual, Taimin could barely detect any motion. Nearby, Selena leaned back against a barrel with her eyes closed. The journey had been arduous, but this last part would soon be over. He wondered what she would make of Agravida. It could be an overwhelming place; utterly different from anything a wastelander would have seen before.

The quadrail began to slow. A higher note, almost like a screech, mingled with the regular hiss of their passage.

"What's happening?" Lars called from his position at the sliding doors.

Taimin climbed to his feet and hurried forward so that he was at Lars's side, staring through the crack in the doors. Forests slid past, but not as fast as before. The trees abruptly ended, to be replaced by more bright fields and a lattice of connecting roads. The quadrail continued to lose speed. They were now following a parallel road, wide but unpaved. A few storage barns moved slowly across Taimin's vision.

"Are we there?" Vance asked.

Taimin spoke over his shoulder. "We're still far from the city. But we're stopping for some reason."

Selena sounded anxious. "Have they found us?"

Taimin didn't know. Ingren had thought he was safe in the closet she put him in last time, but when he left it to join her in another area, warriors had greeted him in Agravida.

He saw through the narrow gap that the quadrail was coming to a halt in an area of open ground. A couple of harvesters stood motionless on the muddy ground, not far from where he was watching. A collection of black barrels, identical to the ones in their compartment, sat in a row.

"How could they know we're here?" Lars demanded as the quadrail stopped altogether.

"I don't know," Taimin hissed. "Stay quiet."

He kept his attention focused outside. Then his breath caught. He saw two tall bonded with curling horns and drab tan clothing. The pair of workers were crossing the dirt to head directly toward him.

Taimin grabbed Lars's arm and yanked him away from the compartment doors. He waved at the others. "Someone's coming. Hide!"

Lars tried to squeeze his bulk through a gap between the barrels. Vance disappeared between two of the black containers. Meanwhile Taimin stood frozen with indecision. He couldn't see anywhere to hide. Then he saw Selena furiously beckoning at him.

Taimin raced over just as the sliding doors were hauled open. Selena swiftly shuffled, cramming herself between the barrels and the rear wall. Taimin followed and brought himself right up next to her. He went completely still.

He could hear Selena's breathing. His own panting sounded just as loud. He wasn't sure if he was visible.

He heard loud thumps as the pair of bonded workers jumped up to the interior of the compartment. Their low, grunting voices filled the silence. As Taimin wondered why they had entered, and whether they knew that four humans were here, he moved closer to Selena in an attempt to hide. She tried to shrink her body to make it smaller. He wrapped his arms around her.

The heavy footsteps came closer. The glimmer of light through the barrels changed; a hulking body created a shadow.

Taimin almost cried out when he heard the hard sound of a hand slapping against the barrel in front of him. Selena tensed. More slaps followed—a series of thuds that shifted from barrel to barrel. The bonded workers were moving around, rapping against the sides of each storage vat in turn. The clatter echoed around the compartment.

One of the workers' voices was louder this time. He spoke Ravange in a gravelly, rasping voice. "All full. It will take time to rearrange them."

"We might not have a choice."

Taimin held his breath. If the workers began to move the barrels, they would be discovered.

"No time," the worker with the rasping voice said. "Let's try another compartment."

Taimin cocked his head to the side as he heard the sound of retreating footsteps. A moment later the metal doors closed with a final boom. Once again they were plunged into shadow. For the moment, the danger had passed.

Taimin felt Selena's body relax. A distant metallic clatter told him that the pair of workers had moved on to a neighboring compartment.

"We should stay where we are," Taimin whispered.

Time trickled past. He counted his heartbeats as the workers finished their task. At last, he let out a sigh of relief when the quadrail started to move again. The familiar hiss was comforting.

Taimin still had his arms wrapped around Selena. He hadn't been this close to her in a long time. He heard Vance and Lars murmur to each other, but still he didn't move. Instead, he reached out and took Selena's hand.

"Selena . . ." He hesitated. She turned her head and met his gaze. "You know why I couldn't tell you I was going, don't you?"

"I know," she said softly. She didn't let go of his hand. Her palm was warm. "I thought you were dead. You know I would never . . ." She trailed off.

"Love someone else?" He gave her a crooked smile. "If I hadn't come back, that is exactly what I would want you to do. But only"—his smile broadened—"if I hadn't come back."

"I'm afraid," she said seriously.

He ran his thumb over the skin of her hand. "So am I."

She leaned in, and as he stroked her hair she whispered again. "Just hold me."

Now that she couldn't see him, Taimin let the worry show on his face. This might be the last time he would have his arms around her. The quadrail continued to speed through this strange land of fields and forests, rivers and lakes.

Soon they would be in Agravida.

———

Selena.

She blinked. She had been asleep, leaning into Taimin's body with his arms around her. She frowned; a voice had startled her awake, but she must have imagined it. There was little sound in the compartment other than the background hiss. Taimin's body was still, aside from his chest, which rose and fell with every deep breath. He was warm and she was comfortable. She decided to close her eyes again.

Selena.

She recognized the crisp, authoritative voice. *Specialist Carter?*

Yes.

How did you find me?

You gave me a link to your location. It works in both directions. You can use it to contact me as well.

Selena's eyes became unfocused, and as she touched her power she realized there was something connecting her to the distant human, in the same way that her lifeline connected her to her body—a cord that she could pull on to bring herself to his location. She wondered if he was able to see her, wrapped up in Taimin's arms, in a compartment filled with huge barrels.

Why are you making contact? Selena tried not to let her hope rise; Carter had been clear when he said that he was too far away to offer any assistance. *I thought there was nothing you could do to help us.*

There was a long pause, making her wonder if he was gone. She was about to speak his name again when his voice re-entered her mind. *It's true that we can't get there soon. But we may have a way to swiftly end this war. Be prepared for me to contact you again.*

I don't understand.

You will. Just be ready.

34

The days passed slowly, and then in a rush. A chill morning found Ruth tending a fire in a long snaking cave, filled with the young and the old, the injured and the frightened. She sat cross-legged and stared into the flames. Leaning forward, she added dried cactus to keep the fire going, more to lighten spirits than for warmth. Now and then she stirred a pot that rested on the coals, but no one was eating.

She had already completed her morning rounds, and nothing needed her immediate attention. At the back of the cave, Gretel was playing with a girl her own age, under the supervision of the girl's mother. All Ruth could apply herself to were the menial tasks that kept people fed and healthy: hauling water, gathering kindling, mending clothing, and pounding razorgrass grain into flour. The cavern held supplies of fresh meat that had to be cooked before it went bad. But with the day still young, she wondered if she should go hunting anyway.

She pondered as she watched the dancing flames. She missed Vance, and wondered where he was and if he was safe. He could be a frustrating man—clever in his own way, but sometimes as foolish as a child—but he always made her laugh and she knew that if she needed him he would be there, by her side, ready to offer any support he could.

Growing tension formed a knot in her stomach. What Vance was doing was risky. He and the others would soon be at the very heart of the bonded city, and if caught they would be executed. If Vance was hurt, she wouldn't be there to help him.

She looked around the cave. A few people chatted quietly. The squeals of playing children contrasted with the somber faces of the adults. Everyone seemed content to stay put, but Ruth felt empty.

In this sheltered place, there was no one in urgent need of care. But at the top of the trail, past the escarpment and close to the wasteland's edge, there would soon be hundreds of broken bodies.

Jerome was there, with Dale and his army. When he left, he hadn't given Ruth any sign of disapproval, but still she felt guilty.

News occasionally came down from above, brought by exuberant messenger boys who acted as if this was all just a game. Ruth had learned that the enemy had plunged into the gray haze that encircled the wasteland where the firewall once was. The war machines would emerge before the end of the day.

Thinking about it made her wonder what she was doing, hiding away like this. She rested her gaze on the fire for a few moments and then came to a decision.

A few people watched her as she headed toward the back of the cave. Gretel was playing in the dirt, using a stick to draw shapes of people and animals. The second girl with her clapped her hands and issued instructions, telling Gretel to add spikes to the animals and horns to the figures' heads.

The older woman keeping an eye on the pair sat on a stool as she sewed a piece of leather. She had a kind, round face, and a curious expression as she looked up to see Ruth coming toward her.

"I can't stay here, Flora," Ruth said without preamble. "Can I leave Gretel with you?"

Flora gave Ruth a slow inspection. "You don't need to tell me—you're going to the battle." She paused as Ruth nodded. "My

Jonah's up there. He's a fighter. There's no way he could sit here and do nothing." She met Ruth's eyes. "And you're a healer. I'm not surprised. You have to go where you're needed."

Ruth was glad that Flora understood, but at the same time she was afraid. Taimin and Selena both said that the battle couldn't be won, and Vance clearly believed them. She knew what Vance would say: he would tell her to sit back down and return to tending the fire. Yet he also realized what drove her, well enough to understand.

She wouldn't be fighting. She would stay back, ready to help where she could. There would be others in far more danger than her.

"Don't worry about Gretel," Flora said. "She's a good child. I'll be happy to take care of her." She groaned as she put her hands on her knees to stand. Opening her arms, she gave Ruth a tight embrace. "Be safe, Ruth. And thank you."

"I'll do my best," Ruth said.

Ruth walked over to Gretel and kissed her on her crown of curly blonde hair. The little girl gave her a quick smile, but was absorbed with her drawing. Then Ruth collected her things.

Her doubts grew as she left the cavern and started walking, but again she told herself that she was doing the right thing. The two suns climbed the sky, with the red sun just below its bigger companion. She hoisted her satchel and headed straight for the trail.

———

A long bulwark faced the gray haze. Made of dirt piled up to shoulder height and packed down until it was nearly as hard as stone, it stretched on and on.

Despite the bright daylight, the smoky air in front of the bulwark was impossible to see far into. High as a mountain, the haze ebbed and flowed in the breeze but never shifted position or dispersed. Just a few hundred paces separated the dirt embankment from the thick gray air in front of it, and a foul odor came from that direction, a mélange of char and mud and rot.

Behind the bulwark waited an army of defenders such as the wasteland had never seen.

Ruth took in the sight as she walked with the afternoon sun blazing on her shoulders. A steady breeze made her wrinkle her nose at the stench. At first, all she could make out was a row of figures. Then as she passed a field of scattered boulders, the line of defenders became more than just a long, thin crowd. She saw dozens of wyverns at the back, snorting and clawing at the ground. The winged creatures were spread out evenly with their riders beside them, some in the uniforms of Zorn's city guard, others not human at all. Regardless of their appearance, all of the riders carried crossbows. They had space to maneuver, and were separate from the rest of the defenders.

Walking parallel to the bulwark, she passed several hundred hunched leather-clad figures with prominent spines: bax, armed with crossbows and spears with glowing tips. There was a time when the sight of so many bax warriors would have sparked fear, but that was in the past.

Among the bax she saw Gorax, wide-bellied and covered in warts, and young Den and Bagrat, all from Gravel Range, on the far side of the wasteland. Taller than those around him, Blixen stood in the very center of the long line, armed with the largest crossbow she had seen. He waited just inside the embankment, ready to duck from enemy fire and return with fire of his own.

Ruth continued to walk. She soon passed the mantoreans. The screen of thin figures stood one next to the other, and every one of the insect-like creatures carried a bow.

The skalen were next. They had come from all over the wasteland, leaving the safety of their mines to fight for their future. A few reptilian eyes glanced at Ruth as she passed, but most of them faced the gray haze. The sinuous skalen carried javelins with green glowing points. Spare javelins were bundled on their backs. Dark, glossy skin reflected the suns' rays. Ruth saw Rathis among them, standing with two skalen who looked like mother and son. She even recognized Kash, the clan leader from the edge of the desert, and Wielan from the mine in the mountain nearby.

A few snub-nosed trulls stood in pairs or waited alone. The least numerous of the defenders, they were also unwilling to follow orders, and would no doubt fight in their own way. Ruth met the dark gaze of a female trull, who surprisingly gave her a nod. She was only as tall as a human, but like all her kind her body was thick with muscle. Her lank hair fell to her shoulders and she wore a coarse vest and leggings. The trull's huge two-handed sword looked vicious, but would be next to useless against a steel machine.

Ruth now approached the area where a continuous row of humans shared somber conversation as they waited behind the bulwark. There were a few bax and mantoreans among them, and in the distance still more bax massed at the flanks. But there were more humans than any other race. Hundreds of settlers and rovers, and a great number from Zorn, stood ready to defend the wasteland. Men outnumbered women, but only by a little. Youths stood beside their elders. Many held crossbows in shaking hands.

Ruth remembered Vance examining the fallen striker and then going on to develop a weapon that could deliver far more aurelium than an arrow. She was proud of him, and regretted how distant she had been at the time. Soon, she would see the crossbows in action. She could only hope that united as never before, the five races of the wasteland could stand their ground and survive.

As Ruth scanned the defenders and wondered where to go, she saw Rei-kika, easily distinguished among all the humans around her. A red-haired soldier in blue uniform—Dale—stood beside the mantorean. Rei-kika had to be advising him. Despite the fact that they were talking, they both had their gazes fixed on the gray haze in front of them.

Ruth kept scanning until she saw a white-haired man in a healer's smock. Jerome was alone on a rocky knoll, behind the defenders but close enough to rush forward when he was needed. Like her, he didn't carry a weapon.

She headed in his direction, but it took him some time before he noticed her approaching. His mouth dropped open.

"Ruth?" he hissed. "What are you doing here?"

He was usually softly spoken, and she was surprised by his harsh reaction. "I'm here to help, like you."

"Vance knows you're here?" When Ruth bit her lip, Jerome shook his head. "Ruth . . ."

Ruth lifted her chin. "I have to do what I can." She stared into his eyes. "Does your wife know you're here?"

"You know she does." Jerome paused and then gave a snort. "Look at us, fools that we are." He checked the wall of haze before returning his attention to her. "I wish you weren't here, but I'm glad that you are."

Ruth's satchel felt heavy on her shoulder, so she set it down at her feet, ready to grab at short notice. She exchanged glances with Jerome and he gave her a steadying look. Like him, she knew her purpose. She was here to do what she could when the blood started to flow.

As she faced the front, where the defenders stood shoulder to shoulder, she saw tension on the faces of all the men and women as they waited to fight for their lives. She also noticed something else. Despite Dale's best efforts, there evidently weren't enough crossbows to go round, and many defenders carried simple spears, bows, and a variety of melee weapons.

The embankment wasn't so tall that she couldn't see above it, and the ground changed as it stretched toward the region where visibility fell away. Rather than red dirt, it shifted to black. She was looking at where the firewall had been.

"What news?" she asked Jerome.

Jerome nodded in Rei-kika's direction. "The mantorean says they are crossing right now. We have two hours, maybe three." He spoke in a grim voice. "There are strikers with them."

Dread trickled along Ruth's spine. She tried to remain as calm as Jerome appeared to be, but it was difficult. It had been easier in the morning, to come to the decision she had made, when she had been sitting quietly and staring into the flames. A puff of wind brought the taste of ash to her mouth. She swallowed.

She remembered what Selena had described. A long line of devastators, rumbling on belts with tongues and grooves. Now Jerome said there were strikers in the sky above them.

A high-pitched shriek made her jump, but it was just a wyvern nearby, struggling as it pulled at the rope in the hands of its rider. She glanced up. The sun was past the midpoint of the sky.

She wondered where Vance was. He might be in the bonded city by now.

The metal war machines were advancing. Whatever Vance and the others were going to do, they had to do it now.

35

One moment the quadrail was hurtling through a rugged landscape of hills and forests, the next cube-shaped buildings flew past, structures that grew taller and taller.

The difference was sudden, but Taimin was waiting for it, and he soon knew without doubt that the quadrail was slowing. He leaned against the sliding compartment doors and peered through the crack, seeing a solid gray wall with only the occasional flash of a white symbol to indicate the quadrail was moving. After a time he saw a symbol slide past slowly enough for him to actually make out its shape. He turned and put his finger to his lips before waving at his companions.

Selena looked anxious as she climbed to her feet. Vance and Lars each hoisted their heavy packs onto their shoulders; the contents were muffled by leather wrappings and didn't make a sound. Taimin glanced at the coil of glowing wire on Lars's shoulder. The big skinner moved slowly and carefully, agile for his age, knowing that to strike the wire against something would not be a good idea.

The quadrail continued to slow. Sometime late in the afternoon, the four humans reached the terminus at Agravida.

The gray wall vanished, to be replaced by the cavernous space Taimin remembered. From his position in the goods compartment, his eyes roved furiously as he checked the pathways between the rows of other quadrails, searching for a group of bonded warriors who might already know of their presence. There were a few bonded about, clearly waiting for someone or something, but their manner indicated they weren't expecting anything out of the ordinary. A tall warrior with curling horns chatted to his yellow-robed advisor, absently glancing at the quadrail as it slid to a gentle halt. A group of workers in tan clothing stood with slumped shoulders, making it hard for Taimin to believe they had once been warriors. Otherwise the terminus was empty.

The quadrail came to a complete stop. Something in the distance hissed. Only the gentlest of nudges and the sight in front of Taimin told him that the journey was over. He turned and met the eyes of each of his companions, making sure they knew to stay silent while they waited. Selena and Vance both looked apprehensive, but there was something eager about Lars; he looked as if he wanted to push Taimin aside and see for himself. They had all taken their turn at staring out at the wide world as the quadrail traveled an immense distance in a single day. Murmured conversations had been filled with words of wonder. But this was different. Now they were in Agravida.

Taimin kept watch as the workers traveled the length of the quadrail. He held his breath as they walked directly past and for a moment he thought they might stop and enter his compartment to inspect the barrels. But they kept walking, and he saw multiple horned heads bob up and down.

Soon a few bonded pairs left the quadrail, having traveled in from the distant farmland, and walked toward the row of elevator doors at the end of the terminus. The area was empty for a time, but still Taimin waited. Then he heard a whirring sound and a clunk. The workers came into view again. They each gripped the handle of a wheeled platform about ten feet wide, loaded up with crates. The workers grunted to each other as their platforms trundled past.

Still Taimin waited, until the terminus was dark and deserted. The quadrail rested where it was, as if gathering its strength for another journey. But Taimin knew that if another quadrail were scheduled to arrive or depart, more bonded would travel through the terminus. Rather than exit, he turned to Selena and gave her an inquiring look.

Her eyes glazed. He didn't know what she was seeing, but the seconds trickled past. After a long time, she refocused and nodded.

"It's safe to go," she said softly.

Taimin turned his attention to Vance and Lars. "Remember: Selena and I have to get to the archive so we can give you directions to the stalk. For a time, we'll travel together, but we'll have to split up at some point."

Vance nodded while Lars gave a grunt of assent. Selena gave Taimin a determined stare. Then Taimin almost jumped when he heard a loud noise. Lars had grabbed the edge of the sliding door and heaved. It glided smoothly, but when the door was fully open it made a resounding clash of metal on metal.

Lars saw Taimin's disapproving look. "Sorry," he said sheepishly, jumping down to the hard gray floor. Vance hopped down a moment later, and then Selena. Taimin was the last to go.

While they all gazed around the terminus, remembrance struck Taimin with force. There was a certain fragrance in the air, not unpleasant, but different from any place he had been to before. The overriding impression was of hard angles, clean surfaces, and a distinct lack of color. There was no dirt in sight, nor rocks or big boulders. Nothing grew: no cactuses, razorgrass, withered trees, or shrubs covered in thorns. The dominant color was gray. Everything that was in this place was here because the bonded wanted it to be.

"Come on," Taimin said. "This way."

This was the third time he had passed through the terminus, and he led his three companions directly toward the elevators.

They followed his lead, and walked silently but swiftly, with no one speaking. He entered the nearest compartment and waved at them to hurry. Then, once they were all inside, he touched the blinking red arrow.

The arrow flashed blue.

The compartment began to move upward.

This particular compartment didn't have any windows; the smooth and solid gray walls gave nothing away. Taimin focused his attention on the shining white symbols above eye level that changed with time. His companions looked stunned, but he had explained what would happen, and they remained quiet.

As soon as the symbols stopped shifting from one form to another, Taimin began to tense. The elevator stopped. The metal doors slid open.

Taimin's eyes darted around. He let out a breath of relief. There were no bonded warriors waiting to greet them.

He checked on the others. Vance looked awestruck by the new world around him, but Lars was grim-faced, as if he shared Taimin's apprehension. Taimin glanced at Selena, who was clearly tense. "Can you . . ."

She nodded, and then her eyes glazed.

Clarity returned a moment later. "We have to wait," she said. "I saw them." She lowered her voice. "Warriors in red and black."

They waited for a few anxious moments before Selena checked again and nodded. Taimin led the way as he left the elevator and took his companions onto one of the moving walkways. Wind buffeted them all, somehow holding them in place as they were whisked along from one tall building to the next, one part of Agravida to another.

A long transparent wall opened up ahead, and then they were speeding past it. Behind him, Taimin heard Vance gasp. He turned and saw Vance, Selena, and Lars all staring. Following their eyes, he was struck once again by what he was seeing.

Selena spoke up. "I thought I understood, but this . . ."

A city of perfectly rectangular buildings filled the vista, some incredibly tall, others half their size, creating a staggered effect. The golden sun hung low in the sky, with the red sun just below it as they both cast long shadows from the steel-and-glass structures. Long bridges stretched from building to building, connecting them at multiple places. Flying machines whizzed through the air. Quadrails glided far below, part of a network of wide streets where other machines sped over the ground. In the center of it all, a vertical lattice that looked incredibly thin twisted in a spiral as it thrust its way up and up until it vanished into the clouds.

Soon everyone was staring at it.

"There it is," Taimin said. "The stalk."

As they watched, a glass-walled compartment left the ground to climb the stalk, gathering speed until it was moving almost too fast for the eye to follow it. A second compartment descended from the sky soon after, plummeting toward the area where the stalk's base was hidden.

The walkway slowed and then came to a halt. Taimin stepped off and headed briskly toward a junction of wide corridors. Selena was just behind him and he felt her reach out and grab his upper arm, pinching it tightly.

"Stop," she breathed.

Taimin flattened himself against the gray wall and glanced back to see the others doing the same. As he watched the junction, a group of bonded warriors passed across his vision. Tall and indomitable, they walked with long strides and occasionally spoke in their guttural language, too low for him to hear. At their hips they all were armed with the field lasers he remembered from his last time in Agravida.

Six of the warriors marched past, but Taimin glanced back at his companions and held up a warning hand. A moment later an equal number of bonded with short yellow horns dressed in robes filed past: the warriors' advisors. Of course, they were all unarmed.

Nonetheless, the sight of the bonded warriors brought home the danger they were all in. Taimin took a deep breath. The sound of heavy footsteps faded away. He turned to Selena, who nodded.

"Come on," Taimin said.

When he looked over his shoulder, he saw that even Lars's eyes were tight. Vance's face was pale as he hoisted his pack higher on his shoulder. With haste they hurried into the next corridor, before turning into another, and then taking an elevator down.

As they navigated the city, they paused frequently and glanced at Selena, waiting for her to nod that they were safe to continue. Some encounters were close, but every time Selena gave warning, so that they were at least able to find an alcove or a side passage to hide in while more bonded warriors marched past. Taimin led the way with growing confidence; he had paid attention during his time in Agravida and had traveled from the archive to the terminus before. Two more moving walkways led them to another junction.

Taimin brought the group to a halt. He rested his gaze on Vance and Lars. "The archive is this way"—he nodded down one of the corridors—"so it's time to split up."

Selena took her cue. While her eyes glazed, Taimin felt the growing tension pouring from everyone around him. The strain grew until she finished casting and turned to the two men carrying the aurelium. "Head that way until you come to a bend," she said as she pointed. "Keep going and there's an archway a little farther. It leads to a storeroom. You'll be able to wait there."

"More than anything," Taimin said, meeting the eyes of first Vance, and then Lars, "stay hidden. Don't do anything until Selena makes contact. She'll help you get to the stalk without anyone seeing you." He glanced at the glowing wire on Lars's shoulder. "Whatever you do, don't ignite the aurelium. Our plan is to threaten them. We have to stop the fighting. That's all that matters."

"Understood," Vance said. He looked as fearful as Taimin felt inside.

But Lars was a steadying presence. "We know what to do." He glanced at Vance. "It'll be fine, lad. What's to worry about? Either they shoot us, we blow up, or we'll force them to back down."

Selena followed Taimin along the corridor, occasionally watching his face.

He appeared confident, but she knew him well. There was worry in his eyes and tension in his jaw. He might have been able to navigate his way through this bizarre city, but he was far from certain this plan of his would work.

It was difficult to believe that he had come here, that he had given a speech and spoken directly to the leader of the entire bonded race. She now understood in a way she hadn't before. The bonded were simply so . . . powerful. Their city was a marvel, and the stalk—the very structure they planned to destroy—was so far beyond her understanding that she wondered if she were dreaming. All of the doors, walkways, and elevator compartments appeared still, but then they suddenly glided and slid. The city's buildings were each the size of mountains. Bright lights rivalled the suns. The natural world was rough and rugged, with humps and curves and jagged edges. There were no smooth lines. There was no whisking from one place to another. Nature took its time.

She thought she had seen enough to fill her with a lifetime of awe. But then Taimin passed underneath a tall, broad archway, decorated with sharp-edged symbols. She realized they had entered the archive.

She stared with wide eyes in all directions and saw a large space with a vaulted ceiling. In one corner, glossy black boxes the size of a big man's hand rested on tables, where oversized gray chairs with sloped backs waited ready for a bonded to sit. But it was the corridors of white panels that drew her eye. Colorful moving images slid across the panels, somehow appearing three-dimensional despite the fact that the panels were flat. She came to a halt, perplexed as she watched them, but then heard Taimin call her name.

She turned and saw that he had gone straight to an area where large pictures covered the wall. Some displayed what appeared to be diagrams, others multiple dots that looked like representations of the night sky. Taimin stood in front of one of the biggest. She hurried over to join him.

He scanned the drawing and soon he was tracing routes with his finger as she reached his side.

She gazed at the image, but it made no sense to her. But she wanted to help, and opened her mouth to ask him what she could do, when something strange happened. Her mouth snapped closed.

She heard a voice. And the voice was inside her mind.

She put a hand to her head, but Taimin was preoccupied and didn't notice.

Selena?

She recognized the clipped, authoritative tone.

This is Specialist Carter. I don't have long. You will remember that I asked you to be ready. I have not been authorized to do this, but I feel it is the right thing to do. Decisions have now been made. I'm here to warn you. There was a pause. *I told you that it would take us years to reach you, which is true. But for a long time now we have possessed a weapon that can tunnel through space itself. What we didn't have was the location of the bonded homeworld.*

Selena's eyes became unfocused. She pulled herself free of her body and there was Specialist Carter, floating beside her, a short-haired man with a hard, angular face, wearing tight clothing with a stiff collar and symbols on the shoulders.

I don't understand, she said. *What are you saying?*

The weapon has been sent. It will arrive soon. Very soon.

He shared an image with her: a spiked metal ball that peeled away at a black vortex, rippling against the void as it sped toward a golden star with a tiny red companion. Selena knew that she was looking at a weapon of pure menace, utterly terrifying in nature.

Carter sounded upset. *I have to be honest with you, there isn't much chance of survival. The weapon is what we call a radiation device. It destroys everything on the surface of a world. The bonded will have no defense against it. But if you take refuge, and find somewhere deep underground, with water and stocks of food, I promise you that if you do survive I will come as quickly as I can to rescue you. Use our link to find me again.*

Selena wanted to scream and cry, both at the same time. *How could you do this?*

I know it is difficult for you to understand, he said, *but we need this war to end. I'm sorry. More than you can know. You gave us the key to victory, yet you are the ones paying the ultimate price.*

You said you would help us! Selena leaned forward to stare into Carter's eyes. *Can't you stop it?*

Even after the weapon was sent, I tried to change their minds, but I was overruled. The bonded will never stop fighting. It's in their nature.

All of a sudden the mystic hovering in front of Selena vanished. *Carter?* She realized Carter was gone. Taimin was talking to her.

She reconnected with her body, but the feeling of horror stayed with her.

273

"Selena?" Taimin asked in concern. "What's wrong? Is someone coming?"

She shook her head and swallowed. How could she explain?

Taimin jabbed his finger against the map. "I found the route Vance and Lars have to take to reach the stalk." When she didn't reply, he gripped her shoulder. "Selena, if we don't do this, everyone in the wasteland will die. Whatever you're worried about, it can't be more urgent than this."

Selena's thoughts were in turmoil. What was the point in continuing?

But then she realized. Taimin planned to force a change in bonded society. He wanted the warriors to give up power. If the elders and advisors took command, there would be peace.

The stakes had become even higher. If their plan didn't work, they wouldn't just doom Dale's army, but the entire world.

She wondered if she should tell Taimin what she had learned. But he needed to focus. And telling him wouldn't affect what they were trying to achieve.

Taimin was still looking at her.

"I'll find Vance and Lars," she said. "Tell me what to say."

36

Vance looked cautiously from side to side as he crept along the corridor. Despite knowing that Selena was guiding him, he kept expecting to walk straight into a group of bonded warriors. Tension clawed at his lower back and he found himself gnawing at his lip. He glanced over his shoulder to check that Lars was still with him; his older companion's presence was reassuring.

The corridor split into another four-way junction up ahead. He heard the loud clatter of heavy footsteps and froze.

Selena?

Her voice inside his head calmed his ragged nerves. *Just wait. They're heading away from you.*

The sound grew distant, and he continued once more. Sweat beaded on his forehead, despite the fact that the temperature never seemed to change in the bonded city. He was extremely conscious of his pack's weight on his back.

Selena directed him and Lars to turn left, and he fought his fear as he snuck along, focused intently ahead as well as casting frequent glances behind him.

"Hurry up," Lars muttered.

He's right. Selena echoed the big skinner. *You have to trust me.*

Vance picked up speed. His jaw was tightly clenched. He reached one of the corridors with moving floors, while Lars came quickly behind him, so that the two men knocked into each other. Lars cursed and swiftly whipped the coil of aurelium wire out of the way.

Touch the arrow.

Vance touched the blinking red arrow, which turned blue, and the floor below his feet began to slide forward. As the walkway grew faster, wind rushed against him, pinning him in place. A transparent wall soon revealed that he was on one of the bridges that connected one building to another.

The sights of the immense city tried to snatch his attention. The golden sun brushed against the top of the tallest buildings. He couldn't believe that it was still afternoon.

The transparent section finished, telling Vance that he was in a different structure. Everything was gray: gray walls, gray ceiling, gray floors . . . He had no idea where he was and would never be able to find his way unaided.

The walkway slowed and then ended.

Keep going. You'll come to a row of elevator doors.

Knowing he had to trust Selena's casting, he strode swiftly along the next corridor while Lars followed close behind. As with many of the other corridors, he passed a series of oversized metal doors. Spying the row of elevator doors up ahead, he began to walk even faster.

He frowned. A light flashed beside one of the elevators. He wondered what it meant. Then Selena's voice sounded loud in his mind.

Stop!

He came to an abrupt halt. His eyes were wide as he turned and looked at Lars.

What do I do? he frantically asked Selena.

Quickly. Turn back. Hurry!

Vance didn't say a word; he simply grabbed Lars's shoulder and hauled the bigger man back the way they had come. As he moved into a shuffling run, he glanced toward the end of the corridor and saw that the elevator compartment was opening. He caught a glimpse of several huge figures in red uniforms.

The corridor was long and wide, with nothing to stop him and Lars being seen. He passed door after door. *Can I go through one of the doors?*

I'm not sure. Selena's obvious urgency heightened his own. *I don't know if you can open them.*

Let me worry about that. The next door in front of Vance was just ahead, to his left. *Is there anyone inside?*

Selena spoke after a brief pause. *No.*

Vance slammed his hand against the light beside the door. He waited in desperation. For a moment nothing happened.

With a slight hiss, the metal panel slid open.

Vance and Lars jumped inside. Ignoring everything else, Vance activated the light on the other side. The door snapped closed behind them.

The two men panted as they exchanged glances. Vance's pulse raced. As relief slowly flooded through him, for the first time he took in his surroundings.

He found himself in a strange room, filled with long benches where tubes, flasks, and bottles lay on every surface. Each vessel contained a liquid or powder in a variety of colors: bright green, sky blue, and the yellow of the golden sun.

Selena's voice returned. *They're coming toward you.*

Renewed fear made his eyes widen. *Did they see us?*

There's no way for me to know.

Lars opened his mouth. "What's going on?"

Vance gave him a glare and cut the air with his hand. He could hear his own heavy breathing, and tried to slow it down but failed.

277

His heartbeat thumped in his chest. He counted the beats, knowing that the warriors outside would be getting closer and closer.

They're at the door.

Vance gasped.

Then Selena's sigh came through. *It's all right. They're past.*

Vance slumped against the wall to release some of the tension. He met Lars's eyes and nodded, before giving the older man a weak smile. Lars scowled. While he waited, Vance glanced at the place he needed to touch to open the door once more.

You can go.

Vance pressed his palm against the light and the door snapped open. Despite what Selena had said, he made his own inspection of the corridor before resuming his path toward the row of elevator doors.

How much more of this? he asked Selena.

You're nearly there.

Unwilling to be taken by surprise again, Vance moved into a jog. He could hear the clunk of the aurelium chunks in their leather casings. The skalen knew what they were doing, he reminded himself. The aurelium wouldn't detonate unless the wire on Lars's shoulder flared up against it.

Vance and Lars rushed into the compartment. Selena issued an instruction to activate the downward arrow. The doors closed.

You can relax for a moment, Selena said. *You're heading down to ground level. This part might take a while.*

Even as he watched the cycling symbols, Vance had a chance to think. He knew from his last sight of the city that he had been high. Now he was heading down, on his way to find the base of the stalk. When he reached it, Selena would help him and Lars position their packs close to the stalk's foundations. Lars would lay out his wire and he and Vance would poise themselves to strike it.

In a strange way, at that point Vance and Lars would be safe. The bonded knew about aurelium and what it was capable of. Taimin would reveal himself and force the bonded to halt their advance on the wasteland.

Vance glanced at Lars; the older man had a tight set to his mouth, but didn't say anything. Vance returned to pondering all the things that could go wrong. In just a few moments his life might be over. At least Ruth was safe with the people who had remained at the bottom of the cliffs.

As the elevator compartment began to slow, the symbols on the wall scrolled from one to another, and then a single symbol became fixed in place.

The metal doors began to open.

Vance readied himself, focused on the gap between the doors that grew wider and wider. He first saw an area of flat, hard ground, different from the smooth gray floors he had seen so far. Fresh air blew into his face. There was blue sky overhead, unfiltered by windows or panels. The golden sun shone directly into his eyes and made him blink.

The elevator doors finished opening. The stalk glistened in the afternoon light, far larger than it had appeared at first glance. From a distance the twisting lattice looked as thin as a spider's web, but now he could see it in detail. The individual strands were at least as thick as his forearm. They combined together to form the climbing structure, bars gripping other bars, until a complete framework curled into the clouds and vanished into the heavens. Without its height, it would have been barely noticeable among the multitude of buildings that surrounded it. But the incredible ladder to the void, located at the city's heart, was impossible to miss.

A collection of cube-shaped storage containers filled the area directly in front of the elevator door. Like hulking rock formations, they spread in orderly rows across Vance's immediate vision and clustered around the stalk's base.

Something screamed.

Vance started as he immediately tried to find the source of the sound. His gaze shot up and he saw a glass-walled compartment plummet from the sky to slide down the side of the stalk like a water droplet. The compartment slowed only at the last moment, and for a brief instant the sound became ear-splitting, but then it faded. Despite the containers in between his position and the stalk, Vance could see all the way to where the compartment touched the ground.

Lars watched Vance with growing impatience. They had yet to exit the elevator, but Vance wanted to hear from Selena before he took a single step, and he ignored the older man as he continued to get his bearings. He focused on the stalk's base. The stalk might have strong foundations, and burrow deep into the ground, but where the compartments were loaded and unloaded he could only see more of the thin lattice.

He began to think that the plan might actually work. The aurelium would release a powerful explosion. Taimin had said the forces that held the stalk in the sky were delicately balanced. If allowed to happen, the explosion would blow the thin strands apart. Taimin was right. They had found their enemy's weakness. All that remained was to deploy the threat.

He heard Selena's voice in his mind. *Wait.*

Some broad-shouldered bonded appeared from behind one of the containers. They had the curling horns of warriors, but none of them had advisors with them and they wore plain, tan clothing. Even their horns were brown rather than the sinister color of blood. Vance knew from the things Taimin had told him that they were workers, warriors who had outlived their bondmates.

The workers stomped toward the stalk until they reached the compartment that had just set down. They entered one after the other. A moment later, without warning, the compartment shot up again. In the blink of an eye it disappeared into the clouds.

As soon as the workers were gone, Lars turned away from the stalk to fix his gaze on Vance. "Well?" he grunted. "Can we go forward?"

Is it safe to go? Vance asked. *Selena?* He waited for her to tell him what to do. Time passed, before he gave Lars an anxious look. "She's gone."

"Gone?" Lars frowned. "What do you mean, gone?"

"She's not saying anything." Vance anxiously looked toward the base of the stalk. It wasn't far away, perhaps several hundred paces. "Selena?" he asked aloud. "Selena!"

"Shh," Lars hissed. "Not so loud."

Vance thought furiously. All he knew was that Selena and Taimin had done what they had set out to do. Their task had been to guide him and Lars to the stalk, and here they were. "If something's happened to them, we should keep going, shouldn't we?"

"We don't have a choice," Lars said.

Vance knew that they would be taking a terrible risk without Selena to tell them the way was clear. The containers might be hiding anything.

"I don't know—"

"Vance," Lars said harshly. "Something must have happened to her. Lad, focus! We have to take matters into our own hands."

"We should wait." Vance let out a breath. "Selena?"

Lars glared at him. "Vance, think about all those people waiting to fight on the edge of the wasteland. You've seen the same things I have. You think they'll survive?" He indicated the pack on his shoulder. "We've come all this way." He fixed his gaze on the stalk. "I'm going."

Without another word, Lars left the elevator and burst into a run. He crossed the space swiftly, heading directly for the area where the stalk met the ground. Vance watched Lars go for the briefest instant and then, with a curse, he hurried to follow.

With Vance just behind, they passed one of the containers and then another loomed on the other side. They ran under its shadow for a dozen paces. Soon they had halved the distance to the stalk. Vance kept his eyes focused on his destination as he sprinted along. Sweat coated his forehead. The stalk was so close that he felt he could reach out and touch it.

He heard a rasping shout behind him.

The sound made his heart give a sickening lurch. The voice was rough and grunting, loud enough to carry a long distance. He ignored it and continued to run. Just a couple of containers remained before they reached their destination.

But from behind the nearest container, a group of eight-foot-tall giants appeared.

With his chest heaving, Lars came to an abrupt stop. Vance skidded to a halt beside him.

Vance took in the sharp horns, the glossy crimson uniforms, the ridged faces and fiery eyes. The six warriors were shouting as they fanned out, but their words were unintelligible. Long black weapons were in their hands, pointed at the two men.

Turning to look behind, Vance saw a second group of warriors heading toward them.

One of the warriors, with a single star on the breast of his uniform, stepped forward and thrust out a finger as he bellowed something aggressively. The other warriors formed a circle until Vance and Lars were surrounded.

"I could spark it now," Lars said under his breath.

Vance looked at the base of the stalk. It was close, but not close enough. "And then we die," he said.

"Might as well take a few of them with us."

"What's the point?" Vance said. He glanced at Lars. "It's over." He slipped his pack off his back and let it fall to the ground. Lars did the same. Then, with a look of regret at the stalk, Lars removed the coil of aurelium wire from his shoulder and set it down.

The leader continued to shout and pointed at the packs.

"I think he wants us to open them," Lars said.

Vance focused on the lead warrior and shook his head. He indicated the green wire and then the packs. "Aurelium," he said, although he didn't know if they would understand him.

They clearly did, and exchanged a series of agitated words. Some of the warriors angrily stepped forward and used their weapons to force Vance and Lars to move away from the two packs and the coiled fuse nearby.

Then the leader shouted something else as he indicated the ground meaningfully.

Vance was the first to sink to his knees. He watched Lars's dark expression as thoughts of resistance crossed the older man's face. But then, with a sigh, Lars knelt also. The leader didn't stop his barrage of harsh commands, but Vance would never understand what he was saying.

Vance wondered what had happened to Taimin and Selena. He couldn't take his eyes off the weapons pointed at him. At any moment the leader might issue an order that would be the last sound he heard.

They had come close. So close. But not close enough.

37

Taimin and Selena turned to put their backs to the map of Agravida. Selena had been farcasting when a group of bonded warriors rushed into the archive. The warriors growled a series of harsh syllables as they pointed their weapons.

"They want us to show our hands," Taimin said.

He and Selena both raised their arms. A tall warrior came forward, uncomfortably close, and for a moment Taimin felt a spike of dread. Then clawed fingers patted Taimin's body, and he realized he was being searched. After a series of brisk movements the warrior soon found Taimin was unarmed. The warrior then moved on to Selena. She tensed, but in moments the warrior was done and stepped back.

"Vance and Lars . . ." Taimin murmured. "Did they . . ."

She gave him a look of dejection. "No."

"Silence!" one of the warriors barked. Taimin didn't bother translating for Selena. Her mouth snapped shut.

Taimin scanned the warriors surrounding them. A few pointed their weapons at him, while others were leveled in Selena's direction. They were strangely expectant, and he wondered what would happen next.

His heart sank as realization struck home. His gamble had failed. He had convinced Selena—the woman he loved—and two of his closest friends, to commit to a desperate plan. He had brought them all into harm's way. Trying to save the army of the wasteland from the desperate battle they were sure to lose, he had all but guaranteed that Selena, Vance, and Lars wouldn't live to see the day's end.

Taimin wondered what else he could have done. He had tried talking. He had sought help in the stars. He had attempted to deliver a powerful threat—to use fear of imminent destruction, perhaps the only thing that might bring about a change—and it had all gone badly wrong.

Just a little more time and the outcome might have been entirely different.

Movement caught Taimin's eye.

He looked past the group of warriors as a figure passed through the archway to enter the archive. Ingren's shining robes and horns matched the color of sunlight. She took swift strides toward the warriors and their two human prisoners.

Taimin saw immediately that she was angry. More than angry. There was wrath in her dark, narrowed eyes. The group of warriors moved apart as she neared and the leader gave a slight bow.

"Elder, we have them," the leader said. He then went on to emit a string of words. His speech was too fast for Taimin to follow, but he heard the stalk mentioned.

Ingren stopped directly in front of Taimin. She rested her seething gaze on him. For a long time she held his stare, and then she shook her head.

Taimin wondered if it was Ingren who would issue the command to kill them. She was an elder, incapable of violence—but did that extend to giving an order to another?

When she spoke, it was in a low voice that conveyed both fury and regret. "You should never have come back."

Hours had passed and still everyone waited behind the bulwark and stared into the wall of gray haze.

Ruth tried to guess how far away the haze was. Behind the defenders, she and Jerome stood on a low rise, where they could see over the tops of people's heads, past the embankment, and into the area that had once been scorched by the firewall. The first hundred paces of open ground were clear, and then the air began to thicken. After that, the dirt changed color and the gray wall clouded the terrain beyond.

Occasionally someone coughed. A light breeze blew the foul air in Ruth's direction. Whenever a defender retched, she tried to tell herself it was because of the stench that stuck to her tongue and clung to the inside of her nostrils.

From her vantage she scanned the bulwark in both directions and wondered if the terrible odor was having the same effect on the other races. At the limits of vision, the bax formed a long row of hunched figures. Spears bristled and their glowing points made up an array of little green lights. At the front, tall for his race, she saw the unmistakable form of Blixen. The bax from Gravel Range were somewhere in there too, but even Gorax didn't have Blixen's size.

The darker mass of skalen held an even greater number of javelins with green tips. She shielded her eyes from the afternoon sunlight and saw Rathis as he prepared to fight alongside his kin. The mantoreans were spread out more thinly, and it was hard to tell the difference between them and their tall bows.

Individual trulls paced back and forth, and when Ruth turned to the other side, she saw that more bax and trulls had grouped on the opposite flank, next to the humans. Scattered along the line, dozens of wyverns strained in the grips of their riders and spread out their wings in restless movements. Intermittent shrieks split the air.

She tried to guess the number of defenders but failed. She couldn't even see to the bulwark's ends. In the expectant silence, she wondered what thoughts were turning in everyone's minds. Were they proud to be standing with so many others? Were they confident of victory, ready to break their attackers and then commence their journey through the haze, to the other side, where they would take the battle to the enemy's heartland? Or were they wondering if they should have made a different choice?

Ruth returned her attention to the haze to focus on the one element everyone was resting their hopes on.

Jerome had pointed out the long line of black rocks, halfway between the embankment of packed dirt and the wall of thick gray air. The skalen had brought aurelium in quantity; Ruth had seen the jars and pouches for herself. Taimin might have taken a small portion of it, but the rest was buried below the rocks. A trap had been set. When the assault came, the ground would erupt. With luck, they would halt the attack before it even started.

Yet there was still an even stronger hope that Ruth held on to. If Taimin's plan was successful, the attack might not come at all. As she struggled to manage her fear, she watched the haze and knew that if no bonded army appeared, the plan had worked and Vance was still alive.

Just inside the embankment, Ruth saw Rei-kika lean over and say something to Dale. Wondering if the moment had come, Ruth clenched her jaw tightly. Dale turned and opened his mouth wide to call out.

"Defenders!" he bellowed. "Ready your weapons!"

Ruth felt the blood drain from her face. The attack was still coming. Taimin's plan had failed. Vance might be dead. Almost certainly he was dead. She tried to tell herself not to let despair take over.

"You came, Ruth, because you wanted to," she heard Jerome say beside her. She looked at him and she knew he could see the anguish in her face. "Have faith," he said.

The humans arrayed around Dale hoisted their crossbows. Spread out at both sides, other men and women readied bows or spears. Wyverns rose into the sky, while their riders lifted the frames of their own crossbows. Across the entire line, a shudder of movement passed from one group to the next as defenders of all five races prepared themselves.

Ruth's heart jolted from a swift beat to a frantic patter. She watched intently. Part of her couldn't believe this was happening. Another more detached part told her that she needed to be ready for the moment when the first injured were carried from the front.

The ground began to shake.

It started as a tremor and grew until a strong vibration traveled up Ruth's legs and set her teeth on edge. Staring straight ahead, she told herself she had to stay strong. She wasn't one of those up front. They were the ones who deserved to be afraid.

Her breath caught.

The first outline appeared through the haze. Then another, and another, until the smoky horizon became filled with moving machinery. At first the shapes were indistinct, but as they rumbled forward she saw detail. The war machines—devastators, Taimin had called them—rolled over the ground and were all exactly the same. Black and menacing, they were each the size of a house and traveled on wheels connected by grooved belts. Every one of them had a dome that crowned the rectangular base, and from the dome a long tube pointed directly ahead.

The traveling row of devastators was wide enough to cover the entire bulwark. With only a short distance from one machine to the next, Ruth realized that there must be dozens and dozens of them, easily more than a hundred. There might even be two hundred. She wasn't sure she wanted to know.

She heard a high-pitched whine she recognized. It made her stomach churn and frayed her already stretched nerves. High in the sky triangular shapes appeared out of the mist, hard to see at first, but then their forms grew larger until they hovered above the machines below. Striker after striker kept abreast of the rumbling ground advance. Ruth tasted bile at the back of her throat. The wyverns were heavily outnumbered.

Her thoughts inadvertently turned to the destruction of Zorn. In an instant the bulwark of packed dirt seemed like barely any protection at all. None of the defenders called out. Dale gave no orders. The faces she saw among the defenders displayed sheer, utter terror at what they could see coming toward them.

It was too late to run. There was only one hope.

The sinister machines would soon reach the line of black rocks, where Dale had set his trap.

38

Ingren continued to glare at Taimin, more furious than he had ever seen her. The bonded warriors pointed their field lasers at their two prisoners. Taimin considered plan after plan and discarded them all. He knew that he and Selena were both at Ingren's mercy.

Taimin took a deep breath. "Ingren—" he began.

She held up a hand and a warrior stepped forward to shove the hard metal of his weapon into Taimin's chest. When she spoke, her tone was scathing. "What was your plan, Taimin? To destroy the stalk? Fortunately we seized your companions in time." She shook her head. "You reckless fool."

The warriors looked on curiously; she was speaking the common tongue and they had no idea what she was saying.

"I thought you had sense, but I was wrong," Ingren said. "I thought I knew you better, but here you are. If you had succeeded, even your precious wasteland would not be safe."

Taimin lifted his chin. "What did you expect? If someone attacks me, I can't just lay down and die. It was the only idea I had. I tried peace. Peace wasn't possible. I had to threaten you with something that would make you afraid."

"With that much aurelium, it would have worked," Ingren said grimly. "That is the frightening thing, foolish human. If the stalk came down the consequences would be catastrophic. Not just for us. For all life on this planet—"

"I know," Taimin said. He met Ingren's eyes. "There was no aurelium."

Ingren frowned, perplexed.

"I made sure it wouldn't work," he said. "The packs are filled with rocks. There's no danger in opening them. You can check for yourself."

"What?" Selena turned wide eyes on him. "Why?"

"I knew that destroying the stalk would mean killing ourselves as well as them. That's correct, isn't it, Ingren?"

She nodded, but her expression was still wary. "Of course it is."

"I needed something strong enough to convince the sky marshal that continuing the fight would destroy everything—not just the ability to wage war, but everything. But I couldn't take the risk of it happening by accident. I wanted to make a serious threat. I didn't want to be responsible for the end of the world."

As Ingren considered Taimin's words, Selena spoke into the silence. "You may not want this world destroyed but there are those who do. And we gave them the information to do it. I'm sorry, Taimin, but the end of the world is coming anyway." Taimin saw that her face was pale. "Soon this will all be over. And we will all be dead." She stared grimly at Ingren. "Yes, even you."

Taimin was confused. "What—?"

She interrupted him. "The man we spoke to, Carter, contacted me. It was just a few moments ago, when we first entered the archive."

"Why didn't you say anything?"

"We had to help Vance and Lars get to the stalk." Selena focused her attention on Ingren. "The man I'm referring to isn't from the wasteland. He works for the five allies, and he's not even from this world." Ingren's face registered disbelief. "He showed me a weapon . . . he called it a radiation device. It's on its way as we speak. They didn't know the location of this world until we gave it to them."

As Taimin realized what Selena was saying, he felt light-headed. He remembered the moving images he had seen in this very room, images of beautiful worlds that shone against the black of space. In an instant the worlds became enveloped by the color red as they burned to cinder.

Together, he and Selena had sought help in the void. Instead, they had doomed their entire world. She had to be wrong. But at the same time, it made a terrible sense.

Selena stared up at the tall bonded elder. "You've been fighting for a long time. They would do it, wouldn't they, if they had the chance?"

Ingren was frozen in place. She looked completely stunned. "It cannot be." She shook her head from side to side. "I do not believe you."

The uniformed warriors watched the exchange, clearly not comprehending what was being said. At any rate, they had their two human prisoners well in hand, and with their weapons ready to fire at a moment's notice, it mattered little if Ingren wanted to learn more about the plot to destroy the stalk.

"Ingren," Taimin said slowly. "You know Selena is a mystic. After I left Agravida, we made contact with a human. There was a five-pointed star on the side of his ship. You know about these things. I'm sure that symbol means something to you. How could I know about it if we hadn't seen it?"

He could almost see the thoughts whirling through Ingren's mind. She knew that what Taimin was telling her was at least possible. Her posture and facial expression conveyed uncertainty, anxiety . . . perhaps even fear.

"Can you find Carter again?" Taimin asked Selena. "Ingren is the only one who can help us now."

"I can." Selena nodded. "Ingren, you can talk to him. He can tell you more than he told me. The fact that he's real . . . That would prove it to you, wouldn't it?"

Ingren's brow ridges came together. "How would I speak with this human?"

"Through me," Selena said simply.

Ingren snorted. "Ha. You humans deceive by nature."

As Taimin watched Ingren, he cast his mind back to a time not so long ago. He had traveled the wasteland with her and guided her, made camp and eaten with her. He had saved her from firehounds.

She had been kind when he had discovered Syrus's homestead destroyed. She had taught him the bonded language. When they reached her world, she never betrayed him. She gave him her promise that he would get a chance to speak for those in the wasteland, and it was a promise she had fulfilled. She had helped him to flee.

"Ingren, what if she's right?" he asked softly. "You value knowledge. Don't you need to know the truth? Sometimes, all we have to go on is trust."

Her lips thinned and she shook her head. "Communication with our enemies is forbidden."

"Elder," one of the warriors grunted in the coarse syllables of Ravange. "Why the wait? Let us kill them all."

"Silence," Ingren commanded.

Resplendent in her golden robes, Ingren stood tensed with indecision. Then she reached up to the collar around her neck, where tiny aurelium beads glowed with green fire. First she unclipped one fastening, then another, until she had removed the collar.

Ingren faced Selena. "Put me in contact with this human."

39

The row of devastators emerged from the smoky haze and rumbled toward the long bulwark and the defenders who manned it. The strikers advanced in the sky above. Just a few hundred paces separated the two forces.

The machines that moved on huge wheels left flattened dirt behind them. Ruth watched as one approached a big boulder. The boulder initially resisted the devastator's advance. But the devastator's nose rose up and a moment later the heavy mass of metal came down again. The boulder vanished underneath. When she saw the area again, all that was left of the boulder was strewn gravel.

Ruth swallowed. The ground continued to shake. The line of war machines steadily approached the black marker stones where the ground had been mined with destructive potential.

Her heart raced. The distance narrowed. This was Dale's core plan. As soon as the enemy was directly above the aurelium, the ground would erupt. The strikers weren't high, just a few hundred feet above the ground and level with the wyverns aloft over the defenders. The explosion might take the strikers down too. Everything depended on this moment.

The attackers came to a halt.

At Ruth's side, Jerome drew in a sharp breath. She turned and they exchanged glances, before returning her attention straight ahead. Her fingernails pressed painfully into her palms. Why weren't they moving? What had made them stop?

A cascade of bright light erupted from every single one of the devastators.

Red flashes streaked from the wide mouths of the tubes that rested solidly on their shoulders. Rapid fire peppered the ground between the row of attackers and the bulwark. The spray of light was carefully targeted, directed on the row of black markers.

The explosion was terrifying.

A great ejection of fire and dirt erupted from the ground as the aurelium detonated. A powerful roar shook the heavens. Ruth clapped her hands over her ears and gritted her teeth. A thick cloud of smoke and flame climbed the sky. It rose up and up, swelling until nothing could be seen beyond the bulwark but a volume of dirt that shot high into the air. The explosion reached to a height of hundreds of feet before the debris thrown up by its force began to fall.

Closer to the cacophony, the defenders all shrank to the ground. The bax looked as if they had been batted down by a giant fist. The skalen were all piled up against each other. Stunned mantoreans were like scattered bones; it was hard to separate one from the next. The humans had flattened themselves. Only the trulls stood tall.

The overwhelming roar gradually faded. The defenders took stock and gathered themselves. One by one, they straightened, until everyone was again gazing past the embankment at a cloud of thick haze.

A wind came up. It tugged at the cloud of smoke and gradually the dust cleared.

Ruth's breath caught.

The row of war machines was exactly where it had been before. The strikers still hovered in the sky. For a brief moment everything was still.

Then the devastators began to advance again.

Taimin didn't know what Selena had done, but Ingren's face was horrified. Whatever had passed between them, something came over Ingren's expression; an urgent fire filled her eyes. If he had needed any further confirmation that the weapon was on its way, he had it now.

Ingren turned to the warriors around her. She barked a series of rapid orders in Ravange. "Find the marshals. Call an emergency session of the assembly." The warriors looked uncertain. "Now!"

The bonded warriors knew that the stalk had been threatened. They had seen an exchange between their elder and two of the humans who had come to do harm to their civilization. Now Ingren had learned something that obviously terrified her.

"At once, Elder," one of the warriors said. He began to nominate some of his companions to join him.

"There's no time to waste." Ingren's eyes narrowed. "All of you. Go!"

The warrior glanced at Taimin and Selena. "But the humans—"

Ingren turned the full force of her gaze on him. "I will take charge of them myself."

"Elder, you cannot defend yourself."

"They are unarmed."

"No," the warrior said forcefully. "It is against all custom. I will not leave you with them."

Ingren drew herself up. She raised a finger and pointed it at the bigger, stronger warrior's chest. "You know me. I am an elder. In the name of the stars, I would not lie to you. There is a radiation device on its way to our world. Do you have any idea what that means?" The warrior looked aghast. "Now go. I command you. Convene the assembly."

The warrior gave a crisp nod. With a wave of his arm, he gathered his companions and the crimson-clad bonded warriors all ran from the archive. In moments, Ingren, Taimin and Selena were alone.

"You two," Ingren said firmly. "Follow me."

Taimin and Selena had to move quickly to keep up with Ingren's long strides. After leaving the archive she took them along one swift walkway after another. Taimin wondered where she was taking them as they traveled the gray-walled corridors and passed rows of metal doors. Meanwhile, bonded warriors and their advisors ran past in the opposite direction but barely gave them a glance. Ingren entered an elevator compartment, and another opened to eject still more bonded, calling in harsh voices to one another as they raced away.

Taimin and Selena exchanged swift glances in the elevator. Ingren's manner was both troubled and frantic. She clenched and unclenched her fists impatiently as the elevator plummeted.

"Is there anything you can do to stop the weapon?" Taimin asked.

Ingren rested her eyes on him for a brief instant. "No."

The compartment slowed and then stopped. The metal doors parted. Ingren immediately resumed her swift pace. Taimin glanced through a long window and saw that the stalk was a distant thin line: they were in a part of the city he had never been to before. Despite the effort required to stay with the golden-robed elder rushing along the wide corridor, he called out loud enough for her to hear him.

"Our friends. Are they still alive?"

"Eh?" Ingren cast him a distracted look. "They're under guard."

They reached a junction and Ingren turned left. A broad archway with blue symbols written along its rim beckoned. Ingren plunged through without hesitation, and Taimin saw that even the nature of the corridor changed beyond the archway. He had become familiar with the gray walls, but now a blue horizontal stripe decorated both sides of the corridor. Metal doors soon appeared up ahead. Ingren slammed her palm against the blinking red light beside them. The light flashed blue. The doors opened.

Ingren's voice was grim. "Wait here."

She vanished through the doorway and the metal panels closed behind her. Taimin realized he was alone with Selena. Ingren had simply left them.

He turned toward her. Her face was pale and there was tension in her eyes.

"Vance and Lars—" she began.

"There's nothing we can do," Taimin said. His brow furrowed. "What happened? Did she talk to Specialist Carter?"

Selena nodded. "To say he was surprised would be an understatement. But I found him and he spoke to her."

The metal doors slid open. Ingren appeared, and now there was another bonded by her side. The newcomer was dressed in the same golden robes as Ingren, marking her out as an elder, but hers were strikingly different. A blue band on the hem and sleeves contrasted with the glossy yellow. Taimin had never seen the costume and had no idea what it meant.

"Do you understand?" Ingren asked her companion.

"I will see it done."

Ingren opened her arms to gather Taimin and Selena, and herd them back the way they had come. "Hurry," she said. "We don't have much time."

40

Ruth watched the row of devastators roll on toward the embankment. She stood with her fists clenched at her sides. After the explosion, the defenders had all been thrown to the ground, but now they were picking themselves up.

It was time to fight back.

Soon the defenders were once again standing side by side. As the devastators climbed the bulwark, Ruth saw Dale and those around him prepare themselves. Dale shouted something. Crossbow after crossbow shifted into readiness. Every war machine crested the bank at the same moment.

Dale cried out again.

The defenders in front of Ruth released a salvo of green lights.

The aurelium bolts shot forward, too fast for the eye to follow. Green flashes struck metal and clouds of flame enveloped devastator after devastator. As the deadly hail continued, each successive strike penetrated deeper until a devastator blew into pieces. Several more devastators exploded from within. Meanwhile the wyvern riders flew forward to battle the strikers, ducking and weaving and launching their own crossbow bolts.

The attack faltered. Now the defenders were able to concentrate on the few devastators remaining. Steel twisted and groaned. Booms split the air. Skalen threw javelins and bax launched spears, but it was the crossbows that struck each devastator to the heart. Ruth felt hope stir when she saw that there were just ten left, and then five.

And then there was nothing but a row of broken metal raised high on the crest of the bulwark.

Cheers rang out from all directions. Ruth heard the throaty voices of bax, the softer tones of skalen, and the clipped sound of mantoreans. Humans roared their defiance. Trulls grinned and bellowed. Ruth cheered with them.

But then the cheers died away.

The ground began to shake once more.

Another row of devastators began to crest the bulwark, shoving the broken metal aside as if it weighed nothing at all.

———

Ingren walked swiftly. She followed a corridor that was far larger than the customary size, and then Taimin almost stopped in his tracks.

He recognized the pair of massive doors: one gold and the other crimson. Beyond he would find a platform supported in the empty air, centered within a vast space filled with rows of tiered seating.

Memories came flooding back. He had stood exposed to a multitude of malign stares. He had given a speech to the sky marshal and the warriors he led. His words had done nothing. He had been laughed at.

He was about to enter the auditorium.

"Selena," he murmured. "You're about to meet the sky marshal."

"The—"

"Their leader."

If Selena's face had been pale before, now it was white. But she set her jaw and straightened her posture as she walked. Taimin thought about the girl he had first met in the wasteland. Selena had changed. He supposed he had too.

As soon as Ingren approached, the huge doors began to part. She waited impatiently for them to open, clearly not in any frame of mind to appreciate the slow, dramatic pace. Taimin and Selena caught up to her, but she didn't meet Taimin's eyes; instead she wore an expression of agitation.

The doors parted. Without checking on the two humans, Ingren strode through the entrance to the auditorium. Taimin and Selena followed behind her.

Ingren emerged onto the platform that jutted out, high above the ground. Chin held high, she approached the central podium where Taimin had given his address.

Selena's eyes were wide as she took in the immense, overwhelming space. The false stars above twinkled against the dome's black background. All of the tiers were at their height or lower, and every direction was filled with bonded in either crimson or pale yellow, in the process of hastily taking their seats. A loud roar of conversation came from all quarters.

The scene was vastly different from the one that had greeted Taimin last time. Usually everything about the bonded was well-ordered, even rigid. Now he was looking at an assembly in chaos.

He called out to Ingren, striding just ahead of him as she headed toward the podium. "Ingren, when was the last emergency assembly?"

She threw a single word back over her shoulder. "Never."

Sky Marshal Jakkar was already settled. Tall even for his kind, with curling horns and metallic armor trimmed in black and silver, he leaned forward and fixed his flaming eyes on Ingren. His advisor sat beside him, shorter and submissive in a pale yellow robe. Taimin remembered her name—Astrin—and that Ingren had spoken well of her. The council of elders spread out behind the sky marshal, matched in appearance to Ingren.

Ingren made her final ascent up to the podium. Taimin and Selena came to a halt behind her. The conversation that poured from all directions faded from a loud rumble to a murmur. All of the warriors who made up the assembly had finished taking their seats and now stirred as they gazed up. From the faces Taimin could see, their advisors looked troubled, but they had no power in this place.

The last voices faded. Ingren swept her gaze over the auditorium. She spread her arms and raised them up, calling for silence.

Taimin glanced at Selena and noticed her staring straight ahead. He didn't have to guess at the target of her grim fascination. "That's the sky marshal," he murmured.

She was breathing heavily. Her expression showed a mixture of fear and disgust. "He's the one? He ordered the attack on Zorn?"

"Undoubtedly."

Selena's eyes narrowed as she stared directly at the sky marshal, which made Taimin think about the battle on the edge of the wasteland. If it hadn't begun already, it would at any moment. He remembered the preparations he had seen, the bonded forces arrayed and ready to deploy. The devastators would easily destroy anything in their path. Strikers would finish the rest. Even if Ruth was below the cliffs, she wouldn't be safe for long.

Ingren opened her mouth, but the sky marshal held up a hand to cut her off. His deep brow ridges came further together and his mouth parted to reveal a cavernous hole filled with rows of yellowed teeth. The fire in his eyes grew brighter.

"Elder Ingren." The sky marshal's harsh voice resounded throughout the space. "What is the meaning of this emergency assembly?"

Selena turned to Taimin. "What is he saying?"

Taimin translated for her, while keeping his attention focused on the podium, where Ingren made a solitary figure.

Ingren called out to address the entire assembly. "I have the most important news you will ever hear." She paused. "Our world's location is no longer secret. Even as I stand here, a radiation device is on its way to Lumea, sent by our enemies."

The auditorium broke out in an uproar. Harsh voices joined together in a deafening rumble. Warriors stood and shouted. Taimin continued to translate, even as sweat beaded on his forehead.

The sky marshal bellowed above it all. "Silence!"

Taimin was stunned by how quickly the voices fell away. The scattered warriors standing sank back into their seats. Once more, there were only two figures that mattered. Again it was Ingren in the direct gaze of the sky marshal.

Jakkar leaned forward. His voice was low, but even so it was clear enough to be heard throughout the auditorium. "Elder Ingren, how do you know this?"

Rather than reply immediately, Ingren gazed down. When she spoke, she addressed those below her. "We have seen the effect of these weapons on our colonies. There is no defense against them." She was clearly trying to reach as many as possible with her words. "I can see only one course of action. We must sue for peace. Our enemies have sought peace before. We have always rejected them. That must change."

An angry, rumbling growl rose up from the warriors. The advisors stayed silent. The sky marshal initially looked astonished, but then an expression of rage overcame his face.

"You would cast doubt upon my command, Elder Ingren?" Jakkar demanded.

Ingren's straight posture faltered. Her gaze lowered and her shoulders slumped. For a moment she was as Taimin had first seen her, when she had served her bondmate Ungar and was bound to follow the warrior's commands. She was an elder, with a far greater degree of free will than an advisor, but he could only imagine how hard it was for her to stand firm.

But he saw her take a deep breath. Her shoulders squared. She lifted her chin and raised her gaze. She stared directly at the sky marshal.

"Yes," she said. "I believe you are no longer fit to lead us." When the cacophony of voices threatened to overwhelm her, she raised her voice above it. "In the past, after victory, we have followed the path of wisdom rather than war. I now speak to all advisors here. I call on the council of elders. We cannot wait for total annihilation before we make the change. This war has gone on for long enough. We have tried the warriors' way, and in this new age of fighting across the stars, war has failed."

Sky Marshal Jakkar abruptly stood. With his size and striking armor, his presence dominated the entire auditorium. "The warriors are ascendant. I will not allow anyone to call for a reversal. Bonded—warriors and advisors alike—what evidence is there that Elder Ingren speaks the truth?"

Ingren turned and indicated Selena. "The human female is a mystic." Apprehension crossed Selena's face as Taimin continued to translate for her. "With her help, I was able to make contact with a representative from the five allies."

Jakkar drew in a sharp breath. "You removed your collar? You let an enemy into your mind?" A glint of triumph came to his eyes. "All bonded, understand this. I have two simple explanations for Elder Ingren's strange behavior. Either her thoughts have been corrupted, or she looks to reversal to save the lives of the humans she cares so much about. There is no radiation device. It is a lie."

Taimin's heart sank. Ingren had come up against the same hard reality he had. She understood that peace was the only path to survival. She had made her plea. But in a society geared only for war, all talk of peace looked like weakness. And, once in charge, the war-makers would never relinquish their position.

He heard a sound behind him.

As the gold and crimson doors opened, he saw Vance and Lars. They both looked shaken. Escorted by a group of bonded warriors, wary of the field lasers pointed toward them, they were forced to back away until they had joined Taimin and Selena on the platform.

Then Taimin saw one of the warriors push another human forward. He caught sight of blonde hair, a heart-shaped face, and frightened blue eyes. Hannah tried to return to the warriors, but they presented their lasers and barked at her to join the other humans.

Sky Marshal Jakkar's voice resounded throughout the auditorium. "We will change the nature of our bond only when all of our enemies have fallen. Elder Ingren, if you are so eager to take up the mantle of power, then you know that there cannot be any of our enemies left alive—and especially not here in our great city. I am sure you will share my pleasure in watching these humans die."

———

Ruth lay on her back, sprawled on the ground. She drew in a gasping, shuddering breath. Her ears were ringing. She could feel bits of dirt all over her face and she tasted blood on her tongue. She turned her head and Jerome's sightless eyes stared back at her.

She had been watching the advance of the devastators when a machine's black dome had rotated. In an instant the machine's weapon had flashed. A streak of light flew from it and struck the bottom of the hill where Ruth and Jerome had been standing. She had experienced a wave of intense heat and then the sensation of her entire body lifting up.

She now grimaced. Pain spiked between her temples. The ringing in her ears grew louder. The clatter of explosions came from all around her, but the sound was distant, as if she had something wrapped around her head. Her legs felt numb. She was terrified to look at her body. She knew the look of surprise that injured people sometimes showed when they saw their own vicious wounds.

Her arms were sore and her hands tingled. Nonetheless she was able to flex her fingers. Taking a deep breath, she craned her neck to peer down the length of her body, but could only see as far as her waist; the rest was covered in dirt. She rolled slightly and pushed onto the ground at the same time. With a groan, she shuffled until she was in a sitting position. She dragged one leg, then the other, until both were free of their confinement.

She looked over at Jerome, but he was beyond help. He looked startled, and his face was unmarked and miraculously clean. But some of his hair was burned and blood coated the back of his crown.

She climbed to her feet. A wave of nausea accompanied another surge of pain in her head. She groaned and swayed as the entire world around her moved. She put a hand gingerly up to her temple and her fingers touched moisture. With a wince, she knew she shouldn't try to move any more.

Something bright and fiery streaked across her vision. A powerful boom shook her senses. In a rush, screams and shouts replaced the ringing in her ears. Ruth realized she was in the middle of a battle. Her eyes darted from place to place. Fear and horror combined to make her blood run cold.

Smoke filled the air, rising from a thousand places. Dirt erupted time and time again as volleys of fiery crimson light streamed from the row of devastators. Behind the bulwark, the defenders fired green-tipped projectiles that arced toward the war machines. High in the sky above, wyverns weaved around strikers ejecting streams of sparks.

Utterly stunned, Ruth watched as a wyvern and its human rider swooped toward the sleek silver form of a flying machine. The wyvern wrapped its limbs around the striker even as the creature's body jerked violently in the volley of fire. The striker began to lose height, still enclosed in the grip of the animal as the machine fell into a spiral. As they slammed into the ground, a roar shattered the air and flame rose up to envelop them all.

Some defenders continued to successfully destroy the devastators. Dozens and dozens of green lights continuously flew from behind the embankment toward the line of rumbling domes on wheels. From the direction of the skalen, a javelin slammed into a black carapace and blew a gaping hole in its crown. Subsequent javelins struck the same place and a moment later the entire machine erupted in smoke and fire as it ground to a halt.

Another wyvern descended from the sky to dive down on a machine's dome, even as the devastator turned to fire on the human defenders behind the bulwark. Ruth saw the rider, a woman, lift her crossbow. The shot was on target, and aurelium tore the dome apart.

Around the battlefield dozens of black devastators lay still and smoldering. But there were many more, rolling forward as they made the ground tremble. Bright flashes continued to dart from their weapons. Dirt flew up into the air time and again. The defenders still held their ground, but Ruth knew at a glance that they wouldn't survive for long. Not everyone had weapons that worked against the thick metal skins. The advancing forces were now close enough for humans, trulls, and bax to charge with swords and axes, but their efforts were futile. Soon the advancing line would finish the job of pummeling the wall of packed dirt.

Ruth saw Dale up at the front, just behind the embankment. He raised his crossbow and his bolt tore a machine apart. But immediately after it, another devastator crested the embankment. Its front rose up before it crushed the dirt wall beneath it. The dome rotated. The weapon flashed.

The bright light struck Dale directly.

Ruth gasped. When the smoke was gone, so was Dale. Even amidst all the chaos, she felt a sense of loss. Dale had defended his city with everything he had. He believed in fighting together, no matter what race someone belonged to. His mother, Elsa, had loved him. He had been brave, and had fought to the very end.

Stricken expressions filled the humans' faces when they saw they had lost their leader. They backed away to shoot their crossbows at the devastator leading the advance. After a series of explosive strikes, they brought it to a halt, but more were closing in just behind it.

Ruth had come to help the injured, but she realized that the attack was far too ferocious; she would never have a chance to help if healing was all she tried to do. She saw a few crossbows littering the ground in front of the wall of dirt.

She began a staggering run. Her eyes were on a crossbow, just behind the nearest defenders. A green bolt was already in place.

She couldn't just watch everyone die.

She had to fight.

41

Taimin watched helplessly as the bonded warriors shoved Vance and Lars forward. Hannah's protests were futile, and the warriors pushed her until she also backed away from their advance. Soon the humans all stood together—Taimin, Selena, Vance, Lars, and Hannah. The warriors kept their field lasers pointed directly at the group trapped on the platform.

Around them, on all sides of the bowl-shaped auditorium, bonded warriors and their advisors watched with expressions of shock. Ingren had defied Sky Marshal Jakkar. In turn, he had just ordered the humans' execution.

Ingren left the podium.

She moved past Taimin. With a determined expression, she walked until she was blocking the armed warriors. An audible gasp shuddered throughout the assembly.

"Elder, move," one of the warriors growled. He had thick curling horns and a star on the breast of his uniform.

"Why are you doing this to me?" Hannah turned toward the sky marshal and pleaded. "I'm not like them!"

As the warriors hesitated, reluctant to follow the sky marshal's orders while Ingren stood in the way, Hannah broke into a run.

She pushed past Ingren and raced toward the armed warriors. For a moment everything was confused. A warrior's long arms came out as he grabbed her. Hannah struggled and he wrestled with her, but he was much stronger, and he soon took hold of her and forcefully threw her to the ground.

Taimin cried out as the bonded warrior lifted his field laser to level it with Hannah's torso. Light flashed at the end of the tube and a sharp crack split the air. Hannah convulsed. Her eyes shot wide open. A black, smoking hole appeared in the center of her chest. Taimin watched as the life left her eyes.

Hannah's death had been shockingly swift. Vance looked as if he was about to be sick. Selena reached out for Taimin's hand. Only Ingren stood between them and imminent death.

"Elder Ingren," demanded the warrior with the star on his uniform. "You must move out of the way!"

"I will not," Ingren said, lifting her chin.

Still on his feet, Sky Marshal Jakkar called out. "Elder, your role is to advise. The warriors are in ascendancy."

Without changing position, Ingren looked back at the sky marshal. "No more. This is a question of ascendancy itself." Taimin heard a metallic clatter and saw the gold and red doors spreading apart once more. Ingren's gaze swept over the entire assembly. "Bonded, if you seek the truth, do not look to me alone."

She thrust out an arm to point toward the doors, and Taimin saw twenty or more bonded walk out onto the platform. They were all elders, with golden robes, but they were also marked out as different by the blue trim on their sleeves and hems.

Ingren spoke in a powerful voice. "I call on the council of mystics." The warriors on the platform turned toward the approaching newcomers. Ingren focused on the bonded mystics. "Speak so that all may hear. Did you see the device on its way to our world?"

The mystics came to a halt. One left the group to step forward, and Taimin recognized the elder Ingren had spoken to earlier.

"Elder Ingren speaks the truth. The radiation device will be here by nightfall."

As soon as the mystic stopped speaking, shouts of panic echoed around the auditorium. For the first time, the sky marshal looked afraid.

Ingren raised her voice again. "This is our last chance, Jakkar. We must communicate with our enemies and make peace. We have no choice."

Ingren tilted her head back and stared up at the domed ceiling, where swathes of artificial stars glittered down at her. As she spread her arms, Taimin experienced a shiver of awe and exchanged glances with Selena. He felt hope welling up inside him. A momentous change might be about to take place in front of his eyes . . . An exchange of power, within a strange race that he had somehow come to know. When humans first met the bonded, these tall creatures had been knowledge-seekers, peaceful and welcoming. Would the bonded become that way again?

Ingren spread her arms and bellowed. "Let there be a reversal!"

The sky marshal roared. "I forbid it!"

But then Astrin, the advisor seated beside the sky marshal, climbed to her feet. The auditorium fell into stunned silence. Taimin could almost see Ingren holding her breath.

When Astrin spoke, her words were loud and clear. "Bondmate," she said to Jakkar. She pointed toward the platform. "These are our mystics. Do you doubt them, and the advice they offer?" Then she put her hand over her chest. "Do you doubt me? The advice I am giving you now, Jakkar, is in the one form that your half of the bond can never ignore. The time for war is over. You must stand down."

Jakkar scowled, and then opened his mouth, before closing it. His face contorted as he wrestled with the realization that his time in power was over. For his race to have a future, they could no

311

longer be governed by primal urges, and the desire for the complete extermination of an enemy, no matter the cost. In his search for total victory, he had risked total annihilation.

He had lost.

Taimin was shocked to see the sky marshal's proud bearing change. Jakkar's shoulders slumped and a look of resignation crossed his face.

"Now sit down," Astrin said. The sky marshal sank back into his seat. "You exist to serve. The bond is in your bones and in your blood. We—the seekers of knowledge and peace—are ascendant."

A clatter resounded throughout the auditorium as every one of the yellow-clad advisors stood. Arrayed behind the sky marshal, the council of elders also rose to their feet. There was something noble about them, with their short, pointed horns, and heads held high, as they spread their arms and gazed up together.

Thousands of voices called out in unison: "We are ascendant!"

———

Selena made sure that she wasn't the only one to see the change in bonded society. As soon as Ingren called for the reversal, Selena summoned her power and set off into the void. After she summoned Specialist Carter to the auditorium, he was stunned by what he witnessed.

Did you see it? Selena asked when the sky marshal relinquished power, along with every bonded warrior. From now on, their role would be to protect and serve their bondmates.

Yes, he said, *we saw it.*

Along with Carter, multiple presences surrounded Selena. They had joined him as he called on them, one by one. Selena saw Carter's ghostly figure, with his short hair, angular features, and crisp clothing. But there was also a shadowy mantorean with multifaceted black eyes, a glowering bax, a stocky trull, and a sleek skalen. They all wore uniforms with five-pointed stars on the sleeves. Mystics from far away, they floated with her, just above her body.

Can you stop the weapon? Selena asked.

She knew that the fate of her entire world rested on his reply.

Then Specialist Carter spoke. *What you are asking for is already done.*

———

Ruth's hands fumbled with the crossbow. A glowing bolt fell out to tumble onto the dirt. She stared up at the devastator in front of her as the dome rotated until the long cylinder pointed directly at her. A rumble came from deep within the machine's belly. Bright light appeared from somewhere inside the cylinder.

She knew her life was over.

The fire inside the devastator's fearsome weapon grew brighter. When the weapon flashed, she would instantly burn to a cinder. Running wasn't an option. She would never be able to leap out of the way.

But then nothing happened. The light within the weapon became dark once more. The devastator froze and the groaning sounds it made faded away.

Ruth's mouth dropped open in disbelief.

She stared frantically in all directions. At the crest of the embankment, the entire row of war machines became still. Weapons were no longer firing. The constant sound of explosions and eruptions of dirt ceased completely.

All of a sudden, without reason, the devastators reversed their motion.

Strangely, the war machines were backing away from the wall of dirt. Meanwhile the stunned defenders watched. One after the other, the rumbling devastators turned until every one of them was facing away from the wasteland. They rolled over the terrain, heading back toward the gray haze. High above the battlefield the strikers also turned. Trailing white plumes behind them, they increased speed until, in moments, the sky was clear. The devastators plunged into the haze. Soon it swallowed them up, and the growing realization dawned.

The battle was over.

The crossbow Ruth was holding dropped out of her hands.

Smoke clouded the battlefield, but a growing wind came up and revealed what had come of the wasteland's final stand. Bodies lay strewn over the landscape, but the dead were easily outnumbered by the living. Bax stood side by side with skalen; stunned trulls looked at the humans next to them; mantoreans lowered their bows.

Ruth saw a familiar figure and began to walk. She took step after laborious step to navigate the long line of defenders standing dazed behind the bulwark. She kept moving until she reached the mantorean who was easily marked out among so many humans.

"Rei-kika," Ruth called.

Rei-kika didn't respond for a moment. She simply looked ahead, toward where the machines had vanished. It was a long time before Rei-kika turned and rested her gaze on Ruth.

"What happened?" Ruth asked.

"They are leaving," Rei-kika said in her clicking voice. "All of them. It is over."

Ruth stared into the haze. No one cheered. Instead, those who had chosen to fight for the wasteland stood in shock.

"They did it," Ruth whispered. "I don't know how, but they did it."

42

More than two years had passed since the change among the bonded. Life moved forward, and it now felt like a long time since the wasteland's inhabitants had anything to fear. The bonded, with elders and advisors dominant, had become a peaceful, gentle race . . . although, with their dutiful, protective warriors, it would never be a good idea to threaten them.

At first, for many, it had been difficult to come to terms with the bonded after the reversal. But Lumea was a special world, the only place where the intelligent beings of the universe—in their six unique forms—came into regular contact. Everyone put aside their differences, both here and in the void.

Taimin sat on a hill with Selena beside him. The golden sun was warm on his face and a soft breeze ruffled his hair. The wind also blew Selena's hair over her eyes and she swept it away from her face in a gesture that, for some reason, always made him smile.

Taimin was weary, but it was a pleasant form of tiredness, more of the muscle than the spirit, a sensation that told him he had put in a good day's work and now deserved his rest. From the hill where he sat with Selena, he gazed out over the broad plain and his thoughts turned idly from one subject to another. He inhaled slowly and drank in the view.

A network of fields opened up to follow a thin river that curved as it cut through the plain. Each field was a different color from the one beside it: dark red, verdant green, bright yellow, and soft brown. A range of healthy crops swayed in the breeze. For a man who had grown up learning to survive in a harsh environment, it was a sight Taimin loved to watch. He knew he would never get tired of it.

To his distant right a long series of cliffs towered over the land below. This was the same plain Taimin had been so curious about when he was a child. He and everyone else had accomplished more than he had thought possible in just a couple of years. He watched as people moved about the farmland; already the most popular lanes were on their way to becoming well-trodden roads. From his vantage he could see Vance and Ruth working side by side in the fields. Vance said something to Ruth that made her slap him on the shoulder, but all he did was laugh and pull her close to kiss her roughly on the side of her head.

Hearing a high-pitched sound, Taimin turned and smiled when he saw Lars and Gretel in the river together. The little girl squealed as Lars threw her high in the air, before catching her and plunging them both into the water.

A collection of homesteads bordered the fields, close enough to create a sense of community. Two more were under construction, and the budding village wouldn't stop there.

Taimin felt a surge of pride when he rested his gaze on a homestead near the center of the group. He and Selena had built their home together. It was sturdy, with stone foundations, a roof of bundled razorgrass, and walls made of wood from outside the wasteland. He had a wide porch with a pair of comfortable chairs, and a storeroom with plenty of food and water.

Unlike the homestead he had grown up in, there was no ditch or twelve-foot-high fence. The wyverns kept to the cliffs, and people were safe as long as they didn't stray too close.

Thinking about wyverns, Taimin glanced up at the escarpment. Tiny specks wheeled in the sky and when he squinted he could just make out the arcs of wings. He often saw Griff—and his growing family. Taimin had also cleared away the rubble of the homestead where he grew up and put a marker there in its place.

He smiled as he wondered what Aunt Abi would make of the wasteland's transformation. She would probably grumble that an easy life would make him soft. He didn't mind the idea at all. His parents, Gareth and Tess, would have been right at home.

"I suppose that soon people won't be calling it the wasteland anymore," he said.

"What will we call it then?"

"I have no idea. It's not for me to say."

"Don't be foolish, Taimin. Everyone listens to you."

"Well . . . I might like to name this plain." He grinned. "But they're rebuilding Zorn, and once it's done they'll probably be the ones to come up with something new."

"You think the bax won't want a say in it? The skalen?"

Taimin chuckled ruefully. "Even more reason to stay out of it."

He continued to gaze out over the fields and homesteads, the river and the people moving about. Another shriek came from Gretel as Lars threw her high. The river gurgled as it rushed along an ancient watercourse the rainwater had happily chosen to follow. Vance and Ruth continued to playfully bicker.

He reflected on the past. Together he and Selena had found a city, broken free of a barrier of fire, opened up a new world, and eventually found a path to peace. Yet that wasn't what Taimin's thoughts were focused on, and it wasn't what made him sleep well at night. He now had a vision for the future, and it was a good one.

"I'm proud of us," he said, meeting Selena's eyes. "Look at what we've done."

"We've found our place. Ever since we met, we said we would do it together." She smiled as she gazed toward their homestead, before glancing at him once more. "And we've still got a lot to look forward to."

He returned her smile, and they once more sat in silence.

After a time, Selena turned toward him. "Do you remember when we stared up at the moon, and talked about other worlds? Do you ever still think about what's out there?"

"Of course I do."

"We never did find out about Earth," she said.

"It's where we come from."

"Yes, but what's it like?"

Taimin's brow creased; her face was animated as she spoke, but he was worried.

Selena had been acting strangely for a while now. Sometimes he saw her, sitting under a tree with her eyes unfocused. He didn't know why she was farcasting. What need was there now?

While he sat looking at her, she leaned in close and kissed him on the cheek.

"I love you," she murmured. "Never forget. I'll always love you."

⌣ ⌣

Taimin woke with a start. He was in his bed. A faint glow of light through the window told him it was a little before dawn. He had rolled over as he reached out to pull Selena close, but his arms found emptiness. He sat up and looked around; she was gone.

He pricked his ears, but couldn't hear any movement.

He pulled on his trousers and wandered through the rest of the homestead. It wasn't like Selena to vanish without warning, and clearly she wasn't inside. His curiosity shifted to concern as he walked out to the porch.

His focus went immediately to the pair of wooden chairs, but both were vacant. The first rays of morning light shone on the brightly colored fields in front of him. He shaded his eyes, looking for Selena's familiar silhouette, but so early in the day there wasn't a single person out there.

Heading back into the house, he threw on the rest of his clothes before returning to the porch and once more scanning the fields. Still no sign of her. His jaw tight, he hurried down the steps and searched in all directions. At any moment he expected to see her smiling face as she walked toward him, perhaps with some fresh water in a bucket or some food for a surprise breakfast. But he couldn't spy her anywhere.

He became increasingly worried. With long strides he left the homestead and walked along the lane that would take him toward the river. They were all learning to swim, and perhaps she had got into trouble. As different scenarios played out in his mind, his heart rate began to increase. What if she had drowned? Or perhaps a dangerous creature had found her. He cursed himself. As the population of the settlement grew, he had become complacent about the threats he had been trained to search for. His footsteps quickened. The river. He first had to check the river.

He had only halved the distance to the river when he heard a roar.

It was a loud, fiery sound, like tearing paper combined with the hiss and crackle of a raging fire. He stopped in his tracks and spun on his heel. The source of the sound was high, somewhere in the sky. He stared in the direction of the cliffs, and when he saw it, he initially didn't believe what his eyes were telling him.

At first it was just a long tail of red flame. But then, as it arced down from the heavens and its position became more vertical, he began to understand what he was looking at. He stared at the huge machine, shaped like the tail of an arrow, as it grew bigger and bigger in his vision. He watched the machine until it vanished in the direction of the plateau at the top of the cliffs.

He didn't understand why the ship was here at first. But then the shock of realization hit him hard.

He started to run.

—————

Selena stopped when she heard his voice calling her name. She turned to face him.

Taimin didn't understand what was happening. She was walking with no possessions, nothing at all besides the clothes she was wearing. The ship that had landed on the plateau was immense, and towered over her. Its sharp nose pointed up at the heavens, where a few morning stars twinkled from high in the sky.

He quickened his stride, leaving behind Griff, who settled to the ground to watch. By the time he stopped in front of Selena, his chest was heaving and his face was flushed with emotion.

"Selena . . ." he said. He trailed off, wondering what he was supposed to say.

She was going to leave him, to explore other worlds without him. She was a mystic. What they had built together wasn't enough.

With a start, he realized something. He knew her so well that he could read the thoughts on her face. She didn't look troubled, or torn. Instead, her eyes were sparkling. She smiled wryly and shook her head.

"This was supposed to be a surprise," she said.

For a moment his mouth was open as he tried to find words. "I don't understand."

Then, out of the corner of his eye, Taimin saw a human leave the ship and walk toward them. His eyes widened as he recognized the smiling man with the square jaw, broad chest, and athletic frame that filled his silver uniform.

Specialist Carter.

"You thought I was going to leave you?" Selena raised an eyebrow. "We're together, Taimin. Always."

"Then why is he here?"

"Think about it for a moment," she said. "We had a part to play in saving the universe. He's here to thank us. And he's going to do something for us, for all of the humans on this world. We have a lot to learn. We're now connected to our own past. He's going to teach us about the world we came from. About Earth."

Taimin understood the gift Selena had given him.

They had built a home, on the world of their birth. Lumea was where they belonged.

But, at the same time, they would learn about their origins . . . about the achievements of the human race, and accomplishments made together with other races. One day, they might even travel to Earth and see it for themselves.

Carter spread his arms and his smile broadened. His face was much warmer and kinder in person. For the first time since the creation of the firewall, humans from distant worlds were reunited.

Together, Taimin and Selena walked to greet him.

ACKNOWLEDGMENTS

My utmost thanks to everyone at 47North and United Agents who has been so supportive throughout all stages of the publishing process, with special mention to my editor, Jack, and agent, Robert.

Eternal gratitude to Ian, for helping make sense of my crazy ideas. I'd also like to credit Jon's help with early development, and my amazing readers: Amanda, Amy, Nicole, Estrid, Sandra, and Rosa.

Thanks to all of you who have reached out to me and taken the time to post reviews of my books.

Boundless recognition must go to my wife, Alicia. We share these dreams together.

ABOUT THE AUTHOR

James Maxwell grew up in the scenic Bay of Islands, New Zealand, and was educated in Australia. Devouring fantasy and science-fiction classics from an early age, his love for books led to a strong interest in writing. He attended his first workshop with published authors at the age of eleven, and throughout his twenties he continued to develop the epic fantasy story he would one day bring to life.

The internationally bestselling four books of The Evermen Saga were published with 47North in 2014. James soon followed with his second series, The Shifting Tides, a sweeping tale of adventure, intrigue, and magic.

A Search For Starlight is the third and final title in his latest series, The Firewall Trilogy.

James lives in London with his wife and daughter. When he isn't writing, he enjoys French cooking, acoustic guitar, and long walks in the English countryside.

For free books and to learn about new releases, sign up at www.jamesmaxwell.com.